"Bonanno's sequel to *Preternatural* presents a kaleidoscope vision of a young woman on the edge of insanity—or else tuned in to emanations from another universe. Eccentric in style, this odd combination of speculative fiction and historical vignette is suitable . . . where experimental SF moves briskly."

—*Library Journal*

"Right up there with some of Philip K. Dick's more paranoid pieces."

—*Locus*

"A complex, occasionally painful book that will amply reward readers of serious SF."

—*Publishers Weekly*

"Bonanno is a bit of a juggler; she thrills in seeing how many story lines and plot twists she can keep in the air at one time. In a lesser writer this would be disastrous, but time after time she catches the last thematic element before the whole thing crashes. A pleasure to read."

—*Booklist*

"Bonanno keeps the pace zipping along. She has written a wonderfully funny, literary novel that manages to stay within the bounds of science fiction while playing with the concepts of the genre, so that even people who do not like science fiction will like this story."

—*The Denver Post*

"Well worth the ride."

—*The Feminist Bookstore News*

Tor Books by Margaret Wander Bonanno

*Preternatural*

*Preternatural Too: Gyre*

# PRETERNATURAL TOO: GYRE

MARGARET WANDER BONANNO

A TOM DOHERTY ASSOCIATES BOOK

NEW YORK

This is a work of fiction. All the characters and events portrayed in this novel are either fictitious or are used fictitiously.

PRETERNATURAL TOO: GYRE



This book is printed on acid-free paper.

A Tor Book
Published by Tom Doherty Associates, LLC
175 Fifth Avenue
New York, NY 10010

www.tor.com



Library of Congress Cataloging-in-Publication Data

Bonanno, Margaret Wander.
Preternatural too : Gyre / Margaret Wander Bonanno.
p. cm.
"A Tom Doherty Associates book."
ISBN 0-312-86671-2 (hc)
ISBN 0-312-87541-X (pbk)
1. Authorship—Psychological aspects—Fiction. 2. Science fiction—Authorship—Fiction. 3. Women authors—Fiction. I. Title.
PS3552.O5925 P75 2000
813'.54—dc21
99-089847
CIP

First Hardcover Edition: April 2000
First Trade Paperback Edition: August 2001

Printed in the United States of America

0 9 8 7 6 5 4 3 2 1

*For my beloved Jack,*
*who teaches me to live in the Now*

"A person is not a thing or a process, but an opening through which the absolute manifests."

—Martin Heidegger

# ACKNOWLEDGMENTS

With special thanks to Greg Cox, for "getting it" the first time, and for editing *Preternatural* with a watchmaker's touch.

And to Ted Chichak, for a lifetime's patience.

# PRETERNATURAL TOO:
# GYRE

# ONE

Karen's mind was filled with voices lately. She wasn't quite sure what to do about them.

Max Neimark had made the most sensible suggestion the minute the film wrapped. Max Neimark, the anomalous leading man who'd parlayed a fortuitous bit of casting as a three-eyed alien on a sixties TV space opera into a career as a respected actor/director/screen writer/producer, had sat across the table in the studio commissary that phantasmagorical afternoon, raised an eyebrow at her, and said in that wonderfully resonant voice of his:

"Maybe you need to write a sequel, Karen," and Karen had laughed and answered:

"Tell it to my editor!" at the same time thinking: *Oh, sure! He thinks it's really that easy.* But Max had been so pleased with himself that afternoon, and the whole experience of having a movie made out of one of her usually invisible little novels had been so magical she hadn't wanted to disillusion him, or herself for that matter. She knew the moment was illusory and never to be repeated.

All of them, the three Hollywood types—Max and Larry Koster, the superhero, and Tessa McGill, the self-made guru—had gone on about their ever so interesting lives once the film was over, wishing Karen well but not giving her a second thought. She'd expected nothing more. Larry had his stud farm and his image to worry about; Tessa, in between concert tours, was off on a vision quest in Tibet, and Max was already in production on his next film by the time

Karen's plane touched down in Newark out of LAX. It was the way things worked, and that was fine. Karen wasn't part of anyone's posse; she was a working writer. It was time she got started on the next book.

However, no one seemed interested, and that was getting to be a problem.

Karen Rohmer Guerreri, forty-something housewife, single mother of a daughter and a son in their twenties, novelist. Not a very exciting protagonist for anybody's fiction, except that she heard voices. That, ewe sea, was how it all began.

*Voices? Did you say "voices," Kemosabe? Hey, we'll give you voices. How many would you like? As many as All There Are?*

*That was how we first identified ourselves to her, yew see, because that was what we thought we were, All There Was in the entire universe. Karen, on the other hand, who has hands, thought we were just characters in her next novel, if you can imagine. Turns out we were both wrong, but imagine if you will how humiliating it was for us—who assumed that, being All There Are, we also knew All There Was to Know—to have her, a mere human (temporal, for pity's sake!) show us the error of our ways. Of course, she also apologized for thinking we were fictional, which took some of the sting out of it, and we, preternaturally magnanimous beings that we are, have been—ahem—grateful ever since.*

*Haven't we?*

*Hello . . . ?*

*Well, don't all shout at once. . . .*

*Which is why we aren't speaking to her lately. She thinks the reason she's so sad is because editors won't buy her outlines, or because that pseudo boyfriend of hers went south on her, or because her parents are giving her grief, raising specters of ancient abuses. But those are as nothing compared to the Absence of Us. She'll see, who has eyes to see.*

To recap Her Back Pages (for those of you who've just joined us), once upon a time Karen wrote a rather odd little novel called *Preternatural*, about a species of intergalactic telepathic jellyfish who had a somewhat unusual way of making first contact with humans. (That's they making all that racket in the background. Awl rite, guise, that's enough now; simmer down!)

In one reality, Karen's convoluted little fiction saved a planet and, on the assumption that there was no such thing as a minor motion picture, became a major motion picture, yanking her out of debt for the first time in years, if not quite making her rich and famous.

In an alternate universe, there had been no movie. The novel had sold a few copies and garnered some interesting reviews, even attracting the attention of the *New York Times*. It hadn't earned enough to make a noticeable impact on Karen's financial situation, but the argument was that it would alter her career long-term.

It had. Oh, it had. Ordinarily, editors took months to reject her work. Now, they did it in a matter of hours. Perhaps this was an indication that she *had* in fact been elevated to a new status as a writer. Or it might just mean that senior editors, overworked as they were, had learned how to use fax machines.

She'd taken to entertaining herself by reading the rejection letters aloud. She'd been shopped around so much in twenty years that she knew many of these editors, and it was easy to extrapolate from their prissy Westchester finishing-school tones and imagine that the ones she hadn't met sounded very much the same:

"The problem for us is that the background seems tired, and the subplot isn't compelling enough to make up for that. It's a novel that doesn't seem to have a real place in the market. . . ."

This one had a reputation, Karen knew, for cutting all the sex scenes out of manuscripts because they "made her uncomfortable," quote unquote.

"As discussed the author writes well but unfortunately the theme doesn't seem to work well with our target audience. . . ." (*Remind me to send her a box of commas for Christmas!* Karen thought wryly.) "We'd be happy to look at anything else by this writer except this particular idea. . . ."

Those were the women editors. Most male editors didn't even bother writing rejection letters any more; they just called her agent and said clever things like "It doesn't work for me."

"It's not anybody's fault, darlin'; it's the tenor of the times," Tony Salda explained, rolling his consonants and cranking up "the Speech": "Since the Time-Warners and the Viacoms have bought everybody out, it's all about 'product.' Nobody cares what's between the covers as long as the stockholders get paid off. Not to mention everyone's had to drastically cut support staff. Senior editors are doing everything but cleaning the toilets these day—"

"Some of them ought to be. . . ." Karen muttered.

"No one has time to actually *edit* any more," Tony went on, ignoring authorial mutterings. "Unless a book comes in which will exactly fit a hole in their inventory, they can't be bothered."

Karen sighed. She knew the answer to this question before she even asked it. "So what are you suggesting?"

"Think about a sequel."

"Tsk, tsk!" Karen chided him. "Language!"

•

Karen's mind was filled with voices lately, but not the ones she wanted.

•

"Karen, I love you intensely, but it's just too complicated. You misunderstood my intentions, that's all. I wish I could explain it better, but—"

"Explain!" she pleaded with him, hearing the desperation in her voice. This was the kind of infatuation she should have had at twenty, not now. "Raymond, please, explain. I'm listening!"

"I . . ." She heard him catch his breath, the way he did when he was at a loss for words. That, or he would stammer. Usually so glib, annoyingly glib, the trained diplomat, never at a loss for words. In a minute he would find them, and they would be bitter, accusatory, because he was angry with himself, not her. What was it in her that made her the scapegoat for other people's inadequacies?

Her ex-husband, given to ten-minute tantrums when he couldn't find his car keys, used to call her hysterical. Her mother, who lied constantly, called *her* a liar when the lies didn't fit. Editors suffering from midlife crises found her "temperamental." Even her landlord blamed her when his wife packed up and went back to Greece, because all women were evil, weren't they?

*Raymond, please, explain. Don't just turn on your heel and walk away!*

". . . intensely. But Jeanne fits my requirements to a T. We're not even having sex yet, but she's exactly what I need. I can't explain it any better than that."

*Last week you said I was exactly what you needed!* Karen wanted to scream. Instead, she sat there clutching the phone, more at a loss for words, professional wordsmith, than he was.

"I really have to go," Raymond was saying. "I've got a meeting in ten minutes. If you had e-mail . . ."

An old argument; she'd only recently acquired her very first—second-hand—computer. As if he'd have anything more honest to say on e-mail. "Go if you have to go," she said and sat there for the longest time, the receiver resting against the bony place between her shallow breasts, dead air against her heart.

•

Karen's mind was filled with voices, but not the ones she wanted.

". . . and your mother and I don't want you writing one of those *Mommie Dearest* books," her father said. Another county heard from. She ought to rip the phone out of the wall.

She knew what he meant, though, as usual, Mr. Accuracy had it backwards. Strident and melodramatic she might be, but Gloria Rohmer bore no other resemblance to Joan Crawford. What Dick Rohmer meant was that he and his wife had lived in fear for more than twenty years that their daughter, always a great disappointment to them, would write a novel out of her bizarre childhood. But Karen prided herself on her credibility. No one would believe her mother even if she came from another planet.

"Right, guys?"

•

Silence.

"Hey, guise? C'mon, talk to me."

That had always been sufficient to summon them before, the voices that lived inside her head and gave her the words to put on the page and earn a livelihood. Sometimes they would come to her unbidden—in the shower, in the wee hours of the morning, in the middle of a conversation with a here-and-now, flesh-and-blood person which made her murmur, "Excuse me a minute!" and grab a pen and scribble on something.

"Eccentric," those who loved her said. "A writer."

"Rude," the rest said or, like her parents, said nothing at all, exerting all their energies to Not Notice.

But the voices had gone away of late, had stampeded like cartoon characters to the other side of the plane to gawk at the Grand Canyon until the pilot requested they return to their seats. Karen hadn't really minded; she'd always known there were many voices, and only some of them were S.oteri.

(Again, for those of you who've just joined us, the jelepathic tellyfish are now officially known as S.oteri, as in *esoteric,* which is a very nice word we'd recommend for your personal dictionary. Oh, and as for that bit of wordplay—*jelepathic tellyfish*—sigh! I'm afraid it's one of their endearing young charms that you'll just have to get used to if you're going to stay with this narrative much longer. Sorry!)

In other words, Karen was confident she could come up with an idea or six for new novels even if the S.oteri were off chatting with someone else or just ignoring her because they could. That was why she'd flown all those other outlines out there—the one for the thriller about neo-Nazis and stolen art, the one about an alien scientist using role-playing games to heal child-abuse victims. (She'd loved the editorial response to that one: "In our experience, child abuse isn't 'hot.' " Uh-huh.)

No response on any frequency.

So when Tony started using dirty words like *sequel*, Karen found herself listening.

But where do you go from All There Are? She and Max and Larry and Tessa and the S.oteri had saved the universe last time, or at least a little corner of it. How was she supposed to top that?

•

"Maybe a few thousand years after our little movie has been bounced off the cable satellites and forgotten," Max had been in an expansive mood that last day, philosophical. "And the possibility of extraterrestrial intelligence, including telepathic jellyfish, is as acceptable to the layman as, say, quarks, we'll have the technology to go pay the S.oteri a visit. Maybe we'll find ways to join with them physically as well as mentally, to form a hybrid third species. Maybe you need to write a sequel, Karen."

Could it possibly be as easy as that?

•

"What are you working on these days?" Karen asked Karen as they drove under the Verrazano Bridge and onto the Belt Parkway, going east.

"Picking up a little ghostwriting," Karen replied. "Tidy up chapters and outline for one writer, put a proposal together for another. Spent last year writing a cops 'n' robbers novel for a rich guy from Hong Kong. It would probably sell if he ever figures out how it ends. It's amazing how many editors love my work as long as someone else's name is on it."

"I hear you," Karen said. On Planet Academia, where she lived, publish or perish was the Law of the Jungle, and similar absurdities were commonplace.

"And I've got an idea for a new one of my own, but it takes place a thousand years in the future."

"That sounds terrific! Even I might read something like that," Karen said, changing lanes. The old car coughed and lurched, and the ubiquitous New York asshole in the car behind them honked just to prove his manhood. "Or do I detect a little uneasiness in your tone?"

From the passenger seat, Karen looked at her sidelong. "Are you kidding? I'm the English major who never took physics, remember? I don't even understand today's technology. How am I supposed to project into the next millennium?"

"Shouldn't be difficult, Rohmer," Karen said. "Go backwards."

Trust a medieval scholar to state the obvious, Karen thought.

Everyone should have at least one friend with the same first name. Karen had known Karen since college; they had always called each other by their last names. Karen Jenner, Ph.D., ex-nun, medievalist, was the kind of friend you could look up at two-year intervals and resume the conversation where you'd left off. Between classes on Marie de France and the Courts of Love, she scheduled guest speakers at her small Catholic college. Karen Rohmer Guerreri, science-fiction writer and alumna, was this week's coup. Barring traffic on the Southern State Parkway, within the hour she'd be surrounded by eager undergrads, telling them How She Broke into the Writing Business.

"Go backwards," Rohmer repeated what Jenner had just said.

"Sure," Jenner said, muttering something very Chaucerian and un-nunlike at a minivan trying to nose into her lane. Even more nearsighted and red-haired than Rohmer, she pushed her glasses up on her nose, ruffled her short Clairol Intense Red hair up out of her eyes, and honked the minivan driver, the frown-lines between her eyebrows evidencing concentration rather than nerves. (She could have qualified as a NASCAR driver.) "The point has been made that if something works, the essential design won't change in a hundred years or even a thousand. Look at shipbuilding. Sails and rudders have changed, but the basic shape of a clinker-built seagoing vessel stayed relatively the same from the Phoenicians to the steam era.

"Or, something closer to home. A teakettle. Tell me the thing we boil water in has changed in thousands of years. Materials, yes. Aluminum or glass instead of bronze or iron. And we set it on a stove instead of hanging it over the fire, but it still has a round body, a handle, and a spout."

They both thought of, and immediately suppressed the thought of, the nursery-song about the Little Teapot. Commonality, parol, shared synapses. Karen immediately saw what Karen meant. That was all good writing was about—tapping that germ of a familiar idea in somebody else's brain and setting it dancing. Sort of like psychiatry, only it paid a lot less. Or like putting water in a teakettle and letting it boil. Rohmer rolled the thought around in her mind.

"Or farm tools, or jewelry—" she suggested.

"Exactly." Jenner tapped the brakes and leaned on the horn as a motorcycle slalomed around them. "A pitchfork, an ax, a hammer haven't changed since Celtic times. Earrings, cloak pins. The Celts invented the safety pin, by the way, no matter what the Egyptologists tell you. The clasp on a cloak pin from 3500 B.C. is no different from this—"

With one hand, she unclasped and passed across to Rohmer the filigreed round the size of the palm of her hand which had been holding a paisley scarf at her throat. "We just call them scarf pins instead of cloak pins. And as we get older and our necks get crepier, we start collecting more and more of them. Nothing like a well-draped scarf to take a few years off you. Next to the right hair color, of course."

Rohmer touched her own throat absently, telling herself it was to keep from watching Jenner take both hands off the wheel at sixty mph to refasten the scarf pin, all but holding the car in the lane with her knees like a dressage rider. Rohmer thought about coloring her hair at least once a week, but didn't, telling herself it was because she liked the asymmetrical way the gray was growing in—roanish, almost iridescent, like an S.oteri.

"Of course, you adamantly refuse to look your age, even without any help," Jenner scolded affectionately. "How old are your kids now? Have you thrown them out of the nest yet?"

"Nicole's twenty-four and engaged. I told you that. And Matt graduates next June. I'm not pushing them out. They'll leave when they're ready."

She smiled. She loved her kids and loved the fact that people always told her she didn't look her age, even though it hadn't been all that important until she'd met Raymond, who was so much younger. Raymond . . . was there anything that didn't remind her of him, even after all this time?

Four years since he'd stalked out of her life, his back arched like a toreador's, a measure of his fury, though he'd softened later. One year, seven months, and an odd number of days since he'd even condescended to call her and, no, she would not call him. Why, then, was no day complete without her thinking about him?

*Think about something else!* Kettles and pitchforks and thumbscrews—oh, my!

"Okay, premise:" she said. "A thousand years from now some everyday things will be so drastically different or even newly created—devices for functions we don't even have today, technologies we can't even imagine because we don't yet have a use for them—that we'd have no clue what they were if we found one lying in the gutter in our own century—"

Jenner was nodding. "Good, good. You're getting it."

"But it's the speed of the thing. Forty years ago, if someone had handed you a computer disk, you'd have been unable to identify it or even suggest what it might be used for. But a thousand years—!"

The car slowed to a creep. They were caught in the eternal bottleneck near JFK Airport. They both sat back and watched the technology roar over their heads in trails of choking hydrocarbons.

"Do you really think technology's going to evolve on an uninterrupted continuum?" Jenner asked, rolling up the windows so they could breathe a little less jet fuel. "It hasn't yet."

"Wars, plagues, religious backlash. Granted. But a thousand years . . ."

Jenner inched the car forward with the rest of the traffic then stopped again. "Odds are we'll still be eating our oaten porridge with spoons and defecating into some version of a hole in the ground. Now, if I understand your field correctly, the spoon will probably be mechanized, or perhaps there'll be some way to ingest the oatmeal intravenously—"

"Or just the chemically integrated nutrients and appropriate amount of fiber—"

"Yummy!" Jenner grimaced. "And your hole in the ground will probably be pneumatically operated so as to whisk the waste away while you're still *in medias res* so to speak. . . ."

Rohmer was nodding at her appreciatively now. "Maybe you should take over my job."

Jenner gave her a sidelong look. "Saw it in *2001*. Talk about your ancient history. . . ."

Rohmer sighed. She hated the technology part of it. All she wanted was to write good stories about interesting characters. But Maxwell Perkins had died before she was born.

"Go backwards," Jenner repeated as traffic began to creep forward again. They were going to be late, no way around it. "Find the future in the past. So what if you guess wrong? Or are you vain enough to think your novels are going to survive into the next millennium for future readers to make fun of?"

Rohmer laughed nervously. "Did Chaucer? I hadn't even thought of it."

•

"What about poetry?"

She had glitter-green nails and an eyebrow ring and probably read a lot of Anne Rice. Why did they always ask about poetry? The answer was simple: Adolescents, if they wrote anything at all, wrote role-playing games that they thought were movie scripts or poetry.

"I've never sold a poem," Karen said, "so I'm hardly in a position to answer that. There are, however, lots of literary magazines that you can submit to—college publications, the so-called 'little' magazines, but—"

"How much do they pay?"

*Oh, this one's not* too *aggressive*! Karen thought. At s/f cons she always made allowances for the loudmouth with no social skills who popped up like a gopher in any sizeable crowd, asking multiple questions, and outshouting everyone else. She'd learned how to handle him in con-text. ("Sir, may I suggest that if you're unhappy with my fiction, you go home and write your own? . . . You have? Who publishes it? . . . Oh, I see, you still have it on your hard drive, but as soon as you get an upgrade—right! Next question!") But college crowds were usually more polite.

"How much do they pay?" Repeat the question, an old time-buying trick. Resist the urge to say, "By the way, honey, eyebrow rings are passé," because Catholic school kids always took a few years to catch up. Counter impoliteness with politeness; it confuses them. "Usually they pay in authors' copies."

"Huh?"

Articulate, too, Karen thinks. "Yes, they send you a few copies of the magazine your poem is printed in—"

"You mean they don't pay in money?"

Karen leans forward confidentially. The crowd is smallish, no more than twenty, and ever-changing, a constant flow of traffic in the back as people stick their heads in to decide if whatever's going on is worth their time, and she's done what she usually does under those circumstances—pulled her chair out from under the table or down from the dais or whatever separates her from her listeners, and brought it into the midst of them, projecting from the diaphragm to make sure everyone can hear her in this more intimate setting. But Little Ms. Eyebrow Ring is breathing on her, and it's time to back her up a little.

"Hon, let me ask you: When was the last time you bought a book of poetry?"

Ms. Eyebrow Ring thinks that's hilarious. "Well, like never."

"I rest my case. . . ." Karen sits back and scans the crowd for a more intelligent question, thinking of cloak pins and pitchforks and a man with warm dry hands and a tender mouth and a voice that wrapped itself around her like a blanket, who simply hadn't bothered to explain his reasons until it was too much too late, thinking: *Maybe it's going to take a thousand years!*

•

"How's about I take the S.oteri a thousand years into the future?" she asked Tony when she called him back, the talk at the college leaving a lingering bad taste in her mouth. Jenner had been extremely apologetic about the lack of turnout, but it wasn't that. She'd played to smaller crowds before. It was quality, not quantity, she needed. Or something.

She needed. On the practical side, she needed a project and an income. Anything else was going to have to wait for a thousand years. Maybe in a thousand years the S.oteri would stop sulking and come back to play. Maybe in a thousand years she'd be able to stop thinking about Raymond, stop lulling herself to sleep every night by imagining his long arms around her, his warmth pressed against her spine, the sough of his breath in her ear, the quiet thunder of his heart. Yes, it was beginning to look like a sequel.

She could hear Tony chuckling to himself. Some of his clients were more thick-headed than others. "How's about you do? But get me chapters and outline to pitch before the first one disappears from the bookstores. We don't want them to lose interest."

He is talking about editors, not readers. Half the time the readers don't even know the book is out there. Karen mutters something about the attention span of gerbils. Tony, as usual, is finishing his thought:

"And, a word of advice: This time don't make it so autobiographical."

# TWO

*Don't make it so autobiographical, he says*! Karen thinks. *Not a problem.* The Midlist Writer had been on the endangered species list since the Recession of '82, and there hadn't exactly been any efforts to reintroduce them into their natural environment in today's market economy; she and her kind would be well and thoroughly extinct long before the thirtieth century. . . .

•

Word had come from the Union Site that the Telekinetics' Credit Account had been frozen again. No one would get paid until after the next elections. There was the subliminal rumble of "strike" throughout the ship.

"Fine, just fine!" Darymon, ship's pilot and the only non-Tele aboard remarked, loud enough for everyone to hear, wired-in or not. He was loud enough probably to be heard even by those behind the Door and offshift. "We'll drift, that's all. Or we'll slo-mo plummet, depending on the physics of it. Get snagged in a gravity well—and if the 'espers go out, too, I won't even be able to tell that—and just spiral down into the nearest star. Take us a few weeks to roast to death, but we will cook, I promise you. See if I care!"

He'd stalked off into his cabin then, his back arched like a toreador's, which meant he was truly angry and not feigning it. When had she had time to notice that? Gret wondered. Well, she was in love with him. And they had been in space for a thousand days. But 'espers weren't allowed to mate with Nulls, not even casually. Since the Wars, it had been Written.

Part of her hoped when they made Touch with the New Species, that would change. Not that Earthbound humans' rules would change, but that Darymon would change, his tone-deaf mind opened for the first time, like the blind man's eyes in the Xtian scriptures. The Writing had never made sense to Gret anyway. As a Null, Darymon was by definition unreadable, and he certainly couldn't Read her, so where was the danger?

Back on Earth, where Teles comprised only eleven percent of the population, she might have risked it, but not here, with so many of her own kind watching and listening. If the New Species could open Darymon's mind, he could mate with her. Or with any other female on the ship. Or all the other females on the ship. Including her or excepting her? Gret wondered. Knowing Darymon as she did, even with his mind closed against her—

The Door whooshed open again. Darymon had the knack of making it sound louder than anyone else could. Like throwing a door open in an old novel, Gret supposed.

"How the hell are you going to spend credits out in space?" Darymon demanded. "The whole argument's specious. By the time we get back from this one, there'll have been three more elections, and you'll all be zillionaires. Get over yourselves!"

*Always the diplomat!* Gret thought, hearing the other 'espers titter. They thought she was so clever, despite her infatuation with a Null.

The 'kinetics weren't laughing. *Just try running the ship without us!* they thought and, for Darymon's sake, scrolled the thought onto the commscreen.

"I can't!" he shouted. "I know I can't! That was never the issue. The issue is loyalty to this mission or loyalty to your fucking paychecks! Which is more immediate here?"

For her part, Gret, being merely an 'esper and not a 'kinetic, had never understood why the 'kinetics couldn't simply take what they wanted, just manipulate the Union's accounts even from this distance and transfer the right number of credits in. But not being a 'kinetic, she had not been initiated into the Mysteries and so didn't know the rules by which the 'kinetics governed themselves. Still, would they really let the ship drop into the nearest sun? Even now, when they were so close?

"It's my own fault," Darymon was raving. "I should have set a blackout on all but official comm at the start of this mission. This is what I get for being lenient, letting you yammer with your kin back home even after we got out of Sending range. . . ."

Gret noticed how his voice cracked every time he said the word *Sending*. It grieved him not to be a Tele. Was she the only one aboard who felt it?

*Please!* she Sent ahead to the New Species. *I know we're not supposed to ask for favors, but I'm sure it was just some genetic glitch that made Darymon a Null. His soul's in the right place, if not his mind. If you could possibly see your way clear to grant him this tiny favor . . .*

There was no answer. Gret hadn't expected one. There were more immediate concerns just now. Like which side would the 'espers take, and would she go along with them?

•

Everyone had expected the next war (there was never any doubt that there would be a next war) to be about technology. That it had been able to begin, take hold, and spread so rapidly, was a function of the element of surprise. No one had expected it to be about power-of-mind.

"Well, they should have," Darymon told Gret during one of their several debates, drinking cha to her jav as usual. He was an historian, among other things. "Ideas have always been more threatening than weapons. And it's always easy to start by burning books and end by burning people."

The War had ended five centuries before either of them were born, but its resonances echoed still in both their lives. Not least of its impacts was in the Writings separating Teles from Nulls, who comprised the majority of humans.

Not that one dared call them Nulls to their faces. *That* had been how it all began.

You see, by the time midway into the twenty-first century when it was established that 'esper ability was a real and measurable phenomenon (at issue had been separating it from the other hocus pocuses of the nineteenth and twentieth centuries: séances, regressions, and so-named "white" magic and the like) it was discovered, quantitatively, that some ten to twelve percent of the population had extrasensory capabilities, realized or not, and that a smaller subset of these were also telekinetic, their talents, once defined and refined, considerably beyond the sideshow capacity to bend spoons or pluck a handkerchief out of a subject's pocket. But as this discovery coincided with the discovery that there were aliens involved, there were accusations of coercion and conspiracy, the usual human nonsense.

Or, in other words, every society had always had those who could foretell the future, read other people's thoughts, and appear to move objects without touching them. The observant observer might have realized that these types proliferated in preliterate times, their numbers diminishing with the written word, not to mention the onset of Christianity. But by the aforementioned century, no one was being observant, because everyone was blaming it on the New Species.

What's to blame? you might ask. Isn't it in fact exciting that humans can do these things? Well, you know how it is. People misinterpret democracy as meaning everyone should be the same, and there's an awful lot of jealousy (not to mention accusations of devil worship) involved when approximately one out of ten of your neighbors can do something that you can't. It was clearly unfair that the New Species should talk to them and not to you, and so you had to do something to put a stop to it, didn't you? Just give those people an inch and, next thing you knew, they had your job, your home, your wife. . . .

Fortuitously, Earth was going through a pretty lush period by then. Budgets for wars had evolved into budgets for space travel, and Mars was beginning to look like a good place to ship all those extra greenhouse gases, not to mention a lot of human hot air. Mining on the red planet had already begun, and there was talk of actual colonization once they got the atmosphere properly balanced. That this would take another two centuries was something no one realized, but the anticipation was enough to keep people excited for a while yet.

So the usual things happened. Unemployment was virtually nonexistent, which sent stock prices tumbling, but by then Wall Street was only one tarnished player in a very big playground, no longer the Big Bully, but a sniveling runner-up to the Nikkei and half a dozen others in countries that a century before couldn't have found *capitalism* in a dictionary. And, as these things happen, some of the presumed-dead socialisms began infiltrating the Big Greedy Economies, disguising themselves as egalitarianisms, and the next thing you knew, the world gradually became a little more equitable.

True, not everyone could have Kobe steak for dinner, but strictly speaking no one starved anymore, either. Besides, too much cholesterol still isn't good for you, even if there are shots for it these days.

Surprisingly, then, it took another couple of centuries for the little niggling disgruntlements to turn into World War III, because it all seemed so silly at first. Here's how it happened:

The idea of aliens from another planet infiltrating Earth by means of telepathic abilities had been dismissed as not worth thinking about as far back as the twentieth century. Those who believed in extraterrestrial intelligence were divided into (A) the UFO School (and we know how they ended up) and (B) the SETI School or, loosely translated, (A) the "they'll come here in ships and dominate us/be our friends/eat us for lunch/bring us the Second Coming" school, and (B) the "they're much too far away to send ships here, but they'll have the same sense of mathematics that we have, and that's how they'll communicate" school. Or, to reduce it even further, would you rather watch Richard Dreyfuss playing with his mashed potatoes or Jodie Foster journeying on the spaceship of her mind?

You couldn't make a movie about a disparate bunch of people like an Eighteenth Dynasty pharaoh and a female messiah and a midlist science fiction writer just sitting around communing with the voices in their heads. There were places for people like that, and nowadays, with FDA approval for Clozapine and other atypical antipsychotic medications, many of them no longer had to be kept in "places" but could return to their normal lives.

And if you couldn't make a movie out of it, who cared?

It was almost impossible, by Gret and Darymon's time, to know exactly what happened back in the transitional days. The Telesper Texts insisted it was a benign revolution, that quiet little sects of New Species speakers began to discover each other and connect; all one had to do was drop the word *jellyfish* or even the word *esoteric* into cocktail party conversation and watch for the telltale reaction. It was at about this time that, coincidentally (or not?), certain medical school faculties and research labs started "calibrating" esper potential in volunteer subjects and discovering that ten-to-twelve-percent figure. They discovered another curious thing as well:

Musicians and artists and other right-brained types tested higher than, for example, accountants or computer programmers, yet many of them were unable to "perform" esper functions on cue unless their creative urges were suppressed. One famous violinist, who'd been in a bad traffic accident (well, you didn't think we'd solved everything by then, did you?) and had never been able to get his fingering back entirely, volunteered to not even listen to music for a year, at the end of which he was able to commune with a writer, who'd recently gone blind, entirely by mind. The two eventually married, but that has nothing to do with our story.

To sum up, then: The very week that an article on the quantification of esper abilities appeared in *Lancet*, and *American Genetics* revealed the existence of a "telepathy gene" (or, as it turned out later, several), the Combined Space Services issued a statement to the effect that they had identified at least the part of space where the New Species' planet was located, and the Worldwide Back-to-Jesus Movement announced that those who trafficked in interspecies "pollution" were an affront to the morality of the entire human race.

You get the picture.

So which came first, the egg of human telepathic ability or the chicken that was jellyfish intervention? (Or was it the chicken of . . . and the egg of . . . ? Never mind!) For our purposes, it doesn't really matter. All you need to know, before we get on with the story of why Gret and Darymon and a shipful of telespers—including Darymon's daughter, the ambassador—are out in space and about to come to a dead stop, is that five hundred years earlier most of the telespers were slaughtered, but the trait survived.

•

Initially, of course, they'd been invited to live in special enclaves, "for their own good." Many, with the ignorance of past histories that passes for innocence or at least trust, took the authorities up on the suggestion and were the easiest eliminated once it came to that. For the next few decades, there were the requisite underground movements, an entire industry in tutorials in how to "fake" the esper tests now required of all secondary school students, even alternative schools set up in backwoods and secret basements. But the War happened as wars happen, except that this time, for a change of pace, the repressed minority eventually won.

Pushed to the wall, telekinetics fight hard, and they fight dirty, but once they've achieved the desired result, like causing an entire unit of extermination troops to turn their weapons on themselves, they're willing to negotiate for the most basic rights and promise not to do it again and, surprisingly for humans, keep the promise. The end result was the Writings, which spawned the Unions, which made it possible for the Eleven Percent to live in harmony, or at least wary coexistence, with their Null neighbors.

And which ultimately led to this voyage, which was about to be scuttled by the very sources that had set it in motion.

Even the dullest Null could see that the New Species, having dabbled in human psyches all this time, was not simply going to go away. Best thing, it was decided, was to go visit them and see what happened next. Cultural exchange, an embassy, a tourist office. At the very least, medical exchange.

Because it was rumored the New Species could heal. Things like brain-stem and spinal-cord injuries which, even though the multiple scleroses and syringomyelias had been nipped at the genetic bud, still happened whenever two or more hurtling objects containing humans collided, or cranes fell or bungee cords failed or people did stupid things like jump off buildings. What the New Species might require in exchange for this technology wasn't quite clear; that was up to the ambassador to find out once the ship arrived.

The ship was run on kinetic power supplemented by esper power, which is to say that once conventional rocketry got it out of the solar system, the 'kinetics used their minds to push it (or pull it, or float it, or "harmonize it with the interstellar winds," depending on which theory you listened to), and the 'espers provided sensor readouts, giving the ship eyes and ears and radiation detectors, and feeding all their data into ship's computers faster than it could be input by mere mouths or fingers. It took a lot of energy. It also took a lot of Teles.

Nearly every 'kinetic on Earth had been screened for the job and, even rarer than 'espers, most of them were aboard. Competition among the 'espers had been fierce, because there were more of them and fewer were needed. And to complicate matters, there were the Conflicting Opinions.

Some had suggested even now, even with the head of the Space Services and any number of public officials being Teles, that this voyage was a ploy, a way of taking as many Teles as possible off Earth and somehow losing them, even though research indicated that ten to twelve percent of the population would carry the trait regardless, and two Nulls were just as likely to produce a Tele offspring as two Teles were. Efforts to suppress it at the genetic level had failed as abysmally as the efforts to enhance it. Factions and subfactions had roiled and turmoiled over the voyage to the New Species' world for more than twenty years before the ship had even been constructed. That was why everyone had been jumpy even before the ship left, and after a thousand days those feelings had been exacerbated by word of the accounts being frozen. It was just one more bit of grit in the eye and the machinery.

•

"How do you think I feel?" Darymon was always upfront about his feelings. "If the lot of you decide to spend the entire voyage never saying a word aloud, you at least can talk to each other. I'm completely isolated. Well, at least my daughter talks to me, when she's not ambassadoring. Without Jeska, I'd have nothing but my holos for comfort."

Because none of his ex-wives had wanted to go along, and Darymon hadn't had time to entice another likely Null female to accompany him on a seven-or-more-year voyage away from Earth and back, the Space Services had provided him with as many interactive holograms as he'd requested as well as the tools to create his own. The holos were whom he peopled his quarters with whenever he was behind the Door.

*Pretty hollow!* someone suggested, and there'd been mental sniggering all around, strong enough to send a ripple through the ship that even Darymon could feel.

"Oh, cute!" he'd protested when Jeska, with a small smile of understanding for both sides, translated for him. "Very nice. I'd almost rather you mutinied outright than tried to kill me with sarcasm. A man can only take so much."

Only Gret hadn't sniggered, but Darymon couldn't have sensed that. Maybe his Jeska had noticed and would tell him. Gret had been careful to let the ambassador understand that their friendship was pure and of itself and had nothing to do with her unrequited love for Jeska's father.

Darymon wasn't joking about mutiny now, not when it looked as if he had one on his hands.

•

*I hate to find myself taking Darymon's side,* Gret began when her shift had unplugged and gone to meet with the shop steward to discuss whether they'd back the 'kinetics or adopt a wait-and-see. *But he's right. What is the point of a strike out here in space?*

"Oh, you're not taking his side because you're sweet on him or anything," Petra said aloud just to be rude.

"It isn't actually *his* side." Gret could be rude, too. She saw one of the academics, the ones who these days literally lived in ivory towers and never dealt with Nulls or the spoken word, wince at the unaccustomed racket. One would think, after a thousand days with Darymon's voice in his ears, he'd be used to anything. "It's our side. To him it's no different than piloting to Mars and back; he's got no stake in what we'll find among the New Species. To us it could mean an entire evolution to a new level of awareness. Even . . ." she hesitated, as they all did, before speaking the part that took on an almost religious significance even to the most cynical of them, ". . . even a physical as well as esper joining."

*Though not for me,* she thought in the innermost part of her mind where no one, not even a 'kinetic, could reach uninvited. *No matter how sublime their minds. I'll stick with my warm-handed, forked-stick Null, thank you.*

"To him, it's just a job," she finished, perhaps too quickly, to shield what she was thinking.

She'd spoken aloud for another reason, which was that it was harder to lie in one's mind. In fact, she was one of those 'espers who couldn't lie at all in any language. But it was easy to reinvent the truth in wordspeak, and the truth she knew was that it was more to Darymon than a job; it was a sacred mission. He simply didn't trust anyone else to look after his daughter.

Under the circumstances, who could blame him? Jeska was barely eighteen, the youngest ambassador to anyone ever. But her power of mind was so pure and so extraordinary, a kind of perfect pitch, with all the concomitant controls and shields, that no one else on Earth had been more qualified to make the Touch.

"I'm frightened for her, Gret," Darymon had confided almost tearfully the night before the voyage left, the last night he was entirely honest with her. "Just thinking of what she's about to do makes me tremble. But I've been fearing for her from the day her mother and I first saw her test scores. How does someone like that come from a dead-Null like me?"

*You're not a dead-Null!* Gret had cried in her mind, Sending as hard as she could in the hope that something, anything would penetrate to him. *You're all potential; you just haven't found your Eye yet! I know you can learn to See, I know!*

It was rare, but it had happened, that a Null had been "opened" through careful nurturing by a Tele, but it had been enough to start a few small brush wars and initiate a great deal more extraneous legislation even in these times. It lay in the same gray consenting-adults moral area that sexual choices had a thousand years ago. But it didn't seem to matter here. Hard as she was Sending, Gret could see she was having no impact.

"You're exceptionally quiet," Darymon had said obtusely. "Nervous about the voyage?"

Gret had never even been offworld before, and here she was taking the first interstellar.

*No!* she thought, and a split-second later said it. "No." *Not as long as it's with you.*

"Well, I am." Darymon drained his cha and motioned toward her empty jav mug. She shook her head. "Not about the voyage, but about what's at the end of it. What if it's all a trick? What if for more than four thousand years they've been planting false images in our minds? Or, should I say, your minds?"

*A true telesper cannot truly lie to another. . . .* Gret began one of the First Principles, but even as she thought it she wondered.

"I'd be turning my daughter, my child, over to an Unknown that could potentially—" Darymon stopped, squeezed his eyes shut, shook the images out of his mind. "I don't even have the words for it."

*They'd have to get past me first!* Gret thought. "I'll be there to look after her," she said.

Darymon's glance said, clearer than any Sending: Oh, *you!* If he said the word *frail* within her hearing again, she'd pound him. She was not frail, but how would he know? Before she spoke, he softened:

"Yes, you will, won't you?" He squeezed her hand. "I'll count on that, Gret; I mean it."

It was then she believed there was hope for him yet.

•

And that was why she had to speak aloud to tell the rest of the Unit that she thought they had a greater stake in this voyage, in encountering the New Species, than Darymon did. To cover for him. He was vulnerable enough, without giving the 'kinetics, elitists that they were, any more ammunition. Gret realized she still had everyone's attention but would lose it in a nanosecond.

*A few simple questions, then. Or one, really. If we go in with the 'kinetics, what do you think we'll accomplish?*

There followed the usual cant about solidarity, as if the 'kinetics would have gone in with them if it had been the 'espers who'd initiated the strike. But after awhile the debate began to spin down under its own momentum. The final decision was to let the 'kinetics go on strike; the 'espers would issue a statement of agreement with them in principle but keep on providing sensor readings.

*It might bring them to their senses,* Jeen, the shop steward, suggested. *If they do bring us to a stop, someone's got to send the message back to the Union Site. And we can keep an eye out for debris and unforeseens. Anything else would be suicide.*

*All we've got to do is yell "meteor shower," and they'll all get serious again!* someone else suggested. There was laughter, and the meeting ended on an upbeat note after all.

•

On the Eye of the World, the S.oteri watched and waited.

•

*No, no, no, nonononono! That's not the way—*

# THREE

—*It happens at all!*

Oh, what's the matter now? Which one of you is that anyway? Or do we have to explain that part all over again?

Premise: The S.oteri are a species with a Common Mind, which is to say that until they bumbled into humans, it never occurred to them that each of their individual members could be individuated. Imagine yourself if every cell in your body suddenly decided to think for itself.

No, huh? Sigh! Okay, we'll go back and explain it from the beginning:

•

Among the older suns, their star system could not be seen from Earth. For the first billion years of their existence, they were blue-green algae, perhaps the most common life-form in the universe. Somewhere in the second billion years, something went *pop!* and thus began diversification. A billion years after that, there were two life-forms, vegetable and animal.

The animal began planktanous and, in a few million years, began to diversify. It branched and rebranched, formed and deformed, complexed and dissolved in slow death-dance decay of constant mutants, sports and efforts valiant and failed, until one form remained. Ctenophore or scyphozoan, or something both and neither? For our purposes: jellyfish.

Pretty creatures, each possessed of a dominant color spectrum from which its name derived—as Gray, Amber, Azure, Virid, Lake, and countless others—but also iridescent, able to alter that color at will. The effect is kind of shimmery, when it's not diaphanous, like gauzy curtains flowing in the breeze. And when you consider that each shift of color also means a shift of mood, a thought process going on outside as well as inside, you can see why they're so appealing.

While there was surface water, the species dominated the surface. As the waters receded, the less evolved succumbed—pulsating gelatinous masses exposed to the stab of merciless sun through tenuous atmosphere—boiling, evaporating, leaving stickiness and shadow on rock like the children of Hiroshima, lasting the chill of night and gone by morning.

Those that specialized into pseudopods, tendrils, and tentacles learned first to sense radiational and vibrational variations and fluctuations in water temperature, alterations in chemical content that presaged evaporation. After a few billion of these, muzzily contemplating their newfound talents, had slowly fizzled in the sun, others learned to propel themselves via these same sense organs, expediently discovered by an expanding intelligence to possess the power of motion, to the shelter of the caves, safety, survival.

Their membranous invertebrate bodies jelled and stabilized, the pseudopods extending long and far and specializing, some to seek out the fungus that is their sole sustenance, some to smell and taste. Some distinguished temperature, light and dark, the sting of radiant danger which was death. Brains elaborated and specialized as the pseudopods did, strange synapses formed a thinking interlinked connectedness, a Common Mind.

As each brain cell specialized, so did each brain become a single cell within the Common Brain, the Common Mind. How many were there? All There Are. How many was that? Only one, the

Common Mind. How did they call themselves? As All There Are, over-against nothing in the universe, they did not call themselves at all.

They Are. They have been but did not know it, until they discovered they were not All There Are. And that happened when they first bumped their telepathic minds up against humans.

And that, for those of you who live in Gret's time, was a thousand years ago, or two or three. Which is to say that one of the most important things you have to remember about the S.oteri is that they owe no homage to time.

And another thing is that they were never quite clear, in communicating with humans, as to when exactly they began. The first contact they were willing to admit to was with a pharaoh named Akhenaton, who lived in the fourteenth century B.C., and they picked some very odd choices after him. But the first time the S.oteri realized this wasn't just a game was when they got mixed up with a midlist science fiction writer and a trio of aging Hollywood types who were convinced telepathic jellyfish couldn't possibly be real. Ever try convincing someone you're real when they think they've invented you?

So don't forget this is a novel you're holding in your hand, a piece of fiction; we want that to be clear from the get-go. So sit back, suspend your disbelief, and trust us. Within the fictional construct, everything we tell you here is true.

•

So here's the premise of Gret and Darymon's story: That a thousand years have gone by, during which time certain intellectual exchanges have been going on between human and S.oteri, but distances in space being what they are, neither side has had the technology to venture to the other's world for a visit. It was incumbent upon humans to make the journey anyway, since S.oteri don't have opposable thumbs.

Not that all is peaceful on Earth at the time (or does that surprise you?). In fact, this very voyage was sufficient cause for controversy so as to be delayed for several decades, a heartbreaker for those who did the initial work on it and died before they could see it happen. The problem was, you see, that within a hundred years of the aforementioned challenge by Karen and the Hollywood types, spontaneous telepathic talents began springing up among more than the usual number of humans on Earth.

At least, if one didn't know about S.oteri, one might consider them spontaneous. The Great Debate had been about whether contact with the S.oteri had contaminated what might or might not have been a normal aspect of human evolution.

Not exactly a megalith playing Strauss for the apes, but a clear violation of the Prime Directive, wouldn't you say?

•

But at the moment we're dealing with a problem of a different nature. One of the S.oteri (oh, yes, the biggest change on their world was being able to see themselves as "one" over against "many." As we say, imagine each cell in your body deciding to think for itself, which is one theory for how cancers get started), a garish little chit who calls hirself Fuchsia, is taking exception to Karen's narrative.

But to begin with, let's lose that bit of dialogue at the start of the chapter, because to be absolutely accurate, Fuchsia doesn't talk like that. Fuchsia has taken to imitating the speech pattern of a particular human, a human Karen knows all too well. The way this human talks goes something like this:

*No, no. That's not the way it happened, no. I never said that, no. You're a liar. No, that's not what I said at all.*

Okay, slow down. Nobody even said this was about you. Now what exactly are you objecting to?

*It never happened that way, and you know it. She's just doing that to get attention. When humans do launch their ship a thousand years from now, it—*

Hold it right there. Are you out of your Mind? There's a human here, and she's listening! You know it's against the rules to tell her what happens next.

Silence.

Karen? I think you'd better explain it to hir. . . .

Karen lifts her fingers from the keyboard, folds them in her lap, takes a deep breath, sighs. Somewhere in the transition between *Preternatural* and its sequel she has finally learned to write on-screen instead of in longhand, but the words still come as slowly as they always have. Any interruption (and there have been far too many of them lately) means a setback. Worst is when it's her subject matter that's giving her shit.

"It's fiction," she says helpfully. It was what the S.oteri told themselves about her for the first half of the original novel; maybe it will work in reverse. "Fuchsia? You do understand the difference, don't you? I'm only making this up in my own mind, and you know how different my mind is from yours. A thousand years from now I'll be dead, and you'll know what really happens, if you don't already, so my little story won't make any difference to you, will it? Fuchsia?"

She is waiting for the one to ponder, then come back with something pithy like *Oh, eye sea. Except that last time you imagined us, and we really WERE. So how do eye know you won't do that again this time?*

In which case Karen can explain that that was just a fluke, or perhaps a result of that renegade Azure's fiddling the minor chords in her mind and steering her narrative in a particular direction, as the most recalcitrant characters are wont to do. But suddenly she's not speaking to Fuchsia at all.

"I don't get it."

Karen sighs for real this time, a sigh from the depths of her soul. "Hi, Mom."

"I can't read that science fiction stuff. When are you going to write another *real* book?"

Loop back: Karen is sixteen years old. She has been in counseling with Father Russell for three years. He is about to send her away.

When she knocked on the door of the impossibly narrow little room where she had poured her heart out to him once a week for three years, she found him as always slumped in the desk chair which he used as a projectile, shooting himself from one side of the room to another, caroming off the walls and bookcases like a black-clad human-sized ping-pong ball. He had that aspect to him, short and round and impossibly cheery, considering the interminable tales of incest and alcoholic brutality and a thousand more subtle forms of abuse he heard for several hours every day from the troubled adolescent girls the guidance counselors referred his way.

Usually, he leapt out of the chair and enveloped Karen in a bear-hug, an unorthodox therapist at best. Today, he remained where he was, hands on the arms of the chair, ready to shoot himself in any direction, but strangely immobile for once, not even swinging the chair from side to side as he did even when the wheels were still. Karen's presence seemed to surprise him.

"What are you doing here?" he demanded from under his eyebrows.

"It's fourth period, my usual time," Karen answered uneasily. Had she gotten the time wrong? She always used one of her study periods to see him.

"Don't you realize I have other people to see?" he demanded. "People with serious problems? Why are you wasting my time?"

The tears burst through the dam then, splashing against the lenses of her glasses in their urgency. Karen clutched her books against her chest, feeling her face crumple, her nose redden, her knees buckle. She backed toward the door.

"I'm sorry, I . . ."

His arms were around her, holding her tight, defending her against the universe. How had he propelled himself out of the chair that fast, much less pried the books out of her fingers and tossed them—where? She could barely breathe, but the sobs came anyway. He loosened his grip and took her hands and led her like a child, sat her down, found his own chair, and zoomed it over to face hers, somehow acquiring a box of tissues in the process. He handed her a wad of them.

"In three years I've never had to use these with you," he marveled, watching her mop at her face. "This is the first time you've cried."

"If you cry, they only hit you harder," she had said.

"I know," he responded, and waited until she'd blown her nose and pushed her stringy bangs out of her eyes. Her face was greasy, violent with pimples no matter how many times a day she scrubbed it. Another psychosomatic reaction—like the constant headcolds and inexplicable rashes, the priest knew, but his client would have to discover for herself—to the relentless psychic assault that passed for a home life among her people.

She was no longer sobbing but shuddered from time to time the way a small child does who has been crying far too long. Between shudders her breathing was so quiet he had to listen for it. He took her hands again.

"I had to shock you into doing that," he apologized. "Because I want you to listen very carefully to what I'm about to tell you. Are you listening, Karen?"

He rubbed her knuckles with his thumb as he spoke. Her skin was incredibly sensitive, and sometimes his touch was rough enough to make her wince, but she never complained, priding herself on her high pain threshold. She knew he did it to keep her focused. If you cry, they only hit you harder.

"Yes," she managed, one more involuntary shudder—the last one in her—touching her voice at the end of it.

"What I'm telling you is this: There is nothing wrong with you."

She waited. For three years she had protested: "No, everything's wrong with me. I'm clumsy, I'm lost in class—can't do math or science or languages or even music—my skin's a mess, boys laugh at me. Last week during Ladies' Choice I asked a guy who wasn't even good-looking to dance, and he sneered and said, 'Get out of here, you skank!' and all his friends thought it was hysterical. Everything's wrong with me, everything." Her mother's words, from the time she was very small:

"You're awkward, you don't know how to dress, you're completely unlovely. You don't even know how to carry on a conversation, you have no friends and you never will, and no man will ever want you."

But this time she didn't speak. This time, after three years of having him peel away the layers of verbal abuse that stuck to her like so much dead skin after sunburn, she knew the truth of what he was saying, and she listened.

"You are one of the most warm-hearted, loving people I have ever known," he went on. "You should hate your parents for what they've done to you, but you don't. You're bright, you're gifted. Sister Patrick tells me you're the best writer in any of her classes, maybe the best writer she's ever had as a student. You're going to shine someday, Karen, but I want you to promise me two things."

Still she waited. He was giving her permission to lead her life.

"I want you to stay in school. No matter how hard it gets, I want you to finish your education. That's one. Then I want you to put as much distance—physically, emotionally, psychologically—as you can between yourself and your parents, and never look back.

"There's absolutely nothing wrong with you," he repeated. "I'd like to throw a net over your mother, but she's outside my jurisdiction, and you're too old for me to have you removed from the household and put in foster care, and I'm not sure that would serve you. You've survived this long; I'm asking you to promise me to survive a little longer."

She nodded. He had taught her the skills to augment her own, her ability to curl up in a little ball when the pounding and the kicking started, her ability to tune out the tirades by humming snatches of Bach in her head. All she had needed was one adult's outside perspective to tell her she'd been right all along, that she wasn't the things her mother said she was, but someone unique in all the world.

"I promise," she said and hugged him back, knowing it was for the last time, but glad.

•

She'd kept part of the promise, finished her education, although she wouldn't consider it finished until the day they put the pennies on her eyes, as her Irish grandfather might have said. And she'd made something of herself, because except for senior editors and Gloria Rohmer, most people considered a novelist to be *something*, at least as legitimate as, say, an accountant or a housewife. But as for putting as much distance between her parents and herself as possible . . .

"When are you going to write another *real* book?"

Gloria Rohmer had never admitted to reading any of her daughter's other books, either. Each one sat untouched on the coffee table as Karen presented it, "To Mom and Dad with love," as unremarked as a box of chocolates. Even more unremarked, in fact, because with a box of chocolates Gloria Rohmer would have remembered her manners and offered everybody one.

The statement about *real* books (as opposed to what?) was just a ploy to deny the existence of the ever-growing stack of published works that defied Gloria's alternate-universe version of her daughter as a social misfit who had never left home and whose sole purpose in life was to look after her parents in their old age. Poor dear, stuck somewhere on the ether between *Mommie Dearest* and *Rachel, Rachel!* And now being imitated to the point of caricature by a jelepathic tellyfish.

"Don't make it so autobiographical," Tony had warned Karen. Well, this wasn't autobiographical. Ask Gloria Rohmer if she'd ever said any of the above to her daughter, and she'd flutter her eyelashes, cant her head like an android, and say:

"Oh, don't be ridiculous! Karen writes that science fiction stuff. She's nothing but a liar. She makes all of that stuff up."

Autobiographical? Not a bit of it. Ahem.

"Fuchsia . . ." Karen begins as patiently as she knows how; someday she will get the last word with her mother, too, "I explained all of this before I began. This is a novel, just like its predecessor. I don't know the future because, unlike you, I haven't seen it yet. Gret and Darymon and everyone else on the expedition is just fiction. And, in fact, if anything I'm writing even remotely resembles what actually happens, I don't want to know about it, because it will spoil my narrative integrity. Do you understand?"

*You're a liar*—Fuchsia begins, using her mother's voice.

Karen no longer needs to hum Bach. The radio is on as she works, playing Beethoven's *Emperor*. That's also new. She used to need silence to work.

"Hey, guys?" she says, shutting Fuchsia out as easily as she does her mother's hobbyhorses. ("Did you know *They* put sulfites in everything now?" *Who's "They," Ma?* "First it was red wine, now it's white wine, too. And salad bars. Every time you go to a salad bar you take your life in your hands. They spray sulfites on the lettuce to keep it looking fresh, and my doctor says more people are allergic to sulfites than even to MSG, and they can make you swell up and die. I used to enjoy a glass of white wine once a year, but I can't even do that any more. Oh, and did I tell you I met someone you went to high school with in church last Sunday? I can't think of her maiden name, but she said to ask you when you're going to write another *real* book.")

"Guys?" Karen demands of the S.oteri through the static. "Did I not explain all of this to you? Can someone communicate it to Fuchsia, because I don't think she gets this science fiction stuff."

The comeback takes far too long, even allowing for the static.

*Karen, um, we'll do that when we get a chance, okay?* The voice, Karen thinks, is Gray's, the one who used to be the sticky-stuff that held the entire Mind together. *We're a little busy right now. . . .*

Karen doesn't like the sound of that, but there's nothing she can do about it.

"Fine," she says, busy herself, hands back on the keyboard. "Don't forget."

*A Mind which cannot forget does not forget,* comes the lofty reply, and Karen smiles inwardly. Hit them in the pride; it gets them every time.

•

The 'kinetics didn't strike after all. A last-minute referendum set aside emergency funding for them until after the elections, and both parties issued formal statements promising that, regardless of who won, the Voyage to the S.oteri was still among their first priorities, and nothing would be done to jeopardize it.

"And I didn't have to say a word," Jeska marveled. As ambassador as well as a Tele, she occupied a curious limbo. And she was so very young.

"We know the truth," her father teased her. They were speaking aloud for his sake. "You used your Powers to influence them even from here."

"As if I were that powerful!" Jeska smiled, basking in his pride in her.

She looks tired, Gret thought, letting a little of the thought leak over to a place where Jeska could hear it. The girl's eyes slid in her direction, acknowledging the thought. They were her father's eyes, the color of cinnamon, with an exotic upward slant which suggested something in the gene pool no one knew about. Back when Darymon used to confide in Gret, he'd told her he had no idea who his father was.

"We're almost there!" Jeska said, sounding like the child she'd still been when they left home three years ago. "How many more days before planetfall, Father? Are we still on schedule?"

"No thanks to the 'kinetics, yes," he grumped, though now that the crisis was over he seemed to have calmed down. "Another three-four days to make orbit, unless those anomalies in their ionosphere pop up again. Synchronous orbit from there, maybe another ten days until we find an optimal landing site."

"I can feel them!" Jeska said eagerly, trying not to interrupt. "They're as excited as we are!"

•

Reluctantly, Karen shut the word processor down. It was time to start packing for the con.

Lately, she'd developed a love-hate relationship with s/f conventions. Back when she was still unhappily married, she'd loved them as the escape they were, no matter that all the drudgework she left behind was still waiting for her when she got back. These days she felt guilty for leaving the work behind and simply allowing herself to have a good time.

But this one was one of her favorite cons, an annual event in the very mid of the Midwest which she'd watched grow over the years from a one-guest show (she being the guest, a self-styled cheap date ready to do one-woman panels in exchange for a plane ticket and a place to sleep) to a two-writer show (the other writer being her old friend Greg whom, since he'd moved out of New York, she only got to see at these things) to "This year we can afford to pay a fee for one of the guest stars from *Trek* or *SpaceSeekers* or *B5* or *Lost in Space,* plus a linguist from the Klingon Language Institute, and a local makeup artist who specializes in alien appliances. Maybe two guest stars next year."

Thus they grew, these little oases of pop culture amid the Wal-marts and the Big Boys, raising funds for the local Make-a-Wish chapter or the Boys and Girls Clubs, the out-front signboard on the Days' Inn proclaiming: "Welcome 'Seekers!", though sometimes they forgot the apostrophe. Less trouble most times than the local Elks' Club, these folks; fewer rooms trashed, less beer-puke in the shrubbery. Karen looked forward to meeting once again with her constituency.

There was Jimmy, the trucker, who called her "ma'am" and, if there ever came a year he wasn't going through a divorce, dearly wanted to write. Ginger with her brave face and the autistic son who drained the life from her the rest of the year; who if she couldn't once in a while get away to a con just knew she would go mad. A former biker, former jailbird who had parlayed four years for assault into a high school diploma, because he came across a *'Seekers* novel in the prison library and the cover art intrigued him all to hell, enough to make him register for a GED course because he had to know what was between the pages. There might be a million stories in the naked city, but there were as many more out on the road.

Up too early, car service to Newark, which was actually easier to get to than either LaGuardia or JFK, which wasn't to say it was easy. Thank God for suitcases with wheels, she'd thought even as she'd dropped it on her instep getting it down from the shelf last night. Sit in the window seat wondering if her bladder could hold out for two hours so she wouldn't have to tromp over the two people beside her. Why, she wondered as she looked down at the cloud cover with this-is-only-a-movie bemusement, did she always get the window seat?

Pin her genuine Franklin Mint collectible SpaceSeekers identi-badge to her coat so the nice young man at the arrivals gate sent to chauffeur her to the hotel would recognize her. Ask him to talk about himself on the hour or two or three until they got to the hotel so he wouldn't feel awkward or put out because he hadn't gotten to pick up the TV stars instead.

Wheel suitcase into room, lock all the door locks, crank up heat or a/c depending on the time of year, decompress, calculate how many hours or minutes there were until her first Appearance. Why did she love it so?

". . . My fiancé was killed in a six-car pileup on the Interstate during that really bad storm three winters ago. Sent me over the edge. Antidepressants, painkillers, booze; half the time I didn't know what I was pouring down my throat. I'd sit there with the remote in my hand watching anything that moved.

"One afternoon I was watching an old *SpaceSeekers* rerun, and I started to cry. I hadn't cried once since they'd told me—not at the funeral, not for weeks. Suddenly, I couldn't stop. The next day I started reading through all the *'Seekers* books I had in my collection and went out and bought more. When I came to your books, they seemed deeper than the rest. I couldn't wait to see how they turned out. A little thing like that made me decide to live again. Isn't that something?"

". . . and after that, eight weeks of chemo. I lost thirty-two pounds and all my hair. It's just starting to grow back. My wife brought books with her every time she came to the hospital; she rigged this little frame thingie to the tray table so I could read them flat on my back. It took my mind off the nausea. Yours were my favorites. I even like your non-Seeker stuff. That last one, *Preternatural?* I felt like it was real. Been looking for jellyfish in the rain puddles ever since. . . ."

"Makes you crazy, doesn't it?" Greg beside her said as they signed autographs.

"What does?"

"The fact that we get to hear this, while all our editors hear are the bean counters? Goddamn, I hate the fact that this has to be my livelihood! I wish I'd win the lottery or rob a bank so I could write just to make people happy."

"You and Kermit the Frog," Karen teased, punching his arm lightly. He hadn't sold a book in longer than she had.

"There's a room party tonight," he told her. "Some of my Romulan friends have whipped up a batch of The Green Stuff."

Karen smiled. "I'll be there."

•

Before she goes, she jots notes. Back when she used to write first drafts in longhand, she could actually use the downtime at a con to get some writing done. In these technologically advanced times, she has to wait till she gets home.

". . . description landing on planet. Barren wastes with traces of ancient water, like Mars? Mean daytime temps? Flora? NO! Fungus and S.oteri, period . . . description mouth of cave . . . dark contrast to strong sunlight outside? Sense of radiation danger even inside their space suits. Atmosphere? Wouldn't they know all this ahead of time? . . ."

•

Atmospherics hissed in Gret's ears inside the helmet; the too-clean air parched her sinuses. All she could think was: What if my nose itches? Thinking it, of course, made it so. She twitched it like a rabbit, her gloved hands clenching helplessly. She didn't need to look at him—couldn't see his face really between the dampers and the glare of that damn white sun—to know Darymon was laughing at her.

"Amateur!" he crackled at her through the comm, though his tone was gentler than she'd heard it in a long time.

He's frightened, too! she realized. The cave mouth was further off than their readings indicated. How could they traverse parsecs with such uncanny accuracy and err by meters planetside?

Inside her helmet, inside her ears, inside her head, she felt the warm throbbing that was They. The others—a dozen altogether, ten 'espers handpicked to accompany the ambassador and her father, leaving all the 'kinetics on the ship, which Gret wasn't at all sure was a good idea—had begun to trudge through the talcumlike dust, unvaried by so much as a pebble, which stretched in eddied, patterned waves from here to the cavemouth. Gret wondered what it was that held her back. The gravity was Earth-normal, the same as the ship's; that didn't account for the vertigo. Was it just having a horizon, agoraphobic, after three years between bulkheads? Or too high a mix of oxygen inside the suit? Gret checked the medRead on her left forearm. It showed resps normal and pulse only slightly elevated, her usual condition. Why did she suddenly feel as if she was walking on her hands?

Tender, tentative tendrils twined about her mind as she forced her feet to move, trudge, one in front of the other. They were here, speaking to her as well as to Jeska who, her father one pace behind her, led the way. They were here, inside her mind already: S.ote—

# FOUR

T*hat does it! I've told you a million times not to do that, but you never listen, do you? You're deliberately defiant, and I'm going to make you sorry. . . .*

Ancient echoes reverberate late at night. Karen thinks she's about to retire to her solitary bed in a Days' Inn in midcountry after a night's camaraderie and a couple of shots of Romulan Green Stuff, whose components she no longer remembers but knows they begin with vodka. Her novel is writing itself on the Cosmic Consciousness, to be retrieved when she gets home and back to the word processor.

She rubs Noxema into her ordinarily wheat-colored eyelashes to remove the mascara she only wears at night as if, behind her bifocals, it really matters except to those who dare get close enough to those incisive blue-gray eyes.

"Intimidating," Raymond used to call them. "They look right down inside me, and they don't blink. Sometimes it's—unsettling."

"Good. I like you unsettled!" Karen had said warmly at the time. What was time? Had it ever really happened?

She rinses her face, brushes her teeth and her long roanish hair, urinates for what she hopes will be the last time before the sun comes up (not middle age but life has given her a nervous bladder), turns off the heat, and crawls under the covers, curling up in one small corner of the king-size bed. (There was something unnecessary about assigning a woman alone a king-size bed.)

She is not drunk. She has been drunk precisely once in her life, and that was four years ago when she and Raymond—when she hadn't had time for lunch and her blood sugar was somewhere down in her socks and she and Raymond—

No, she is not drunk, but there's a pleasant softness around the edges of her thoughts, which more often late at night feel like pebbles in her shoes, broken shells lying in ambush just under the sand on a beach, but this night or early morning are muzzy-friendly and still buzzing with something nonspecific but strangely comforting. Thus she is surprised when a wave of nausea begins in her gut and works its way into a full-blown spinning in her head. She sits up in the dark.

"Shit!"

Glances at the clock and, by reflex, takes her pulse. She suffers from sinus tachycardia, a fight-or-flight response that can kick her heartrate up to anywhere from 90 to 130 beats per minute. For this she takes Inderal, a beta-blocker that does what her adrenoreceptors apparently cannot. Sometimes she manages to wean off the little orange pills, but chronic stress can trigger the pounding all over again, the viselike headache, the low-grade fever, the sensation that someone's standing on her chest, all of which made walking across the room feel like running a marathon. Being Karen, she copes.

But it isn't her pulse this time; that's ticking away at a gentle 78—normal for her. The nausea has passed, and she wonders if it's something she ate, since this time last year she was diagnosed as lactose intolerant as well.

*You're beginning*, she tells herself, *to sound like the My Illness Is My Life brigade!*

Don't get her wrong. Karen is as compassionate as she knows how to be, but if you've ever been to a con, you know the type. She is invariably gravitationally challenged, somewhere in the vicinity of an excess of one hundred pounds, and her monologue goes something like this:

"Hi, I'm so glad to meet you. I'd shake your hand, but my

asthma's been so bad all week I can't even get out of this chair. That's not to mention my allergies, and I have a heart murmur, and my doctor says my blood sugar and electrolytes are way out of whack since I hurt my knee this time last year, and if I don't have surgery soon I'll be on crutches for the rest of my life, but the state wants to cut off my compensation since I got this part-time job and . . ."

All she'd usually said, Karen thought, was Hello. What she should say is: Have you considered therapy? Because if you'd truly been loved and accepted as a child, you wouldn't have any of these problems. . . .

The nausea has passed, and the dizziness doesn't seem so bad now. She lies back on the pillow again, thinking: Migraine? She gets those occasionally, too, now that she's slouching toward menopause. She closes her eyes to search for the aura, that dead spot in the center of her vision which presages the flashing lights and six to eight hours of impervious headache and blurred vision if she doesn't take her feverfew.

The cure used to be four aspirin and a heavy dose of caffeine. She likes the herbal cure much better. When exactly was it she started dabbling in herb lore?

In any event, there is no aura, hence no migraine. That's a relief. But is the dizziness getting better? Karen sits up again.

"If it's a piss you want, then 'sooth, take it. Pot's under the bed as ever. Only quit flopping about, will you? One of us ought to get some sleep!"

The voice was female and familiar, as was the language. English, Karen thinks, remembering that Kit speaks not a word of *langue d'oc.* There was also the familiar warmth of her on the other side of the straw-filled pallet, her soft and oversized self taking up more than her fair half of the narrow cot, and Kit's smell of sweat and yeast and bread flour, not so very different from her own, which was only a little more sour from the brewery. On the morrow they were to gather the spring's first chamomile flowers for sleeping potions, under the full moon as the Old Ones had since before time, though the priests warned against women being out after dark where the incubi lurked.

It was all familiar, as familiar as the grunt and snuffle of the sow who shared their quarters, welcome warmth on winter nights though she should be in the pen outside by now. But Kit swore the sow could hear when last year's shoats were being slaughtered for the New King's feasts, and kept her inside until Richard's troops were back on the roads of Poitou and all the sow's children were bacon. It was the sow's shifting her great weight in the straw in the corner that had disturbed her roommates' dreams.

It was all familiar, but it shouldn't be.

"I'm sorry. I was dreaming," Karen said, remembering to say it in English.

Usually it was automatic: *Langue d'oc* with any within the keep or on the rare occasion when she went down to the abbey, her smattering of *langue d'oyl* for when the queen was in a confiding mood and chose to share her thoughts with a lowly brewer's widow, English when with Kit or anyone else from the island side of the Channel. She especially remembered it for Kit, who got so homesick whenever they came to the mainland that hearing anything but English gave her another excuse for tears. Pity the queen sometimes had a craving for Kit's rustic barley bread that the finest French *patisseries* couldn't satisfy. But when one first awakened, it sometimes took a minute or two to sort through all the tongues in her head.

"What was you dreaming about?" Kit asked sleepily.

"That I was somewhere else, another time and place. And that I might've been a little drunk."

"Oh, aye! Don't I know how that goes! And who was it plied you with the drink, then? Was he pretty? Did his cock crow for ye?"

"It wasn't like that," Karen said. "Mayhap I was drinking 'cause he wasn't there."

"Left ye, did he?" Kit yawned and burrowed into the pallet, tugging at the sewn-together sheepskins that were supposed to cover both of them. At least once a winter Karen wanted to cut the stitching down the middle and give each of them a fair half. "Not wi' child, I hope. Though hardly, at your age, I suppose. You're not the queen."

Queen Eleanor had given birth to the last of the royal eaglets when she was forty-four. His elder brothers referred to young John Lackland as the Pustule. Some things did not improve with age.

"Mayhap I was younger in the dream," Karen offered, knowing it wasn't true. Before she could say anything further Kit began to snore softly.

So much for conversation. Karen lay back down, the husks that filled the pillow slip rustling familiarly. She stared into the dark, using the slivers of bright moonlight that pierced the wooden shutter on the room's only window, trying to think this through, only to discover that she needed to piss after all. With a sigh, she reached under the bed for the cracked earthenware bowl, castoff from the kitchens, which did service as a chamberpot for both of them, though Kit's bladder, being a generation younger, didn't need emptying as often.

Karen slipped out of the bed, the shock of the cold stone floor against her bare feet almost making her let go before she could even squat over the bowl. As she was finishing, the sow lumbered to her feet and tiptoed over to sniff at her.

"Never you mind! Get back where you belong!" Karen gave her hairy hide a shove out of old practice, then slid the steaming pisspot back under the pallet where the sow couldn't get at it. Her thumb instinctively found and rubbed the chip missing from the edge, where Gervase, the flighty sous-chef, had struck it with a stirring spoon in a fit of pique once when the Young King had insulted him, telling him his peacock aspic tasted like slops.

*The Young King's been dead seven years and more, the Old King since last summer,* Karen thought, fingering the chipped bowl, evoking memories. *Eleanor's only fear now is that she'll lose Richard in this new Crusade. . . .*

It was all of a piece to her, broken crockery and broken families. The Plantagenets loved to hate each other, and often their internecine quarrels could decimate whole countrysides. A brewer's widow needed many skills beyond her craft in order to survive.

Karen lay back on the pallet listening to Kit's untroubled breathing. The girl's life was as simple as her mind: Live one day at a time. When one had lived as long and seen as much as her bedmate had, one took a longer view.

Long enough to look into the future?

"Grethe, I just thought of something." Kit had wakened suddenly, propped herself on one elbow. "What if we were taken by an incubus when we went to gather the herbs? Would the priest shrive me, do you think, if I got with child that way?"

No hope for sleep now. All solicitude, Kit's bedmate sat up yet again. "Are you, girl?"

Kit began to sob then, clutching at the older woman, drenching her thin linen shift with tears and not a little snot.

"Grethe, what am I to do? He talked so sweet to me I had no need of drink to go with him. Now it's three weeks since I should have bled and me breasts all tender, and I don't know, I just don't know. Do I have the babe? Do I ask the midwife for a potion to free me of it before it's too late? Do I burn in Hell either way?"

"Hush, baby, hush." She stroked the girl's flaxen hair, trying not to notice the head lice; only her own knowledge of herb lore saved her from getting them. "There's no God so cruel He'd send the likes of you to Hell, who's all heart and generosity—"

"Or all twat, to . . . to hear *him* tell it. . . ." The girl's voice was muffled, and the sobs had become hiccups. "What am I to do?"

"A practicality first. Will he marry you?"

"Nay, he canna, for he has a wife already." Hiccup.

"I was afeared you'd say that." Sigh. "Can he keep you as his leman then? Will he?"

Snuffle. Hiccup. "He said he would."

"Well, then. Do you want the babe?"

One last hiccup, and Kit pulled away, wiped her snotty face on the backs of her hands and her hands on the sheepskin. Her smile gleamed in the filtered dark. "Aye. More than anything else in the world!"

"Then you've no need of incubi."

Kit actually giggled and pulled the sheepskin up under her chin. Only then did the realization hit her companion like a shock wave: *My name's not Grethe; it's Karen!*

Isn't it?

Once again she was out of bed, only slightly disturbing the sow this time; she grunted irritably as Karen/Grethe took her heavy cloak from the hook behind the door and slipped her bare feet into her wooden-soled pattens.

"Where are you going?" Kit asked plaintively. "Did I upset you that much?"

"It isn't you, sweet. I need the air is all. Or maybe an incubus of my own to soothe what ails me. . . ."

•

The first thing she thought, squinting at the scene beyond the door once she heard Kit slip the bar back into place behind her, was: I'll fall over my own feet; I left my glasses back in the room! But what room, where, when? She really had awakened in an outbuilding of a castle in Eleanor of Aquitaine's time.

Powerful, that Romulan Green Stuff. Unless there was another explanation.

Of course. "Hey, guise?"

Remember to speak softly; there are figures afoot on the parapets and in the darker corners. Sentries kept the watch out over the countryside in any land where the queen's train stayed. Where

Eleanor herself might be beloved, her son Richard was usually more hated and feared. Karen craned her neck and squinted up at the cowled and chain-mailed figures in their ordered march, wondering if any of them fantasized what she would in their place—the sudden arrow out of the dark that, lodged in the throat, meant certain and, one hoped, swift death. Richard himself would meet such a fate a few years hence.

"Wait a minute!"

The bifurcate thought process was rattling her. She knew without a doubt, now that she'd remembered it, that she was Karen Rohmer Guerreri—sometime twentieth-century novelist, occasional dabbler in medieval history whose favorite films included *The Lion in Winter*, but seriously, folks!—who was apparently having a very weird dream.

"Well, fine!" Karen muttered. "And if I run into the queen, and she happens to look exactly like Katharine Hepburn, then I'll yell 'Cut!' and step off my mark and ask the director 'What's my motivation for this scene?' or maybe just click my heels three times and—"

In the dream, if that's what this was, Karen knew herself as a brewer's widow named Grethe, for whom the latter half of the eleventh century was home. Kit and the sentries and the armorers working the open forge—set at the far end of the keep beneath the walls so the noise wouldn't bother the royals or their retinue nor the stray spark catch any of the other buildings on fire, medieval man's worst terror—even at this hour, its demonic heat softened to a satisfying glow as it spilled across the rutted bailey to where she loitered, uncertain, were not actors, extras, stuntmen, but real people whom she'd known all her life. This *was* her life, and the future time and place she'd told Kit about were actually the dream.

Except she was never nearsighted in her dreams.

Nor was Karen about to surrender her first reality that easily. Once upon a time, the S.oteri had tried to alter her immediate past, and she'd refused them. Now they wanted to tinker with whole centuries? Not if she could help it.

She had a couple of kids up there in the twentieth century—her daughter was engaged, her son graduating from college—even as she somehow knew Grethe was childless. And while Karen knew without knowing how she knew that both she and Grethe had any number of dear friends in their own time and place, she was not about to surrender hers for Grethe's, not even, cuss him, Raymond. And then there was always her career.

*Are you serious*? she thought, crossing the open places with carefully measured steps, sidestepping the occasional goat and a flurry of chickens (thinking: Aren't they supposed to roost at night?) and the opaque, wheeled humps that were peddlers' carts whose owners slumbered in or under them, waiting to do a brisk business in furs or silks or sewing thread, spices or spoons or cooking pots on the morrow. What career? Sixteen hundred eighty-seven copies of *Preternatural* sold out of a five-thousand hardcover print run is a *career?* The royalty statement stamped across the top with the greatest obscenity in the midlist writer's vocabulary—*UNEARNED*—meaning that while the publisher's earning his money back, the author hasn't sold enough copies to see a royalty, again—you call that a *career*?

When they write my epitaph, Karen thought, it will consist of that single word: UNEARNED. As if because my name isn't Grisham or Clancy I haven't earned the right to live, to be a person with a livelihood, a profession, much less a career. Better to be Grethe, the brewer's widow, who knows how to make beer and gather healing herbs and whom Queen Eleanor sometimes—as a jape or sincerely?—seeks when she needs advice. As long as mankind had a thirst and aches and pains and a need to prognosticate beyond the morrow, she'd never want.

Enough with the self-pity! she told herself. As Tessa McGill would say: Focus and click! The obvious explanation for all of this was that it was really just jellyfish all the way down. If she hadn't been able to wake herself by now, this wasn't a dream.

Finally, none of her dreams, she thought, as her open-toed patten went *Squish*! into something she could just *imagine,* had ever been quite so . . . er . . . tactile. All she had to do was wipe the whatever-it-was off the sole of her shoe, step beyond the light from the open forge, search the dark for the telltale sparkle of S.oteri, make them stop playing around and send her home.

Unless there was some reason why she needed to be here.

Was she really Grethe? Were jellyfish the simple explanation for all the reincarnation theories, or was she caught in some *Quantum Leap* rerun with an S.oteri standing in for Al?

She found herself drawn toward the forge, where there would be armorer's sheet metal or a pot needing mending or maybe even a polished-brass mirror in which to seek her own reflection, and maybe catch the twinkle over her shoulder, or a subliminal giggle or two, which meant it was all one big joke and any minute now she'd wake up in that king-sized bed in Middle America, her glasses and her beta-blocker and her Chapstick on the nightstand where she'd left them, all's right with the world.

The face she saw in the dented surface of the pewter serving plate was her own, down to the last laugh-line, her long roanish hair done in a practical plait over her left shoulder, tied with a bit of leather thong. She was who she was except—oh, this was cruel! A dozen of her teeth were gone.

Well, wasn't that true in either reality, the only difference being the wonders of modern dentistry and porcelain crowns? But that upper incisor, deadened and discolored by a root canal when she was twenty, had been a sore point until she'd been able to afford the cap four years ago; she'd been forty-three before she'd dared to truly smile.

In this time and place, no one over twenty had a full set of teeth.

Did that mean she'd be free to smile even with that gap in the center of her mouth? She set the platter down and fought back a sting of tears.

"You'd think they'd be too drunk to throw the things quite so hard," came a gruff voice from the dark behind the heat and light. "Herself was livid and banished that particular fool from the table for a fortnight for not being *chevalier.*"

The voice belonged to a hairy, barrel-chested man who looked exactly the way a smith ought to look—bearded, bare-armed, sweat-streaming, wearing little but boots and hose with a leathern apron over, tufts of hair sprouting even on his massive shoulders, hammer upraised left-handed over a fire-reddened horseshoe held in the long fire-charred tongs.

"How they expect a man to get the real work done when half my time's squandered on hammering the dents out of their toys, God knows." He wiped his brow with one great muscled forearm. "Good morrow, Grethe. Up early."

"I am that, Jaime dear," she acknowledged, knowing his given name to be James, Jaime to his friends, though most had dubbed him Vulcan for his profession. "Spoken by one who never seems to sleep."

"Not while there's horses to be shod and mail mended," he acknowledged. "It's said Richard's making the rounds of his holding to make sure there'll be no trouble while he's in the Holy Land. Warming up for one battle with another. Will they never have enough?"

"Of fighting? Not as long as they've got male parts. It seems the two go together," Karen temporized, amazed at the words coming out of her mouth, easy as from long familiarity, as if she and Jaime had had this conversation or similar ones a thousand times before. Even as she spoke she found herself knowing the kinds of things about him one learned out of long friendship, about the sorrows he'd seen in his thirty-odd years, including the wife and two of his five children taken by the pox the summer King Henry died. At the same time a different part of her mind was ticking over with an older—or younger—reality.

The predawn breeze as she'd trod the mud of the bailey had swayed the hem of her long cloak and the flimsy shift she wore beneath, ruffling her leg hair until she wanted to scratch and, in fact, here against the heat of the forge, she surreptitiously stood on one leg and worked the long toes of her other foot out of the wood-soled shoe to rub her calf with them. Leg hair? Since when?

She remembered some of the silliness of the early '70s feminist resurgence (that's 1970s, to set the record straight)—bra burnings, refusing to shave one's armpits or leg hair. She'd shrugged it off the way she did most mass movements. For one thing, she never wore a bra; for another, unshaved leg hair made her itch. So there.

So here. Whoever was directing this movie had thought of everything, right down to the authenticity of missing teeth and unshaved leg hair. And armpits, too. No wonder she could smell her own sweat, especially here in the warmth of the forge. But everyone smelled the same; no one would notice.

"Good thing for me I've a trade that rids me of the fighting choler," Jaime said, beginning to hammer the cooling horseshoe into its proper shape. "Not for me to go over the ends of the world and die of pox or the infidel's arrow, no matter it get me into Heaven."

"Aye," Grethe agreed absently. "There's some say that was what popes and kings had in mind, to rid the land of the useless and the younger sons. . . ."

Jaime thrust the horseshoe into a leathern bucket filled with cold water; its cooling hiss gave emphasis to his next words.

"So it's been said, but there's some as ought to be careful how loud they say it." He watched her narrowly, though there was concern in his honest brown eyes. "Have a care, Grethe. You always were one for an opinion."

In either century! Karen thought. "If I can't trust you, Jaime, who can I trust?" she asked, tossing her head to make light of it.

His answer was to put a finger to his lips and choose another raw metal bar from the heap and heat it in the fire. "It's only that the rest of us don't get to talk to queens."

Loose lips sink ships, Karen thought out of another era, nodding her understanding and gathered her cloak about her. "Good morrow to you, Jaime. I'll be drawing off the first brew of the month day after next. Shall I bring you a mug?"

His heretofore solemn face split into a grin. "As always. Good morrow, Grethe."

Okay, fine, she thought, picking her way back across the rutted mud, heading for the brewery. She was here. Here where in at least one reality she knew what she was about, for she knew that "here" was the fortress of Chinon in what would one day be France, but now was a river junction between the oft-disputed borders where Anjou, Touraine, and Poitou met, just up the road from the Abbey of Fontrevault, where Henry Plantagent had been interred the summer before, and where Eleanor herself would one day come to rest, along with her favorite son.

Richard I, Count of Poitou, and by the grace of God and his father Henry's death, King of England, who had come to his coronation wearing the pope's white cross and was sworn to do what his predecessors could not: reclaim Jerusalem for Rome. A little more than a year from now he would lay siege to the city of Acre and, having captured it, order the cold-blooded slaughter of something like five thousand unarmed Saracen prisoners. For this history would dub him Lionheart, the most gifted killer of his generation.

To say as much aloud, both Karen and Grethe knew, meant certain, if not always swift, death. Groundlings were not to offer opinions on the matter of kings. Better to go about the round of her days, head for the brewery among the hunched out-buildings clustered inside the mote before she even returned to the hut she shared with Kit to wash and dress. She'd have to accept the situation for the moment at least. No point in getting hysterics. Who would she share them with? The issues were survival, not blowing her cover, and figuring out if this was just some telefishic jellypathic whim or something important.

Like changing the course of the Third Crusade? It seemed to be on everyone's mind, including her own, or at least Grethe's. Did she remember enough history to find her way? Or would she have to rely on Grethe's knowledge of the times, limited as it was to hearsay and probably hampered by the inability to read?

*Could* she read? Karen wondered, unconsciously slipping the barrier between her two *personae*. There was nothing out here under the sky to read. With a flash of persnickety pride, she recalled sounding out a passage from Eleanor's *Book of Hours* when the queen was conferring with some local lord over the disposition of a charter and had forgotten Grethe was in the room. Of course she could read, in Latin at least, which was the only language that mattered. Not well, but she could read. She'd prove it to herself the next time the queen summoned her into her chambers.

Which Eleanor would, she knew, when Grethe brought the new brew for the steward's approval and learned from him if the queen wanted to see her. More often than not, the queen did.

Slow down! Karen told herself. One step at a time. The cocks were stirring and the sky beginning to lighten. She let herself into the brewery with her very own key, kept at all times either in an inner pocket of her cloak or on a belt around her waist, along with her personal spoon, a plain copper one to suit her station, for eating from the common bowl. The brewery and the armory were the only places within the keep that wanted locking. Eleanor insisted on it.

Breathing in the familiar sweet-sour smell, Karen went to the shelves at the back of the big dirt-floored room and found the covered earthenware jar that held the hawthorn berries.

Hawthorn, Grethe knew, calmed erratic heart rhythms. She dosed herself with the dried berries steeped in wine every morning of her life. Who needed beta-blockers?

As she stood on tiptoe to return the jar to its shelf, her right foot began to throb. She looked down to see the spreading purplish bruise across the top of the arch where yesterday, eight hundred seven years from now, she'd dropped a suitcase on it.

# FIVE

God, Karen thought, I hate time-travel stories! I never understand the physics of them.

Of course there were some writers who insisted there was no physics to them, that because time travel was impossible in real time, it was a sacrilege to write about it in fiction. Karen had always figured that was their way of saying they didn't have the skills to pull it off. Her best advice had been from a gentle little man with more published titles than she had eyelashes who had winked at her and said, "My dear, it's fiction. The only rule is to make it work!"

Thank you, Mr. Stubbs, she thought, but this isn't fiction. Does your wisdom still apply?

She fixated on the bruise across her instep, made by the impact of a forty-dollar twentieth-century suitcase. As long as she could see it, feel it, she could juggle both realities, the Now and the once-was/hadn't-happened-yet.

For now, survival. Eat your oaten porridge out of the common bowl, assume you have the same antibodies as everyone else hereabouts, and are no more likely today than yesterday to catch anything from the muddy farm lad with the mouth sores sitting shoulders-and-elbows beside you on the long bench slurping his. More important, in your case, was to determine beforehand that after being soaked and boiled overnight to soften the husks, the oats are served up with fresh butter and a dollop of salt the Irish way, instead of with milk and sugar, Quaker Oats style. Butter's allowed on your diet, whole milk isn't, unless you want to spend the rest of your day doubled over on the privy.

But her contemporaries already know milk makes Grethe ill; that and her age and outspokenness have earned behind-the-hand mutterings of witchcraft since her husband died.

"Extras for you," Kit had smiled on her, arriving to serve in the refectory after early Mass—more out of a need to flirt with her man than any piety, Grethe knew—to hand her two slices of her best bread, thickly buttered, when everyone else got one. "You get much thinner you'll be no good for warming me next winter!"

"From the look of things, young Kit, you'll soon have something else to warm ye!" one of the plowmen remarked with a nod and a wink, and everyone about the long tables laughed, including Kit. Everyone except Grethe, known for her seriousness, too.

Kit always gave her extra bread, she knew, because everyone else got a mug of warm, foaming milk with their breakfast, "straight from the teat," the cowherd's wife said every morning as she ladled it from the bucket, inviting comments about the generosities straining against her own tight-laced kirtle. They were a merry bunch, and Grethe felt at home with them for all the sidelong glances at her because she couldn't drink God's own milk and presumed to gossip with queens.

Well, all right, a small triumph, Karen thought. How to survive as a lactose intolerant in a century where peasants live on fruits and vegetables in season, grains and roots and milk products with the occasional egg or bit of meat thrown in. At least no one will be insulted if I don't try the new cheese. It can't be any worse than being a compulsive label reader in my own time. (Yes, dammit, my own time. Don't lose sight of that, not even for a nanosecond, and don't give me that What is Time? crap!) Grethe's managed to survive to middle age in spite of her infirmity; she'll do so even with me occupying her body and brain, or is it the other way around?

Now if only my eyes didn't ache already from squinting without my glasses. . . . And what do I do in this time and place if I get a migraine?

Feverfew, the answer came to her. She and Kit were gathering herbs tonight, remember? She'd have to check all her supplies on the back shelf of the brewery beforehand to see what was wanting, even though most of them couldn't be gathered until late summer or fall.

For now, live in the Now, until you either find a lurking S.oteri and grab it by its nonexistent throat, or figure out on your own what happens next.

•

Earlier, she'd gone from the forge to the hut she shared with Kit to find the girl already at the chapel, the mossy-bottomed water bucket empty, the slop bucket full. She dealt with them both, though it was the younger woman's turn, and set about putting herself in order. Once a week, she knew, after Saturday's labors were done, she and most of her peers would repair to the bathhouse just outside the walls or, if it were overcrowded with soldiers as it had been from February until Richard's troop departed, walk with a group of the other women across the bridge and down the road along the river valley to the abbey where the nuns would allow laywomen to use their bathhouse if they joined in the vow of silence and didn't linger overmuch.

It was a bit of a trudge unless the weather was sweet; there was to be no lewd talk or silliness, but the nuns were generous with their firewood, which made the bathwater hotter, and there was no fear some stray foot soldier had lingered behind the woodpile to spring out for a quick grab at a tit or bottom as the flock of naked women scattered shrieking like chickens before they rallied and beat him off with bundled twigs. Grethe had enjoyed such pranks when she was younger, but these days she preferred to soak in peace. The luxury of steaming her pores and washing her tumble of hair was just that, a luxury, and only to be indulged in on the eve of the Lord's day.

Absent the luxury of a daily bath, she managed a quick splash of cold water on face and neck and arms every morning (taking time this day, now that she was Karen as well as Grethe, to notice that every mole and scar and freckle was just where she'd left them. One scar in particular, a jagged lightning bolt from a childhood appendectomy, wanted serious explaining in this century; how had the S.oteri managed that?). She'd save the waste water to wash her feet just before she donned a pair of hose and cloth shoes in the cold months, the open pattens when the weather was warm.

Today would be a day for bare toes, she decided, rebraiding her hair. Her linen sleep shift would be abandoned in the warmer months as well. Laden down with layers of fabric during the waking hours, any woman was relieved to sleep as naked as God made her. For today, her woolen skirt and kirtle were belted over the linen shift with the stout leather belt that held her key ring and her spoon. There was a stained linen apron in the brewery that went over the lot, she knew. Neither fussing with veil nor wimple (a working woman needed her movements and her peripheral vision unhampered, and who cared if her neck was aging? was Grethe's philosophy) she tied the chinstrap of her little white cap, tucked all but a few tendrils of hair up under it, and set off for the workers' refectory to break the fast with the rest of them.

The more pious went to Mass every day, but Grethe, it seemed, had been angry with God for taking her husband with a sudden fever and only appeared in the chapel on Sundays, fulfilling the letter of the law lest she burn in Hell otherwise. Even Queen Eleanor had noticed. It had been, in fact, the reason the Queen summoned the brewer's widow the first time.

•

"Only Plantagenets have the right to quarrel with God, Mistress Grethe. That is what you're called, is it not? What makes you presume to the right of kings?"

Grethe had stilled her quaking heart and mastered her stammering tongue and, eyes lowered and curtseying, replied, "I've no quarrel with God, Lady. I'm only not speaking to Him until He ceases His quarrel with me."

The overdressed ladies and fluttering, pointy-toed courtiers draped about the chamber in various stylized poses had tittered over that, but a gesture from Eleanor silenced them. Her face, gray-green eyes fixed on Grethe's, remained as serious as her question.

Eleanor of Aquitaine's face had been as oft-described by her contemporaries as Mona Lisa's in her time but none of them, Grethe/Karen thought, had got it entirely right. The eyes were either gray or green depending on the light, not blue or hazel as some careless later researchers claimed. The face was not Kate Hepburn at all but entirely Eleanor. Heart-shaped in her youth, perhaps, but all chin and cheekbones now, paler than parchment, with a scattering of broken capillaries when seen up close, perhaps the sun's legacy from the time when she and her Amazons had ridden bare-breasted with Louis of France, her first husband, on the Second Crusade. The entire face was patinaed with a map and web of fine lines, legacy of a life of thinking on her feet from the age of fifteen when her father's death and the size of her lands made her the most marriageable prize in Christendom. For more than half a century, Eleanor had fought for the right to be herself and not some man's property. Every battle was etched on that face.

No telling the color of her hair, tucked under the stiffest, most immaculate white veil-and-wimple Grethe had ever seen, though it was probably completely gray by now. Eleanor was twenty years Grethe's senior, but the erect carriage, the eyes and voice and steady hands beneath their signet rings, were those of a woman in her prime.

"If God is a man, as our prelates claim," that voice had said in the silence of the tapestry-hung *solar* whence the Queen had summoned Grethe, "then your method wants rethinking. The way to handle a quarrelsome man is not with silence, but to quarrel back."

Certes you should know! Grethe had bitten her tongue to keep from saying as the courtiers tittered anew, and this time Eleanor allowed it. Your last quarrel with your husband, Henry, had him imprison you for fifteen years!

"Respect, Lady, but as God is not my husband, I know His moods not well enough to understand His quarrel with me. I can only answer with silence."

The storied face had smiled then, though Eleanor's eyes had been dancing throughout.

"You loved your husband, did you not?" she asked with the right of queens.

"More than my life, Lady," Grethe had answered at once.

She had expected more tittering (imagine loving a spouse in these days, when anyone schooled in Eleanor's Court of Love knew you married for property and loved adulterously) but before the hangers-on could react, Eleanor sighed. The sound reduced the room once more to silence. Even the dogs rooting among the rushes seemed to respect the mood.

"You have my envy, Mistress Grethe," the queen said. "I loved a husband once, and he too was taken from me, but by his own wayward heart, not the hand of God. Still . . ."

The admission seemed to tire her. The gray-green eyes moistened for a moment, then went whimsical again.

"Think you you'll ever marry again?"

" 'Tis sorcery to foretell the future, Lady," Grethe had said, not knowing why she said it. "I am no sorcerer."

"Are you not?" Eleanor asked after a long glance in a longer silence, then dismissed her with one hand, for the benefit of those around them listening in. The understanding in that glance was why she summoned Grethe thereafter.

•

It was no secret that the queen consulted astrologers, though she pretended to make a sport of it. This was one of the most educated women of her age, made regent in her son Richard's absence. The instant she'd gotten word that Henry was dead she took upon herself the ruling of England, personally hearing the grievances of those from all classes, freeing the misjudged and those too long awaiting trial in Henry's odoriferous prisons, filling those same cells with those she deemed recreant.

She'd joined Richard for his Christmas court in Bures on the mainland, then went with him to Anjou to set things right in the lands of her birth, where they'd gone to hell in the last frantic addled days of Henry's reign, then settled in Chinon to sign charters and treat with ambassadors of every stripe from Antioch to the Vatican and back again and, in between, to interview the occasional peasant woman on her knowledge of the future.

No one needed a knowledge of the future more.

And Karen got the distinct impression that Grethe had foretold it for her, on more than one occasion. Would she know what to say when the queen asked her next? How much was too much?

•

The trouble with time-travel stories, Karen thought as she went through the rote of skimming froth off the fermenting vats and clearing the new beer (her knowledge of how to do these things ingrained in Grethe's memory, hence automatic to her) is that they have to have a beginning, a middle, and an end. Would that real life could be contained within a four-hundred-page manuscript or a forty-seven-minute TV episode!

No point in questioning whether she was supposed to be here or not. Her peers had accepted her as Grethe and nothing in Grethe's behavior struck them as odd or out of place. And the very fact that it was already established that Grethe sometimes foretold the future for the queen seemed to suggest that she should continue doing so, up to and including prognostication on the impending Third Crusade.

If this were the movies. But real life was so messy; there were no rules here. What was she supposed to do?

"Not a damn thing until I get my hands around an S.oteri!" she said aloud, with only the mice in the corners to hear her. "I mean it, guys; I'm not playing until I know the rules. You can keep me here forever. Or can you? How long before I go missing in my own time?"

That was another thing about time-travel stories. Usually the protagonist wasn't missed at all, because no time passed in her own time while she was "away." Was that the case here?

Silence. What if those rules were different, too? What if she was stuck, inverse Rip Van Winkle, living out her life before her life? What about her son's graduation, her daughter's wedding? More immediately, what about her novel?

"Well, I suppose I could keep working on it here," she told herself, then didn't know whether to laugh or cry at the thought. Grethe might be able to read a smidge of Church Latin, but her writing was limited to the dates scrawled on the sides of the vats and a bit of figuring on a flat piece of wood to remind her how much to pay the corn merchant before the next delivery. It was as much a sin to teach a peasant woman how to write as it was to prognosticate the future.

Nothing for it, she decided, but to go through the rote of her days—including getting up at moonrise tonight to gather herbs with Kit—until she got the lay of the land.

•

If it was about the Crusade, she thought, on her hands and knees in the soft fragrant earth beneath the moonlight, a clump of delicate chamomile in one hand as she combed the long grass for more with her other, she still had time. It was only early May. Richard was still knocking heads and hacking up disloyal retainers in the length and breadth of Poitou. About a month from now he would come north again to meet with Philip of France at Gisors, where the two would plan their military assault upon the Holy Land. It would take weeks to muster their troops at Tours, and they and their thousands would not set out on the road to Vezelay until July.

From there they would wend their way along the Cote d'Azur and end up in Sicily just as winter set in, the storms on the Mediterranean making further passage impossible until the spring. It would be a full year from the time they set off on the march until Richard made his decision about the prisoners at Acre.

This is *my* knowledge, not Grethe's, Karen reminds herself. She can see Karen Jenner at the lectern, hear her drawing parallels between decisions made in wars long past and a little thing called Vietnam which had colored all their lives then. Grethe couldn't possibly know any of this because it hadn't happened yet.

She sat back on her heels to rest her aching knees. There had to be a better way to gather herbs! In later centuries, nearly every castle and churchyard would sport an herb garden, those in Shakespeare's time becoming legendary, but here in glorious 1190, they grew wild along the lanes and in clearings in the woods, and some of them had to be gathered in darkness.

Chamomile was particularly tricky. The tiny white flowers shut at nightfall; it was almost impossible to see them even under a full moon. One had to gather them largely by feel and by their distinctly sweet smell, because it was the way it had always been done, probably since the cave. Karen heard Kit sigh, saw the girl stand, rubbing her lower back.

"I think I've found all I can, Grethe. Shall I see if the raspberry's in flower?"

"Go to," Karen acknowledged. "But only a few, remember. We'll want the berries at midsummer."

"Aye."

Raspberry flowers could be gathered standing up. Pregnant or not, the girl was simply lazy. Karen watched her saunter toward the canebrake separating the dense wood from the clearing.

Focus and click: Grethe doesn't know the future; you do. But not really. You can only imagine what might happen if Richard *doesn't* kill all those Saracen prisoners next summer.

She'd spent the day in the brewery going through the motions, combing her memory for everything she knew leading up to the slaughter at Acre. Bless you, Jenner, for giving us history along with the literature!

"History has it that Richard, after his sappers breached the walls and he captured the city—something two years' siege by the other Christian forces couldn't accomplish—took all the adult males, mostly merchants, as his prisoners. It doesn't say what disposition was made of the women and children." Dr. Jenner waited for the nervous laughter, watching Karen Rohmer, who got it first, smile grimly. "Richard sent a ransom note to Saladin and waited.

"This was the same Salah al-Din who, when Richard came down with the tertian fever at the start of the assault, had fresh fruit sent to the king's tent, packed in snow his servants had run down from the mountains miles away. Imagine the infidel knowing more chivalry than the Christian king whose mother had invented it! Richard appreciated the gesture when he was ill, but his actions suggest he was implacable once he recovered. Whether Saladin ever received the ransom note remains moot to this day, but the ransom was not forthcoming.

"Then Philip of France, hearing of troubles with his barons on the homefront, not to mention having lost all his hair and fingernails to some unspecified Eastern plague, decided he didn't want to play at Crusades any more, pulled his troops out and sailed for home, leaving Richard with a fraction of the men he needed to hold Acre before marching on to take Jerusalem, and a horde of unransomed prisoners to feed.

"Would a more 'modern' leader have made the magnanimous gesture, sent them back to their lord Saladin with a note: 'Thanks for all the fruit, and if you're ever in Poitou, let's do lunch,' and changed the face of history? What would the Islamic world do without Christians to brawl with down the centuries? Not long before, Richard had tried to secure the peace by offering his widowed sister, Joanna, as a bride to Saladin's kid brother, al-Dil or Safadin, until Joanna pitched a Plantagenet fit and got the pope to back her and make Richard call it off. In the wake of all of this, what was on Richard's mind?

"Did he stand on the parapet and look down upon those thousands of men at prayer—because the chronicler tells us he waited until they had obeyed the muezzin's call and knelt in prayer—and imagine he was God? Or did he merely convince himself he heard the voice of God, and that history would thank him for what he was about to do? Didn't the Saracens' own creed tell them that those who died for Allah went straight to Paradise? Did Richard actually think he was doing them a favor?

"In truth, we'll never know but, gifts of chilled fruit or no, Richard reasoned that he needed the ransom to feed his own troops. When the deadline had passed, he acted, ordering the prisoners gutted in the market square, and went on to Jerusalem which, as history tells us, defied him. In essence, the Third Crusade was a failure. On the way home, Richard himself was kidnapped and held for ransom. It took his loving mother two years to buy him back. . . ."

•

Her mind full of voices that hadn't spoken yet, Karen pulled herself to her feet in the moon-spattered dark, shaking clods of dirt from her apron, and stuffed the bunches of chamomile into the sack slung over her shoulder. Chamomile, raspberry—what else could be gathered this early in the year? White-oak bark for headaches, she thought, and set off for the edge of the wood, at the same time wondering where Kit had vanished.

Sounds of giggled lovemaking from the raspberry bushes answered that question. Of all the places to choose! Foolish girl would end up with thorns in her backside. Karen/Grethe cleared her throat loudly before calling out.

"Ho, Kit! I'll be by the stand of white oak for the nonce. After that, I'm for home."

"Aye!" she heard, muffled no doubt by an extra pair of lips. "Don't go without me!"

"I'll not." As if you didn't have someone else to walk you home if I did! Although what would the neighbors say, much less his wife?

Karen found the white-oak thicket by old habit, steadying herself against the gnarled, almost ground-sweeping branches of these elderly, unpruned giants. Finding the places where Grethe had made her cuts the spring before, she pulled out her small clasp knife and began to cut the inner bark away anew, taking just enough for a season's needs without damaging the deeper layers. The work was automatic and left her free to think.

•

Before Richard ever got to the Holy Land, Eleanor would be with him on two occasions. Once, briefly, to see him off at Tours, the words of the Crusaders' theme song *Lignum Crucis* or "Wood of the Cross" echoing in her ears as liveried knights on horseback and countless foot soldiers marched out through the main gates onto the long road, the song evoking memories of the time half a lifetime ago when she herself had ridden on crusade. Karen could only picture the barely controlled chaos of that scene—messengers running in and out with dispatches, jongleurs and troubadours distracting king and nobles alike until he roared them out of the chamber, squires fluttering about refilling winecups, a jealous and rheumy-eyed Philip Augustus glowering in a corner as the better-dressed and better-looking Richard, who was *his* vassal for God's sake, stole all the glory.

Enter Eleanor under full sail to kiss her son goodbye, a few tasteful tears bedewing those parchment cheeks. No time to whisper in his fuzzy little ear: "Don't kill those Saracens when you have the chance, Richard dear. Be merciful. History will thank you!"

If she wanted to. Who knew Eleanor's mind? Not Grethe, the brewer's widow, and certainly not Karen.

There would be a second opportunity during the Sicilian winter, when Eleanor arrived with Richard's bride, the hapless Berengaria who, history suggested, loved women as much as Richard loved men. Poor Eleanor, trying to fight nature and give England an heir, because the nearest alternative was her youngest son John Lackland, a.k.a. "the Pustule," whom his mother had caught pilfering from the exchequer before Richard was even across the Channel, and whose ineptitude would result in Magna Carta and the beginning of the end of monarchy.

Could Eleanor, would Eleanor, sometime during the marriage feast, lean across the table to her bright-eyed son as a servant refilled his winecup and say, "Richard, a word with you about this Crusade . . ."?

Hopeless! Karen thought, folding her clasp knife, bundling the oak bark with a bit of grass-string and adding it to her store. Let's make a few dozen assumptions here: Suppose I was destined to be here, because the S.oteri haven't been just watching us, but actively tinkering with our history, which was a question Max and Tessa and Larry and I kept asking them without ever getting a straight answer. Ergo:

It's up to me, or at least to Grethe, to make predictions for the queen at her express request. Am I to wait until Eleanor takes me into her confidence and says, "You know, Grethe dear, I'm worried about that lad of mine, so impulsive, don't know how he's going to comport himself once he gets to the Holy Land; he's always been irritable in the heat! And Philip's whining and carping is worse than a woman's, and enough to drive any man into a killing frenzy, particularly—oh, don't give me that horrified look; we both know he and Richard did more than kill deer on all those hunting trips, and if some later poet has something to say about *women* scorned, well, he never had to deal with Philip Augustus, who has his father's mealy-mouthed piety overlayering an ambivalence about his sexuality; remember, I was married to the man. . . .

"So let's suppose a situation arises," Eleanor goes on, "in which my son Richard has to choose between good policy and his temper. Do we have any doubts which way he'll go? Now, if before he marches down the plank to board his deep-drafted dromond in the harbor at Messina and sets his face toward the south and east, what if his mother tells him of a vision she had in which he was asked to choose between mercy and expediency? What do you think, Mistress Grethe? He was always headstrong as a boy. Think you this time he'll defy me just for the sake of defiance, or for once in his life will he listen?"

And all Mistress Grethe will be able to do, Karen thinks, wondering if Kit's finished fucking yet, is agree with the queen, because peasants always agree with queens if they want to die of a ripe old age. So where's the harm?

No guarantee Richard won't kill his prisoners anyway, but at least I'll have tried to prevent it. And what if he listens?

Picture a future in which Muslim and Christian have been allies for eight hundred years. Spain made that much stronger for not having to fight its Moors, and it and England as a combined force conquer the Americas. Kiss the Indians goodbye; prolong slavery well into the industrial age. Beirut and Sarajevo might still be among the garden spots of Earth. And all the Jews dead long before Hitler.

Which is not to say Richard's showing mercy at Acre would necessarily kick start any of that, but what if it did?

Karen's heart begins to pound so hard it staggers her. Please God, she thinks, don't lay this on me! I'm a writer, remember? I'm not supposed to have a life!

# SIX

She can just hear Raymond, with his degree in international relations, dismissing the whole thing.

"What-if scenarios. We must have done a zillion of those in grad school! You can't possibly calculate all the potential variations. And you can't make policy if you think that way. You'd be paralyzed."

I'm not trying to make policy! Karen thinks. I'm trying to survive and get back where I belong. And because I *can't* calculate all the variations and you're nowhere around to advise or even argue with me, I'm not making any moves unless I can see that current history's somehow been altered by my arrival, and so far I don't see it. Maybe it only works that way on TV.

She gathered her wits about her, along with her cache of leaves and bark, and made a decision: Unless something other than an S.oteri told her to do otherwise, she would do nothing more than watch and listen. For all she knew, her own existence, mixed European ancestry being the tangle it was, might depend on it.

•

"Guerreri . . ." strangers would muse when they met her. "You don't look Italian."

"I'm not. That was my married name."

"You should drop it and go back to Rohmer," some of them suggested. Karen would shrug.

"Professionally, I'm kind of stuck with it," she'd explain. "It's the name readers know me by." Yeah, all sixteen hundred of them! she'd think without saying. "Besides, it puts me closer to the front of the alphabet. That's important when you're on the 'New Releases' shelf in the big bookstores."

They'd nod and laugh appreciatively while she waited for the next question:

"Rohmer. What's that, German? You look more Irish."

"A little of both. The Irish is part English, maybe. No one on that side of the family could read until this century. And the German side's half Bohemian, with maybe a little Czech mixed in. Or we could be Jewish. Depends on which day of the week my father's telling it. His family was strangely secretive about their origins."

And my father tells me a different version than he tells anyone else, she'd think, suppressing that thought as well. Again she can hear her mother's voice: "Oh, Karen writes that science fiction stuff. Nothing she says is the truth."

•

So maybe, she thinks, wrapping her cloak about her as she waits for Kit to pull herself together so they can go home, if I speak to Queen Eleanor and if she believes me and if she feels the same way I do and if she speaks to Richard and if he manages to control himself and set his hostages free, return them to Saladin in a gesture more magnanimous than bringing snow down from the mountains, a gesture that says, like a Laurence Koster Production: Yeah, mine are bigger than yours and they clank louder and history will remember me for this, if, if, if . . .

Richard's troops might have more energy for not having to slaughter a few thousand Arabs and be able to take Jerusalem, and maybe one anonymous crusader, say one of Frederick Barbarossa's bowmen, instead of surviving to beget eight hundred years' worth of Rohmers, might fall at the gate or die of plague and never see home.

Or, maybe, if Saladin's so impressed he *gives* Richard Jerusalem, and Islam and Christianity make peace, their next move will be to eliminate everyone's favorite scapegoat long before pogroms or Hitler, and a different branch of my family, under another name, those who in the time line I remember were probably forcibly baptized in lieu of death, might never exist at all and neither will I.

That is, if I'm just Karen, and not Grethe. My present situation seems to suggest I'm both. How can I prove or disprove that?

The scuffle of careless feet in the underbrush behind her made her turn. A tousled Kit, still tying the lacings of her kirtle over her abundant breasts, last season's leaves in her hair, came shambling toward her.

"Ready as you are," the girl yawned. "They'll have to make do with day-old bread on the morrow. I'll not be stirred out of bed till midday."

"S'truth, looks as if you've been stirring aplenty, in bed or out!" Grethe remarked dryly, picking the debris out of Kit's hair. The playboy of the Western World, she supposed, would be halfway home to the village by now. The things some women settled for! Not she, who'd had her husband all to herself the whole of their lives together.

Hadn't she? Then why could she conjure neither a single memory nor even a name or a face?

The thought was enough to make her stop still on the winding deer track which did duty for a road.

"What is it?" Kit hissed, who startled at every snap of a twig. "Did you hear something?"

Her soft body moved closer to Karen's; in another instant she'd be clutching at her. Karen hushed her with a gesture.

"Not heard, lass. Thought I saw something."

The moon was past its zenith, a chill glimmer behind the soughing, new-leafed trees. A different slant of light danced far ahead of them on the twisting path. Warmer, pinkish, glittering like a migraine aura, always just out of reach—oh, Karen knew the type!

S.oteri. A deep pink flutter—rose, cerise, magenta? No, she

thought, searching the thesaurus in her mind: fuchsia. But is it truly Fuchsia, the one Karen had to 'splain things to only a day or so ago, or a trick of the light, one of the familiar ones like Lake or Amber playing at color changes just to be mischievous? Whatever, it was definitely S.oteri. The sight was almost a relief. It explained how she'd gotten here. Now, how to grab the damn thing and make it take her home?

•

There was a Third Thing, sight unseen. At first, the Common Mind had not been pleased. It wasn't the not-seeing; S.oteri couldn't see. But why hadn't it met this third species while it was still all of one Mind? Yet, the Third Thing offered something irresistible. It asked only one thing in return:

> {*Choose one from among you at random to suit our experiment. Now that the One is individuated into as many ones as All There Are, choose one, any one, no special qualifications. This is a pass/fail exam, no retakes. If the least of you is not the best of you, as well as every gradation in between, we shall seek elsewhere.*}

*It could be dangerous*, the residual resonance of the Mind suggested.

*Tertium Quid,* Latin for "the Third Thing," which was to say neither human nor S.oteri, evidenced indifference:

> {*Dangerous? Perhaps. But if you want what we offer . . .* }

It had almost been enough to make the Common Mind demur. Almost. The most important thing was to Know. All right. Reach down into the bingo tumbler and choose a number, any number: Fuchsia.

*Oh, God, not Fuchsia! Can we toss the marker back when no one's looking, choose a different one? Of course they're looking. Tertium Quid apparently has eyes in the back of its head. Shit!*

Azure, once the rebel, now the cornerstone, drew in hir tentacles and shuddered: *Not Fuchsia! We can do better than that. You know what S/HE'S like! There's going to be trouble. Yew'll sea.*

The Mind glanced sidelong, which had not eyes to see: *As if ewe aren't the resident expert on trouble! Ewe aught two Noh.*

Yet, though the choice was random, according to TQ's demand—the price of interaction with this third species, which offered something no S.oteri should be without, available only through this limited-time offer—the Mind offered Fuchsia instruction.

*Word up. This is a very serious responsibility TQ's offering you. Telekinesis, do you know what that means? It means not only will you be able to drift through currents of time within the Mind, but actually, in act, for real. And, while we're not entirely sure because TQ won't entirely tell us, it may be possible to move things around, if you get our drift.*

*Think temporal. This is serious. TQ won't let us limit or control you, but if you fuck up, baby, it's all our asses. Which have not asses, get it? Which is to say, we're reasonably certain that if we piss TQ off, the very least it/they will do is yank the telekinetic power out from under us and never give us another chance with it, or anything else, and who knows what else it has to offer? And there may be punitive damages we can't even begin to imagine. So buck up; don't fuck up, baby. It's up to ewe.*

But Fuchsia, caught up in the riff in hir own mind is, as usual, not listening. That's why Karen's caught hir sparkling in the road.

•

Kit's labored breathing reminds Karen of the here and now . . . er, the there and then. As the silence lengthened and her companion kept frowning at the path in front of them, the girl, skittish by nature, threw her heavy arms around the older woman's neck, pulling her close.

"What *is* it, Grethe? What do you hear, or see? You're so still you're frighting me!"

"Hush, child. I'm trying to think!" Grethe/Karen answered more harshly than she'd intended, prying the girl loose. As if at the sound of her voice or perhaps the sudden movement, the pinkish glitter glimmered and vanished. Karen could hear it sniggering. "Damn!"

"Grethe!" It came out a breathless squeak, almost like the one Kit used in lovemaking.

"It's nothing," Karen said more gently now, squeezing Kit's hands as she had this morning to reassure her. Real life or phantoms were equally frightening in this time and place. "I thought I saw a light upon the road. Didn't you?"

"What manner of light? Like an interloper with a lamp, or fairy lights? I saw nothing."

"Then if you saw nothing, there was nothing to see." Karen began to move forward again, putting a swaying confidence into her stride she didn't feel. "How could I see anything when you've the better eyes? Or did you think I don't know they call me 'Squint-Grethe' behind my back?"

That brought Kit to giggles, for it had been her lover who'd first called Grethe that. Grethe's nearsightedness was not uncommon in one her age but made her a joke among her peers all the same. Even her husband had—

Had what? The memory of a memory flickered and faded. She'd almost had it, then it was gone, as if it weren't her memory to remember. Added to the bruise on her foot, it was something to hold onto. Taking the younger woman's hand, she walked purposefully out of the forest toward the main road, past the abbey to the castle keep.

•

For the life of her, she couldn't remember her husband, whom she'd supposedly loved as much as that very life. Not even his name or the suggestion of a face. She lay in the graying dark beside the softly snoring Kit and stretched her hands out, trying to limn a face in the dark, a face looming over hers as his body did, joined in all the right places, moving in conjoined and timeless rhythm that was love.

Had he been tall or short, stocky, slim, her own age or, more likely, older? Women wore out quickly in those days, Eleanor's stamina notwithstanding, and men, needing new wives to rear their numerous children, remarried often. Had he been a mentor, father figure, or a wild and boyish lover, both, neither? Karen saw the new day's light between her fingers, nothing more.

She tried to conjure him in daylight, in the brewery, instructing her in his art, as if he knew he'd not only need a helpmeet while he lived, but she would need a livelihood when he died. She searched for his footsteps in the worn floor, his written mark on a cask or bit of foolscap (would she recognize it as his?), some scrap of a garment that had once been his. Nothing.

She conjured some younger version of herself slipping up behind him to wrap her arms around his chest and lay her cheek against his back, feeling the strength of him beneath his coarse linen shirt as he labored.

No! she thought. You don't know that. You're extrapolating, writing fiction when it's never been more important to stick to fact. Maybe he refused to teach you anything, and you learned by watching him on the sly, remembering how much of what to mix in the fresh cold water from the spring, how long to brew it, how to clear it, how to—

She clenched her hands into fists, lowered them to her side, sighed. The memory wasn't there. That was good. It proved she wasn't really Grethe, only borrowing her skin for a while. That meant she didn't have to say anything to Eleanor at all, just fill the queen's ear with platitudes if she asked and go back to the brewery until the pink glimmer on the road got tired of toying with her and sent her home. Why, then, did it make her feel so melancholy?

What was it like to love someone more than your life? Karen no longer remembered.

•

*Lowered them to her side, sighed.* Fuchsia mimics, smirking.

*Awl rite, that's enough of this foolishness. Stop this at once!*

*Uh-oh!* Fuchsia, furtive, is about to be caught. How careless of hir not to think of including the memories of Grethe's Jacob in the mix! Well, for one thing, s/he'd forgotten about that human tendency to attach to individuals rather than a Common Mind. For another, there wasn't Time—

*That will teach you to act out of anger!* a little voice that ought to have been hir own taunts nastily. There had to be a way to retroactively rectify the error, since Fuchsia never made errors. Meanwhile, how to keep the Mind from finding out what s/he's been about?

*Nothing, nothing!* s/he protests like a child, before the question's even been asked. She tries on the Official S.oteri Voice to throw them off: *Moi? Not doing anything in particular in this particular era. Just mucking about, watching a day in the life of a castle keep, learning my Earth Human Western European Medieval History 101 like a good little jellyfish. Why do you ask?*

S/he can't sustain the Voice, of course, and lapses into hir own, made individual by the Awareness of Humans, for which Karen is in large part to blame:

*It's none of your business what I'm doing! You said yourself the whole idea was to go off on our own and experiment. Don't you DARE talk to me in that tone of voice! Don't you DARE tell me what to do*!

All the while frantically accessing hir own memory to find Grethe's memories of Jacob the Brewer, scrolling through the file to find him. Is this the one? Eyes as blue as the sky in October; even an S.oteri which has not eyes to see can see them. Grethe might choose a blue-eyed man where Karen mightn't, too wary of finding herself looking back at herself in his eyes. Yes, this was Jacob: deep-chested, slightly hunched of shoulder, white-haired, considerably older than his childbride even when he chose her, deep-voiced, too, and gifted of hand. No heavyhanded man of his own time, but infinitely gentle, and oh so willing to teach the eager youngster everything he knew about brewing as well as the larger world. Small wonder she'd loved him so.

Now to infuse those memories into Karen's memory before it was too late. *Damn! Careless, careless, careless and, as if that wasn't bad enough, you forgot all about that bruise on her foot from the suitcase, too!*

*A bruise, you say? Hey, wait a minute, what about the scar on her belly? You've never adequately explained—*

*Ahem. Weed like a word with ewe. . . .*

*Oops! Damn!*

Is s/he actually hiding hir hands behind hir back like a four-year-old, who has neither hands nor time?

*If you haven't done anything wrong, you've got nothing to worry about,* the Mind tells Fuchsia, thinking: Ahem! Believe us, please. Would we lie? *Ahem. We'd just like a word with you, honest. Just tell us what you've done with Karen.*

*Karen? Um, Karen who?* Thinking: This telekinesis stuff actually works! They really can't see where I've put her, which has not eyes to see. Then again, if I sit here thinking on my own much longer without answering them—

*Oh, you mean* Karen! *What makes you think I've—? Oh, don't be silly! Last I looked, she was writing another novel about something or other. Troubles with her editor and her love life and her DNA donors and even the landlord, I hear, as if short of rape and pillage everything in the category of Murphy's Law has already happened to her, poor dear! You'd think she'd welcome the chance to vanish into another time line when things were simpler, and rape and pillage were all the average woman had to worry about.*

All the while thinking: Leave it to Karen to stir up so much static over the Third Crusade that even the Mind has noticed! This one can't leave anyone's history alone, not mine, not hers. Hmm, maybe I can use that. . . .

•

It was the same every month when she drew off the new brew. Grethe filled her best tankard, wrapped it in a clean apron, crossed the bailey with it held before her like a chalice, entered by the kitchen entrance, and delivered it up to Gilbert, the sommelier. Beer was for peasants. The royals and their courtiers drank wine, often sugared or mulled in the English fashion, and even the lowest of them wouldn't admit to a taste for grain brews, but the first drawoff of every month had to pass muster anyway. Eleanor required it.

What Gilbert didn't know was that he wasn't the first to taste it. Grethe had already stopped by the forge with a plainer tankard for Jaime. He was still licking the foam off his mustache appreciatively by the time she arrived in the kitchens.

Gilbert invariably took advantage of Grethe's hands being full of the foaming tankard to have a grab at her ass, pulling her close enough to smell his sour breath and making some coarse remark. Grethe tended to ignore him. Necessary rituals. He would take the tankard, making sure to brush the back of his hand against one of her breasts; she would look him straight in the eye as he lifted the brew to his mouth and tasted, her intimidating gaze (thank you, Raymond!) making him cough a bit as she stepped back out of his reach as much as his grasp. Silly twit! It wasn't his pleasure she waited on.

Still, wait she would until he'd nodded his satisfaction with her beer if not her mood, spiriting the less-full tankard away to one of the pantries; he'd send a kitchen boy round to the brewery with it empty later. Grethe would pass the time with whoever was in the kitchen and didn't think themselves too grand to gossip with a brewer's widow (unless Gervase, the sous-chef, were about, in which case the rest of them would all be too busy looking busy, and there'd be no time to chat), lingering to see if the summons from upstairs would come. More often than not, she would leave then and go about her business until the next drawoff.

Only sometimes would the rustle of brocaded skirts and the sudden drop of bows and curtsies among the kitchen staff alert her to the summons from Eleanor, in the person of her eldest daughter by Louis of France, the Countess Marie.

"Mistress Grethe, good! Methought I'd find you here," Marie

would invariably say, as if it were happenstance, and not that she'd been scanning the bailey all morning from the upper windows to await the brewer's widow's arrival. "My mother, the queen, wishes to speak with you."

"At once, milady."

Grethe would follow the countess at the requisite distance, up the endless stairs and down the angled, echoing corridors, past drowsing dogs and drowsy pages and smoke-grimed tapestries wafting in the draft, dodging piles of old rushes and the scurry of mice and the drip of pitch from the torches in the wall sconces until they reached the *solar* and Eleanor.

Eleanor managed, whenever possible, to arrange herself against a backdrop of the sky. The arched "modern" windows of the sun room, limned in the newer, more radical style history would dub "Gothic," airier and more daring than the squat, pragmatic "Romanesque," framed the erect figure sitting so that her perfectly straight spine barely touched the back of her chair, the parchment-white face framed within the frame of the window arches by the frame of a snow-white wimple. The young eyes in the weathered face were clear with thought but clouded with troubles.

Young eyes in a weathered face. Like Jacob's eyes, Grethe remembered with a start. It was the difference in the color that had fooled her, but the look—of unfathomable sorrow—was the same.

Karen stood stock-still, visited by an almost-memory.

•

His eyes were looking down into hers, the same color as the sky above his white-framed head.

'Tis a saint, the little girl thought. I am died and gone to Heaven and am visited by a saint. But why does it still hurt?

"Rest easy," he said, and she recognized the voice as Jacob's. Jacob the Brewer, whose wife Elspeth was the midwife then and sometimes taught small Grethe about herbs. It was only the sun behind him that had made his dark hair look white. Jacob's voice was as warm as the hand that held her own small one. "I know it hurts, but I know you to be brave. Lie very still and breathe this. It will hurt less."

He held a scrap of cloth to her face, and she breathed a camphorish sweet smell which made her head swim but also made the knifing pain in her right side seem less urgent. There were voices, other faces looming over her, blocking out the sky.

"Let it die!" she heard a too-familiar voice, the man who called himself her father. "It killed its mother being born, and it won't behave itself like a girl. Let it die!"

The pitchfork, Grethe remembered then. She'd been running in the stables with some of the lads her own age from the fields, running wildly with her hair streaming, mostly because Wat had tried to put his dirty fingers up inside her. When he grabbed her long skirts, she'd tripped and tumbled and the pitchfork—

She inhaled sharply, and the pain returned. Was she going to die? Jacob said she wasn't, her father said she should. Who was right?

"What are you saying, man?" she heard Jacob's resonant rumble overriding her father's higher-pitched whinny. "Do you want her not?"

"She's none of mine! Take her if you want her. Mayhap you might get some work or other out of her."

Grethe felt rather than heard him retreat, like a cloud moving away from the sun. She didn't understand what the rest of them were sniggering about. Something else blocked the sun from her face then; Jacob was crouching over her again. She felt his strong arms slide under her knees and shoulders, lifting her slowly, slowly to spare her further pain.

"Sure, Jake, take her, do!" someone she couldn't see cat-called as they moved toward the room at the back of the brewery, where Elspeth would treat her wounds and where she would live from now on. "She's young for the kind of work a woman does best, but mayhap if you break her in early—"

Grethe winced as the big man turned on them with her still in his arms.

"Dare say that when I'm empty-handed!" he growled. Grethe could feel it vibrating in his powerful chest and knew there was danger in his face. Again she felt rather than saw the rest of them step back and sidle off.

She slipped into unconsciousness then, from shock and from whatever potion he'd had her breathe to ease the pain. When she woke, she heard Elspeth's voice before she could open her eyes.

"It's a clean wound, for all the source of it," the midwife was murmuring. Grethe frowned with concentration, trying to understand what was being said. "There was no matter from her gut to poison her, and I've stitched her and dressed her with the drawing poultices. It may have damaged her woman organs, though. Whatever man gets her may find she cannot bear."

"She's only a child. . . ." Grethe heard Jacob murmur. "That rabble—"

"Devil take them!" was Elspeth's pronouncement. "Do we keep her, then?"

"Not without your say-so, wife."

"Then we keep her."

And they did, and the pale, stick-legged Grethe flourished beneath their care, remembering fondly the nights by the fire when Jacob sang and Elspeth combed the tangles out of her roanish hair. Remembering, too, the wasting sickness which took Elspeth, and which even her herbs couldn't cure. Grethe and Jacob sat with her through the nights and days as the tumor grew in her breast, and her body shrank around it.

"Promise me something!" Elspeth whispered one winter afternoon when Jacob had gone for a moment to deal with the corn merchant, and she and Grethe were alone. Grethe was fifteen at the time.

Grethe had smoothed the whitening hair off Elspeth's brow; the sickness had aged her decades in only weeks. "Anything, my chosen-mother, anything!"

"Be wife to Jacob when I'm gone. No sense the two of you passing each other like ghosts the rest of your lives. No sense you giving yourself to some lout who won't know what he's got—"

"Mother—" Grethe started to say, but Elspeth wouldn't hear it.

"—and besides, you know how to run the brewery."

Despite their knowing that Elspeth was dying, the practicality made them both laugh. Grethe thought about it. She'd seen the sidelong glances Jacob had given her as she'd grown to womanhood these past two years, and they'd made her flush with pleasure. There was no mystery to the sex of him, not with all three of them living in the one room and sometimes, in the coldest months, bundled in the same bed. But wed the man who'd been more father than her father ever was to her? Well, why not? She knew how he would cherish her.

"As you put it that way, Elspeth mine, how can I refuse?"

The older woman squeezed her hand with her last strength. "Done, then. I can die in peace."

Before the sun came up, she did. After Grethe had washed the body and dressed it and laid it out for the neighbors to view, as she and Elspeth had done with countless others, she went looking for Jacob, finding him hunch-shouldered with grief in the darkest corner behind the casks. She sat on the floor behind him and rested her cheek against his back, feeling his sobs.

After an eternity, he reached for her hand and kissed the palm of it.

•

*There!* Fuchsia thinks, triumphant. *It's working! Rewrite my history, will you? What do you think now? Are you Grethe or aren't you?*

•

Karen swayed slightly on her feet, wondering if the queen would notice. If it was true memory and not fantasy, was she truly Grethe?

Did that change the rules? What would Eleanor ask her? What would she answer?

"I had a dream last night, Mistress Grethe," Eleanor said without preamble. "Perhaps you can tell me what it means."

Only then did Karen notice that the room was empty. No one was ever alone in a medieval household, and royals for their own safety surrounded themselves with guards and pages and footmen if only to protect them from their own kin. Countess Marie had motioned Grethe into the *solar* and then slipped away, the swish of her skirts lost in the sound of the closing door. Even the dogs had been banished; there was no one here but Eleanor. Arguably the most powerful woman in the Western World and certainly among the most alone.

"Certes I shall try, Lady."

Eleanor's long hands were folded in her lap, resting on a bit of needlepoint one could tell she didn't care for. She was better at painting; a new-begun miniature on an easel by the windows, angled to catch the northern light, attested to that. Better still at drawing up writs and agreements with her lawyer's mind and elegant hand—

(Now, how do you know her handwriting's *elegant,* Karen wondered, when no sample of it survives? Stop writing fiction! Pay attention!)

But ladies did needlepoint, and even queens, if they wanted their subjects to respect them, the menfolk to take them seriously, and their ladies-in-waiting to feel comfortable around them, occasionally must succumb to custom.

" 'Tis because my mind is so full, I thought to empty it," Eleanor answered Grethe's unasked question, as if the two knew each other's minds too well to need the pretense. With that she tossed the lot of it—fabric, frame, needle, silks, and scissors—into the fresh rushes, intermixed with pear blossoms, Grethe noticed approvingly, on the flagged stone floor. "I dreamt of Richard."

"Did you, Lady?" Grethe's hands were clasped beneath her

apron—damp with the new beer that had spilled out of the tankard when Gilbert jostled her—to stop their trembling. Please! she thought. Please say you dreamt he had a fever and recovered, nothing more! Or say you dreamt he married and had a dozen children. Say he turned into an eagle and flew away over the trees. Say anything but what I know you're going to say, so I can work around it!

"He was in the Holy Land. . . ." Eleanor's voice took on a dreamy quality; she had lapsed into *langue d'oyl,* the language of her childhood, where even Grethe would have trouble following her. Could Karen use that? Eleanor's eyes were further clouded, and something seemed to sparkle in them. "It could be no other place for, God's breath, I know it well! Almost I could feel the bite of sand fleas yet again! My son was eating something from a basket of fruit, methinks it was a fig. Have you ever seen a fig, Grethe? They grow where I was born, and all through the southern regions, but not here. And you've never been further south than here, have you?"

"I fear not, Lady." Keep talking! Karen pleaded. Talk about the fruit, about the snow it's packed in, about the man who sent it, but don't go any further! Has Grethe ever fainted? Would that do? Or shall I just plead stupidity? Gosh, your Highness, not a clue!

"Well, then, I need to tell you that a fig is a fruit quite different from a pear or apple, which has but few seeds. The fig has countless seeds, which are found throughout its sweet flesh, so tiny one devours them along with the sweetness, scarcely knowing that they're there. . . ."

Eleanor's eyes cleared suddenly and fixed deep on Grethe's.

"Richard made to eat the fruit, but someone—man or woman, I know not—burst into the tent. Yes, I forgot to mention he was in a tent, and he'd been ill. The fruit was a gift. . . ."

Keep talking! Karen pleaded, but Eleanor shook her head slightly, to clear it.

"The voice said: 'Stay your hand, King of England. Do not eat of this fruit, and history will glorify you for it.' "

Eleanor looked fixedly at Karen. "What say you, Mistress Grethe? Clearly the fig was only a symbol for something other. What think you it means?"

[GLITCH]
[HICCUP]
[oops!]

Glitch and hiccup and oops, and suddenly it is no longer spring but early winter. Suddenly the trees on the rolling hillsides beyond the arched windows were bare of the leaves that had already turned their myriad rusts and reds and yellows and browns and crimsons, and the *solar* was empty. Someone had forgotten to close the shutters against the cold. Eleanor was well across the Alps on her way to Navarre to collect the Princess Berengaria and present her to Richard in Sicily, and Grethe hadn't said a word.

A spattering of leaves blew across the flagged stone floor, teasing at Karen's pattened feet. Even her garments were different, a heavier kirtle, hose on her feet, though the apron she wrung in her hands still felt damp from the brewery. She hadn't spoken. Someone, something S.oteri had prevented her. The Third Crusade would go on without her, history remain the same.

An exercise in futility. And she was still eight hundred years from home. Had the S.oteri, one or many, vanished along with Eleanor and left her stranded here? She stood empty-handed in the empty *solar*, until she heard the scream.

# SEVEN

It was Kit, who'd broken water all over their shared bed and was well advanced in labor by the time Grethe arrived in the hut. How had she heard the girl scream from within the castle, high up in the *solar?*

She hadn't. Karen had. What is the sound of one S.oteri sniggering?

"How long since your water broke?" Karen/Grethe asked at once and practically, barring the door behind her. The midwife, she knew, lived in the village below the abbey. An hour or more to find her and fetch her back, assuming she was at home and sober. Where Elspeth had been midwife in her time, none had trusted Grethe, who had no children of her own, to birth theirs.

"Sunup!" the girl gasped, flat on her back with her legs splayed, panting with pain and fear.

"And the pains?" A post-LaMaze Karen wanted to say *contractions,* but Grethe, being a Christian, knew her Genesis and a woman's lot, and spoke first.

Kit winced as another contraction took her, holding her breath until it passed. The worst thing she could do, Karen knew, but she said nothing.

"Small ones from the very beginning," the girl said. "But when I tried to get up to tell someone, they got so bad I couldn't stand. I've been lying here ever since, trying to keep quiet, hoping they'd stop. My mother always said they'd stop if you lay still. I'd not meant to scream, but that last one felt like it was ripping me in two."

*Your mother was an idiot!* Karen wants to say, but Grethe restrains herself.

"Once you've lost your water, you'd best pray they don't stop, lass," she said instead, calculating. Sunup. It was twilight now, say four-thirty in the afternoon. What was wrong with the child, to wait so long?

"It's bad-omened," Kit answered Grethe's unasked question. "The midwife said today was ill-starred for birthing. I've got to wait until the morrow."

*The midwife*, Grethe thought, gritting her surviving teeth, *intended to be drunk all day and hadn't wanted to be disturbed!*

"Nonsense!" She did speak up this time. "The best day to birth is the day God decides the babe is due. Is that your best shift?"

"Aye."

"Then take it off and put on the other one. Or do without, if you're warm enough. This is only going to get messier."

Her peremptory tone seemed to focus Kit, who sat up, slid off the bed and, meekly, did what she was told. While she was taking off the good shift (fluid-stained on the back, Karen noted, but no blood. Was that a good sign or a bad? She racked her brains, trying to remember the childbirth classes. It was more than twenty years since she'd done this, and she'd been on the receiving end of it) and putting on the mended one, Grethe took the bucket to the well for fresh water and to wash her hands. A gaggle of shawled and chap-cheeked gossips, having heard Kit screaming, was gathered at the door.

"It's her time, then?" the stereotypical toothless crone—her avatar a decade or two hence, Grethe thought—demanded immediately.

"Aye." Karen scanned the group of a dozen or so, seeking a child to run an errand.

"Need you help, then? Wat's youngest's gone to fetch the midwife, and I've birthed thirteen myself."

And all but two of them in their graves, Grethe thought, but decided to be diplomatic.

"Goodwives, I thank you, but as it's her first, there's no hurrying it. We'll wait for the midwife." Who will be too drunk to stand! she thought as, squinting in the gloaming, she found the volunteer she needed. "You, Alix. Go to the kitchens and ask your mother has she any sour wine to spare."

"New wine would be better, for you and the lass!" one of the other women suggested amid a great deal of nudging and winking. The girl, Alix, realizing she wouldn't be allowed inside the hut to see what was going on any other way, stood on one foot waiting to see what would be decided.

"The sourest she has, Alix, lass. Hurry now."

She watched the girl scamper off, seeing herself at a long-lost age, filled her bucket from the well and began to move away, parting the crowd with her forward motion. Still, they trailed after her, surrounded her in a miasma of her own good beer intermingled with onions and rotten meat and rottener teeth. When she reached the door of the hut, Grethe had to physically bar them from entering.

"Goodwives, I thank you for your concern, and those who wish to linger outside the door in this chill air, I cannot forbid you. . . ."

Where are these words coming from? Karen, the writer, wonders, still searching the corners of her eyes for jellyfish. Whoever was scripting this was better at thinking on their feet than she was. Against the disgruntled murmur of the gathering ("Outside? Does she mean we cannot all crowd into that tiny room, filling it with our stale breath and body heat and fresh bacteria?"), she plunged on:

". . . but Elspeth, my mother, taught me skills I have not begun to use. As you know me, let me practice these skills now."

Gratefully, she saw young Alix silhouetted against the light from the kitchens, staggering a little under the burden of an earthenware jug of wine dregs from the kitchen, best antiseptic to be found in these parts. A prolonged and barely muffled moan coming from within the hut gave her the impetus to shake off her auditors and slip away.

Door closed and barred from within, she set to work.

•

"Please, Grethe, please, oh, please! I'm going to die!"

"No, you aren't, lamb. You're just going to have a baby. Most natural thing in the world. Hang on!"

Grethe had washed her hands in the wine and, hoping she knew what she was doing, examined the girl, clearing the mucus plug sealing the placenta, which prompted a flow of clotted blood and increased the intensity of the contractions. When she stuck her hand inside again, she thought she could feel a change in the shape of the cervix. Was it dilating the way it was supposed to? Ten centimeters, Karen remembered, the number stuck in her head from her long-ago/not-happened-yet LaMaze classes, though how she was supposed to measure that—

It had all come back to her in a single gestalt; added to Grethe's fledgling midwifery, it would have to serve.

If nothing else, Karen thought, this may turn out to be the most medically sound delivery of the century! The hardest part was convincing Kit she knew what she was doing.

"Roll over on your side and tuck your knees up," she'd ordered her as soon as the contractions intensified. "Or you can walk about if you're restless, but don't sprawl on your back. Feel better? Now, breathe as I've instructed you. Don't argue!"

"But what about the birthing stool?"

It was one of two ways it was done in these parts in these times. The parturient sat upright on a short, hard, backless stool—a milking stool would do—either holding onto a rope tied to the rafters or, more frequently, held up by two well-meaning kinswomen while a third knelt between her legs ready to catch the infant in her unwashed hands. Karen's back ached just thinking about it.

The alternative, if there were four volunteers about or at least two strong ones, was to make a hammock of a sheet and bounce the woman up in the air with each contraction until the infant's head appeared in the birth canal and she could finally bear down. Probably more distraction than practicality, it was out of the question anyway with only Karen in attendance.

Kit expected a birthing stool. Her gimlet-eyed stare, between contractions, told Karen she would not be trusted unless she gave a credible answer to that one.

"We'll not need a birthing stool. I know a better way. Are you breathing as I told you to?"

Kit shook her head, clamped her jaw stubbornly, her eyes widening now with more than the usual fear. Karen could read the thoughts as they scrolled across her simple mind: Grethe's never borne and never before officiated at a birth. She doesn't believe in omens; her methods are unorthodox; she dares prognosticate for the queen, and says we do not need a birthing stool. Neither Abelard nor Duns Scotus nor all the learned men in Christendom were needed to tell simple Kit that, ergo, Grethe must be a witch and, QED, she and her baby were doomed.

Wisely, Karen waited, hoping to soothe the girl with body language where words would only frighten, stroking the vast heaving mound of her belly as much to comfort as to time the contractions. Betimes she stroked Kit's hair, crooned to her, bathed her face in cool water, and gave her little sips to drink. Still she could feel the tension in the girl's entire body, hear her shallow breathing as she held herself back. They'd never get anywhere this way. Karen took a cleansing breath of her own, steeled herself, and barked:

"Breathe!"

Startled, the girl obeyed, but soon was panting again out of fear. Karen leaned very close to whisper in her ear.

"If I am indeed a witch, you are powerless. Hadn't you best do what I bid you?"

Numbly, aware her thoughts were being read, Kit nodded.

"Then breathe as I have told you, and no harm will come to you or the babe. . . ." I hope! Karen prayed. If anything went wrong now, Grethe's life wasn't worth a sou. Squashing down her own fear, she took Kit's hands. "Ready now? Inhale deeply . . . that's it. Now pant like a dog at midsummer, keep panting until the pain eases, just like that. Now let the breath out, all the way out, like blowing out a candle. There you are. Now, again . . ."

Was this the first time in history a woman had been more afraid of the midwife than the birth? Karen wondered. No matter, as long as it worked.

It did, for the next several hours. In that time, Wat's youngest—a snot-nosed brat of eight, barefoot even in this weather, no doubt insulated by his several layers of dirt—returned from the village to report the midwife in her cups and wishing Grethe Godspeed but offering no assistance. Alix's mother sent a pigeon pie and some new wine to keep the new midwife's strength up. Karen demolished the former and was mixing a little of the latter with some water to keep her head clear when Kit, who had calmed enough to actually drowse in the precious seconds between contractions, suddenly entered transitional labor.

"Grethe, I need to push. It wants out of me; I can't hold back. I need to push, Grethe, now!"

Calmly (how dare she be so calm?) Karen stuck her fingers into the void once again. The cervix was fully dilated, but she couldn't yet see the head. Almost. "Not now, love. Not yet. Breathe for me a little longer."

"I can't, Grethe, I can't!"

"You will, or be damned! Pay attention now: Sit up and grasp my hands. That's it. Now sing me something."

The girl's eyes widened at what she considered sheer madness. "Sing you something?"

"Aye, you heard me: Sing. You can't push if you're singing, and it's not yet time to push. Sing!"

Shakily, struggling against the overwhelming urge her hormones and a few million years of evolution were screaming at her, the girl began a wobbly, offkey version of "Wood of the Cross" in an illiterate's fractured Latin. Knowing the words and the melody both, though she'd never heard either before, Karen—thinking: Why this? Why not some bawdy lay ballad instead, when more humans have died of religion than of flu?—joined in at the end.

"Again," she ordered Kit. "All the verses yet again, and don't rush them, and then I'll let you push."

"Grethe, I can't—"

"Yes, you can, love, and you will. Do it."

This time she sang the whole thing through with Kit, realizing: Grethe isn't here. This is just me and the S.oteri. Which of us knows the words? I'll never live this down!

"Grethe?" It was a whimper, and only Kit's plaintive tone reminded Karen of who and where she was supposed to be. The girl was clutching her hands like a drowner, panting in desperation. "Please?"

One final grope inside confirmed a small, wet newborn head presenting in the birth canal, pushing mightily toward light and life. Karen wiped her hand quickly on her apron and grasped Kit's two hands again, pulling back as hard as she did.

"Yes, now, Kit darling . . . push!"

•

Somewhere after midnight, they were done. A small and perfect pink girlchild lay mewling against her mother's breast. There was no keeping the neighbors out now. As they jostled each other to get nearer the bed, wiping snotty noses with dirt-seamed fingers before touching the uncanny softness of a newborn cheek, Karen quite literally washed her hands of them. The sooner the infant adapted to the contagions of her time, the better her chances of survival.

And as she walked beneath the stars, her back aching no doubt as much as Kit's from the strain of the past few hours, she took off the sweaty cap that had held her hair back all this time, undid the plait, shook her hair out beneath the sky, and came to terms with it: She was entirely Karen now and had been since she'd taken charge of Kit's labor when no one else would. Wherever Grethe was, it was Karen who'd delivered. Whatever impact that might or might not have on Grethe's future, there was nothing she could do about it.

Was that all it was about, then? Was that why she'd been dragged back here, to deliver a baby Kit could have delivered herself once the increasing pain got her over her mother's bad advice? Or could she? There was a certain amount of danger in letting the labor lapse once the amniotic sac had broken, a certain amount more if one pushed before the cervix was fully dilated. Could such nuances have added Kit's infant to the century's fifty-percent mortality rate?

And what about the impact on Grethe? What if the baby had been meant to die? What if, barring Karen's presence, Grethe had panicked and refused to help? Having quite literally lived with her eleventh-century avatar these several days—or was it months?—Karen thought she knew Grethe better than that.

Would the neighbors ask Grethe to deliver their babies from now on? Would that put the old midwife out of business, or create a dangerous rivalry? What convolutions had Karen set in motion here, or was all of this as it would have happened anyway?

No way to know. No way to know if Grethe's skills would have been up to the challenge even without Karen's assistance. And, dammit, it had been exciting! Nothing comparable, except birthing her own, to the flush of triumph as the small life had been propelled into her hands, slick and bloodied and squalling all hell loose. But had she sacrificed her own future for Grethe's and the child's?

*I want to go home!* Karen thought, feeling suddenly as if it had been she who'd given birth. She crouched in the shadow of the well, biting her knuckles to keep from crying it aloud.

The stars spun round. Karen felt her gorge rise and started to retch. She started to bow her head but then, defiant, tilted it back, closing her eyes to control the spinning. Would it be this easy?

*C'mon, guys; I really don't want to play any more. Take me home!*

•

Gray and the Mind contemplate Eleanor, by the Grace of God, Countess of Poitou and the Aquitaine, once Queen of France and finally Queen of England, as she sits in her *solar* at midday serenely painting a miniature. The subject is the countryside as seen from the Gothic-arched windows of her seat of government at Chinon, overlooking the spires of the abbey church of Fontrevault, which would one day house her tomb. There is no reference in her painting to the muddy, rutted castle keep just below her window or to the small lives that transpire in it.

The more observant observer, who had eyes to see, might notice an uninspired bit of needlepoint, perhaps abandoned by a lady in waiting, dropped forgotten among the rushes and wilted pear blossoms on the flagged stone floor. Unlikely as it might seem within the confines of a medieval demesne, Eleanor was alone.

*I told you so!* Fuchsia tells them, trying not to sound too smug. *Where did you get the idea that Karen was here? She isn't here, so there!*

There is no other noise but a sibilance of brush strokes and the sound of one queen humming. The song might have been *Lignum Crucis,* "Wood of the Cross."

The Mind exchanges glances. The alibi doesn't satisfy, but . . .

A few hundred miles away, in a Celtic stronghold during Julius Caesar's time, someone was beginning her day with a very bad headache.

•

*No glitch or hiccups this time; I've got yew rite wear I wont yew . . . snrk! Tee/hee . . .*

•

What was it like to witness the end of the world? Grainne had been pondering that throughout the spring and for most of the summer as she watched the enemy build their siegeworks just beyond her city's walls. By now, having a fair idea what was to come, she pondered a new thought: How much longer?

"We are forty thousand strong!" Ryalbran had regaled those gathered at the feasting the night before. ("If you count the babes and ancients!" someone else had remarked to much guffawing, gallows' humor. "Shall we teach them to fight?" There followed a riff on toothlessness and incontinence in both babes and ancients, and it might have gone on all night or until the beer ran out if Glewlwyd, who was king that summer, hadn't reminded them half-sternly that the Young Crow still had the floor.)

Through all of this, Ryalbran stood on his dignity, as if it were all he had.

"We have sufficient stores to last a winter and a summer more without planting the outermost fields, if they insist on keeping us from them," he went on, his poet's hands stuck into his sword belt because Grainne had once pointed out that he gestured too large, especially when he'd been drinking. "We . . ."

*He moves just like Raymond,* Karen thought. *In fact, he even looks like him!*

Then she reminded herself that she was not Karen but Grainne, the Ugly, and Raymond was two thousand years from being born.

Hold it. Not again! Yes.

Oh, yes, she had it figured out this time as soon as she'd awakened this morning to the sun needling at her through the miniblinds, making her think: The con must be over, because I'm home.

Then she realized the angle of the sun was wrong, because the miniblinds were not miniblinds at all. The light was poking at her vertically instead of horizontally, which was enough to make her sit up and pay attention, only to find that the sun was coming at her through the walls of a house of undaubed wattle, a house built of sticks like the Second Little Pig's, made from the small green saplings, no thicker than a woman's wrist, which were harvested regularly to keep the great stands of forest healthy by weeding out the spindly new growth which would otherwise have, literally, sapped the great Mother Trees by sucking all the nutrients out of the surrounding soil. So the Arverni, as all their Celtic brethren, cultivated their old growth forests even as they revered them.

Houses, then, were built of thin saplings lashed together, and roofed most often with thatch. In the cold months the walls were lined with hides to keep the cold out, sort of, not that it mattered because the Celts were a hardy lot and didn't mind the cold—as if it ever got that cold in south-central France—and since there was a fire going year round anyway, what better way to get rid of the smoke, in addition to the smokehole in the ceiling, than to have walls that breathed?

Lastly, in these Roman times, at least one wall of every house was actually a section of the *murus gallicus* (or so the Romans called it, and having won the war, they got to write the history afterward) or "Gallic wall," a box-shaped redan of timbers filled with rubble and faced with stone which encircled the entire *oppidum* or fortress city of Avaricum and its forty-thousand-plus inhabitants, for what better place to build one's house in these Roman times but snug up against something twelve feet thick and virtually impenetrable?

Except when the sun shone through the far wall into the eyes of those who had drunk too much the night before and didn't remember how they ended up tumbled back into their narrow shelf bed and oblivious when the rest of the city was up and about. As usual, Grainne slept alone, on the far side of the hearth from Sequanna and her oft-absent warrior husband and whichever of Sequanna's offspring were passing through at any given time.

And Karen knew all of this before her eyes had completely focused against the glare of the same sun under which she'd been born but under very different circumstances.

Meaning that Fuchsia had done hir homework a little better this time, and the illusion was more airtight. But having slipped up that first time in Eleanor's court, s/he'd have a hard time convincing Karen now.

And as a final insult, s/he'd given her someone else's hangover.

Karen—or rather Grainne, who was apparently to be her avatar in this life—had drunk too much beer the night before because Sequanna had asked her to keep Glewlwyd company and do her mightiest to preserve the mood behind his bleak smile for one night in spite of the Romans' intention to wipe them all off the face of the land. The summer-long siege was one thing. But if one more messenger arrived with one more tale of shrieking slaughter from the lands to the east and north, the Old King might wish his people still killed their kings once a year, that he might avoid the decisions the coming days would force him to make.

•

Some years earlier, in the city of Rome, a crude man, an upstart, a nose-picking, toe-picking, armpit-and-crotch scratching common soldier named Gaius Julius had, by reason of his gift for slaughtering civilians of a barbarian bent, been made proconsul of the Province of Gaul, with the typical effrontery with which the Romans claimed every bit of land their eyes fell on, as if there weren't several million souls already inhabiting it. Taking this to mean that all of what would one day be northern Europe was his own personal toy, this Julius thought to win immortality, or at least an emperorship or, if nothing else, make the trains run on time, by annihilating every man, woman, and child in what he called Tripartite Gaul, so that his own kind with their incestuous marriages and their vomitoria and their blood sports and their lead-lined drinking cups (which some say would be their downfall more than the barbarians at the gate) could raise their standard over it and have it for themselves.

At least, that was the simple version of it.

The complex version had to do with a confluence of seemingly unrelated events, including an attack by the Celts upon a Greek principality known as Massilia, which happened to be an ally of Rome, and the migration of the Helvetii, nearly four hundred thousand strong, from their land between the mountains because of pressures from the Teutones to the north, and the resulting intertribal turmoil—as if any Celt who owned a spear and a horse needed an excuse to create intertribal turmoil.

The Romans under Julius-the-eponymous-Caesar (from which whee get *kaiser* and *czar*—whee!) began by slaughtering two-thirds of the Helvetii and sending the rest into exile back to the very lands they'd scorched before they'd taken to the road. The reasons he gave had something to do with his people's still smarting from their one and only defeat by a Celtic tribe called the Volcae Tectosages nearly twenty years earlier. He needed a scapegoat to keep his troops happy, there weren't any *shtetls,* all Celts look alike, and the only good Celt—well, you get his drift.

And what did any of this have to do with the Arverni of Avaricum, of which Grainne/Karen was apparently a citizen? About as much as a twentieth-century European Jew had to do with the death of Christ (even that was the Romans' responsibility, which you'd know if you'd been paying attention). Honestly, Gentle Reader, we're surprised at you! You're asking for reasons? How, after being on this journey known as Western Civilization all this time, can you possibly ask such an ingenuous question?

And Karen, still smarting from all those D's in high school Latin ("All of Gaul is divided into three parts. . . ." Yeah, so what's your point?) can't help thinking: A thousand years after I'm dead, Hitler will be considered a military genius for his invasion of Poland, and ninth-graders will be busting their heads translating his as-yet-undiscovered memoirs: "All the Jews were divided into three parts: Those we locked in the synagogues and burned, those we marched into the woods and shot, and the rest we gassed. . . ."

In spite of herself, she finds herself making a mental note for her novel, a bit of dialogue between Gret and Darymon and the S.oteri about the course of human history; it almost made her head stop pounding.

Except that prognosticating a future which included S.oteri was what had gotten her in trouble with Fuchsia in the first place.

*Um, Fuchsia, dear friend, I know you're responsible for this. Okay, you've made your point. Just send me back to my own time, and we'll negotiate. Maybe I can write my novel without including S.oteri or just give them another name. Hey, far be it from me to risk copyright infringement on a minor thing like that.*

All the while thinking: Hah! Just get me back to my own time, and I'll rat you out to the Mind, and the novel goes on. I've been standing up to bullies all my life, remember me?

That is, of course, unless the Mind's involved in this, too, and since when does it have the power of telekinesis, anyway?

Maybe since I started writing about it?

Uh-oh. Maybe Fuchsia's right. Maybe I am a danger. Maybe I can change the course of history, mine as well as theirs. Maybe—

"You truly are going to sleep the day away, aren't you?" Grainne sat up and squinted at the squat form of dark-haired Sequanna, who was holding out a cup to her, one of her better incised earthenware designs. "Head hurts? I'm not surprised. Drink this."

"Thank you!" Grainne/Karen remembered as always to look directly at Sequanna when she spoke. Sequanna had lost most of her hearing in the same skirmish where she'd earned the scar on the lower-right quadrant of her belly.

•

It couldn't properly be called a battle, and neither of them had wanted to fight that day. Nor were they sure if they'd ever wanted to fight at all but, girls as well as boys, they had all learned to ride almost before they could walk, and could handle both knife and spear before they'd lost all their milk teeth. Those who earned it, like their childhood companion Flidias, would from puberty to death carry a sword.

Flidias was still fighting alongside the men, though she was a grandmother several times over, and the years or maybe too much drink had coarsened her and added a heft no amount of riding could work off. It was ironic that of the three she would end up with only superficial scars.

Fighting was like breathing to their kind. The sheer number of tribes which called themselves Celts, yet cherished different gods and different sacred places and different kinship lines and any excuse to steal each other's cattle or whack heads off ought to have been a clue. Their names rolled off the tongue as soon as a child learned to speak, a reward given to the one from each seven-year who could recite the most of them at the summer games.

Grainne had won in her year. She could still see her mother glaring at her, narrow-eyed. Most parents were proud of a child's accomplishments. Only this one behaved as if everything the child learned somehow detracted from the woman who bore her. Still, the little flame-haired brat had sung loud and defiantly:

"Atrebates, Belgae, Remi
Allobroges and Iceni
Nervii, Ubii, Vindelici
Ordovices, Boii, Breuci
Tolistobogii
Bituriges
Caledones
Gallaeci
Lemovices, Carnutes, Regni
and the Volcae Tectosages . . ."

"And we are—?" Glewlwyd, who was much younger and bore a different name in those days, and who was only Lord of the Games and never dreamed of to be King, had prompted her.

"Arverni!" young Grainne had crowed proudly, knowing without looking at her that her mother's scowl had deepened.

Most parents who named a girlchild Grainne did so as a kind of nervous superstition, because the child was exceptionally beautiful and to call her "Ugly" spared her being stolen by spirits.

"Not you!" Grainne's mother had shrilled at her from the time she was four. "I named you Ugly because you are! Ugly and clumsy and stupid, and no man will ever want you!"

To spite her, Grainne had grown to be bright and graceful and, if not beautiful, at least passing handsome. As for men, many had wanted her, and she had chosen among them, and only one remained forever out of reach.

But, to get back to the reasons the Celts fought each other, they were many. A cattle raid, a "stolen" bride (though Grainne had never known one to go unwillingly), even a careless word spoken in drink could set one or several hundred at each other, with the survivors turning the event into some great historic moment to be recounted afterward in endless drunken poems, no matter how silly its origins were in fact.

Thus Grainne and Flidias and Sequanna and a few of the boys of their year had been out larking on their horses that spring day—as yet too young to be bespoken, and so free to pretend they were still children—when a gaggle of Aedui droving a herd of clearly Arverni cattle ahead of them crossed their path. In order to hide their cattle-thieving, it was clear to the cross-eyed Aedui leader—who was barely old enough to sport a beard—they'd have to kill these Arverni youngsters and then claim ignorance once the then-King sent his messengers to inquire.

Knives were drawn, a spear or two was thrown, there was a great deal of shouting and wheeling about of horses and a choking cloud of dust raised. Grainne and her horse simply didn't get out of the way fast enough, and one of the Aedui knives grazed her belly and, as her horse stumbled, throwing her forward—

No. That didn't explain Sequanna's loss, the ringing in her ears from the combination of the fall and the bleat of carnyxes, the animal-headed, bronze-throated battle horns that were only brought out for serious battles, and which would one day drive the Romans to despair. Theirs was a small skirmish in a bigger battle, one that was still sung of to this day, though Sequanna could not hear her part of it but only lip-read it if the singer wasn't too drunk—

No. Make up your Mind! Fuchsia scrambles to rewind the tape and edit simultaneously. . . .

All Grainne remembered was dust and blood and the screaming of horses, the ground shaking beneath their hooves once she was thrown (and chariots; she was sure there had been chariots), a fire lancing through her gut and the demon howl of the carnyxes (Yes!), and when her head cleared there was nothing but dust and trampled ground and one of their boys and three of the Aedui dead and Flidias Wildhair looking down at Grainne from horseback, shaking her lime-stiffened locks and sucking the blood from a flesh wound across her upper arm.

"It's over. Can you stand?"

"Sequanna . . ." was all Grainne managed to say. If she could breathe she could stand, she decided, refusing to notice how much blood she'd lost. It ran down her thigh and dripped about her feet as she pulled herself upright, inspecting the wound in between pressing the edges of her tunic against it to staunch the flow. Most annoying, it had seeped into her crotch, and the littlest brats would taunt her about it when they got back to the city, mistaking it for menstrual blood unless someone set them straight.

Her head was spinning. Why was she thinking of these things now? Where was Sequanna?

Unhurt, it seemed, at first, Sequanna stood off aways, on the edges of where the battle had been (a dozen combatants or a thousand? Why didn't that part come clear in Grainne's memory?), a look of absolute horror on her face. She had her hands clasped over her ears. Her mouth was open, trembling as if she were weeping, but no sound came out. Seeing Grainne was wounded, she ran to her. Through all of this, Flidias did not dismount. Her horse finicked, shifting from one foot to another, anxious to get away from the stink of blood.

Sequanna tumbled into the dust beside Grainne and put her hand to the wound. Strangely, it not only instantly ceased to hurt, but ceased to bleed as well. When Sequanna took her hand away, Grainne was strong enough to walk. She clasped her friend's hands in gratitude.

"What did you do?"

Sequanna only shook her head. "I . . . I can't hear."

# EIGHT

This was how it was for them. The RealWorld was not some sky-borne paradise or wait-until-you-die afterlife, but here and now and always—just over your shoulder, just under your skin, as near as a drink from a sacred spring, the feel of a good horse under you, the scent of a breeze, the touch of a loved one's hand, the laugh of a child, the smile in an old one's eyes. And the sacrifice of an OuterWorld gift was rewarded with one from within.

Undistracted by the voices around her, Sequanna learned to listen to the InnerWorld. From that day forward she came into her own as *filid,* a natural healer who also sometimes saw the future as if it were the present. Karen's time would misconstrue the word as *seeress,* a kind of Cassandra.

Sequanna would have been horrified at the thought. As she and her kind saw it, she had simply been given an extra door to the RealWorld that hearing people lacked.

It was this philosophy which made it possible for life to go on despite the Roman legions camped on their doorstep.

They'd arrived—metal-chested, red-skirted, hairy-legged—as soon as the roads were passable in the spring.

Since the last century there had been treaties made between certain tribes and the Romans, and the treaties had been kept. It was in everyone's interest. Trade with Rome meant trade with the tribes to the far East, and trade was always desirable. There wasn't a Celt alive who didn't cherish silks and wine and gemstones and silver in exchange for their amber and iron and bronzework and pottery and salt. Give a Roman trader twenty-two minutes, he'd give you the world. And if it was a fight the Celts wanted, they could do what they had always done and would always do, as any visitor to an Irish pub can tell you, and fight among themselves.

But when the Helvetii, possibly the largest of the tribes at nearly four hundred thousand strong, torched their own villages and set out from their cramped territory between the mountains to seek more fertile land, it made the Romans twitchy. As if the nose-picking, balls-scratching Julius—who, it was said, sought to distract his constituency from both his common ancestry and his penchant for falling-down foaming-at-the-mouth convulsions so that he could be emperor someday—needed an excuse to kill Celts.

"If he were one of us, we'd revere him for his infirmity," Sequanna opined when Grainne translated for her what the latest drunken courier had reported to the assemblage about the leader of those monolithic thousands digging their trenches and siegeworks and churning up dust in the woods and round about the *oppidum*. "Why is it we know he's gods-touched, and the Romans can't see it?"

Grainne, who was a potter not a philosopher, had only shrugged. "Maybe it's because they live in cities. Their feet touch marble floors and paved roads. Or neither, being clad in silken slippers. They no longer remember the scent of the earth."

"And so they lose touch with the spirits inhabiting it." Sequanna had considered that, nodding as she accepted it. One or another of her grandchildren had wanted her attention then, getting it by launching himself at her knees and clinging there until she pried him loose and went with him to see what he was tugging at her about. "Pity we can't capture yon Julius and introduce him to our ways. It might stop the killing."

Meanwhile, life did go on. The outer fields beyond the walls could and often did go fallow in bountiful years, and there were fields enough within the walls to sustain them, as Ryalbran had pointed out to the assemblage last night, even if the siege lasted a year. Thus, the potters continued their pottery making, the glass-makers shaped their strands of beads for trade, and everyone tended the fields and cows and chickens, and the ironmongers plied their trade in making sure every chariot's wheels were newly rimmed and all the swords were tempered. The only difference was that the salt traders went wanting because no one could smuggle the salt in from the mines to the north, and all the cattle drovers had left, sneaking out in pairs and singly when the moon was down, and moved their herds to far-flung fields the Romans couldn't police without spreading themselves too thin. There were shortages, but life went on. Men and women still ate and drank and coupled and made babies; young ones grew and old ones died; flowers bloomed and berries ripened; horses foaled and shoats were weaned, and there was still plenty of beer.

The Romans, sour and solitary, ate their field rations and the occasional stolen chicken, beat themselves off in their sweaty tents or did each other the Greek way, and cursed the epileptic Julius whenever he was out of earshot. Still, they'd kill for him, or at least for the patch of land that was promised each of them if he survived twenty years in this business. The job sucked, but you couldn't beat the pension plan with a stick.

•

As for the drinking in Glewlwyd's house the night before, that was from desperation. The Old King was dying, not of Romans but of a heart that leaked half as much blood backward as it pushed forward. Simply breathing was an effort for him, and he could no longer mount a horse. What he ought to have done, some suggested, was have himself tied on and lead a suicide raid against the legions to get the gods' attention. But Glewlwyd clung to life, waiting for the Archdrui to come with the autumn equinox and read the entrails and tell him what to do, whether it was to die or to live, whether alone or to take his people with him. In the interim, a true Celt, he opened his coffers and bought drinks for the house.

"The gods may wait that long, but the Romans won't!" Ryalbran had chafed. "Glewlwyd should give over and let someone else be King."

"Someone else like you, pussy eater?" someone had hooted and the debate began all over again. Aside from fighting and breeding, what any Celt liked best was to drink and argue.

Had he not been so impatient, Ryalbran might have been more listened to. Who in Avaricum knew the Romans better? Kidnapped as a child by a rival tribe, he'd been sold into Rome and came of age there, his dark hair and inch-long eyelashes and unusual cinnamon-brown eyes—unusual for one of those almost universally pale-eyed northern barbarians, anyway—making him a kind of pet in an elderly noblewoman's household. He never did any true slave's labor but was taught to read and write and orate ("That last was where they made their biggest mistake!" Sequanna had whispered to Grainne, and the two women had giggled and hugged each other as tears of mirth coursed down their faces) and made a scribe and keeper of the household accounts.

What else he became to the old hag as he grew to his full height and his voice deepened and his pretty face began to show signs of downy hair, no one asked and Ryalbran did not volunteer. They could picture her, her face inches thick with paint and her breath foul with wine, having outlived three husbands, and fearful her old bones could not stand the passions of a mature slave, choosing the Young Crow's innocence. How many nights did she command him to set the ink and quill aside and do her service with a different manner of tool? Ryalbran spoke of his past to no one, except Grainne. For some reason he told Grainne more than he told anyone, even the women he slept with.

The story of the "battle" where she'd earned her scar was what had first caused the Young Crow, who'd been born a decade later, to revere her.

"To be so young, and not even fully trained as a warrior, and to have fought so bravely—!" He could not finish his thought. What bizarre hyperbolic version, Grainne wondered, had he heard? Or was he only regretting that he'd been too young to fight those who had enslaved him?

"We were ambushed by cattle raiders," she'd tried to set him straight. "I didn't get out of the way fast enough. I suppose if I hadn't run into somebody's sword, they'd have carried me off and I'd be a slave in some other tribe today. The rest was largely exaggerated."

"Still . . ." Ryalbran had looked at her with awe. At the time, infatuated with him, she'd let it be.

"We each do what we have to do to survive," she'd tried to comfort him. He himself had escaped Rome in his teens and found his way back to his tribe with no training and no knowledge beyond what his father had taught him of rivers and streams and sacred places to use as guidelines. He'd been overcompensating ever since, throwing himself into battles, earning too many scars, including the one that had nearly severed the tendons at the back of his right knee, in order to still the whispers of "Roman pussy boy" that dogged him when his companions had been drinking too much.

•

I never had any of those conversations! Karen thinks as they come flooding in on her with each sip of whatever it is Sequanna's given her: But Grainne did, and I remember them. And as if that's not complicated enough, I've got to deal with Grainne's feeling about Ryalbran what I feel for Raymond, and neither of us getting any. Just what I need!

She had to sift her own memories out of Grainne's before the two became intertangled, as they had with Grethe in Eleanor's time. Fuchsia was getting better at this, and there was no telling where it would end.

Sequanna had gone to stir something on the open hearth. Oatmeal again! Karen noted. At least some things were consistent. A milch cow lowed and shifted its feet and contemplated her from its enclosure in one corner. Half a dozen small children, at least two of them Sequanna's grandkids, skittered around playing some chasing game in and out of the open doors. Karen took advantage of the distraction to assess her situation.

Fact: She had been sleeping naked under a light summer cloak thrown over her as a blanket, still wearing her amber jewelry and with the lime not yet washed out of her hair. Meaning Grainne really had been too drunk last night to do more than slip out of her clothes and fall on the bed. So far all of this was Grainne, including the blue-inked spirals of tattoos twined about her shoulders, thighs, and upper arms, giving the lie to one theory that only the Druids had tattooed themselves. There was clay under her nails, which reminded her that she, like Sequanna, was a potter, an artist/artisan (no class distinctions in this culture, no separation of the Grishams from the midlist writers, any form of art was a connection with the InnerWorld, the RealWorld) with a lifelong place of honor in her society.

She also still had the bruise across her instep from a twentieth-century suitcase. Good. That was her touchstone, her connection to herself as Karen, and to the future she'd come from. Taking another sip, Karen continued her inventory:

What surprised her, until she thought about it (less sugar and more minerals in the diet), was that she still had all her teeth. Closing first one eye and then the other, she noted that she was somewhat less nearsighted (because there was nothing to read?). She wondered if she was still prone to tachycardia. She did know, with the part of her brain that belonged to Grainne (did a knack for rhyming come with the territory in this preliterate culture?), that there were hawthorn trees in the woods and, assuming she could dodge the Romans, she could harvest the berries to keep her heart rhythm under control if need be. Lastly, her arms and legs and even the space between her eyebrows were as smooth as if she'd been plucked.

Which, of course, she had been. Apparently, she and her kind spent a great deal of time bathing, sitting in sweathouses, gazing at themselves in polished bronze mirrors, and plucking their entire bodies with varieties of iron tweezers.

Karen Jenner's lectures on the design of things came back loud and clear. The only thing missing was the reek of jet fuel from JFK.

This is not my knowledge, Karen thinks. Yet now it is. But this time I'm leading someone else's life with far more ease than I care to admit. If only I had a legal pad and a couple of pens, I could almost get to like it here. Of course, it might have helped if I'd read Graves's *White Goddess* the way I was supposed to in undergrad so I'd know what was going on.

Or would that only have complicated the issue? Who said Graves or any modern scholar really knew what was going on?

The brew she was drinking was one of Sequanna's secret potions—a tisane steeped dark enough to obscure the bottom of the bowl and always the cure for what ailed one. Karen swore she tasted ginseng.

No. Not possible, not in this time and place. Or was it? Until this summer's siege, the Arverni had traded with the Romans, who traded with the world.

"The last of the root I got from the Helvetii *ovate*. She claimed it came from a land where it snows all the time," Sequanna answered the unasked question. Reading minds from faces was only one of her many talents. "Though I wonder how plants grow if there's always snow? I wonder, too, if she survived the fighting."

"I wonder will we," Grainne countered, drinking deeply.

"I've been thinking about that." Sequanna squatted on her haunches before Grainne's cot. Grainne/Karen frowned at her until she smiled sheepishly and sat on the bed beside her life-long friend. "Is it madness to live as if everything is normal?"

The question was as practical as it was philosophical. There was no difference to their kind. Sequanna had three grandchildren staying with her and a fourth on the way; her daughter Aoife, whose husband was one of the absent cattle drovers, was due with her first any day now. There were ways of smuggling them out to kin in other places, but were they safer on the open road than behind a twelve-foot wall?

Yes! Karen knows, not knowing how she knows. If you send them south to Gergovia where Vercingetorix has his camp, they'll at least have a chance.

Or will they? Did everyone die at Avaricum when the legions finally abandoned the siege and attacked? Grainne can't possibly know yet, and Karen's knowledge of this era's history is far too sketchy.

"Is it better to allow the future to destroy our joy in the present?" she counters, temporizing. "Or shall we live as we have always lived until we must do otherwise?"

Sequanna smiles and shakes her head at her. "How much *did* you have to drink last night?"

Grainne/Karen sets the tisane aside. "Too much, obviously." Her head has stopped pounding, but now she can't stop yawning.

"You really are lost among the Old Ones today. Maybe you're evolving into a *filid.*" Sequanna pats her shoulder, tucks the cloak up over her, and begins to shoo the children outside to play. "Go on, sleep it off. Join me in the pottery later."

•

It was one thing, Karen thinks, to be stuck in a century which one at least recognized from the movies, in a medieval court populated by a few hundred souls most of whose functions one at least vaguely understood. Quite another to be stranded in a major city in a century so far removed from her own that blatant faux pas were inevitable.

Yet Sequanna had accepted her as the person she was supposed to be. And because Sequanna did, the rest of the city would as well.

First premise: Avaricum *is* a city.

Why is it one hears *preliterate* and thinks *primitive?* This was no rustic way station, no clearing in the woods, but a true metropolitan area with a population the size of Flagstaff, Arizona or Wheeling, West Virginia or the average state university campus. It's because, Karen thinks, the Romans won the war and got to write the history after. Ever since, Western culture has derived from the Roman model, and Catholic high school kids are saddled with Caesar's dead Latin.

Wouldn't it be a hoot, she thinks, if I could save Avaricum and have them join forces with Vercingetorix to the south, whip Caesar's pantsless ass and, when the time comes, not have to suffer through second-year Latin after all? A Nation Once Again, indeed!

What the hell was in that tisane anyway?

She finds herself, as an excuse for lying abed instead of getting up to face the day, sorting her knowledge out of Grainne's, only this time she finds it sorely lacking. Jenner's medieval classes helped her wing it in Eleanor's time, but except for the aforementioned second-year Latin, an old issue of *National Geographic*, and a lot of neo-Druidism peddled by some of her Wiccan friends, this time she's really stuck.

Rather like an S.oteri trying to comprehend human society? Now, there's a hook.

"Um, Fuchsia?"

Karen is alone in Sequanna's house now, except for the cow; even the children have left her in peace. She knows the little pinkish jellyfishic snot is watching her, but is s/he listening, too? Karen sits crosslegged on the cot, the summer cloak tucked around her breasts for modesty. The lime in her hair is beginning to itch, and the amber necklace is suddenly chill against her awakening flesh. To her it suggests she's becoming more fixed in this reality.

"Look, I know you're responsible for bringing me here, and if there's a reason . . . well, fine. But if it's just to prove the point that you *can* . . . well, that's fine, too, because there isn't much I can do about it, is there?"

Silence. Karen scratches at her scalp, raining little flakes of dried lime down over her shoulders, breasts, and legs—no Head & Shoulders in this century—clears her throat and tries again.

"Hey, I'm impressed, okay? Now let's end the game and send me home, because maybe I'm spoiled, but I kind of have this thing for flush toilets. There is also the minor detail that before the summer's over most of these people will be dead, and since I've already figured out that you're not going to let me do anything to prevent that, any more than you let me change the course of the Third Crusade . . . hello?"

Silence. Karen tosses the cloak aside and hops off the cot now, getting annoyed. Ordinarily she's not the type to go striding around naked when there are no locks on the doors, but Grainne is a pre-Christian Celt, and this is no big deal for her. Neither is railing at the gods when they fuck with your life, particularly when there's one behind every bush and tree.

"By the rowan that is my name's emblem, by the whitethorn that gives me heart, and by the yew that presages death, I caution you, Spirit!" Holy shit! Karen thinks: Is that coming out of *my* mouth? "You will answer to me and do my bidding, or woe to you and your household!"

She loves the texture of the words on her tongue, words which, she now remembers—though without knowing whose memory it is—were the one true thing that bound all Celtic tribes together, an entirely oral language which was as readily understood as far east as Olbia as it was to the north and west in Hibernia and which, even in her own time, would really only have two variations in two surviving branches, so that a Highland Scot could understand a Breton as easily as two drunken Irishmen could understand anything either was saying at all.

It is her tongue, and she is speaking it, and that in itself feels glorious. But she's not getting any answers.

"All right for you!" she says in a moment of entire Karenness. She hears tittering outside and wonders if the children are peeking through the withes at her—old Grainne communing with the gods again—or if it's only jellyfish. For effect, she shakes her fist at the sky. "I'll play your game for now, but if I do, I'll win it!"

Wrapping the cloak carelessly about her, she picks her unerring, callus-footed way along the stone-paved street to the sweathouse, thinking: They can't read my mind; not yet! They can't tell how terrified I am. . . .

•

For something which ostensibly doesn't have a face, Fuchsia is getting very good at frowning. Right now s/he's wearing Grainne/Karen's mother's scowl. *Don't you DARE speak to me in that tone of voice, don't you DARE!*

TQ Is Watching You.

You do remember Tertium Quid, don't you? Tertium Quid is to the S.oteri as the S.oteri are to humans. That is to say, way ahead of them in some respects and untested yet in others.

Or perhaps it is to say all species are created equal. Do you find it interesting, Gentle Reader, that you accepted the arrival of TQ in this narrative without any problem at all? Think about it: You don't know what it/they are, or where it comes from, or even *if* it comes from. What if it exists on the same planet as the S.oteri and they don't even know it?

Yes, I know. We told you in the first book that the S.oteri and the fungus were the only living creatures on their world.

What if we lied? And, by the way, who's *we,* Kemosabe?

Confused yet? Let's add yet another dimension: What if the S.oteri are actually a species of parasite dependent on TQ as the host? Alternatively, what if TQ is really the fungus which, after a few million years, is tired of being eaten and has evolved an intelligence of its own and a desire to fight back?

No, huh? Okay, try this: What if TQ is really an inner dimension of the S.oteri, a heretofore unexamined aspect of the Common Mind, which ain't so common any more, which occupies the same temporal space or lack of same and is or isn't one and the same? Kind of a superego to the S.oteri id? Are you paying attention?

Anyway, you don't know what TQ is and you don't really care, do you? You just want us to get on with the story. Okay:

So TQ watches. It knows what Fuchsia's up to but has a manner of Prime Directive of its own. Much as it would like to pluck hir out by the roots and give hir a good shaking, it has to play the game out by its own rules or what's the point? So it watches and waits, drumming its fingers, waiting for hir to go too far. But what's "too far" to a Third Thing? Not necessarily the same as too far might be for humans who, in this century alone have given us a couple of world wars, a few dozen genocides (don't bother counting them), and the notion that the right to eat is incumbent on your political persuasion, especially if you're a child. So what do you mean "too far," Kemosabe?

Put it this way: The S.oteri, as you know, are still having trouble with this concept known as Time. By contrast, TQ is very much aware of Time, which it perceives as a weave of multicolored strands sometimes interwoven, sometimes wrapped around each other, sometimes dangling in midair, sometimes knotted and doubled back on each other, sometimes looking like something the cat's gotten into, all snarled and chewed and saliva-sticky. At least, that's a metaphor simple enough for your little human minds. Okay so far?

So as far as TQ's concerned, things happen or they don't happen. If Hitler's father had beaten his mother so severely that she miscarried, would the Third Reich have started without him? If Karen dies along with the other forty thousand Arverni when the Romans get tired of scuffing their feet in the dust and breach the walls of Avaricum, does it matter? Well, maybe to her loved ones back in the twentieth century, but not to the course of literary history, not at sixteen-hundred copies sold.

Tertium Quid's not concerned with any of that. It's watching Fuchsia, to see if s/he'll go too far.

However far that is.

# NINE

B*ut the Colors don't blend any more.*

Azure, protoMessiah, is the only one who notices.

There is a Common sigh. Much as the Mind has agreed to let bygones go by, it can't help remembering—which never forgets—that it was Azure who got the Mind into this tangle with humans in the first place. And we are still not of one Mind as to whether that was a good thing or not because, very simply, if we hadn't gotten mixed up with humans, we might still *be* a Mind. But then again, we'd have been that much less interesting to Tertium Quid, now wouldn't we?

As if we're at all sure whether *that's* good or bad. Meanwhile, there's this to contend with: *The Colors don't blend any more.*

*Not now, dear,* Gray answers Azure, which is no answer at all. And not all of the Mind agrees.

*What does s/he mean, "the Colors don't blend any more"? I think we need to address that, don't you?*

*Well, certainly; I couldn't agree more. In fact, I was thinking the very same thing myself. . . .*

*You know, I thought there was something fishy going on. . . .*

*"Fishy"? What do you know from "fishy"? Have you ever even so much as seen a fish, much less smelled one? Pretensions to metaphor, indeed!*

Alarums and excursions. Dissension in the ranks. Here we go again. . . .

*Oh, all right.* Gray sighs again. This may take a while. *What do you mean "the Colors don't blend any more"?*

*I mean, you know how sometimes we all sort of swirl together like chocolate milk into a single color which is actually all colors or no color and thus has many names?* Encouraged by the silence, Azure plunges on. *And you know how at other times we exchange colors or become each other's colors, like I did with Lake last week—*

Sigh. *Yes, dear. Go on.*

*Well, it doesn't work as well. Something—someone—is missing. And from what I understand of the vision thing and the causative factors behind color spectra, all evidence indicates it's Fuchsia who isn't there. Um, I mean, here.*

This time there isn't even a sigh, more like a *tsk!* of impatience.

*Well, of COURSE. That's because Fuchsia's involved in TQ's telekinesis experiment. S/he isn't here. (Or is s/he?) Or weren't you paying attention?*

*Or, worse, are you envious because Fuchsia was chosen and not you?*

*But*—Azure begins but does not finish, because someone is calling hir.

•

"Azure-blue, where are you?"

Finger-combing her hair in the bath house—she's left Grainne's fine-toothed bronze comb and the intricately embossed mirror, gift of a former lover, back at the house—Karen speaks it aloud. What does she have to lose? She and Azure were each other's touchstones during a previous adventure. If she has an ally left among the S.oteri, it will be Azure: "Azure-blue, where are you?"

It is her softest voice, the coaxing-a-kitten-out-of-a-tree voice, the We-were-friends-and-I-helped-you-once-and-now-I-need-your-help voice.

But Tertium Quid is having none of it.

•

{Resonance,} it tells Azure. {False positive, old memory, echo on the radar screen, contaminated double-blind study, pay no attention to that man behind the curtain, you've got a bad disk, that's all, recalibrate your instruments, cross-circuiting to B, you know you still have trouble distinguishing past/present/future and that's all this was.}

*But—which one? Past, present or future—?*

{Yes. Besides, we just got finished telling you: NEVER MIND! You didn't hear what you thought you just heard.}

*But—*

{We're still getting the bugs out of the telekinesis software; that's why you thought you heard it. Except you didn't hear it. Something we were doing with Fuchsia spilled over into your mind, that's all. Okay?}

•

Okay, Karen thinks: No response from Azure. She is, as she suspected from the beginning, entirely on her own.

There had been an exasperating languor to her days in Eleanor's court, as if by not yet understanding the rules, she could do nothing but wait until the scenario played itself out. Here in the Celtic RealWorld there was an episodic quality, as of some scenes being fast forwarded while others moved at normal speed. Karen knows somehow that she will be spending less time here than she did in the eleventh century.

And make no assumptions about her abilities here, Gentle Reader. Back in Chinon she had the ear of the most powerful woman in Christendom and look where that got her—up to her elbows in another woman's privates delivering a baby that could have delivered itself. So just because she got drunk with the Old King last night, it doesn't necessarily mean a damn thing. For one thing, every tribe's got its king, and most choose a new one annually, so Glewlwyd's overstayed his welcome by a decade or two. For another, he's dying.

For another, Karen no sooner has her hair combed and her fibulae fastened than she finds herself standing the palisades with one of a legion of wannabe New Kings.

This is Ryalbran, whose name means Crow, and who reminds her uncomfortably of an unrequited love she left behind in what used to be her own time, right down to the impatient way he moves, hands on his hips, heavy brows drawn together in a single knot above his cinnamon eyes. He is the same height; his shoulders are as broad; his deep brown hair recedes to precisely the same point on his brow, with the same single recalcitrant curl tumbling into his line of vision as he moves. He even limps slightly on his right leg when he's tired. All that's missing is the bureaucrat-blue suit that goes with his government paper-pusher job and the designer-frame glasses for him to push up on his broad nose as he talks. And talks and talks and talks. Even that is the same.

"The longer we wait, the stronger they get," Ryalbran grumbles, indicating the Romans with a thrust of his jaw. "Fight, surrender, or slip off into the night—we must do *something!*"

It makes her wonder. Are there duplicates or even multiplicates of each of them scattered throughout time? The thought makes her shudder. She hates alternate-universe stories even more than time-travel stories. If it's true, then no one is unique. They are all fragments of a broken mirror, protosouls, illusory. Maybe her editors were right all these years: Nothing any of them does matters at all.

"Glewlwyd says he will decide with the Equinox," Ryalbran goes on as they watch the cloud of dust through the trees which, coupled with the bleating of their short trumpets, means the Romans are practicing maneuvers again.

" '—because the Equinox signifies siring and fate,' " Grainne recites with him. They were both, she remembers, schooled by the Druid for a year or two and know the significance of each of the holidays in their thirteen-month year. In fact, Ryalbran could have *been* a drui, but for reasons which in a later century might be attributed to Attention Deficit Disorder, he lost his nerve.

When Ryalbran clamps his jaw shut, suspecting she's making fun of him, Grainne completes the thought. "It is because as king, Glewlwyd is father of us all, and because none can change his fate or his tribe's without first knowing what the gods want."

To which Ryalbran replies: "Glewlwyd is a fool!"

"You, of course, would do things differently," Grainne suggests archly, noting that the Roman fortifications have grown since the last time she'd climbed up here. It puts Karen in mind of all those Westerns she watched as a kid, only this time the cavalry is outside the walls and the Indians are waiting for them to attack instead of the other way around.

And we all know how all those Westerns turned out.

The Roman siegeworks, barely a few months old, looked almost as permanent-looking as the walls of Avaricum, which had stood for several generations before any of them were born. The main rampart, made of stone and earth packed four meters high, was reinforced with a wooden palisade all but identical to the one Grainne and Ryalbran stood upon. A V-shaped ditch deep enough to cripple a horse stood before this, with trenches filled with sharpened saplings before that. It was like watching carpenter ants destroy a forest to build a nest of shavings, simultaneously repellant and compelling.

Rumor of circular pits dug at random in the sacred wood, with sharpened stakes or iron spikes projecting upward from them, had all but the most adventurous afraid to leave the confines of the *oppidum*. It had become a kind of grim entertainment to climb to the top of the great wall and peer across the however-many meters to where the Roman soldiers were doing the same thing, to see what progress was being made.

This war of nerves, in between hot-blooded spontaneous skirmishes, with the Celts invariably on the headlong and hopelessly outnumbered attack, had been going on all summer. Avaricum with its forty thousand citizens comprised a solid inner ring, around which the broken ring of Roman fortifications, built to the undulation of the land, interspersed among woods and streams and outcroppings, formed an imperfect but slowly strangulating noose. Anyone from either side who ventured too close to the others' fortification was forfeit, though with partisan variations.

The Romans, lacking the luxury of hauling slaves back to Rome from this distance, had gotten into the habit of simply gang-raping and killing anyone young and pretty of either sex. The Celts killed clean and hacked off heads, displaying them on their battlements. The remains of one, fly-buzzed and over-ripe, adorned a pale just over Ryalbran's shoulder. Grainne might not have noticed the stench, but Karen did. So it was true that rotting flesh really did smell sweet. The writer makes note.

All trade with the outside had been stopped; there was no one on the roads. Glewlwyd's bravado in doling out the beer and Ryalbran's prognostications fooled no one; they would not last the winter. Avaricum would yield, or starve, or last until Gaius Julius got bored and set off for some less impervious town. Or until the snows came. The debate between whether or not the food would run out before the cold drove the Romans south where they belonged was what informed Glewlwyd's macabre, almost-nightly revelries.

To Grainne it was as it should be. To Karen it all seemed so unnecessary.

"Do the Romans really think they can starve us out before the winter comes?" she wants to say aloud, but can't. "I can understand their not wanting to attack a city this formidable without softening it up first, but what I don't understand is why we let them build their goddamn siegeworks without shooting them all first!"

Not bad for an old hippie, dyed-in-the-wool peacenik, eh? TQ finds this internal exchange entertaining. How long before Karen realizes she's thinking post-artillery, not pre–bow and arrow?

She figures it out before she opens her mouth, but the whole thing still seems a waste of time and manpower. Look, she wants to say, we can see the whites of their eyes. We can wave to them, blow kisses, shout obscenities or best wishes, throw water balloons. Send them fruit packed in ice like Saladin did . . . er, will . . . and they'll all come down with dysentery and go home. (Maybe that's what Saladin had in mind?) Why does it always have to be "This town ain't big enough for both of us"?

". . . outpsych them . . ." Ryalbran is saying. At least, that's how Grainne's knowledge of her own tongue translates it in Karen's ears. But until she's sure that's what she really heard, Karen will take it with a Grainne of salt. "To know the Romans is to understand two things: One, there is no end to the manpower they can muster, and two, they fight so differently than we because they are afraid of death."

Ryalbran came of age among the Romans. He knows. Grainne presumes to rest her hand upon his arm.

"Tell me what you know," she says warmly, while Karen thinks: Maybe he's the key. Maybe if just one person listens to him instead of laughing, he'll find the focus to do what needs to be done. Whatever that is.

She does not hesitate to speak in this time. She knows Grainne better than she had time to know Grethe, and knows that she would say this.

•

All right, then, what does Karen know? That a fibula is as familiar as a safety pin, and that if the Celts didn't invent tweezers, given their obsession with body hair, they ought to have. She knows about the silences, which are S.oteri-induced. She knows what Grainne knows.

Grainne exists in a world without telephones, computers, motors of any kind. Karen the Writer has long since learned that, just as there are no blank walls (molecules all the way down), unless one lives between worlds as Sequanna does, there is no such thing as silence. Karen has stayed in places in the country that have driven her mad with animal noises—screeching grackles, bugs with six-foot wingspans that roared all night like power mowers, pterodactyls disguising themselves as blue herons in a state park in Oregon. So just because there are no Harleys or boom boxes in this part of the world doesn't mean it's quiet.

It is a different kind of silence, flavored by the hammering in the forges (a chariot has to have iron fellies on its wooden wheels, or else what's the point? Hit a sharp rock and your wheel cracks). Resonance of pickaxes in the distant salt mines which were the Celtic lifeline to the trade of three continents until the Romans came. Shuffle of hooves, snorts, and bleatings that were livestock, noisier still when there had still been horses and cattle. Ubiquitous chickens, children. Night-whimpers of lovemaking, the sound of a quarrel in any tongue, laughter and singing and a pipe, universal musical instrument wherever there is wood to carve one.

Grainne is part of this people, and it is part of her. She, and now Karen through her, eats their food and sleeps in their beds and shares their stories and spends her days making pottery where she used to scratch words on paper.

Pots are useful; try cooking a stew without one. Pots are beautiful, art as much as craft; much nicer to cook your stew in something incised with the literally endless spirals which latterday scholars would insist symbolized a Celt's-eye view of eternity than in a plain old hollowed-out lump. Grainne's memory is filled with a lifetime of working at Sequanna's side, elbow-deep in the wet clay (as a result, both women have beautiful hands), sharing stories that are as much mimed as spoken over the whir of the potter's wheel and Sequanna's deafness.

Pots are needed. Pots are appreciated. As is Grainne's gift for storytelling around the fire at night. Karen had not noticed before that her voice has gotten deeper with age, less strident. It pleases her. If she ever gets back to her own time, she'll appreciate it more.

But what is her own time? Maybe this is her time now, no going back. Which means her days, like those of Avaricum, are numbered. And there's nothing she can do but savor these her people, as yet untainted by the Christianity which, along with a lack of minerals in the water, would make every other Irishman a drunk and the rest manic-depressive.

If this were a novel, Grainne would be some sort of catalyst, a pivotal character, at the center of things, able to effect outcomes. Here she is on the fringes, as unaware in this city of forty thousand of the doings of the Druid in their private tumuli as Karen would be if her neighbors were running a coven or a crack den back in New York. Here in the RealWorld it is all about hearsay, back-fence gossip with a soap-opera quality, overlayered with Karen's smidgens of badly taught history and learnings on her own to get in the way of her thinking clearly and knowing what to do as she climbs the rustic-runged ladders to the palisades to watch the Romans seal her fate.

Karen the Writer wonders if she should be taking notes. But notes on what? As she takes every spare minute away from the pottery to walk the streets past the glassmakers and the coppersmiths and the patronage hall where the deputies of subordinate tribes would have come to pay homage to Glewlwyd, could they get through the Roman cordon, she not only raises eyebrows ("Poor Grainne's been without a man too long. Can no one still her restlessness?" Nudge-nudge, wink-wink. Some things are the same in any century), but questions.

She is looking for evidence of the Cult of the Skull, one of those temples with carvings of human skulls embedded in the lintels which were found at other Celtic sites and which, coupled with Roman accounts of rampant human sacrifice and the bad rep Druid have in any post-Christian century, would prove that these people, like most of their neighbors, engaged in wholesale killing, either in the name of their gods or just for the hell of it.

What drives her? Some revenant of twentieth-century righteousness, a way of feeling less for them when they die?

Feel less for Sequanna, her almost-sister? Less for her elfin daughter, Aoife, who Karen knows will not live to bear the child she carries? Feel less for Maia and Rosmerta, Glewlwyd's wives, with whom she shares giggling bath-house gossip every morning, or for Ferchu, the songmaker, with his voice like bells, or one-eye Arawn with his entire whimsical face puckered around the sword scar which, as his drinking buddies are wont to say "nearly let his brains out, except there were no brains, you see"?

Feel less for Ryalbran, when she will go to her grave in whatever century wondering if the love she feels is Grainne's for the Crow, or Karen's for Raymond, or some cavewoman's unrequited love which she hasn't lived yet?

There's a horrible thought. Has she lived these lives already, or does she have to go back through more of them? Is this the answer to reincarnation after all?

*Stay grounded!* she warns herself. One lifetime at a time, please. *Ergo*, to borrow a Latin word: Grainne has no memory of human sacrifice, and in her walks about the city Karen hasn't found a temple to the Skull (which is where the Celts believed the soul lodged, so to behead a man was to prevent his soul from reaching the afterlife)—yet. Does that mean there's no such thing? The Cult of the Skull may be no more religious or significant than Halloween in her time. Imagine the conclusions a thirtieth-century archeologist would make about the Cult of Styrofoam or the Cult of the Mouse Named Mickey? ("These artifacts were found, with an alarming similarity, in almost every midden and landfill thus far unearthed. . . .")

The Writer makes note: Use this for Gret and Darymon. Remember them? Once upon a time there was a novel called *Preternatural Too*, in which a ship full of thirtieth-century humans went to visit the S.oteri.

God, Karen thinks—or is it gods?—I think I'm losing my mind! Again.

Okay, make a mental note and get it over with (no writing things down—where, with what?): I have not seen any evidence of human sacrifice, and Grainne has no memory of it. Therefore, I do not know if such sacrifices (A) consist of random bloodletting among babes and virgins and whomever the Druid are pissed at, the way it was reputedly done in Babylon and all those other pre-Christian motherCultures, (B) are a handy way of offing thieves and lowlifes, (C) comprise an early form of eugenics, (D) only occur at certain times of the year, this not being among them, or (E) never occurred at all, and those wicker baskets filled with screaming humanity hung over firepits the Roman chroniclers described were nothing more than bad press. Figure if Hitler had Goebbels, Caesar must have had some pretty peculiar advance men of his own. (Use that, too, for Gret and Darymon.)

So, no up close and personal tidbits about human sacrifice, not here.

•

". . . a place of cold and darkness," Ryalbran is saying. Has Grainne been listening? All she wants to do is look at him, watch the play of moods about his mobile face, listen to his voice, which flows like honey no matter what he's saying. "And this they consider a *reward.* Those who have been evil don't even get that much. They simply cease to exist. The gods stop thinking about them, and they're gone."

Grainne feels a chill, though the day is warm enough to raise a sweat on her upper lip. The Celtic SpiritWorld is one of eternal youth, eternal summer, coexisting with the RealWorld here and now. Spirits and shapeshifters slip between the two worlds all the time. There is hope. What the Romans believed could drive any people to despair.

"They really are alien, then, aren't they?" Grainne wonders, looking out over the treetops at the siegeworks. It's as if the sentries she sees there have each grown a second head. "And in that case, we have no defense against them."

"None," Ryalbran agrees grimly.

"What I do not understand . . ." Grainne lets her thought drift off; Karen's getting in the way. "Is why, if that's what they believe, they don't devote themselves to luxury, to extending that life as long as possible, if it's all they have?"

Ryalbran's laugh is bitter. He is thinking of the woman who owned him. "What do you think they do in that gilded city of theirs? The richest ones buy infant slaves and have them killed so they can bathe in their blood and draw the essence of youth from them. I've heard—"

Grainne's hand is on his arm again. "Have you actually seen this?" she demands.

Ryalbran shrugs her off but answers her. "Not personally, but—"

"Then do not speak of it unless you know," she says heatedly, "for thus is misinformation born!"

She leaves him fuming but looking after her with something like admiration.

•

Aoife, Sequanna's youngest, walks with Grainne from the pottery this day. The late afternoon is pleasantly warm, with a prevailing breeze that hints of autumn. The two women, sun-sensitive like all their kind, wear shallow, wide-brimmed straw hats which Karen finds strangely anachronistic.

Of course, she thinks, straw wouldn't have survived the centuries, not even in the elaborate Bronze Age graves where leather goods and imported brocades were preserved with the bodies of the wealthy. Imagine Jenner's reaction if she could come back to her own time with a factoid like that!

Aoife is small for a Celt, among whom Karen at five-foot-six is considered average size; the top of her plaited straw hat bobs just at Grainne's shoulder. Her belly bulges like a melon, but she is as light on her feet as a deer. And all of fifteen. Looking down at her, Karen fights back tears.

Aoife is chattering away the way adolescents universally do, her mind skipping from one subject to the next the way her feet skip over the ground, barely touching. Grainne, like Karen, is an excellent listener.

". . . and so when Cumaill learnt I was carrying his child, he asked would I go on the cattle-drove with him. He'd planned to spend the summer about, you see, even before the Romans came. And I was all for it, because as you know my kind are strong and can ride horse without incident almost to the day we deliver. In fact, Auntie Flidias claims one of my great-grandmothers actually birthed on horse during a cattle raid, but you know how Auntie Flidias loves to have a go at the truth."

"Oh, I do indeed!" Grainne concurs. Aoife had given her an odd look out of the corners of her almond eyes when she first asked the question ("And why aren't you with your husband so close to birthing?"), since it was something Grainne should have known months ago when the decision was reached. There had been a moment's panic in Karen's heart when the girl actually stopped skipping along the road and turned to her, hands on her slender hips, small dark head tilted as she contemplated why Auntie Grainne would ask her something she already knew.

She knows! was all Karen could think. She knows, with her mother's kind of foresight, that I'm not who I seem to be. That is, I am, but I'm also someone else, someone who doesn't exist yet. That is—

Oh, for godsake, relax! she told herself in the next breath. If Sequanna, who is *filid*, can't tell who else you are, it's all an S.oteri's game, so just play it. What's the worst they can do, sacrifice you to the gods? You're going to die in a few days or weeks anyway!

That thought has left her strangely indifferent. Some part of her still thinks Fuchsia won't go that far. Will s/he? Karen's more afraid of being found a fraud than of dying. It's a Writer Thing.

But in the next moment, Aoife had gotten a knowing look on her heart-shaped face and thrown back her head and laughed aloud, shaking her dark hair back in untempered glee.

"Oh, I get it! You're training me. Mum says I've got the makings of a storyteller. You want to see how good I am at doing what you do—telling the base of the story the same way each time but varying the adjectives now and then."

"Something like that," Karen/Grainne concurs with great relief.

"All right, then," Aoife says. "I'll show you where the decision was reached."

The two resume their walk. The Roman cordon still has gaps in it. There is an earth-walled tunnel beneath the city's outer walls, which once was used to haul the waste away. Long since hidden by brush on its outer end, it is a way into the wood for those who need to pray or tryst or carry on business with the gods.

Karen wants to say: No, let's not go that way. It's dangerous. If you're a true storyteller, you can tell me what happened without taking me there. Grainne knows better. They leave their straw hats at the inner mouth of the tunnel, and she follows Aoife into the damp-smelling walkway without protest. Pushing aside the shrubbery and slipping in among the sun-spattered trees, she tries not to feel the presence of a stray soldier, off to piss in the woods, happening upon them with sword drawn. Besides, they'd hear him clanking, wouldn't they?

•

"It was here." Aoife points. A lively little spring bubbles out of a cleft in a rock in a clearing, running off into the leaf mold and probably drying out within a hundred yards, but sacred as all springs are, because it meant not only fresh water but a direct link to the spirits who lived in the ground.

"Mother was communing with Sulis, who is her favorite because they are both healers, and asked in conversation the sex of the child I'm carrying."

"And—?" Grainne prompts.

Aoife cradles the bulge in her two hands, beaming. "As you already know, a boy. But I must not tell it that way, must I? I must tell it as if you've never heard it before. Well, what happened was—"

A man stood in the clearing, the diffuse sunlight glowing off his pale skin. He had not been there a moment ago, and neither of them had heard his approach—neither footstep, crack of twig, nor stillness among the birds had warned of his coming; yet he was there, and a big man, too, to move so silently—yet neither woman was alarmed by his presence. Clearly, by the silence, he was a shape-shifter or something else magical, else the birds would have given him away.

Karen the Writer puts his age somewhere around seventy. He is bearded, white-haired; she tries not to think of Merlin. Erect and strong, he carries a walking staff but does not lean on it, though Grainne somehow knows he has walked the length of continents and could tell about it. He wears only sandals and a heavy gold torque about his neck. A woolen cloak, too warm for the day, hangs over one arm, and the strap of a leather travel bag is slung across his virtually hairless chest.

Grainne was accustomed to the casual nakedness of her people, whose penchant for fighting naked, lest cloth fibers get into their wounds and fester with killing infection, were further proof to terrified Romans that these were simply barbarians. But Karen's eyes travel down this sudden magician's fine-muscled body and stop however briefly at his best ornament, framed in a crown of silver hair. His own eyes are watching her. The color of the sky in October, they are at once the merriest and the saddest eyes she's ever seen.

His eyes were so very blue. They brought Karen's eyes away from the pretty cock swaying against his sinewy leg, and her first thought, having chanted to her own personal god every morning, was: Azure-blue, is this you?

Her second, with a jolt of recognition, was: My God, it's Jacob!

# TEN

This really wasn't fair. First Raymond and Ryalbran are each other's avatars, now Jacob and this man, whoever he was.

"Govannon," he answers, in a rumble of a voice that is exactly Jacob the Brewer's before Karen has asked the question. "And you are called Grainne, but you are not. Ugly, that is."

If Karen is startled by this, Grainne is not. "And what else do you know of me, stranger?"

"More than wants telling in this time and place." He shifts his weight and somehow the cloak is about his shoulders, not quite covering his nakedness, at least not the part that keeps holding Karen's attention. His eyes are merry to see that hers are drawn there. He holds out his hand to Aoife. "Aoife, child and mother, I may be a stranger to you, but your mother knows me. Tell her the Thunderer requests the hospitality of her hearth."

•

Fast forward, telescope, fade out/fade in. Somehow it is night, and they are at Glewlwyd's feast, the stranger, Govannon, as much a part of the gathering as anyone, for it is Celtic custom to invite any passerby to join the night's feast without question. Only later, when he'd eaten and drunk his fill, was he asked what business had him on the road. Even in these Roman times, no one is rude enough to ask how a solitary traveler managed to pass through the lines unseen.

"My mother was of Olbia, far to the east, an ancient site. . . ." he is telling the assemblage, though it is Aoife who sits at his feet, spellbound, while Grainne manages to busy herself at the roasting spit, finding the cooking more interesting than her troubled thoughts. Still, his voice follows her about the huge smoke- and noise-filled room, and his body is no less appealing for its being covered from shoulders to knees with a borrowed tunic. "She was taken as slave by the one who called himself my father, who came from the land of the Boii, though he was not of them."

Meanwhile Karen, who hates to cook, is thinking: *This is it! This man is the key. Maybe he's an avatar of Azure, maybe not, but his knowing the lingo and the lay of the land doesn't fool me. He's as much out of time here as I am, and he and I together can—*

Can do what? She hasn't figured that part out yet, but she's working on it.

"I never knew his origins. Perhaps he didn't, either. . . ."

He is too polite to spit on the floor when he speaks of the man who sired him, but he makes a gesture that implies it.

"As a consequence, I was slave until I talked my way to freedom. . . ."

"And how did you do that?" Ryalbran, interested in all stories to do with slaves, wants to know.

Sky eyes meet cinnamon eyes, and elder studies younger as much as the other way around. Grainne, watching, stops turning the spit where the boar roasts, until the warning hiss of fat in the fire brings her to her senses. When the boar is done, Glewlwyd will offer Govannon the thigh, the Hero's Portion.

"That is a way that can only be learned, not taught," Govannon answers finally. When Ryalbran snorts in disgust and is about to protest, it is Sequanna, lip-reading as always, who stills him.

"He means you were born with one mouth and two ears," she scolds the Young Crow. "As you can hear, listen!"

Yes, Sequanna knows Govannon, though they had never met. They have recognized each other out of the SpiritWorld that spills over into Real. Grainne has heard her own name mentioned more than once, and Karen wonders what's going on. But she knows she has to speak to him, no matter what.

He is named for Govannon, god of thunder, god of the forge, prototype for the Roman Vulcan. Grainne knows the name; Karen provides the context. Mesmerizing as he is, she refuses to accept that he's only what he says he is. He, like Jacob, is a figment of Fuchsia's imagination.

So what does that make Ryalbran, or Raymond? Or Grainne or Grethe or Karen?

•

It is late in the night and early in the morning when Glewlwyd finally asks his question. Being a king, he cannot ask it directly, but has to play at diplomacy. "It is a rare man who willingly walks into a city under siege, Thunderer," he observes.

Govannon's smile is gleaming and full of wolf-white teeth. "Then I am that rare man, Gray Hero."

Glewlwyd's old heart can bear it no longer. "Why are you here?"

Govannon's smile goes grave. "To give you what you need."

And somehow everyone gathered there, from Karen to the youngest brat asleep in its own drool on the floor, knows what that is. Govannon is offering himself as sacrifice to the sacred pit.

•

Archeologists had for decades puzzled over the meaning of the subterranean pits or shafts found in the excavations of several Celtic cities. Many of them predated the Bronze Age and were up to forty meters deep. Some scholars dismissed them as simply overzealous middens, dumping pits for the bones and broken pottery any city left behind in its landfills, for it was bones and broken pottery they found there. The rest lumped them with the sacred shafts of ancient Greco-Roman cultures—a way for mortals to dig their way to the underworld.

But the Celtic shafts were dug straight down, often with wooden supports built into the walls, like mine shafts. Later (decades, centuries?) they were carefully filled in, layers of potting clay striated with layers of charcoal from cooking fires and the forges as well as ordinary soil, dotted with small clay figurines of gods and sacred animals as much as bones and potsherds. Too, many of the shafts had a log or sharpened tree trunk set upright at the base of them, around which were found traces of blood, human as well as animal. And most were sealed over for as much as four meters with stone masonry as carefully dressed and fitted as that of the cobblestones in the city streets.

Grainne, of course, knew what the shafts were for, but even without her knowledge Karen would have called the scholars idiots. Did they need crossbeams and a crown of thorns to understand? Quick enough to believe the Roman scribe Strabo's accounts of wicker baskets filled with screaming humans roasted alive, how could they not see what the shafts were for?

Helpless, Karen watches the dialogue of two old men—one a fool, the other, she somehow knows, at least as wise as her Jacob (and since when had he become hers?), hence wise as all the world, who was offering to die in Glewlwyd's place, so that the Old King would be free to make whatever decisions he chose without waiting for the gods, and act against the Romans.

*No*! Karen wants to shout. *Don't kill him, because not only does he deserve to live the whole of his life and die in bed, but because he could be my way back home!* While all Grainne is thinking is how sweet it would be to feel that powerful body against hers, but warm and living, not cold in death.

(And lest we accuse Grainne of fickleness, Gentle Reader, what with Ryalbran in the same room watching all this as closely as she, let's remember she's been waiting for him to come to his senses for as long as Karen's been pining for Raymond, and enough is enough.)

But before either of her personae can utter a sound, a roar goes up from all those still awake and not too drunk to understand what's just transpired. The deal is struck; the sacrifice will take place in a day or two when the Druid decide it's best. There is much smiling and backslapping, and Govannon seems happiest of them all.

Grainne knows the procedure. The Druid and the *ovates* and perhaps a *filid* or two (Can she prevail upon Sequanna to stop this, or will her childhood's friend, with her special knowledge of the flimsiness of the boundaries between Worlds, go against her for the first time in their lives?) will prepare themselves with much chanting and fasting to preside over a dawn ceremony in which Govannon will take Glewlwyd's name and be led to the place of sacrifice. There will be more chanting until the moment when the new-named Old King steps off the edge of the Earth and plunges to his death. His death throes will be studied and interpreted so that the living Glewlwyd will know what to do.

Karen, knowing Grainne wants the same thing she wants, decides she is free to do whatever she can to save her own personal Merlin. But how?

•

He has indeed been offered the hospitality of Sequanna's hearth and is led there in the hour before dawn to sleep and take his leisure until the Druid summon him. Fighting exhaustion, Grainne/Karen trails after him, as miserable as a child. Sequanna and her ever-changing brood are long asleep. Now is the time.

"Govannon?" Her own voice amazes her. "I must speak with you."

She hears rather than sees him yawn.

"Can it wait until the morrow? I have eaten far too much, and I am very tired."

"How many morrows do you have left? No, this cannot wait."

It is very dark, yet she can see the blue of his eyes and the whiteness of his hair and beard. She feels his breath on her face, then the brush of his hand. All night she had been staring at his hands in order to avoid his eyes, which had danced about her, drinking her in as his mouth drank in his host's best beer. They are the strangest hands she's ever seen.

"Is that all it is, then? You want to talk to me about my death?" He does not wait for her to answer, in fact silences her with a finger on her lips. "Then it *can* wait until the morrow. And it shall."

She hears him turn away from her, and almost instantly he is asleep. As she listens to him breathing, she knows more than ever that she must have him. Where else in the universe will she ever find another man who doesn't snore?

•

There is a universe in Govannon's eyes.

"You know how it is," he is telling her. "Religion has killed more men than the flu. But at least my death will give the old fool a day or two less to procrastinate."

They are sitting in the shade of the housewall where it joins at a right angle to the *oppidum*. Sequanna has as much as told Grainne to take the day off.

". . . and as many more as you need. Any pots you throw today will be worthless anyway. Don't speak!" Too many people have been telling Grainne that lately. Her dear friend clasps her shoulders and looks deep into her eyes. Because she cannot hear in this world, only in the next, Sequanna's gaze is daunting. "The heart knows its own reasons. Those who would tell you 'He's old, and he's going to die' don't know what you know. Go to him, be with him, come what may."

The way she words it makes Grainne/Karen question her. "How much do you know of what is to come?"

Sequanna's gaze almost falters. "The size of it, and approximately when. But who lives and who dies—no."

Karen is aghast. "These are your children and grandchildren you're talking about. Why don't you speak?!"

Sequanna shakes her head as if to say: *I thought you understood these things!* "I can only speak when the goddess is upon me, elsewise no one will believe. You know this. And if they don't believe, my words might send the fate in a different direction than it was intended. Besides, now we have Govannon."

It was this attitude that had kept Karen awake all the night before, amazed and not a little repulsed at how everyone from Glewlwyd to Sequanna to little Aoife rejoiced in Govannon's offer. How, Karen asks herself, can she feel anything for these people when they would send such a man to his death?

Only Ryalbran, she noticed, stalked off in what she thought was disgust while everyone else was celebrating. She has not seen him since. Nor thought of him, for that matter. She is studying Govannon's hands, feeling the rumble of his voice.

". . . What Glewlwyd ought to have done was let as many of the old ones and children as possible slip away as soon as his scouts saw the Romans on the road, then negotiate. Or send his fastest runner to the horseherds and then on to Gergovia for reinforcements. Vercingetorix is only over the next hill."

If the Celts as a whole ever had a hope of remaining whole, Vercingetorix was that hope. Once Caesar was finished with Avaricum, he would march on to Gergovia, where Vercingetorix would give him a real battle. History would record that Rome lost forty-six centurions that day, which meant four thousand foot soldiers dead. Vercingetorix would not defeat Rome, but he would make it stop and think.

"It's all mental exercise anyway. . . ." Govannon is musing. "Imagine if Rome didn't destroy us? The way we breed, we'd overrun the planet faster than India. And imagine a future in which the likes of us got to write the history!"

This is a modern man speaking.

"What do you mean by 'the likes of us'?" Karen asks carefully.

"I think you know," he answers solemnly, though his eyes are smiling. "For you are Grainne, but you are not."

"—ugly, that is," she says, finishing the sentence for him. His compliment makes her smile in spite of the grief she's feeling.

"That wasn't what I was going to say," he answers.

She does not know what to say, but studies his hands instead. They are Jacob's hands, if Jacob was ever real—big square hands with long, blunt fingers. She used to think she only liked men with hands like Ryalbran's, like Raymond's. Hands with delicate tapered fingers, almost feminine, like Benn's in *SpaceSeekers*. She'd been wrong. Or she was changing.

"How do you know what I am?" she asks him, almost like a child. "And how do you know what's going to happen? Are you *filid,* like Sequanna? Or are you a shape-shifter? Not just the namesake of the god, but the god himself?"

"You know better than that." His words are chiding, but his tone is gentle, as if the most important thing is that she trust him. "For you are no more of this time than I."

Karen, barely breathing, lets her silence answer.

•

Fast forward, telescope, fade out/fade in. Somehow they have talked the day away, and it is hazing into evening. Beyond the tree line, even the Romans are still.

"But what is Time?" Govannon asks finally, though it's as if no time has passed. "And what of you? You don't belong here, yet you stay. You ask why I offer myself to death. What do you call what you're doing?"

Don't think she hadn't thought of it, slipping away under the moon some night, and at worst offering herself in servitude to some other Celtic tribe. Maybe she could be the one to summon Vercingetorix, if she only knew the roads. Did Grainne? Even if she couldn't accomplish that much, all she had to do was remember which tribes were siding with the Romans this week, bring one of her pots along by way of curriculum vitae to show the kind of work she could do, and—

If this were the movies, she'd be shifting in her seat, disgusted, ranting at her character on the screen like something out of Mystery Science Theatre 3000:

"What's the matter with you? Why are you sitting there mooning over a man who wants to die? Save your ass, dig under the wall if you have to, but get the hell out of town!"

Until she met Govannon, she had no idea why she stayed, stuck in the middle of a plot without an ending. All she can do now is shrug. "I guess I'm looking for an answer."

When he touches her—no more than an arm around her shoulder—she knows why.

"I am not that answer," Govannon says. "You are."

•

As if in a dream, Karen sees Flidias Wildhair and Ryalbran the Crow ride up through the fog. Where have they found horses in this horseless town? Their hair is limed, and they are ferocious with purpose. Fat Flidias wheels her horse about and announces in a voice much too loud:

"We are riding out to Vercingetorix, or to death! Nothing less!"

Ryalbran for once does not speak. His jaw is set; his eyes are grim. He looks down from a mount as skittish as he and contemplates the sight of Grainne with Govannon's strong presence beside her. Something like envy passes over his face (why is it some men only desire a woman when another man chooses her?) then he nods with satisfaction, as if to say: *See? I told you you'd get over me!* before digging his heels into his horse's flanks and galloping away.

Grainne watches, unmoving. It is only a dream.

•

The Druid have let it be known that the auspices are best on the morrow. They will come for Govannon with the dawn. All of Avaricum, save for the sentries on the walls, is welcomed to bear witness.

"Don't they realize that would be the best time for the Romans to attack?" Karen muses. When the breeze shifts this way, they can hear the distant chanting, not unlike a Plains Indian chant, complete with drums. She and Govannon have repaired to a borrowed house. (Its owner wisely took his family on the cattle-drive with Aoife's beloved Cumaill and the rest of the drovers while the Romans were still on the road.) The place has been empty all summer, yet somehow it's been swept of chicken droppings and festooned with flower garlands. Sequanna's hand is at work here. So, too, with the bundle of herbs and one of her best glazed pots left beside the hearth to brew them in, a love potion. Karen appreciates the thought, but knows by the way her body tingles that it won't be needed. "I always thought that if the Soviets were going to drop the Bomb, they'd do it on Superbowl Sunday, because no one in the States would be paying attention—"

"—Except for you," Govannon observes whimsically. "You hate football!"

She has stopped questioning how he knows what he knows. As seems to happen in times of acute emotion, like delivering Kit's baby, her pretext for being here—last time Grethe, this time Grainne—has fallen away, leaving only Karen. She has already decided to follow Grainne's desire and sleep with this man if he asks her. She can't get pregnant any more, had her tubes tied when she was forty. No time-line anomalies, then, no danger of being her own great-grandmother, just a decision between two consenting adults. Grainne had wanted him so much she could taste it. Well, so does she.

He knows it.

"I have said before I will not call you Grainne. As I am Govannon, as often called the Smith as the Thunderer, will you allow me to call you Arianrhod?"

She did not understand the name even as she did, but that was not important now. She would consent to anything he asked, if only—"I still don't understand why you have to die!"

Meaning, she thought but could not say, that they were all going to die if the Romans had their way, so why his particular, individual death in such a particular, horrible fashion?

He took her face in his big, strange hands, seeing in her eyes what was reflected in his own. "Yes, you do."

Tears started in her sea-blue eyes. She saw the reasons in his sky-blue ones and nodded. He kissed her brow. His eyes were younger than the dawn sky.

"It would please me if you passed the time with me," was all he said. She started to speak, then thought the better of it. "I ask only the joy of looking at you," he went on. "Or whatever else, in whatever wise, you wish."

She was in his arms then, clinging to him like a child, rubbing her face against the smoothness of his hairless chest. She was going to lose him no matter what. Why not surrender to the Now?

"What I wish—" she murmured against the clot in her throat, feeling the softness of his beard against her brow, his breath in her hair (if this wasn't Real, nothing was) "—is what you wish. Oneness. Completion."

*A sense of closure.* The phrase taunted her from her own time, spoken in an S.oteri's voice. She wondered if any of them would be watching. Fine, let them watch! Maybe they'd learn something.

She felt rather than heard the chuckle in his throat, which was not unlike a sob. "Do you offer yourself to me? Even though you do not know me?"

It was a whimper. "Yes!"

He tilted her face up. His smile was winter, though his eyes were autumn sky. "Then surely I can offer you no less."

•

It was the longest night since the world began, and also the briefest. Had any man ever made love to a woman as Govannon did to Grainne? As the moon went down, she accepted the new name he gave her, Arianrhod, his Silver Wheel. Finding her willing, he shaped her to her truest form. The far trees echoed with her joy.

He must have cast his magic on her, for though she meant to keep the watch until they came for him, sunrise found her sound asleep. She had asked herself if she'd be brave enough to watch him leap into the pit. At the least, she meant to be in the throng and look into those ageless eyes one final time.

Instead, she slept. Even their coming for him (Had they still been chanting? Had they brought the drums?) did not awaken her from what had to be a stupor, unnatural. Not the stir of their feet in the dust outside, nor the gathered breath of them as they walked behind him to the clearing where the pit awaited, disturbed whatever she was dreaming. Only the late thunder of a breathless afternoon woke her, bladder full and stomach empty. It was late, too late by half.

On the bed beside her, where her hand would find it, lay his golden torque. Whatever else he'd worn or not worn, he'd never been without it. Karen let out a cry and rushed to the doorway. The sunlight struck her like the flat of a blade.

Gone.

Was it only the immediate neighborhood that had emptied itself of humanity gone to witness? Surely the entire fortress couldn't be so empty, not with the Romans so near. But with Govannon gone, only she and Sequanna now knew for certain what the Romans intended.

Was Govannon already dead? He would not, she knew, have clung to those last hectic minutes of life, would not have needed the not-so-ritual push, but would have stepped off into the air with the same jaunt in his step with which he'd first approached her to read the future in her eyes. She pictured him floating slo-mo graceful to the lightless depth of the pit, streamlining his elegant body to hasten the moment, embrace the sharpened pale even as hours before he had embraced her, and with the same true love.

She doubled over, feeling the pain in her own liver, her own belly. Had he died quickly? Please, please, whatever gods there were, let it have taken him quickly! She saw him brace his big, strange hands against the crumbling earthen walls, clots of dirt spattering his spun-silver hair, pushing to drive the stake deeper and have an end to it, saw him turn himself by sheer force of will—a trickle of blood flowing past his wolf-white teeth and through the softness of his beard to spill in droplets into the dank earth—so that one last time he could see the sky, match its color to the color of his eyes, the bluest eyes in all the world.

It was over, and only the thunder to awake her, thunder out of a clear blue sky, then a cloying pallor to the sun as somehow clouds boiled up out of nowhere, transforming a lowering firmament. Thunder, she thought. Thunder for my Thunderer, my Govannon, ancienter god than even Vulcan. It was the thunder that told her he was dead, and she had slept through it—bewitched, it must have been—a bitter thing.

The sky closed around the sun like a fist, washing the world in greenish, sickly light. Let the priests omen that how they might. A spatter of raindrops laid the dust, and a sudden rush of footsteps meant the watchers were returning from the spectacle, seeking shelter in their thatch-roofed wooden houses. Thunder grew from rumble to ear-splitting cracks, momentarily blinding. There was the shriek of a tree struck and sundered somewhere within walking distance. Scattered drops became a torrent, a solid sheet of wet. Above on the palisade, the sentries hooded their cloaks up over their lime-bleached hair, thinking: Even the Romans aren't fool enough to attack in this!

Yes, they are, Grainne thought. At least Gaius Julius is. They would see. Absent Govannon, she no longer cared, thought almost with welcome of her own death in the melee. Sick at heart, she tried not to think of how the heavy rain would fill the pit with turgid mud, drowning that clean, delicious body, obscuring the gleam of his blood until he vanished beneath it, one hand held outstretched in a manner of blessing, the last of him to disappear beneath the flood. Would the mob return in the morning and fill in the pit, leaving him for the centuries? Would they have time before the slaughter began?

"Noooo!" Karen heard the howl of her own voice, which last night had howled with joy. She clawed at her face, tore her hair as she swayed in the open doorway, oblivious of the rain. The few strays who hadn't the sense to come in out of the rain—a glimpse of dark-haired Aoife scampering like the child she was, garments plastered against the swell of belly which was by now the most of her—if they noticed Grainne at all, assumed her howling to be no more than ritual mourning for the sacrificed Govannon, and paid no heed.

Should she rush out into the rain in one last attempt to tell them what the morrow would bring?

They wouldn't believe her. Govannon had been sacrificed so that the gods would provide an omen, perhaps a miracle, perhaps even turn the Romans away. Only Sequanna knew differently, and if they didn't listen to her, why would they listen to Grainne?

"Nooo!" Karen howled, a child's protest to the universe, and as equally unheeded. "It's not fair, it's not fair! No fair, no fair; I don't want to play any more. I want to go home! Damn you, take me home!"

*Not yet!* Fuchsia gloats, grabbing and tossing her yet again.

Karen's head slammed against a wall. There was the reek of burning and a taste of crumbling plaster. Past the stars of pain that bloomed across her vision, a little burst of pinkish-purple danced in the corner of her eye. Bombs were falling.

# ELEVEN

Iridescing, first pink, then purple, Fuchsia trips a fine fandango. In all hir immortal life s/he has never enjoyed hirself more. Think how clever s/he is! The Common Mind is chasing hir round about the confines of itself trying to find out what's become of Karen, but s/he's obscured her oh so well, Fuchsia has, that even though the time lines are disturbed for the instant Karen is tossed through them, rippling like a pond-dropped stone, the Mind can't follow.

Besides, it's busy chasing Fuchsia. Catch me if you can, s/he dares it, knowing that, ass over tentacles, it can't run any faster than the gingerbread man. O frabjous day! This really is almost too much fun.

S/he'll bounce that self-righteous human back and forth in time until she's ragged, until she doesn't trust her own mind, until she surrenders this notion of tampering with S.oteri fates. Then bounce her back to that king-size bed in the middle of Middle America a thousand years before or after give or take a century or two, without the Common Mind's ever having a clue where she's been and what she's caused. As for Tertium Quid—

Oh, *that.* That . . . that Third Thing. As if who asked it to butt in anyway? (Does it even have a butt? Or is that *butt* as in butting heads? Language is as limiting as it is freeing, after all.) But Fuchsia's been so caught up in hir little sadistic game s/he's forgotten all about being under observation by that Third Thing.

Is it truly a Third Thing, or part and parcel of the Mind? And if the latter, what part exactly? Ego? Superego? Id? All of the above? Yes. It hasn't butted in to Fuchsia's game so far, so maybe it can't see what s/he's about. Or, better, doesn't care. Fuchsia whirls in a tangle of tentacles. So there . . .

•

Fast forward, telescope, kaleidoscope, cheap f/x like something out of *Vertigo*, fade out/fade in.

Karen's head slams against a wall. There is the reek of burning and a taste of crumbling plaster. Past the stars of pain that bloom across her vision, a little burst of pinkish-purple dances in the corner of her eye. Bombs are falling.

*Bombs?!* Wait a minute!

Was it as far back as first grade that her generation learned to "duck and cover"? Make it late 1950-something. What better way to rear children full of hope and promise than to teach them they can survive a nuclear holocaust by hiding under their desks?

That is, the girls got to hide under the desks. Breeders of the next generation of Catholic cannon fodder, after all; what else is a woman for? The boys had to lie on their stomachs in the aisles with their hands clasped over their heads.

The amazing thing was, no one ever laughed. No one chanted "I see London, I see France . . ." in spite of the view offered by thirty or so eight-year-old girls of all shapes and sizes crouched amid the dustbunnies under their vintage 1930s (complete with old-fashioned inkwells) school desks in their regulation parochial school, just-below-the-knee, loden-green wool jumpers, as observed by thirty or so eight-year-old boys and one wizened nun. Even the "slow" kids and the class clowns seemed to grasp that this was Real.

And the nun's assurances that they'd still be alive after the Bomb dropped hadn't fooled a one of them.

•

*All right,* Karen thinks as the stars and molecules clear from the kaleidoscope of her peripheral vision: *Bombs, then.* Not further backward, which had been her worst fear—because if she thought she was winging it in Eleanor's time or Caesar's, try the La Tène culture for shits and giggles—but forward. What century? Where?

She thinks: I spent my childhood and half my adolescence jumping at every loud sound because if it wasn't the Russians or the Chinese about to drop the Bomb, it was the Cubans launching missiles, or two passenger planes colliding in midair just above my head (which actually happened; you could look it up), and before that (I must have been all of nine, staying up late to watch the *Million Dollar Movie*) it was Godzilla, and all that summer every time I heard thunder I thought the monster had swum all the way from Japan and was walking up the Narrows looking for me. . . .

When maybe what I was afraid of wasn't that at all, but an inkling of some future time, past time, Fuchsia's pastime, when I'd end up, déjà vu all over again, here. Wherever here is, now.

"Excuse me, *Fraulein*, but you should not let the child play so near the entrance. Two nights ago, a child died in the next street from the same cause—"

Karen knows that voice. Oh, God, she knows that voice! But this time it is not addressing her.

"Listen, old man, if I want your opinion, I'll ask for it. Otherwise, go fuck yourself, okay?"

Karen steadies herself against the cellar's shaking and finds some boxes in a corner to sit on, feeling the back of her head for a bump. No one seems to have noticed that she was fool enough to be standing. She wonders if anyone's noticed her at all. Did she just arrive or has she been here since the shelling began? Drawing on her vast experience out of a childhood of watching war movies, she knows where she is. She can almost hear Laurence Olivier doing the voice-over for the BBC:

"Berlin: April, 1945. Civilians, long enured to the vicissitudes of almost nightly air raids, now take to the shelters in earnest. The Russian gun emplacements, set every twenty metres along the road from the east, pound the city relentlessly night and day. Their shrieking adds to the general din of bombs and small-weapons fire, street to street.

"There is no gas, no electricity, in some streets even no water. People no longer wait for the shooting to stop to emerge from their shelters like pale, disheveled rats, but clamber out in spite of the danger, bracing themselves against the few standing walls as the earth trembles beneath their feet, in search of food, water, someone to share a cigarette. No longer praying for victory, now they merely pray for it to end. . . ."

Now that she knows where she is, Karen takes stock of who she's supposed to be.

She doesn't need to look at her face to know it's still her own. She recognizes her own hands, big-knuckled, freckled, and blue-veined, just as they have been in every century before. Her hair feels strangely heavy. Reaching up to touch it, she finds it back-rolled, held together with hairpins and covered with a net. Very Joan Crawford, she thinks with a shudder, being an expert on Mommies Dearest. Regardless of the effort at style, however, she can tell it hasn't been washed in a week or more. She wonders if she has lice. She wonders if she stinks.

Heavy gold-rimmed glasses, one lens three times thicker than the other, pinch the bridge of her nose. Feeling her teeth with the tip of her tongue, she is aware of gaps where the back crowns ought to be and a strange texture to the front ones. They are crowned, probably with gold. She is visited with a vision of countless gold teeth pulled from the corpses of the dead in the camps. Along with all her infirmities, she still has all her knowledge, then.

Feeling her heart pounding, she finds somewhere to sit, on a steamer trunk not far from where she hit the wall, and continues taking inventory.

She is wearing a housedress, a short-sleeved, flower-print cotton dress with buttons down the front, an apron and a ratty cardigan over it. To judge from her resoled shoes and practical ankle socks and the ration coupons in her apron pocket, she is just another *Hausfrau* caught in the midst of Armageddon, trying to survive. And the torque is gone.

She'd had it in her hand a moment ago, intended to hold onto it as her last remnant of Govannon. When she felt the dizzying pull of Fuchsia's mischief yet again, she'd clasped the heavy gold neck ring against her breasts, determined to take it with her no matter what. Had it flown out of her hand when she hit the wall or merely dematerialized in order to stay in the time where it belonged? What else had she expected?

Still, she feels desolate, unreasonably so. What she has to remember Govannon by has nothing to do with gold.

She touches the arch of her right foot where she dropped the suitcase several lifetimes ago. The bruise is still there. Good.

Neverless, she does not flinch as the Russian shells shriek overhead and land in the next street or the one beyond with a rhythm so regular she might almost set it to music. None of the dozen or so souls sharing the cellar with her reacts normally any more; this war has simply gone on too long. Even the little girl, no more than three or four, clutching the sleeve of her mother's coat and watching them all with eyes too big for her face, does little more than blink too hard each time the man-made thunder falls.

It was the young mother—a twitchy blonde in a fur-collared coat (And were those actually silk stockings? Laddered and bagging at the ankles, but definitely silk), chain-smoking in a time and place where cigarettes were currency and even nonsmokers carried them deep in their pockets for barter—who had shouted at the old man sitting with his big hands resting on his knees against the far wall when he expressed concern for her child. She sits closest to the door leading out of the cellar to the street, staring off into space and tapping one foot impatiently, behaving, Karen observes, as if the entire thing were a personal inconvenience, something on the scale of a missed taxi making her late for an appointment.

*Never mind them just now!* Karen thinks, though she can't take her eyes off the little girl. She knows what she will see if she looks closely enough at the face of the man with the big hands. He will be Jacob, or Govannon, or whatever his name is in this time and place. No, she can't deal with any of them now. She has to find out who she is first.

Should she wait until someone speaks her name? What if they are all strangers here, as often happens, people passing on the street when the onslaught starts, who rush into the nearest open doorway, stumbling down a stranger's steps to a cellar as dark and uncharted as the depths of hell, and often already packed full of a humanity crying out as with one voice: "No room, no room! Go somewhere else!"

And as, night after night, block after block, district after district crumbles to dust and rubble, there are fewer places left to go.

All right then, old war movies notwithstanding, don't feign amnesia and ask someone else who you are. There has to be a better way.

Papers! Of course. Everyone in Berlin must have papers. One carries them everywhere in a little folder like a passport, waiting for the inevitable uniformed flunky to demand to see them. They are always on your person (in the bath? in bed?), even as you're running down the stairs in the middle of an air raid. Gives a whole new meaning to "Don't leave home without them." Karen grubs in her pockets.

The right apron pocket holds the ration coupons. Well, that makes sense. Being an orderly Kraut, she would keep anything associated with food in an apron, wouldn't she? And the left pocket holds her currency, a handful of loose cigarettes—Camels, to be precise. Now how the hell did she acquire American cigarettes? Don't examine that one too closely. Where the hell are her papers?

Cardigan pocket, of course. In the left-hand pocket of the outermost garment, as if to say to the nervous young sentry (their average age is sixteen nowadays; all the rest are dead on the Russian front): Watch now, I'm not using my dominant hand, and I'm reaching into my pocket very slowly, so you can see I'm not going for a weapon, just my papers, as you asked. I'm older than your mother, too old for you to want to sleep with me, and I'm not threatening you in any way, so be a good lad and just examine my identity card and let me be on my way, *ja?*

She pulls them out and peers around for better light to read them by. No such thing. She'll have to wait for daylight. Just as well. She's almost afraid of what she's going to see.

There are two men seated shoulder to shoulder on the bench beneath the stairs, stairs which lead to the ground floor of the building above, which Karen begins to remember is a bakery. She also knows that the short, squat man beside the tall one works there. Or did, until the bakery shut down for lack of flour. She remembers also that Timothy has bad lungs. Even through the freight-train roar outside, she can hear the gasp-and-wheeze that passes for his breathing.

She knows about Timothy, but not about herself. Well, wait for it. Fuchsia's playing hir cards close to the vest this time, who has no vest but, apparently, plenty of cards and no restrictions as to time.

"Would you care to come and sit by us, my dear?" Timothy wheezes now, and Karen knows he's not addressing the high-strung blonde. "I'll move my fat ass over and make room. I want to introduce you to someone."

It causes him such an effort, how can she refuse? Besides, they may all be dead in a minute or three. And this way, at least, she'll learn her own name.

As she gropes her way along the uneven dirt floor, a shell strikes the house across the street. Karen staggers, as much knocked off her feet by the noise as the impact. Through the ringing in her ears, she hears muffled shrieks and muttered prayers from those at the far end of the cellar. In the momentary flash of light, she notices two things. First, that the little girl stands transfixed, never uttering a sound, her small hand worrying the fabric of her mother's coat sleeve, that's all, and second that the whole of it is being observed by the saddest eyes in all the world.

"Margarethe," Timothy is wheezing, "this is my friend Johann. Johann, this is Margarethe, my upstairs neighbor whom I've told you about."

"My pleasure, *gnädige Frau,"* Johann rumbles formally. Instead of clasping her hand when she offers it, he kisses it. On the edge of hell, his eyes dance.

The building across the way has caught fire, and in its desultory light Karen watches the scene unfold as if entranced. Where Eleanor's court ran on normal time and Celtic Avaricum on fast forward, Hitler's Berlin runs in slow motion, and it is an effort for her to move.

Yes, Johann is Jacob, and Govannon, and something else she can't yet identify. And Timothy is Timothy, a short, broad, balding man with overlarge eyes behind thick glasses, whose every effort makes him wheeze and sweat profusely. Karen/Margarethe remembers him as a gnomish orphan of ten, newly apprenticed to the baker when she, a bride of twenty, moved into the flat upstairs with her new husband.

Timothy lived in the room behind the shop where the ovens were, and he and Margarethe had become fast friends, almost brother and sister, gossiping in the street in front of the bakery as the years passed and her children grew and she and her man made plans to travel once the war was over, until one afternoon when an Allied bomb falling in the next street broke all the windows in their flat. A shard of glass the size of a kitchen knife had lodged in her husband's throat and abruptly changed their plans.

So in this century, too, she is a widow. This is getting to be a habit. Can't Fuchsia dream up better fictions than that? All right, it's what you've been given; work with it. Her name is Margarethe and, though she can't remember anything about her husband, except that she thinks they were happy together, there is a sense that all of this has been slapped together at the last minute.

And it comes to her that Johann's name is not really Johann, but she's not supposed to know this yet. Nor is she supposed to know that he is a contact for something that has no name, but which among other activities has been smuggling Jews and other undesirables out of Berlin and its environs since the insanity began.

Johann himself is a Jew who has somehow eluded the cattle cars and the ovens, who for his own private reasons chooses to live his life at the heart of the Horror, as if to say to the Nazis: Go ahead and kill me, try! Somehow Margarethe knows this, and it somehow explains the American cigarettes in her pocket, though Karen's not clear how. It just occurs to her that this time Fuchsia's not even trying to make it real.

American cigarettes and men with many names, a virtual Grade-B movie, only Karen refuses to play. She slips her hand out of Johann's and is about to say something, when the Russian artillery makes it moot.

Apparently the shell that struck across the street was only rehearsal. The one that strikes the bakery is the final take. Karen watches as if from a distance as the inferno roars down the stairs—in slow motion, as with everything in this time. Fire and brimstone-bits of shrapnel bloom like some murderous flower, tearing chunks out of wood, brick, human flesh as they bypass the three of them beneath the shelter of the stairs, sucking all the air out of the place, caving in floor beams and walls. A support wall gives way, burying the anonymous lot in the back of the cellar without time to catch their collective breath for a collective scream. As for the blonde and her little daughter—

Karen does not remember moving, but she seems to have literally flown across the cellar, and the child is in her arms. She wraps herself about her, slamming her own elbows and knees as they hit the floor but protecting the little one, sheltering her with her body as however many pounds of wood and plaster and brick and decades, even centuries, of ancient debris pound her into the floor. Shriek and groan of floorboards splintering, a seeming endless crashing, as if the whole building would come down on them, an all too common eventuality in this time and place.

Karen finds herself, strangely detached, listening to each sound, feeling each new layer fall with a kind of bemused curiosity to see how long it will continue. (And to think her biggest worry used to be osteoporosis!) Aside from making sure she isn't crushing the child, she simply waits it out. Is she going to die here, after all she's been through? It's just too silly.

The little girl is screaming now, wailing a mix of terror and anguish ("Mama, Mama!"), struggling in Karen/Margarethe's arms as what's left of the building at last settles itself in some manner of egalitarian compromise between the forces of gravity and those of irony and, after a final weary groan and a final shower of choking dust, decides not to fall on them after all. There is a kind of eerie silence.

Karen realizes her ears aren't working right after all that noise. Inordinately, unnaturally calm, she shifts her weight and arches her back to discover she can move her shoulders and her legs a little and, once she's done spitting a few centuries of filth out of her mouth, she can even breathe.

Beneath her, more bones than flesh, the little girl is still shrieking, her fragile rib cage pumping like a bird's: "Mama, Mama!"

"Hush, *Liebling,* hush!" Margarethe whispers in her ear, the child's fine hair tickling her nose. "It's all right. Mama's gone away for a little while, but I'll take care of you!"

Thinking: Damn right Mama isn't here! Mama's a broken-backed doll with a smear of red that isn't lipstick smudging her pretty, pouting mouth, while her doll eyes stare at the night sky where the ceiling used to be. Someone else will be looking after you from now on, little one; Mama's gone away for good.

How does Karen know this when she's still half-buried under the rubble and can't see a thing? It's because she's seen the dailies, and that scene's been shot already. The seams in this little melodrama are showing. Fuchsia's losing hir touch; Leni Reifenstahl s/he ain't. Well, if she can get herself and the kid out from under this mess, Karen thinks, she's going to set that smarmy little jellyfish straight!

Only problem is, she still can't quite move her legs enough to get out of here. Broken? No, she feels no pain. Just stuck. Well, that can be remedied. Still clasped in her arms, the little girl has calmed enough so that her shrieks have devolved into sobs. She is sucking her dirty thumb, the sobs shaking her entire small body convulsively. She can turn herself enough to burrow into Karen's neck, her free hand stroking Margarethe's cardigan the same way it had her mother's coat sleeve moments ago.

Karen feels one of her eardrums pop violently. Suddenly she can half-hear. Someone's calling her. Timothy.

"Margarethe? For God's sake, answer! Don't be dead, dear, please don't; I've lost too many already! Johann, for the love of God, help me get this shit off her!"

More sounds. Hands scrabbling, the scrape of debris being moved, the weight on her legs and back gradually easing, more dust sucking into her lungs, making her cough convulsively. Only when the two men have pulled her to her feet, and Timothy has taken the child from her arms, and she stands with her hands on her thighs coughing up the crap in her lungs, hacking and spitting while Johann supports her shoulders and feels her back and limbs expertly for injuries, and she is trembling almost as much as the child was a few moments ago—Timothy's presence seems to have calmed her—does Karen realize: She has saved a life in a time that's not her own.

Oh. My. God.

*Now* what!?

Her knees buckle and Johann holds her, easing her down onto the bench beneath the stairs. Timothy, seeing the wordless horror on her face, tries to relieve it.

"Yes, the mother's dead, but the child's unhurt. Don't worry, dear; we'll take care of her. If she has a father, we will find him. If not, Johann has connections. We will get her someplace safe. Besides, the war is almost over. It isn't just rumor this time."

"But, you don't understand—!" Karen gasps, but can't go on. There is still gunk in her throat, and she feels herself choking on it as much as on what she's just done. Time lines, the future, are just abstracts over against the reality of a little girl with eyes so dark they're almost black, white-blonde hair, and a solemn look on her tear-stained, sooty face that is almost adult, certainly far too old for her years.

There hadn't been time to think. And if there had been? Would she—could she—have stood stock-still on her side of the cellar and watched the little girl die?

Well, how does she know Margarethe wouldn't have done the same? She seemed like a compassionate person for the brief few moments Karen knew her. A mother herself, she could not have let another woman's child die.

Could she?

Karen's other eardrum opens at last, but the eerie silence continues. The shelling has stopped. It's almost as if the entire city is waiting to learn what Karen will do next. Has she affected the time line already?

The little girl snuggles against Timothy's broad chest, still sucking her thumb, her huge eyes closed, dozing. An occasional hiccup shakes her, but she sleeps, her eyelashes painting shadows on her dirty cheeks. Where has all this light come from? Somewhere, somehow, a wintry sun is rising on a new day in shattered Berlin.

Karen buries her face in her hands. Johann sits beside her, his strong arm around her shoulders, silent, comforting.

*Let me die here,* Karen thinks. *Have the Russians got one more shell to spare, a little one, small enough to just kill me? Let me die in this time and place so I don't have to go forward and find out what I've done. . . .*

She feels the tug, the familiar nausea. Here we go again. But it's different this time.

# TWELVE

Fuchsia, in hir mental screening room, is running the whole show. Writer, director, producer, casting (and she's seriously thinking about replacing that Karen bitch), editor, light and sound mixer, Foley operator, gaffer (who can make Karen stand the gaff), Best Boy (meaning there's a concomitant Worst Boy, or maybe only a Second-best Girl?), stunts and extras, blue screen multiscreen morphing 3-D virtual reality special f/x. Picture hir little transparent jellyfishic self, tentacles tangling, turning knobs and toggling toggles (Fade to Black and out. . . . ), having a helluva time in time out of time just in time after time and time again. Thanks to TQ, s/he knows where the power is; no one can stop hir now. Where shall s/he bounce hir victim this time, when there is no time like the present?

*What are you doing?* The Mind again. *Stop this at once!*

Oops. Oh, darn. That's what happens when you don't pay attention. Fuchsia feels hir tentacles trembling, slides them away from the controls, leaving everything bleeping and whistling like the con of the *Enterprise*, shields down, deflectors at maximum, environmental controls offline, can't change the laws of physics, hurry and fix everything before the next commercial, crawl through the Jefferies tube and run a Level-1 diagnostic on that—

Oops. Heh-heh. Hi, there. (This is Fuchsia, playing at ingenuous.) Who, me? Nothing, nothing at all. Why do you ask?

(As for Karen, she hangs suspended, unawares, floating in a little iridescent bubble of not-Time, thinking she's been having a terrible nightmare complete with sound and special f/x, on an apparently unlimited budget, not Industrial Light & Magic making molten lava by shining a red light under a sheet of plate glass smeared with five pounds of Vaseline (imagine the smirk on the cashier in the pharmacy when the crew approached the register with *that*) but real state of the art stuff, and cheap old standbys, too, like pellets of explosive embedded in the sides of trees and buildings to explode on cue so they look like rifle shots or Russian shrapnel, adrift while the Powers of the Universe—which read: the Common Mind—try to figure out how, lacking TQ's telekinetic powers, to get her out of Fuchsia's clutches and safely back on the ground without anyone's getting hurt.)

*All right, that's enough of this foolishness. Put it back. Put it down gently, but put it back!*

Meanwhile, all parties concerned can't help thinking: Someone's going to have to pay for this.

•

Karen wakes, alone in a king-size bed. She sits up with her heart pounding and gropes for her little orange pills thinking: Oh, my paws and whiskers! Don't I have a panel with Greg at ten this morning? Am I already late?

No, that was yesterday morning. This morning there's a brunch for the speakers and any of the paying customers who aren't too hung over to move. Which makes Karen think very seriously about what she remembers from the night before. Only then does she notice that the sun's not up yet.

Weird dreams. She can almost hear the snort of Kit's sow and feel the warmth of summer sunlight through the vertical pales of Sequanna's house, the cold sun over Berlin. Slowly, analytically, she reviews each dream sequence, almost tempted to write them down so she won't forget them. As if she were likely to. Usually, she is the observer in her dreams, as in much of her life. Since when has she become the participant?

Weird dreams. She slides out from between the sheets of the king-size bed (sleeping perched on one edge, she's barely wrinkled it), studying her feet as they hit the floor. The bruise across her right instep is still there. And though it means she'll have to tie one sneaker more loosely for the next few days, she wants to weep with relief.

Dreams. That's all. No more booze before bedtime for you! Strange perimenopausal changes in metabolism and the need to empty your bladder more often have you sleeping at a lighter level where the wild things are, and it's put you all out of whack. That's what it is. Relax!

Nevertheless, it is a good half hour before the beta-blocker kicks in, and the elephant that sits on her chest every morning has shuffled shamefacedly away. For the next hour, as the gray turns to sunrise, Karen ponders. As we say in the Writing Business: I can use that! Save it all on your mental hard drive, in the windmills of your mind, grist for the mill and any other cliché you can think of (and even a few you can't), in the hope that somewhere in an outline someday you'll somehow be able to convince an editor that what the world really needs is a story about a time traveler mixing it up in the Crusades and with the ancient Celts and in Berlin in '45, and when they pat you on the head and tell you they don't see how it will accommodate their target audience and anyway it's *much* too ambitious for a writer like you, you can tell them to—

Her thoughts are squirreling; her stomach growls. She half expects to be picking the debris of a Berlin cellar out of her hair. Enough.

It is not until she is in the shower that she notices it—a fairly new, rather largish, oval-shaped bruise on the inside of her left thigh. That's odd! she thinks. How could I possibly—? Well, I must have bumped it on something. How many times have I noticed bruises in the oddest places and not known how I've gotten them?

On the *inside* of your thigh . . . ?!

It's a reach, even for the fiction writer. There's only one way she could have gotten it, and she doesn't even have to examine it closely to know that it's exactly in the shape of a man's mouth. She flashes on a memory of wolf-white teeth and the bluest eyes in all the world. Sad eyes, merry eyes, sparkling at her in despite of death as he . . .

Karen feels herself tingling. A little dizzy, she leans back against the wall of the bathroom, eyes closed, her wet hair plastered to her shoulders and dripping down her back. She can still feel his hands on her, caresses her own arms in remembrance, then drags herself back to the Now.

Ridiculous! Phantom lovers; what next? Vampires crawling up the walls, voices in her head, telepathic jellyfish? But the bruise is real, incontrovertible. All right then, why doesn't she have a bump on her head from the cellar wall in Berlin, bruises on her elbows and knees and back from hitting the floor and having all that debris fall on her when she saved the little girl? Either all of those dreams were real or none of them were.

She strokes the bruise absently and finds herself smiling. Then there are tears in her eyes. Karen never cries. If you cry, they only hit you harder. She dries her hair, climbs into her clothes, and goes off to meet her public.

But the rest of the weekend has a dreamlike quality to it. ("Are you all right?" Greg, all solicitude, takes her elbow when they meet at the breakfast buffet. "You look worse than I feel. How much *did* you have to drink last night?" Karen's only answer is a wan smile.) The flight home is more unreal than usual.

(She has always had that problem with flying: Nothing beyond that little window can possibly be real. Clouds like mounds of mashed potatoes, fields laid out like jigsaw puzzles, cities that are nothing but strings of Christmas lights against the scariness of dark. Thirty thousand feet in midair? Yeah, right! As easily believe in gremlins on the wing.) She drags her suitcase up the stairs to the apartment in Brooklyn with a kind of relief. Never mind the mound of junk mail and the dozen unreturned phone calls. She is home.

In among the catalogues and Visa bills is an eviction notice. Someone once told her landlord that owning a two-family house makes you God. Karen laughs out loud. *This* is real.

•

Alarums and Excursions: This one's called "Putting the Toothpaste Back in the Tube."

There is static on all the wavelengths, S.oteric reckonings:

*. . . Let's see . . . Govannon left no offspring, you say?*

*Well, not by her.*

*All right, but check him down the time lines anyway . . . Now then, Kit's baby—*

*—would have delivered itself. She was right about that as well. And it was Grethe, after all, who first stood in on the delivery. . . .*

*Right. And we're relatively certain there's no way she could have materially influenced either the Crusades or the armies of Rome, but let's keep an open mind until all the returns are in. Now, just run a line on the little girl in the cellar, and . . .*

*Are we set? Everything back in its place now?*

*Eye think so. Hard to tell. Temporal anomalies being what they are . . . whatever that is. We're still too new at this to be sure.*

*Which is why,* Gray says with a malevolent *occulus* on Fuchsia, *we shouldn't have been fooling with it in the first place! Why couldn't you have been content to just bend spoons or juggle oranges, at least until you got the hang of it? Are you going to tell us Why?*

Apparently not. The pinky-purple one is in a purple funk, not talking. The Mind has half a mind to pick it apart tendril by tendril until it tells all, but restrains itself.

Tertium Quid, meanwhile, is nowhere to be found. Found itself other playmates and left the S.oteri in the dust? No way to tell. Meanwhile, does Fuchsia still have the power? No one's going to take the chance of finding out.

*Whew, that was close! Okay, you* (to Fuchsia): *Don't move a muscle. We're not taking our eyes off you from now on. Just sit right where you are and—I don't know, read a book or something.*

Fuchsia glowers and sticks a tongue out, which has no tongue or is it several? Hard to keep track of these things any more.

•

"I don't understand why he wants to evict you," Anna said on the phone.

Karen's been having a few alarums and excursions of hir—er, her own. She processes them in order of importance. First, make sure the check really is in the mail. She signed the contract for the sequel to *Preternatural* months ago. The advance money finally arrives, and it's just enough after taxes to live on for a frugal two months. How she's supposed to finish a 400-page manuscript in that amount of time . . .

"Sorry, darlin', there's nothing else in the pipeline," Tony tells her ruefully, meaning the several ghosting projects he's put her name in for are either still pending or their editors have chosen someone else. "Try to make this last while I see if I can scare up something else between now and the holidays."

Okay, she's gotten away with this for eleven years. Time to start checking the classifieds for a Real Job. That is, after she gets back from Housing Court. Meanwhile, say hello to her kids, answer mail, return phone calls. Oh, yes, and get back to the manuscript she hasn't touched since, it seems, about 50 B.C.

The colorful little message slips were stuck under a magnet on the fridge, the one place in the house where she and Nicole and Matt are guaranteed to intersect at least once a day. Nicole, at twenty-five, is leaving the nest, moving in with her boyfriend right after the New Year. In the meantime, she has watered the bonsai and left her elaborately looped handwriting on the phone messages, among them: "Call Anna Bower RE: TV show."

Absently checking her supplies of herbs in the little bottles on top of the fridge (where she's kept all the pills and vitamins, out of harm's way, ever since the kids were toddlers, and still keeps them, force of habit, to this day) while she waits for either a person or a machine to answer the phone, Karen marvels at how many of them there are. She'd thought she had only hawthorn and feverfew to supplement her E's and C's and stress-formula multis, but the herbs seem to be breeding, because she doesn't remember buying that many. Wasn't short-term memory loss another symptom of impending menopause? There was a supplement for that—ginkgo, Karen thinks. She can't remember.

She also can't remember if she recognizes Anna Bower's name or not. Somehow she thinks she should. The area code is northern Virginia, where Karen's attended several cons, but neither the number nor the voice is familiar, though the reason Anna's calling is.

". . . and like everyone else down here, I work for the Fed. Just your typical government flunkey at the typical desk job. But in my Real Life, I run a little sci-fi show on one of the public-access channels," Anna is saying. She has a wonderful voice, devoid of any regional accent, deep and mesmerizing. "We're very low budget. Usually we just review new books and movies, show clips if we can get them, in-house commentary on the latest episode of *X-Files* or *B5* or whatever and, occasionally, interview a writer or two, usually locals. We pay their gas and tolls, and they see it as an opportunity to flak their latest book."

"I see." There are probably more s/f writers per square mile in the Maryland/Virginia area, Karen knows, than anywhere else on the planet. Does it have something to do with being so close to Foggy Bottom, a black hole if there ever was one?

"But—surprise!—we've got a certain amount of funding we have to spend before the end of the fiscal year, so we've decided to host a round table with a couple of out-of-area writers as well. Would you be interested?"

Yes, Karen thinks, the eviction notice in the corner of her eye.

Yes, please. Give me something familiar to hold onto after these nightmares, past and future!

"Marie Englund tells me you don't fly, so we'd Amtrak you down," Anna adds, mistaking the silence for hesitancy.

"Oh, I'm over that particular phobia now, thanks to Max Neimark," Karen says.

There is an odd sort of silence following that, as if Anna is puzzled by the information. If part of her avocation is reviewing new s/f movies, she should know about *Preternatural.*

"Oh, right," Anna responds vaguely, not asking for an explanation, which puzzles Karen further. "Well, then, I guess we could fly you down—"

"—but Amtrak's cheaper," Karen offers, aware that these groups always function on a shoestring. "I don't mind, really."

"And by the time we got you to and from the airport, it would probably be quicker to take the train," Anna supplies, sounding relieved. Karen knows most of her fellow writers are awful babies—needy, demanding. By contrast, she makes a point of being accommodating. "And I thought, if you wouldn't mind, you can stay with me. I live alone, now that my daughter's on the road, and you can have her room. It isn't fancy, but it's private. . . ."

*[Don't stay with her. There's going to be trouble. You know you make a lousy houseguest. And there are other considerations, things we can't begin to explain until they happen. Don't stay with her; we're warning you!]*

Oh, shut up! Karen thinks impatiently. If the dreams were to be believed, she'd been nothing but a houseguest for the past several millennia. And compared to some of the places she'd been staying lately—

"I'd like that," she says, trying to sound as if she means it.

". . . don't understand why he wants to evict you. I mean, you do pay your rent and everything?"

Karen realizes her concentration has just glitched. Has she missed only a few seconds, or has Anna been talking for a while? More to the point, she doesn't remember telling Anna about the eviction notice. She latches onto the key word in the last sentence and comes back to Earth.

"Oh, you mean my landlord?" she asks ingenuously. "Because he can. Because he thinks women belong in the kitchen, and I piss him off by being able to support myself without a man around. Because his wife left him and went back to Greece, and somehow that's my fault."

"Oh, of course." Anna's laugh is as musical as her voice. "Silly me, what *was* I thinking?" She grows serious. "When's the court date?"

"The week after Christmas. I've talked to some people. It's not as critical as it sounds. If I get a judge with half a brain, I can plead for a six-month extension. Once Nicole's out, I won't need that much space anyway; I'd be happy to look for something smaller and cheaper. I just wish it had been my decision to make."

"Can you handle it?" Anna asks seriously.

"Do I have a choice?"

•

And thus it is, Gentle Reader, that this thing called Real Life intervenes in Karen's thought process for the next little while. The landlord does indeed take her to court, and the judge does indeed give her a six-month extension, which is exactly what she was hoping for. The whole adventure is so soap-opera unreal (she'd never been in a courtroom before) she seems to sleepwalk through it. In recent weeks she's dealt with Nazis and Romans and Plantagenets; what's a scumbag landlord or two? That is, if the dreams were real.

She watches her daughter leave the nest with a minimum of heartbreak. Nicole is an adult, after all, and they will end up calling each other once a week to chat like the old friends they are, giving the lie to the usual mother/daughter stereotypes. Her own mother could have given Joan Crawford lessons, and Karen has had to invent herself; her children are the better for it. Still, the rooms her elf-child (prototype for the dream of Aoife?) leaves behind seem emptier than they ought to be, as if a chill wind is blowing through them.

Karen and Matt will find a better place barely a block away the week after he graduates, with honors. Mother and son are very much alike and will coexist without getting in each other's way. In the interim, Karen sets about interviewing for a Day Job. It's not as if she hasn't had one every decade or so, though it's a pain in the ass faking a resume (Tell them the truth? Not hardly. "What do you mean you're a 'writer'? Yeah, right! So how come you're not a millionaire like Stephen King?"). It also puts the lie to her having once made a movie with Max Neimark, doesn't it? Maybe that was in some alternate universe. Or maybe that part was the dream.

Out of curiosity, she gives Jenner a call, only to be told she's giving a paper at a conference in Basel and won't be back for a week. In that week, Karen has three job interviews and soon forgets about calling a second time to verify a few of the finer points of life in a Plantagenet court.

A month or so later, she orders a stack of books on the Celts and a couple about World War II from the clearance pages of the Barnes & Noble catalogue. The UPS truck will arrive on a weekday while she's at work; she'll find the little yellow "Sorry We Missed You" sticker on the front door when she gets home. The books can't be delivered without a signature; two more tries and they'll languish in the warehouse for a few days before being shipped back to the distributor. Karen wonders if everyone else on the planet has someone waiting at home for UPS while they're away.

So much for research. They were only dreams, weren't they? Elaborate and very detailed dreams which segued more or less smoothly one out of the next, but dreams nevertheless.

The bruise on the inside of her thigh has long since faded; it's almost enough to make her wonder if it was ever really there. In Plato's Cave there are many mansions. Meanwhile, in the thirtieth century:

•

The cave where They lived was farther away than the humans had expected, except when it was closer. It was also larger than they thought, or was it smaller? The instruments were useless once the suited visitors stepped under the lip of the entrance, their connection with the ship severed by some unanticipated interference and all the spatial readings off the dial.

"Nothing," Jeen's voice crackled in everyone's ears.

"That's odd!" Darymon shot back. "My numbers just shot up to maximum. Jeska, Gret? What are you reading?"

"Dead center," both women replied simultaneously, and Gret thought she saw the flash of a grim smile through the younger woman's visor. Hard to tell. The polarized visors had adapted to the absence of light in the cave sooner than their eyes did.

"Shit!" they heard Darymon mutter. "What about the medReads?"

"Fine," everyone said simultaneously. As long as they had those, they'd know how much air, ergo how much time, they had left.

*It also means,* Gret thought to Jeen and Jeska, *that it isn't anything "real" that's affecting the readings. It's They. And if They decide to play with the medReads as well—*

*Why would They do that?* Jeen wondered with an almost religious fervor Gret had caught him at before.

"All right, forget the instruments, then!" Darymon said before Gret could answer. The silence had gone on too long for his taste, which meant he knew his crew were Thinking behind his back. "Somebody tell me what it 'feels' like. Give me a reading, an intuition, a scent, anything!"

He couldn't help the sarcasm in his voice every time he spoke of the way Teles "felt" their environment. He was especially impatient with those who tried to describe what they were receiving in terms of sense of smell. Jeska had learned that rather forcefully when, barely three, she'd described an impending earthquake as "smells like old socks, Daddy."

"You have to learn to explain it better, honey." Darymon had tried to be patient once they'd crawled out from under the bed and found all the dishes shattered on the kitchen floor. "Old socks don't knock the roof off your house."

"These almost did!" the girl had answered matter-of-factly. Poor Daddy, she'd thought: He'll get it one of these days!

But, back to the cave. Of the seven in the landing party, three described it as being huge, quite literally cavernous, cathedral-ceilinged; three said it made them feel claustrophobic, and it was all they could do to keep from crouching out of fear of hitting their helmeted heads. Darymon was of the former group, Gret of the latter. Only Jeska said simply: "It just is. Size doesn't matter."

The others, all except her father, couldn't help a little mental tittering at that, which made the girl demand to know: *What? What's so funny? What did I say?*

*Later, Little One*! was all Gret would tell her. *We mustn't keep Them—or your father—waiting.*

The psychic kinship between them was stronger than ever. In an earlier millennium, Jeska might have been a musician or a composer, Gret a writer or something like that, and they'd have recognized each other instantly out of the kindred realm of creativity. That there were no longer novels or symphonies in their time meant that the creative expressed themselves in Tele terms and still managed to make the eighty-nine percent envious.

"Shouldn't one of us stay outside, just in case?" Jeska asked, a gloved hand on her father's arm.

"In case what, hon?" Darymon was scowling at the dark ahead, as if willing his headlight to shine stronger.

"Well, like they do in old movies. In case all our instruments go dead and someone needs to warn the ship. . . ."

*Little One,* Gret interjected, *it's not our instruments They're playing with, but our minds.*

That thought terrified, because it meant that even though Darymon was a Null to humans, They were able to Reach him. What that might mean to the expedition, much less to everyone on Earth . . .

Trudge on. Big or small, the cave seemed to go on forever, upslope and then down, turning back on itself a dozen times, a glow-walled maze more frustrating than an ancient computer game, and with much more at stake. (The fungus was what caused the glow, Gret was the first to figure out, remembering the endless tales of the Fungus Amongus which had intrigued humans ever since the First Contact). Was it some sort of joke? Were They laughing at the bumbling forked-stick humans shuffling through the stone-floored tunnels looking for something that wasn't there? Had anyone stopped to think that S.oteri might be invisible? The Voices, like the instruments, had gone staticky and silent the instant the humans had entered the cave.

*Anyone bring breadcrumbs?* Jeen wondered dryly. *Or at least a ball of twine?*

"How much oxygen do we have left?" Gret, always the practical one, said aloud. Well, someone had to.

•

Karen, ever practical, spends her days typing reports in a medical office and her evenings and weekends working on *Preternatural Too.* Her agent, concerned that the Day Job might be interfering with the flow of things like sleep and a social life and a chance to do the laundry, checks in on her periodically.

"It's going fine," Karen reassures Tony, which he decodes as meaning: Some days it is, some days it isn't. "You'll be proud of me. This time I took your advice and made it less autobiographical."

Which is sort of kind of true. Granted Gret, whose creativity expresses itself as telepathy rather than fiction-writing, is very much like Karen, but all the other characters are pure fiction, aren't they? Well, except for the S.oteri, and they're so real to her by now they seem like fiction. She doesn't know anyone like Darymon or his daughter Jeska, and she marvels at her gift for, godlike, creating something out of nothing. Why, her powers of description alone ("His eyes were the color of cinnamon, with an exotic slant to them. . . .") are positively breathtaking!

•

*Okay, okay, whee here ewe. This is supposed to be a science fiction novel, write? So wear are the aliens, the Bug-eyed Monsters, the* dei ex machinae *to keep this turkey narrative moving, hanh? Isn't that what yew were about to ask us?*

*Well, in case you're wondering why you haven't seen more of your jellyfishic friends outside of Karen's novel, it's because we're off humans for the duration. Yore really not all that interesting, if yew must know, so weave decided to let you spin out your little lives without us for a while. Weir into other, more important things.*

*And if it's Bug-eyed Monsters you want, just check out your landlord or your next-door neighbor. Humans are sometimes the weirdest aliens of all.*

•

The TV seminar goes well enough, considering Marie Englund and Paul Jonas, two of the best talkers this side of Harlan Ellison, are among the other guests at the roundtable, and before the cameras even start rolling they've gone into their Can You Top This number until, as polite as people tend to be down there below the Mason-Dixon Line, Anna has to stop the shooting in front of a live audience and ask them to put a sock in it *[Oh, whee like* that *phrase!]* and give the others a chance to speak.

Karen moves through the weekend feeling positively two-dimensional. One minute she's in ancient Gaul, the next she's in a windowless room in a medical suite typing scintillating sentences containing phrases like "neurovascular deficits" and "varus or valgus stress," the next she's in Housing Court, the next she's on TV. Only her downtime with Anna after the show provides a little respite from the dizzy-making and not a little dangerous kaleidoscope (whirling bits of broken dreams, like multicolored glass, sharp-edged) that has become her life.

". . . can't believe you're an s/f writer, and you've never read Asimov, or any of the big names, for that matter," Anna is saying, pleasantly enough, not quite using her television voice, but drawing out the interviewee nevertheless.

"Always afraid to," Karen shrugs. "Afraid they've already stolen the best ideas. All I can hope to do is take the same four story lines that exist in the entire universe and try to write them differently and, I hope, better. Besides, I realize it's sacrilege—" she suggests, watching Anna closely; she's gotten into trouble before for what she's about to say, "—but Asimov's characters just lay there. They're mouthpieces for clever dialogue, not people. Although that seems to be true of a lot of s/f writers," she amends herself, only getting in deeper. She can see Anna wants to object but is being the gracious hostess.

"Go on," she says.

"I mean I *have* read them. Pieces of them. Always have to give up after a couple of chapters. They just leave me cold. But they also have inadvertently shown me my niche in this business. I may not understand ion propulsion drives and subatomic particles that may not even be there, but I create damn good characters."

*[The best of 'em having been a bunch of interplanetary telepathic jellyfish! Don't forget about us, huh?]*

They are decompressing in Anna's living room in Alexandria over a glass of their respective poisons—scotch for Anna, tequila for Karen, who was impressed that Anna thought to ask what she liked to drink, and stopped at a package store on the way here from the studio. Anna, a voracious s/f reader, has everything Asimov and the other Big Names has ever written. Karen, making a tour of the room, has to marvel. Not only are the novels arranged in alphabetical order by author—she'd have expected that from someone as detail-oriented as Anna—but each author's works are arranged not by title but by chronology, by the year each one was published. Karen used to know someone else who did that, but right now she can't remember. Sneaking a peek at the *G's,* she finds herself represented there in her entirety, at least the s/f novels, even the ones that are out of print.

"I've got your mainstream novels in the other bookcase," Anna indicates with a nod of her head. And so she has, all four of them, even the one that sold eight copies before the publisher went bankrupt. These, too, are in chronological order and are the only novels tucked into shelves crammed with history books and political texts; Anna is a history buff and—incongruously, to Karen's mind—a lifelong Republican. "Got to keep the s/f separate from the rest."

"Of course," Karen says, unable to shake the feeling she's had ever since Anna parked her little imported pickup in the lot out front, and they took the elevator to the eighth floor, the distinct feeling that she's been here before.

No, check that: The déjà vu began when Anna met her at Union Station in a truck.

It isn't that she doesn't know several people who drive trucks and, as it happens, most of them are women, but there are usually reasons. Marie drives a big red Ram, but Marie is a big woman who keeps a couple of Morgan saddle horses; she needs the truck for the trips to the feedlot and, besides, it suits her personality. But what does little Anna, barely five feet tall and a committed urban dweller, need with a pickup?

"I move a lot," she explains, and Karen finds herself trying to picture someone Anna's size who, if she isn't fifty is close to it, lugging furniture and mountains of boxes by herself but finds it's an image she can't conjure. "Or at least I have been. No more. I've finally decided this late in my life not to let who I'm with determine where I live. I've been through too many relationships since my divorce, and from now on I'm staying in my own place. If whoever I'm with wants to move in with me, fine, but no more doing that complicated ownership thing with some guy. Getting his CD's and videos mixed in with yours, fighting over which set of dishes belongs to whom—"

"I hear you," Karen says over the background music which, so far, has stayed with instrumentals, operatic overtures mainly. If it moves into vocals, she's going to have a problem. Her nervous system has never been able to distinguish opera singers from fingernails on a blackboard.

"Besides," Anna says, pouring herself another scotch and pointing to Karen's empty glass with a question in her eyebrows; Karen shakes her head, No, "my daughter likes it here. When she gets a chance to visit."

Every available surface, as well as virtually every wall, sports a photo of Anna's daughter, Angelica, a cellist with the San Francisco Philharmonic. Something of a prodigy, Angelica had been playing with local orchestras from the age of twelve. Anna's face and voice become transported when she speaks of her only child.

Last night, when she first arrived, Karen was too tired to do anything much besides fall into bed in the guest room, but this night she's had far too much time to look around. The strangeness does not dissipate, but grows. Even the photos of Angelica seem familiar to her, but in an entirely different context which she can only see in the corner of her mental eye. If she tries to examine it front-on, it slithers away like a jellyfish.

Karen does take that third shot of tequila after all. At least she'll sleep well tonight *[Guess recent experience has taught you nothing, hunh?],* and tomorrow she'll be on an early train home. With luck, she'll leave the strangeness here, downwind from Our Nation's Capital where it belongs.

"So who are your heroes?" Anna asks.

"Hm?" Karen wonders if her attention has glitched again. It's always done that when she's overtired, but lately—

"Whom did you read as a kid? I mean, I got into s/f because I thought that was all there was. The library in the town where I grew up was an old church, and the s/f novels, mostly paperbacks, were lined up on shelves in the foyer just as you came through the front door. I'd sneak away from home on summer mornings just to enjoy the air conditioning, and I'd sit on the floor in that foyer and read all day. Literally started with Asimov and worked my way through Zelazny. It never occurred to me to enter the main room or to take one of those books home. My brothers would've destroyed them anyway. That bunch destroyed everything they put their hands on. . . ."

Her voice drifts for a moment, and her face takes on a pained look. She literally shakes it off.

"So who were your heroes?" she repeats, as if to draw attention away from herself.

"*Jane Eyre,*" Karen says quickly, wanting to know more about Anna and hoping to make short work of her own preferences so she can get back into her friend's half-revelations; to the best of her recollection, this is the most Anna's ever opened up to her. "Or any orphan who rose above her station, really. Any story that proved that brains and resourcefulness were better than simpering and guile. I loathed Scarlett O' Hara. She reminded me too much of my mother. And I used to wish I was adopted."

She's said too much, and Anna's giving her a thoughtful look. "Rotten home life?" she asks as if casually.

"Isn't everyone's?" Karen counters. She's feeling way too vulnerable to talk about it. Must be the tequila.

"That's interesting," Anna says, leaning forward from where she's been sitting cross-legged on one of the two small couches, mirroring Karen's posture on the other side of the coffee table. "I've heard a lot of people say they wish they'd been adopted. That nightmare/fantasy every kid has at least once, of having been left on the doorstep. It's always intrigued me, because I was. Adopted, I mean. Though not necessarily left on the doorstep." When Karen says nothing to that but leaves her expression open as if to say: I'll listen if you want to talk about it, Anna goes on: "You mean I've never told you?"

"No."

"The story goes—and I have to filter some of it, because my mother was as much a fabulist as yours is—"

Karen doesn't remember telling her that.

"—that I was brought over here from Germany just after the War. My father, bless his drunken soul, would have us believe he was something important in the OSS, but for my money he was just another GI stuck in Berlin during the Occupation. But whatever the truth of how he got saddled with me, I was supposed to be a Christmas present for my mother. As if she didn't already have four of her own, but she'd had a hysterectomy the year before which, for a Catholic woman of that generation meant her usefulness as a woman was ended. . . ."

Karen laughs with her, though both of them know it isn't funny.

"So he drops me into this mass of freckled redheads, all of three or four years old (they couldn't tell for sure because I had no papers, and I was so small and not a little undernourished), recently deloused, tired and cranky and speaking not a word of English, but insisting that my name was Anna, so they let it be. When he was in his cups—as if he wasn't usually, up until the day he died—the old man'd tell some fantastical story about two men stopping him in the street outside the Allied records office and telling him some tale about my mother's been killed in the shelling. . . ."

# THIRTEEN

The background music suddenly gets very loud, and it's rampant with sopranos, but that's not the only thing that's making Karen's hair stand on end. She's hugging herself, holding herself very close to herself, thinking: *Don't extrapolate! Berlin was a very big city, then as now, and thousands of people died in the shelling. Don't get ahead of yourself; it's nothing!*

Anna sees the pained look on her face and gets up to turn the stereo down.

"Wagner, of all things. You'd think I'd have some innate aversion to it, something almost at the genetic level, being Jewish." Karen's staring at her in a way that might unnerve the average person. "Well, at least I assumed, coming from Germany, and with these eyes and the dark hair. Though I'm told I was blonde as a child. But Wagner . . . I can't help myself. I love it."

*No!* Karen is thinking: *No, no, no, no, no!* Not a dream, then, but a series of realities which have changed the reality she knows now. The kaleidoscope whirls, and suddenly life is made of flying bits of multicolored glass.

Still misinterpreting, Anna shuts the stereo off. "I'm sorry. You did say you hated opera . . ."

Karen nods, numbly. Something else is trying to break through here, and she really doesn't want to see or hear it.

". . . and I'm being a bad hostess," Anna goes on. "I should let you go to bed; you must be exhausted. Honestly, when Marie and

Paul started going at it I wanted to—Karen, speak to me. What's wrong?"

"I *am* tired," Karen admits, taking off her glasses and rubbing her eyes as if to emphasize the point. She looks up at Anna, still standing beside the stereo, through the fog of her myopia and wonders if that will make things better. In fact it makes it worse. Mostly what she can see is Anna's eyes, large and almost black and superimposed over the face of a smudge-faced child in a Berlin cellar. She's going to have to find out for sure. When she puts her glasses back on, Anna's face looks older. She'd misjudged her age. Over fifty, then, if she was a child of three or four at the end of the war. Taking a deep breath, Karen says: "Tell me more about it. Did your father ever give you any more detail?"

Anna sits on the other couch, tucking her feet up like a child; the effect is even more unnerving. She wraps her hands around her scotch glass, contemplating the melting ice.

"My father drank Irish whiskey," she murmurs, lost in the past. "Single malt. Funny, have you ever noticed how some serious alcoholics are very picky about what they'll drink? My mother kept gin in the house for martinis, but he never touched that. Strictly a single-malt drinker. He'd have told me this stuff tasted like iodine."

She took a sip, then put the glass down. "Which it does, but anyway. Yes, he talked about it a lot. Especially when he was dying and looking for a way to explain himself. He told me the man carrying me was so fat he could barely walk. He found that funny in a city where people were eating rats by then. There was an older man with him whose English, he said, was excellent. He was the one who explained about the shell hitting the bakery, and about everyone else in the basement being killed except the two of them, and the child—me—and the woman who saved her. Threw her own body over her—me, I mean—apparently, almost as if she knew the ceiling was going to cave in.

"My father, being the cynic he was, didn't believe a word of it.

Couldn't figure out what the real story was, but then I latched onto his finger the way a kid that age will do, and suddenly the fat man had done a handoff somehow, and I was in his arms. It was the eyes, he said, that made him go through the red tape to bring me home instead of just leaving me in the infirmary with the others. I mean, there were thousands of us.

"So I was the lucky one," Anna concludes, looking at Karen finally with tears luminous in her dark eyes, her expression belying her words. "I always wondered who the woman was, and why she didn't keep me, or bring me to the Americans herself, or whether she was pure fiction. I wonder if she's still alive. How old would she be now; what became of her after the war. . . ."

Both women let the silence go on far too long. Anna finishes the last swallow of watery scotch with a grimace and gets up to go to bed. "Interesting story, huh? It's yours if you want it."

Karen is taken aback. "Wh-what do you mean?"

Anna continues to study her with concern. "I meant you could use it in a novel someday."

"Oh." Karen seems to finally notice how strangely she's behaving. "Yes, you're right. I may someday. Thank you."

•

Amtrakking home. The sound of the wheels is mesmerizing, the scenery just boring enough to induce a state of trance. Karen is thinking:

What if fiction were as messy as real life? No editor would buy it, for a start. The current batch have trouble enough recognizing fiction when they see it. Picture what today's editors would do with some of yesteryear's classics:

"Now, that part near the end where her employer's house burns down, and he goes blind and ends up marrying her? We feel that's *much* too downbeat an ending. . . ." When, Karen wondered, had book editors, emulating newspaper editors, perhaps, adopted the papal *we?* "We feel that Rochester's first wife should simply find a good therapist and the right medication to control her bipolarism. Then they can agree to an amicable divorce, and he's free to marry Jane. Although, would she want to marry him, necessarily, now that he's not blind? I mean, was it really love or just pity? Unless it was for the money, but wouldn't that make her a less sympathetic character? Unless, of course, she has plans to set up a charity or something."

Karen's always tempted at this point to ask "Why don't you just write this one yourself?" But she already knows the answer: "Oh, but *you're* the writer. Okay, let's try this:

"Jane and Rochester do marry, but forget the pregnancy. It does nothing to enhance the narrative. Or let her miscarry; that's always good for narrative tension. Then he's mysteriously murdered, and she inherits all his money and finds herself a young lover while she's on a cruise to Cancun. She's implicated in the murder, of course, in which case we can bring the first wife back and have her testify at the trial.

"Oh, and that business about her being an orphan? *Much* too negative. What if she's an ambitious working girl from Staten Island with a kind of psychic insight into the stock market or something like that. . . ."

Music by Carly Simon. Definitely Oscar material, if it ever got that far. But let's try something a little closer to home:

"First of all, our attorneys are adamant on the point that you'll have to issue a written disclaimer that to the best of your knowledge no such family named O'Hara ever owned a plantation in the South called Tara, because the possibility of a libel suit, in the event that any living person can prove that Scarlett was a blood relative—You do see our point, don't you?

"And all those references to 'darkies'? Not at *all* politically correct. We've talked to our attorneys about that as well, and they're very concerned about the possibility of a class action suit; you'll simply have to change that to something else. Afro-Americans—is it Afro-

Americans they want to call themselves nowadays, or is it African-Americans? Honestly, we see so few of them up here in the rarefied air of the publishing arms of film companies run by accountants and owned by multinationals whose sole purpose is to churn out generic blockbusters that can go straight to film that—no, now, wait a minute. We did have one at the front desk for awhile. What was it she called herself? . . . No, I *know* her name was Gwendolyn, except when she changed it to Shanequa and started wearing her hair in those funny little braids; what I meant was, what is it *they* call themselves these days? You know, *those* people—"

(Do you get the impression that senior editors might really be jellyfish all the way down?)

"—*and* we actually have a black writer on our fall list, or is she part Chippewa Indian? Or is that Native American? All right, Afro, African, whatever. So change that. And the dialogue! Not acceptable. They're going to have to speak Standard English. None of this dialect stuff. It sounds too much like—what's that stuff they wanted to teach in the schools in California?"

"Ebonics," Karen supplies, unable to help herself. "But that's not what—I mean, slaves and overseers both spoke that way. There are first-person accounts, even actual recordings from freed slaves who survived into this century. . . ."

They are giving her that blank S.oteric we're-not-listening look.

"What*ever.* You simply have to change it. *And* you'll have to find a synonym for *slave.* Freedom-challenged, maybe? We'll leave that up to you, but *slave* is just too . . . icky, no; can't have it. Our attorneys will help you with the wording."

(Yup, jellyfish, all right. No question about it.)

"Lastly, that part where Scarlett pulls the radishes out of the garden, and she says: 'As God is my witness, I'll never go hungry again'—Is that it? Not only are we concerned about offending the Religious Right with what might be construed as a defamatory reference to a deity, but there are certain atheist groups which might demand equal representation. One of our publicists suggested the use of the term *Goddess* instead. Or you can just have her say 'I'll never go hungry again'. . . ."

Sigh. All right. The train jolts into Penn Station, late as usual, and Karen drags her suitcase with the gimpy wheel toward the subway thinking: Where do we go from here?

•

Raymond. She says his name aloud. "Omigod, Raymond!"

The photos of Angelica should have triggered something. Angelica is Raymond's daughter, not Anna's. Isn't she?

Every detail is exact: the musical talent, the orchestras she's played with, the battle for custody when she was a kid. Karen listened to Anna talk about her all night and still it didn't register. She had admired the photos, not realizing she'd seen them before, kept them in the corner of her eye all evening, not realizing that while the girl may have the same general coloring as Anna, their features are not the same. Thinking back, Karen realizes she was struck by the fact that the girl didn't look at all like her father, whom Anna was adult enough not to cut out of the family photos when they split.

The only one Angelica looks exactly like is Raymond.

How could she not have seen?

Home now, Karen rummages through every drawer and file cabinet, every box full of papers crammed into closets and under the bed, looking for the accordion folder where she keeps her correspondence with Raymond. It is nowhere to be found. But that's not conclusive. She's misplaced things before.

"Oh, no!" she says aloud, a warning to any earless pinky-purple coelenterate who might be listening. "I wouldn't lose something as important as that!"

There is nothing. No inch-thick stack of letters, no photos tucked into a little glassine envelope from the post office to keep them unthumbprinted and undamaged.

*[Maybe you threw them away? Tore everything up, burned it, danced*

*around the funeral pyre of the death of your relationship? If you could even call it a relationship! Letters and phone calls and unfulfilled promises . . . you have no friends and you never will, and no man will ever want you. . . . ]*

Karen stops her rummaging, narrowing her eyes at something she can't even see. "Oh, no you don't! Now you've gone too far. If I was that angry, I'd remember it. And what the hell do *you* know about relationships? And if you're not speaking to me, then *don't* fucking speak to me. Make up your Mind!"

*[Oops . . . ]*

•

Not a trace of him. Not a mention of him in her telephone log, no card in the Rolodex. Nary a letter from him, not a trace on paper or disk of her letters *to* him. No Russian pocket calendar nor Soviet ruble tucked into her wallet as mementoes . . .

Raymond, like Anna, had a government job, worked with visiting economists from the former Soviet nations. In fact, had the same job title, probably even the same desk in the same cubicle in the same featureless high-rise in the shadow of the Air and Space Museum. They even drank the same brand of scotch. It was all coming back to Karen now. He'd given her the little bit of paper currency from the former Soviet Union as a gentle joke.

"A ruble for your thoughts," he'd said, and she'd added:

"Meaning, now that there's no more Soviet Union, you can't tell if this sucker's going to be worth a fortune or nothing at all?"

He'd groaned. "Must you always find hidden meanings in everything?"

He was being rhetorical; she'd answered him honestly. "Yes."

She'd folded the ruble and kept it in her wallet, along with the photos of her kids. She'd kept Raymond's photos separate, because she didn't have the negatives and couldn't replace them if they got damaged. But she'd wanted something of his close to her even when she was on the road.

•

Gone now, all of it. The time line has glitched, hiccuped, leaving Karen with a residual dizziness, and suddenly none of it makes sense any more.

She'd seen where Raymond worked, didn't need to visit Anna there to know it would be identical. Even the *apartment,* for God's sake, should have tipped her off. It was one of a series of apartments Raymond had lived in between relationships, before he met his current wife. The guest room where Karen had just spent the night had been occupied by a roommate then, a roommate who, from the little she'd seen of him, owned exactly one pair of boxer shorts and a lot of black socks and never turned off the TV.

Forcing herself to remain calm, Karen reexamines her phone log and the Rolodex. Wherever Raymond was supposed to be, she found Anna's name.

Raymond was gone. In spite of the disparities in age and gender and origin, Anna had taken his place, slipped into the time stream, into his life, as if he'd never existed. Almost. Never mind the sudden sex-change operation; Anna was fifty-something, Raymond not yet forty. And Angelica was only eighteen in the reality Karen remembered. Maybe that was what had thrown her. In this Anna universe, the girl was in her early twenties, nearly Nicole's age. It had momentarily fooled her.

It was the handiwork of someone not yet used to the concept of time. The seams were showing. Pay no attention to that man behind the curtain. Karen knows who's responsible.

•

"Hey, guise?"

She has gone to the place inside herself where the words come from or, rather, where the ideas and images shape themselves into words, where the characters emerge from the fog as disembodied voices, distinct personalities to whom she must give form and substance, backstory and structure and forward momentum.

"I am not kidding now. Something's horribly wrong here, and I am not moving until you speak to me, and we get it squared away."

Thinking: If we can.

Her focus is not entirely pure. She has never been able to entirely do that Zen thing and empty her mind, because someone's always whispering offstage, fidgeting before their entrance, fussing with a costume, fumbling a prop. Right now she is thinking:

Long before she met him in real life, Raymond turned up in her novel *Preternatural* as an adolescent character named Johnny, just one of several dozen characters, not counting a planetful of S.oteri, she'd been juggling at the time. But Johnny's time line had been hinky from the outset, slithering in and out of the narrative so that sometimes he was in his teens and other times he appeared as the adult she would meet at a con just after the book came out. Part of her immediate response to Raymond was the feeling that she'd known him all her life.

Which made no sense since he was more than ten years her junior. But she'd still been riding the wave of What Is Time? and anything had seemed possible.

Was it possible that Raymond wasn't real? Could she have imagined him? Or only stumbled accidentally into some little air pocket in the time line where he existed only long enough to break her heart and disappear?

"No, excuse me. That's much too simple an explanation. And what about Anna?"

And, for that matter, she thinks without saying it aloud, what about all my other selves? And Ryalbran and Johann/Jacob/Govannon (especially Govannon)? For a dizzying moment she wonders what would happen if she encountered any of *his* incarnations in her present life. But she'll keep that to herself for now.

*[Anna exists because you rescued her in Berlin. If you hadn't been there, she would have died.]*

"But you were the ones who put me there. That's what affected the outcome. You knew there was no way I was going to stand there and let that little girl die."

*Now, wait a minute, that wasn't all of us*, some of them start to say, but one voice, louder and more pay-attention-to-me than the rest, thrusts through:

*Well, then, whose fault IS it?*

There comes a point, in the middle of the worst crisis, where a terrible clarity is born. Karen's known all along she wasn't speaking to the entire Mind, and now she knows why the voice sounds so familiar. Though her whole world has just warped and twisted round about her in some widening we're-not-in-Kansas-anymore gyre, she'll know how to handle Fuchsia from here on.

"Hi, Mom."

It's too much of a leap of logic for even a Mind to bear. Reaching out a tentacle, it snags Fuchsia by the throat.

*WE CAN'T HAVE THIS!* it snarls, not a little testily. *You've got some explaining to do. . . .*

•

Karen listens to the explanation, which isn't so much explanation as confirmation of what she suspected ever since she woke in Eleanor's time sharing a room with a sow. One S.oteri with a newfound skill and not the brains to use it has used her to fuck the time line.

"Well, that's a relief," Karen says when Gray had told the tawdry tale. Fuchsia, despite repeated proddings from the rest, had clamped hir lipless jaw and refused for once to utter a sound. She looks like nothing so much as one of those mean-spirited old women whose mouths disappear after years of being pursed in disapproval, leaving them to draw a false mouth outside the lines with lipstick, fooling no one. "Not that I didn't figure you guys were behind it somehow."

*Oh, no you don't! Don't tar us all with the same brush, please. We've long since diversified into individual minds, and the rest of us won't be held responsible for what SOME of us have been up to!*

"Well, yeah, but the rest of you left hir unsupervised with this new toy, so I think you have to be held accountable for that much," Karen says, then stops herself. She will not be drawn into their petty squabbling which, she knows, can last millennia. "Let's not get distracted here. All I'm asking is that, now that you've screwed things up, you just unscrew 'em and put 'em back the way they were."

*Um, it doesn't exactly work that way.*

"What's that supposed to mean?"

It is her old cohort Azure who steps in now to clarify things: *It wasn't whee who gave hir the power. Yew sea, there's this Third Thing—*

*Oh, no, you don't!* Gray is intervening hastily. *You can't tell her about THAT—!*

*Why knot? I was only going to tell her what TQ gave us, not the whys and wherefores. Can't you trust me enough not to tell her about—?*

*About what? There you go again, about to spill the whole thing. Remember, there's a difference between past/present/future. You can't just—*

*Oh, yeah? And has any of you figured out what it is yet? How do you know I wasn't going to—?*

They're all mixed up in it now, hissing and squeaking and yammering, squiggling around like so many Gummi-worms. Karen's head is pounding. She wants to scream but speaks very softly instead.

"You know, I'm halfway tempted to write you clowns out of the narrative entirely and go with someone else."

That stops them in their tracks. Does it mean she knows about the Third Thing?

*Aw, now, Karen,* Virid says, *are you sure you want to do that? It's not as if we haven't been of tremendous help to you in the past. . . .*

While Azure asks: *Are you sure you can get away with that? What will your editor say? I mean, there we are, right there in the outline, plain as day. In fact, I think there may even be something in our contract with you which clearly specifies. . . .*

And so it goes, until Fuchsia, watching all this and realizing the focus has shifted off hir entirely, clamps hir jaw even tighter, clenches hir knotty little fists, stamps hir feet in their tottery high heels and shouts, *Pay ATTENTION to me!*

The rest of them freeze in horrified tableau. This sort of thing never went on when they were all of one Mind. Karen sighs. It's all too familiar to her.

*You haven't got the nerve to write ME out of this, because you need me to fix it. That is . . .* (Fuchsia flutters hir eyelashes, which might have looked cute when s/he was four, tries to play coy, but just ends up looking ridiculous.) . . . *IF I decide to.*

"So you admit you're responsible," Karen prompts hir quietly.

*No, no,* Fuchsia is shaking hir head so violently you'd think it would twist right off. *I never said that, no!*

Karen rolls her eyes. This conversation is hopeless. She looks to Gray for a little common sense.

"Well?"

But before Gray can answer, Fuchsia feels the attention shift away from hir again, and the sensation is so unbearable s/he starts to shout:

*You changed my future, I've changed yours!* s/he gloats, and Karen finishes for her: "Nyaah-nyaah!"

The pinky-purple one is so livid now that s/he's gasping like a fish and nothing but hot air is coming out of hir mouth.

"Will you, for God's sake, *do* something?" Karen demands of the rest of them, an edge to her voice. "This may be amusing to you, but it's life and death to those of us who experience such things."

She can tell by their blank looks that they're not going to do a damn thing. Or maybe:

"You can't, can you?" she asks with a writer's instinct.

There is a universal shaking of heads now, except for Fuchsia, who's looking extraordinarily smug.

Karen's legs feel wobbly. She didn't realize she'd been moving around the room, appealing to one or the other, any of them, to try to see it from her point of view. She sits down, hard. Her point of view is suddenly very scary.

"But there is this Third Thing Azure mentioned." She is feeling her way, but somehow knows TQ must be spoken in upper case. Whoever/Whatever it is, that's a pretty impressive power it's tossing around. She can't say much about its judgment, however, in giving it to Fuchsia. Okay, she chides herself: Pay attention! "Can it—they—whatever, put everything back the way it's supposed to be?"

*What makes you so sure the way you remember is the way it's supposed to be?*

"Don't play at sophistry with me, just answer the goddamn question!"

*Weir knot sure.*

# FOURTEEN

Karen glowers at Fuchsia. "Let's get started," she says before she has time to think about it. "We've got a lot of work to do."

But first:

*Does Raymond really mean that much to you?* It's Azure again, genuinely puzzled, as S.oteri always are, at the affection these so very *separate* beings have for each other.

"It's not about that at all!" Karen snaps, not entirely answering the question, thinking: Of course he means that much to me. But whether he does or he doesn't, he belongs here. He had a life here. He has a right to live that life, not be consigned to nonexistence. Or, well, maybe not nonexistence exactly, but some sort of alternate existence, in a different time or place. Someplace, she tries not to think, where I'll never see him again. Maybe he really is/was just Ryalbran, or Johnny, and there never was a Raymond at all.

Isn't that the nature of Fuchsia's problem, not understanding the difference? In which case, clever little twit, s/he's done a damn good job of making hir point. But enough. Time to get real. Karen's almost tempted to go through her notes for Johnny in *Preternatural* to see just when and where and how she created him, and if he's really Raymond, and if, just maybe, that's all Raymond is, a character in one of her novels, a fictional construct, and nothing real at all.

Except she threw away her notes. She always does, as soon as she submits the manuscript, destroys every trace of the thought process that went into it. No one's going to James Joyce her, second-guess her, scuffle together the odd bits of paper she leaves behind and reissue some posthumous version of *Preternatural* (and yes I said yes I will Yes.) comprised of floor-swept fragments and scraps stuck in the back of a drawer claiming, for the price of a trade paperback and as big a percentage as the publisher can swindle from her heirs, that it's more authentic than the original.

She was getting ahead of herself. Wait till you're dead, she thought, before you start worrying about that stuff. Raymond is real; you know he is. Don't let them distract you.

"This isn't just about Raymond," she says. "It's about the Big Picture. If even one of you has telekinesis and doesn't really understand how pulling a temporal being out of its own time can have inexorable consequences, you could potentially 'disappear' us all."

She grabs Fuchsia by a tentacle.

"Let's go, kiddo," she says. "We're going to solve this together."

*Haven't you forgotten something?* Gray asks mildly. *What about Anna?*

•

Karen hadn't even thought about that. Why can't time travel be as simple in real life as it is in science fiction?

"I don't suppose you'll tell me whether or not Anna belongs in this time line?" she wheedles, only now noticing that half of the S.oteri—or half of those she's met; she's still not entirely sure how many of them there are because they're not sure themselves—a good percentage of them, let's say, have left the room, as if this particular little melodrama is of such minor interest to them that they've decided to go for coffee, pick up their e-mail, walk the dog. Which is all the answer Karen's going to get.

If Karen does nothing, just stays where she is, putting one foot in front of the other for the rest of her life and pretending memory is dream, Anna can quietly lead her life, never suspecting that she was meant to die as a child in a Berlin bomb shelter. Her daughter, Angelica, even though she's a few years older than she used to be in

Karen's former reality, will still be a gifted musician playing for a major symphony orchestra, and history will proceed apace. There will be minor or perhaps not so minor glitches, as the changes in her time line impact others.

The two other second-best cellists, for example. Are you following this?

Okay, Premise: Angelica I, Raymond's daughter, born in 1980. She enters a cello competition at the age of twelve whose first prize is a year as guest soloist with a regional symphony orchestra. Whoever comes in second that year gets a check for $500 and a "Lotsaluck, kid!" That kid will most likely start junior high as usual and, maybe in a fit of artistic temperament, give up the cello. That's the way these things go.

Premise: Angelica II, Anna's daughter, born in 1975 but, in all other respects, identical to Raymond's daughter. At the age of twelve—when Raymond's daughter would have been only seven, and not yet that sufficiently proficient—she enters a cello competition which . . .

Get it? One of two potential rogue second-best cellists roaming the world thinking: if I'd only won that contest when I was twelve, I wouldn't be standing in this bell tower looking down at people through the sites of a high-powered rifle thinking they all look like so many ants, and all I'd have to do to stop the pounding in my head is—

Ridiculous! Everyone knows cellists can't shoot straight; they haven't got the fingering.

But we had you going there for a minute, didn't whee?

Karen's memories of Raymond will fade in time; he will exist on the same plane as her fictional characters and maybe, like Ryalbran, in other times and places and, for all she knows, they both might be the better for it.

The alternative is to go back to Berlin and stand by as the little girl with the big, dark eyes is buried under the rubble and dies. No more difficult than watching a Save the Children commercial without becoming Mother Teresa. Then that s.o.b. who broke her heart can go on with his life, never knowing it was Karen who gave it back to him. How much of a choice could it be?

And what makes her so sure it's a choice that has to be made? There are so many potential variables.

There's also the fact that Tertium Quid Is Watching You. Karen's pretty sure all of this is some kind of test, of the S.oteri as much as her. Even if it isn't, someone has to make Fuchsia *see,* acknowledge that humans are as valid as s/he.

This is Karen, who can't even get her own mother to acknowledge her existence. Lotsa-luck, kid!

*What are you going to do, Karen?* Azure asks softly. Karen hadn't noticed s/he was still hanging around, half expected hir to float off with the rest.

"What's it to you?" she asks a little crossly. She's still got Fuchsia by one tentacle, and the little wretch is starting to squirm. "You already know the outcome, if you search hard enough for it."

For a moment Azure seems to be doing just that.

*I just wanted you to tell me, to be sure.*

"Well, I'm not. You're going to have to wait just like everyone else."

*But you are going back in time. That means—*

"It means *I have to know*. That's all it means so far."

Suddenly everyone else seems to have come back into the room. The Mind has decided it can make Fuchsia send Karen back in time, but it isn't about to let Fuchsia go along.

*We believe s/he's done enough damage,* Gray tried to explain. *Let's face it, even though we have no faces: If we can't control hir, how are you going to? If s/he slips away from you for even a nanosecond—*

"I'll cope," Karen says, thinking: That's going to be my epitaph, in whatever century. Here Lies Karen: She Coped. The thought chills her. Is she even sure she's going to die in her own time? Maybe she should dump her notes before she goes. But the Mind is still fussing about Fuchsia.

*No, we're sorry. We can't allow you to—*

{Let hir go with her.}

Karen doesn't so much hear as feel it, like the rumble of a subway under her feet. Interesting! she thinks. So the Mind really is taking orders from this Third Thing. Maybe. The thought gives her hope rather than fear. About time someone took a little adult responsibility here.

The Mind thinks differently.

*Talk about your* deus ex machina! *Pushy bastard(s), telling us what to do. . . .* While carrying over all of them, Fuchsia howls:

*I won't! I won't, I won't, I won't, and you can't make me!* Yammer and bubble, rumble and squeak. Karen yawns. This may take awhile. She concentrates on getting a tighter grip on Fuchsia, which is about like trying to hold onto a well-greased toddler with the strength of a Rottweiler and four or five times as many limbs. Finally:

{You will.}

And it isn't clear if TQ's addressing Fuchsia, Karen, or the Mind. Because, yes, she said, yes, I will, yes. And following the rumble, there is an uneasy silence, while Karen thinks: There's more here than just the threat of taking the telekinetic power away. I wonder what it is exactly? But she has no time to wonder because the Mind says:

*Well, you heard the order: Go with her!*

As if it were the Mind's idea all along! Which Fuchsia likes about as much as going to the dentist, but knows it's part of the test and so, with all the charm of a twelve-year-old spewing pea soup and spinning her head around backwards, s/he plants hirself in front of Karen, purses hir lips to remoisten the lipstick on that phony mouth, and says:

"So?"

Holding the little wretch on her lap all slimy-squiggly, like a kid in a wet diaper waiting for the rollercoaster to crawl up that first big hill before plunging down, down—(well, Gentle Reader, you did want to know what size they were)—Karen braces herself for—whatever.

•

Too late, she thinks: I should have researched first. Should have called Jenner for a refresher course on Plantagenets, borrowed Matt's *World at War* videos and learned a little more about Berlin in April of '45, gone to the library for a brushup on the ancient Celts. Too late too soon. Are we there yet? Soon . . .

•

Margarethe and her little imaginary friend were apparently not in the cellar with Tim and Johann and little Anna and her mother all night, but spent the earlier part of the evening threading their way along Zoostrasse looking to see a man about a dog.

At least, so it seemed to Karen. She "arrived" crouched by a pile of rubble, dry-retching from the journey. The sight was so familiar that none of the other citizens scurrying past her—reprobates like herself defying the curfew, risking death for matters which at the time seemed more important than such a commonplace as death—paid any mind or stopped to help her. She stood up slowly, checked the pockets of the now-familiar apron and her cardigan to see that everything was in place, allowed herself the vanity of making sure her hair had not escaped its net. Her scalp itched. Okay, it was real. She did all of this one-handed. The other still had a firm grip on Fuchsia.

Silly. If the little beast had telekinesis, s/he could as easily hurl Karen down a well or into the sun or into the path of an incoming shell (they could hear the *pum-pum-pum* of the Russian guns in the distance, and while the shells were not yet striking the Museum district, they would) to make hir escape; there was no point in holding onto hir. Either the Third Thing was controlling this scenario or it wasn't. Karen let go of the tentacle. As if knowing there were limits to how much s/he could get away with, Fuchsia followed.

Karen knew she had to meet someone (a man, of course; men did all the important things in wars) and it had something to do with the handful of Camels in her apron pocket. A stupid place to put them, she thought, scoffing at her alter ego's ingenuousness; it was the first place that would be searched if she were stopped. But Margarethe was wise enough to know, where Karen didn't, that this late in the war she'd be shot first for violating the curfew and her pockets rifled later, so where she hid things or even what she hid didn't matter. And while we're on the subject, what was she doing out in the middle of the blackout anyway?

Focus and click; don't get distracted. You're here to meet someone, to pay him off with the cigarettes, only a dozen of them, so it can't be any great thing he's going to trade you for them, but what is it? Information, false papers, a weapon, ration coupons? Are you in business for yourself or working for some Third Thing? The memories, not being Karen's, are not there, and Fuchsia refuses to help.

One thing neither the war movies nor the documentaries ever told you about war was how bad it smelled.

There was the sweet-rot smell Karen remembered from the severed head on the palisades at Avaricum and, when she stopped to think of it, every half-cratered building she passed was a makeshift mausoleum holding body or bodies that would be razed into the rubble when the city finally began to tear itself apart prefatory to putting itself together, sort of, in an unnatural patchwork of four cities which would take more than forty years to reknit as one. Some buildings merely folded in on themselves, dusty but perversely neat, taking their inner secrets with them. Others were jagged-toothed monuments displaying their dead. Tattered curtains flapped from vacant window frames, exposing here a chair with burst, burnt stuffing, there a split mattress ticking. Bathtubs teetered two storeys high, hanging precariously from their plumbing, the floor tiles beneath them spattering down like autumn leaves but deadlier on passersby. Family photos stood exposed against stained wallpaper. A scrap of shirt, a smash-faced doll, a shoe sometimes with what was once a leg still protruding, and everywhere that miasma of a smell. And rats. And a dog or two or whole packs of them, rack-ribbed, foaming, desperate, their fights gone ferocious in the dark at night whenever there was a hiatus in the shelling. Sometimes they fed on each other.

There were toilet smells, too, of vomit sometimes, of urine constantly, puddles against walls that didn't want examining, but most of all a fecal stink, not only from ruptured storm sewers and dank courtyards where people whose water closets held no water or who no longer had a water closet or who simply found their bowels letting loose at the slightest provocation (dysentery was so rampant no one bothered mentioning it) found whatever furtive relief they could, but as if the whole city's bowels had simply let go. This was the scent over all, Hitler's legacy, nothing but shit all the way down.

There were respites, freshets of a clean breeze springing up unexpectedly, places where wildflowers had sprouted in the empty lots the summer before. The trees still bloomed in Unter den Linden. Incredibly, there were still birds. Sometimes children could be heard playing, their clear voices, even laughter, carrying like bells through the smoky, dusty air.

But for the rest, war is all hell. It also stinks. Karen wishes she could make Fuchsia smell it.

Don't hold your nose, don't cover your face; you're a Berliner, you're used to it! Karen tells herself. Strangely, she finds herself wanting to laugh.

There is a story connected with John F. Kennedy's famous speech at the Berlin Wall in a time which, from Margarethe's perspective, hasn't happened yet. Anyone who knows their history knows he was trying for solidarity with the crowd, trying to tell them he understood from the heart the distress they felt at having their city slashed down the middle by this cicatrix of a wall (Can you believe the nerve of him? Preppy rich kid with his pants around his ankles most of the time, when he wasn't trying to find himself a controversy in Cuba or Vietnam he could turn into The War to Make His Presidency Memorable), and decided, probably on the advice of his handlers, to conclude his speech with what he thought would be a rousing turn of phrase in German: "*Ich bin ein Berliner*—I am a Berliner!"

Now, to those of you who never took German 101, what he actually said translated as something to the effect of "I am a jelly donut."

Okay, this is your jellyfish speaking: *Ein* in German, in all its variations, is what is know as an indefinite article. It means *a* or *the.* Except when it's not needed, as in the case of someone from Berlin who, when asked where s/he is from, will answer "*Ich bin Berliner,*" loosely translated as "I am Berliner." Kind of like saying "I am American," rather than "I am an American," only not, okay? The indefinite article is definitely not needed, you see.

Well, Kennedy didn't see. Or didn't do his homework, which preppy rich kids have a tendency toward. Much easier to pay someone else to crib for you, as his little brother Teddy figured out in time to have someone else take his exams at Harvard. *Ergo* Kennedy, being raised Catholic, might have known his Latin (Irony: Irish kids learning the language of the conqueror. Are you paying attention?), but he didn't know from Shinola when it came to German. So how was he supposed to know that *"ein Berliner"*—a Berliner—was a kind of pastry? Like a Danish, get it?

(Well, if you're from New York you do; everyone else in America calls it a sweet roll or a bear-claw or some damn thing. Then there are the Brits, who call cookies *biscuits,* when everyone knows biscuits are what you serve with red-eye gravy. And you wonder why we jellyfish—who aren't even fish or made of jelly—are so easily confused?)

Bottom line: What Kennedy really said was "I am a pastry/a Danish/*ein Berliner*" . . . the Walrus, whatever. And he wondered why so many in the crowd were silent, and the rest were applauding nervously (polite bunch, those Germans, except when they're loading you into cattle cars) so as not to laugh.

Which has nothing to do with Margarethe, who is here in the shadow of possibly the largest antiaircraft tower ever built, looking to meet her contact, except that Karen, her *doppelgänger* (another good German word) finds it amusing in a retro sort of way.

•

About the antiaircraft tower: At the start of the war, Hitler's architect, Albert Speer, had three huge steel and concrete fortresses built, each with 128-mm gun emplacements on the roof to strafe the skies nightly in an attempt to bring the enemy planes down, to defend the city of Berlin. A veritable honeycomb of small rooms below housed munitions, replacement troops, and toward the end, refugees, the wounded, and—in the case of the Zoo *flakturm,* the largest of the three—the valuables from the Berlin State Museums, including crates of small artifacts stacked like apple boxes, priceless oils removed from their frames and rolled like so much unironed laundry, and the three packing boxes containing the so-called "Trojan gold," found by accident sixty years before by an inept German archeologist named Schliemann and smuggled out of Greece in what amounted to blatant theft.

The stolen trove would be stolen again when the Russians took over the *flakturm*, but that was some weeks away yet. The gold would end up "lost" in the basement of Moscow's Pushkin Museum until 1987.

•

All of which also has nothing to do with Karen or her *doppelgänger* Margarethe, except that the *flakturm* is a presence, looming over her, blocking out the sky. She is not so close that it might offer her protection (it is *verboten* for civilians to come too close, at least until the bombing starts, when there are too many of them for the sentries to keep away. On the upper levels, the corpses are stacked three deep—there aren't enough personnel to move them out, and nowhere else to put them—some of them bleeding all over priceless artworks), just close enough so she cannot see the sky.

As if she'd want to. The sky rains death, in a place where there is already enough death.

"Why did you bring me back this far?" Karen asks Fuchsia. "The controversy's over my saving Anna's life, isn't it? Let's cut to the chase." She waits. "Or is this part of it? Is there something I'm supposed to do or see here that will give me a clue?"

Fuchsia doesn't answer. S/he also, Karen notices now that they're both in the same time and place, never quite touches the ground. Any other time she's ever seen an S.oteri—and most times she hears but doesn't see them—they've had that hovering quality, suspended as if in the liquid environment that was their origin. Well, that might be useful for her novel, but it's of no help to her now.

You're here to find Raymond and put him back in his own time frame, she reminds herself. Then what the hell are you doing in Berlin, when Raymond has no German ancestry? Does he?

•

On the road to a con. Raymond was driving. "I was nineteen before I found out my stepfather wasn't my birth father. Nineteen! And trying to tell my mother that I was going to drop out of school and marry Andrea, and what does she say but 'I wish your father'd done the same for me!' Now, how was I supposed to take that?

"So naturally I asked her what she meant, and then she told me that the man I always thought of as my daddy had adopted me after he'd married her. That the skunk who impregnated her skipped town before I was born. And here I was, looking for—I don't know, not sympathy, not from *my* mother; that woman's never had a lick of sympathy for anyone but herself—but something. Some kind of pat on the shoulder and 'Well, son, I'm proud of you for doing the right thing by her' or even 'Well, son, you do what you have to do.' Instead, she somehow turned the damn situation around to where it was about *her*, not about me and my life at all. . . ."

Karen had been there the night, years later, when Raymond's mother finally told him his birth father's name and how he'd skipped town before his son was born, adding that she didn't know or care what had happened to him since, or even if he was dead or alive.

"James Elliott Stuyvesant . . ." Raymond had said the name over and over as he drove away from his mother's place. "Like Peter Stuyvesant? What the hell does that mean?"

"That you're not a goddamn WASP after all," Karen suggested. It was a bone of contention between them; she always made it sound like one word. "Goddamnwasp," she'd say, just to get a rise out of him, "purveyors of every evil in America from slavery to Watergate." It made him sputter and curse and knit his shaggy brows together, and in the early days she'd loved to watch. Toward the end, too late, she grew gentler in her teasing. "It means you're at least half Dutch."

"James Elliott Stuyvesant. Would you like me better if my name was Raymond Stuyvesant?"

"No."

It wasn't the answer he'd expected. He'd glanced sideways at her in the light of an oncoming semi on the nearly empty road.

"I don't care what your name is or was. I'd just love you."

•

Stop this at once! she scolds herself like an S.oteri. The sounds of the shelling were coming nearer. She had to do whatever it was that Margarethe had to do and then get back to the cellar beneath the bakery. She wasn't even sure where that was.

"You're not doing this right!" she tells Fuchsia. "Where are Margarethe's memories? I'm supposed to know what she knows. What am I doing here?"

Maybe Margarethe's contact has something to do with Raymond, she thinks. Maybe he's an American? Or maybe, she thinks, with a sidelong look at Fuchsia, who still has that smug look on hir lipsticked face, I'm being distracted so that I never get back to the cellar and Anna dies!

*"Bitte, Fraulein,* do you have the time?"

After years of blackout, most Berliners have developed a kind of night vision, punctuated by the lightning flash of artillery against the night sky, but no matter how hard she peers into the shadow of the *flakturm,* Margarethe cannot see him. She realizes with amazement that the guns on the *flakturm* have been silent all night, as if by some prearranged signal. Otherwise, she could not have waited this close, would have been deafened long ago, and most certainly would not have heard the stranger's voice out of the shadows.

"No, I'm sorry!" she answers automatically. "I don't have a watch."

"No matter." She still cannot see him, but knows who he is, almost wonders if he's actually here, or if, being a magician as much as a time traveler, he is projecting his voice from the cellar of the bakery. "I only wanted to point out to you that it isn't safe for you here. Your contact won't be coming tonight. Perhaps tomorrow. You should go home before it's too late."

"*Danke, mein Herr,* I will. You—"

"No names," he interrupts her, and she knows he is gone. She also knows by now that she's done what she was supposed to do here this night—wait for someone who didn't show up, then go home. She even knows where home is. Now all she has to do is—

She hears the familiar drone above the low-lying clouds. Any minute now they'll begin to drop their load of deadly eggs, carpet bombing, street by street. Above her, she hears the metallic groan of the gun emplacements moving on their turrets, getting ready. If she wants to have any hearing left she'd better—

"Let's go!" she tells Fuchsia and, not waiting to see if the little monster's keeping up, she sets off, determinedly, knowing the way home. She's only taken a few steps, picking her way among broken cobbles in the flickering dark, when something else occurs to her.

The identity papers in her pocket. They will list her full name, date and place of birth, current residence. She will have evidence to bring back with her, something to research when she returns to her own time.

She will not be able to read them in the dark of the cellar, and there won't be time later. Now, by the light of the demonic fireworks, deadly auroras sparking all around her, she will take them out and read, and know.

No. Where her surname had been, in the upper-lefthand corner, there is a large black smudge the size of a thumbprint, a scorch mark from some previously survived firestorm. Even the *Margarethe* is in danger of obliteration, the first downstroke of the *M* in its antique Gothic typeface singed about the edges.

Do jellyfish have thumbs?

Something explodes at the end of the street, rocking Karen back on her heels; she clutches the papers to keep from dropping them. A rain of brick dust showers onto her head and shoulders, pinging off the thick lenses of her glasses, stinging her eyes. The shrieks of incoming *(Wheow! Wheow! Wheow!)* drown out the background thunder of the Russian guns *(pum-pum-pum)* until they are the only sound. Then the big guns atop the tower begin:

*DAH-DAH-DAH-DAH-DAH-DAH-DAH-DAH-DAH!* It is all the sound in the world. One could almost believe that Sequanna, deaf to this world and two thousand years dead, could hear it in her grave.

This is getting real. Karen shoves her double's identity into her pocket, grabs a handful of Fuchsia and, staggering, starts to run.

# FIFTEEN

Karen and Fuchsia, who has for the moment reduced hirself to a shapeless pinkish glow that no one but Karen can see, tumble into the cellar, not down the inside stairs from the bakery but through the street entrance, which is where the supplies are delivered, or were, before the war and rationing.

(Margarethe remembers man-sized sacks of white and rye flour, brown and white sugar offloaded from trucks with diesel engines and tossed from the man on the truck to the baker's son at street level to Timothy standing broad-armed in the cellar, great milk cans rolled down a ramp from horse-drawn farm wagons, vats of rich sweet butter, dark blocks of unsweetened baker's chocolate dense as bars of gold, raisins and almonds, currants and walnuts, several flavors of jam, great sealed tins of cinnamon, nutmeg, allspice, poppy seeds and caraway, the precious *kümmel* that was also made into an aperitif, not as sweet as the Italian anisette, but as redolent. Candied cherries and citron for winter fruitcakes, brandies, too. Memories whose ghosts lingered in the dusting of flour on the cellar floor, the distinctness of yeast that had seeped in sweet ferment up through the floorboards as far as Margarethe's flat. If she inhaled deeply enough, she could still smell it.)

*What are you doing?* Fuchsia demands, resuming hir more familiar jellyfishic shape, though no one else seems to notice. It's the first time s/he's spoken since they've gotten here.

"Cinnamon," is all Karen will say, defiant. Let the little monster only imagine what it's like to smell. Can't smell the bad things? Can't smell the good things, either. Too bad!

Fuchsia fidgets as if s/he's about to ask "What's cinnamon?" but stops hirself. S/he has dogged Karen's footsteps all the way here, through unimaginable danger. Unimaginable for hir anyway, because it won't affect Fuchsia, but Karen knows that even with TQ watching you, this ain't the Universal tour, kids. A girl could get killed this way.

They've found the cellar, and the latch on the old wooden doors is undone—gone, really, ripped away from the splintering wood, probably the first night the bombs started falling. Feeling her way down the steps in the pinkish phosphorescence of Fuchsia's glow, Karen wonders if her own personal S.oteri is bound to go with her no matter what, or if s/he could just as easily float off on hir own and create more havoc. Well, worry about that if you lose sight of hir, and not before. For now, you're here and you're safe, as safe as any living thing can be in Berlin, April '45.

"For Chrissake, watch where you're going!" a voice shrills out of the dark as Karen lets the door close behind her, and her foot impacts against something soft on the second from the last step. "There are other people here first!"

"Sorry!" Karen manages as the high-strung blonde inches over a fraction to grudgingly let her pass. Why wasn't she visible in the jellyfishic glow? Too much sensory input or not enough. At least all the dramatis personae are here, Karen thinks, smiling at the little girl, who seems as unaffected by her mother's rages as by anything else going on around her. Why does the mother insist on sitting so close to the outside? Where has she been, this late in the war, that she doesn't realize what Allied ordnance can do? Even a machine gun, strafing through that flimsy door—

As if in answer, Karen hears the nervous chatter of automatic fire in and around the other noises. It's a wonder anyone can hear. She is groping her way along the wall to where, this time around, she knows the interior stairs are, and Johann and Timothy will be waiting for her, bracing herself to hit her head against the wall again, when—

"Excuse me, Fraulein," a male voice says, "but you should not let the child play so near the entrance. Two nights ago, a child died in the next street from the same cause—"

"Listen, fat man, if I want your opinion, I'll ask for it. Otherwise, go fuck yourself, okay?"

No, Karen thinks: No, no, no! In the first place, the bomb hasn't fallen in the next street to knock me back against the wall, and in the second place, that's Timothy she's cursing at, not Johann.

She hears Fuchsia snickering.

"You little transparent bitch!" Karen can't help herself. Let them think she's loony; who isn't, this late in the war? "You're changing things around again. Stop it!"

*How do you know this isn't the way it's supposed to be?*

"I don't—!" Karen begins, then stops herself. They *are* staring. More to the point, not all of them are there.

She feels her way across to where Timothy sits. She can hear him wheezing before she is able to make out the shape of him in the dark.

"Ah, Margarethe, my dear! You've made it back safely. I can't tell you how you had me worried. I thought—"

"Where's Johann?" she interrupts him rudely.

"Johann?" Timothy repeats, looking at her strangely. It's almost as if he doesn't recognize the name.

"You . . . um . . . said he might be here tonight," Karen temporizes. Nothing is going according to the script. She is holding Fuchsia firmly by the top of hir little domed head now and can feel hir giggling. She gives hir a little shake; anyone looking at her, not seeing Fuchsia, would think she had some sort of palsy. No one notices. More people than not have developed tics and psychogenic nervous disorders during these nightmare years, tics which will never go away. Better not to notice them. Timothy doesn't notice either. He is clearly wracking his brain for something else.

"Did I say that? Forgive me. Sometimes my head aches so badly . . . but if you say I said it—Ah, but here he is now."

With a remarkable sureness of step, as if he's made this journey a thousand times before in light and dark, the older man feels his way down the interior steps.

"Good evening, all." He nods to them formally. If there is irony in his eyes, it is not in his voice. And though he is still not following the script, his presence steels Karen for what is to come.

Through all of this, whenever there is a flash of light from outside to illuminate the scene, she has kept the little girl in the corner of her eye. The solemn eyes, dark as molasses and as liquid, peer up at her out of a too-old, almost wizened face. Looking at her now, she can see the adult Anna, nascent and still forming. What if she snatched her now, before the shell hit, and bolted into the night? No way of knowing how it would change things, any more than knowing if Sequanna and her kin would have been safer from the Romans on the road, or if Richard the Lionheart listened to his mother.

Instead, she waits, letting the scenario play out until the time comes. She must do only what Margarethe would do and, unlike Grainne and Grethe, she has had precious little time to learn Margarethe. She can guess that she is brave, else why would she wait to meet a stranger in the shadow of the *flakturm,* inviting several kinds of death? She is practical, too, carrying her life in her pockets, wearing a sweater and sensible shoes, prepared for all contingencies. Is this enough to go on?

Johann is watching her. At least this time around maybe she'll have time to ask him: Who are you? What are you? Are you sent to monitor the situation, or do you belong here? And what of me? Am I entirely a pawn?

No time. She feels the incoming shell as an atavistic prickle at the back of her neck, seconds before it strikes. Here we go again. . . .

•

"Margarethe? For God's sake, answer! Don't be dead, dear, please don't; I've lost too many already! Johann, for the love of God, help me get this shit off her!"

The scene replays; she feels them pulling her out of the debris. She is holding the squalling child tight against her own body, feeling her draw in each sobbing breath as if it were her own. She could not have done it differently.

She surrenders the child to Timothy, surrenders herself to the touch of Johann's hands, thinking *So there!* This is what Margarethe would do. I know!

"Thank you!" she says to Johann. Over his shoulder, Fuchsia is twinkling malevolently, screwing up her whole face the way Karen's mother does when she's angry, which is most of the time.

No time. All in a whirl and without preamble, they are moving backward again.

•

"You've overshot it, that's all." Karen sneezes from the dust. "We *really* don't belong here."

*Um, yes, I know,* Fuchsia admits vaguely.

"Well, what are you waiting for? It's only a discrepancy of half a century or so. Fine-tune the thing and toss us forward a little. Just give me a minute to settle my gut and—"

*Um, I don't think I can.*

"What?!"

Among the myriad things Karen had meant to ask and hadn't was whether they would return through time in reverse of the way they'd come, from Berlin to Avaricum to Chinon, or if they would travel in reverse chronology, Berlin to Chinon to Avaricum or, since all of this was on a whim and none of it made any sense anyway, why not alphabetically, *A* to *B* to *C,* except they'd begun with *B,* so there was no way of telling—

Guess again. She and her sidekick had arrived in None of the Above. They were lurking in a hayloft in a city somewhere in southern France, on the eve of a coronation.

"It's too soon!" Karen hisses at Fuchsia, as yet another throng of celebrating townspeople, decked out in their best (which is to say they've actually bathed and changed their clothes), saunters drunkenly past, strewing rose petals in their wake beneath the streaming multicolored banners and the fleur-de-lys on field of azure which was the standard of Louis of France. Young Louis was having himself crowned a second time on the glorious occasion of the coronation of his bride of three years, the eighteen-year-old Eleanor; the boy did love his ceremonies. "We're supposed to be in Chinon in 1190. You've overshot and put us somewhere else fifty years earlier. I can't be here, now, because Grethe won't be born for another two years. You've got to get us out of here!"

She'd arrived in the hayloft in her usual state, head whirling, stomach churning, back in Grethe's skin and clothes and station, right down to the beer-damp apron. She'd figured out what time it was by the events transpiring below them. (Thank you, Karen Jenner!) Now if only she could remember the name of the city where Eleanor was crowned. . . .

There was a cathedral, large enough to accommodate the several thousand here from the four corners of Christendom to attend the coronation. The big bronze bells bing-bonged without respite, so close they'd have rattled the fillings in Karen's teeth, if she still had fillings. But cathedrals were the reasons most hamlets became cities, common as dirt, without even a Hard Rock T-shirt to tell you what city you were in. She'd research all that later, after they got back, if they ever got back, but for now—

"Okay," she says to Fuchsia gently, more patiently than perhaps she should under the circumstances. "Try to remember exactly what you did and maybe between us we can figure out how to fix it. Maybe that's part of the game."

Thinking: It is just a game. This is no longer about me or Fuchsia or anything but the Third Thing. I think.

*I just thought about Eleanor, and we ended up here. I'm sorry!* This is a side of Fuchsia she hasn't seen before, and Karen's not at all sure she likes it. The critter's positively diffident, unsure, almost vulnerable. It's unsettling. *Maybe you could pass yourself off as Grethe's mother?*

"Not exactly!" Karen hisses in hir nonexistent ear, disturbing the chickens roosting in the rafters above them. So far every scenario but Berlin has involved chickens. This is getting tiresome. "Maybe if you thought about someone else. Someone like . . . like Kit, for instance, who won't be born for decades yet. Focus on her, and we'll get back to Chinon."

*I don't think it works that way. . . .*

"You've got to do something!"

"I can't!"

It's not a voice in her mind but a little squeaky sound coming from somewhere in the gelatinous center of something so transparent you can almost see it thinking. This is what a voice would sound like if you didn't have a mouth.

*All we can do is wait until the Third Thing rescues us.*

"I see." Karen says, suddenly all solicitous. She wants to pat hir little head, give hir a hug, something. "You're not very good at this, are you?"

Very softly, Fuchsia answers: *No!*

"And if you had your druthers, you'd put everything back the way it was so we could both go home." Fuchsia doesn't answer. "But it will rescue us? This Third Thing? You're sure about that?"

*I think so.*

"Swell!"

Just then there are footsteps on the ladder leading up to the hayloft, and neither time nor place to hide. Karen is thinking of plausible explanations when a head appears followed by a body. A wiry lad of ten or so, his head too big for his body and his clothes too small, swinging an empty basket in one hand, literally walks through Fuchsia, muttering to himself.

" 'Fetch the eggs, Reynard!' says she. Everyone else in Bourges is gathered outside the gates to see the queen ride up, but not me! 'Maman,' says I, 'they aren't laying, what with all the excitement. The bells ringing all day has 'em blocked up.' But does she listen?"

Karen and Fuchsia, huddled like conspirators, watch him scuff through the straw with his bare feet, occasionally uncovering a small brown ovule to scoop into the basket.

"Can he see us?" Karen wonders in a whisper.

*I don't think so!* Fuchsia answers in a kind of wonder.

" 'Fetch the eggs, Reynard,' says she." The boy rolled another small treasure into the basket none too gently; his auditors could hear it crack. " 'Then run 'em over to the chandler's like always, and his woman'll give you this week's candles in swap.' 'Maman,' says I, 'the chandler's closed this day. So's the whole town. Bolted shut, except for us, gone to see the king and queen.' But does she listen? No . . ."

He squeezed the next egg too hard, and it splattered in his hand. He cursed and flung the mess blindly. Where some of it ran down his arm, the rest should have struck Karen square in the face. Instead, it kept going over the edge of the hayloft, lost in the barn below.

"The devil with it!" the boy finished sourly, carrying the half-filled basket toward the ladder. "I never get to have any fun!"

In his wake, Karen and Fuchsia cling to each other in a kind of giddy relief.

•

"We're invisible!" Karen is almost dancing, then she stops. "And we're in Bourges."

*How do you know that?*

"Because the boy, Reynard, just said so. And I don't know why that name sticks in my head, but it does. But we're safe from discovery as long as no one can see or hear us."

*The chickens did. When you were yelling at me just now—*

"I wasn't yelling!" Karen says, too loudly. There is a flurry of wings from the rafters. A feather or two floats down; Karen sneezes. The sneeze evokes a further response. All right, so the chickens can hear them, but—

Karen moves closer to the nearest one, a fat brown hen who's decided to roost on a low beam instead of above their heads with the others. She stands less than six feet from the creature and stares her in the eye.

No response. Karen waves her hands. Still nothing. The hen has her head stuck down into her neck and seems to be dozing. Karen moves closer, narrowing the gap by half. A city kid, she isn't about to get any closer to something with a beak. Still no reaction from the chicken. Again Karen waves her hands. The hen comes out of her reverie and stretches her neck as if to pay closer attention.

Karen waves her hands again. The hen is giving her that sideways look that any animal with eyes on the sides of its head will do when it's studying something.

*What are you doing?* Fuchsia asks, intrigued.

"Shut up a minute!" Karen says crossly, and the hen startles. Muttering disapproval, she hops off the beam and stalks away with as much dignity as a hen can muster.

"Well, that settles that!" Karen announces, sitting back down in the straw beside Fuchsia. "Humans can't see us and probably can't hear us, and if they do, they'll only think we're ghosts. Animals can only hear us, but that's okay. It's consistent with the folklore in these parts, although most people believe animals can only hear the spirits and speak to them at certain times of the year. In any event, it means we're safe from discovery until we're rescued. *If* we're rescued."

•

They were also, being "spirits," neither hungry, nor thirsty, nor tired. It was possible to sit in the hayloft all that day and into the night without needing to eat or drink or nap or take a leak or even, Karen noted, take her beta-blocker.

What they did have time to do was talk.

"Tell me honestly," Karen begins, knowing an S.oteri can't do otherwise, "Raymond's time line has nothing to do with Berlin, does it?"

*No.*

"But Anna's does, obviously. But was it necessary for me to be the one to rescue her, or would Margarethe have done as much without me? Then again, would Anna have taken Raymond's place if I hadn't rescued her? I mean . . ."

Fuchsia doesn't answer. It's like playing with a pendulum. One got yes/no answers, or silence.

"All right," Karen sighs. "One down, two to go. Maybe. Or maybe we don't have to go back through all three time lines. Maybe the answer's at Chinon. Any hints?"

*No.*

" 'No, the answer's not at Chinon' or 'No, no hints'?"

*No.*

She had to keep talking. If she stopped she'd panic, wondering where the rest of her was, stuck between dimensions since she was only partly here, wondering if TQ would rescue them, wondering if they dared leave the hayloft. It might be fun to pop in on the coronation or just take a stroll around town, but what if TQ came back in the meantime and found them gone? Nothing to do but wait. And talk. Keep talking.

•

". . . cinnamon," Karen is trying to explain. "What must it be like not to be able to taste or smell?"

*What must it be like not to taste radiation and know which is dangerous and which not?* Fuchsia counters, arranging hir tentacles around hir in a pattern only s/he understands. *Or not hear all the minds in the Mind and have to speak with words?*

"Point taken. We each have different definitions of what we call senses. I keep forgetting we're both 'blind' in certain ways. And speaking of senses—you don't have a mouth anymore."

Fuchsia is looking at her oddly. In the absence of eyes, Karen's learned to tell what an S.oteri is thinking by the angle of their little domed heads.

*I never had a mouth.*

"But you wore lipstick, back there. In my time."

Fuchsia shakes hir head. *Uh-uh.*

Karen realizes something else. "You don't *sound* like my mother anymore, either. I must have been projecting—something."

Very softly, Fuchsia says: *No.*

"Come again?"

*I was the one projecting. I thought if I screamed at you the way your mother did when you were little it might make you stop writing.*

Karen tries not to think of diaries read and novels ignored. "Why would you think that? It's never stopped me before."

*She isn't very nice,* Fuchsia observes. *Why did you write all that ugly backstory for her?*

Now we're getting somewhere! Karen thinks.

"I didn't. That's the way she really is."

*What do you mean by "really"? You saw how I tweaked the reality back there in Berlin. You do the same thing when you write.*

"I do not! I don't have that kind of power, and even if I did, I wouldn't use it. That's the whole crux of the problem. It's the reason we're stuck here, thanks to you!"

For a moment all Karen can hear is the refrain: "Another 'real' book . . . another 'real' book . . ." until she realizes this is genuine inquiry.

"You know, this is the first time you and I have actually *spoken,* without that . . . that other, phony voice getting in the way." She sighs, settles herself more comfortably in the straw. "I really appreciate that."

The light outside is fading into a late summer evening; only by Fuchsia's warm pink phosphorescence can she see hir. "Let me see if I can explain it with a little story. . . ."

•

"Once upon a time, there was a little girl. She was about four years old, and she had a terrible earache. She was running a high fever, and she was in a lot of pain. Her mother and her grandmother didn't know what to do, so her father brought her to the hospital. There the doctors did surgery to remove the infected mastoid cells and make her better, but for as long as she lived, she would be able to reach behind her left ear and feel a hollow place where the mastoid bone had been. And for as long as she lived she would never trust anyone to tell her the truth, and this is why."

Karen finds Fuchsia snuggling up beside her like a small child listening to a fairy tale. The tilt of hir little domed head says s/he is paying rapt attention.

"You see, the little girl's mother had very little education. She was frightened of doctors and believed that people only went to the hospital to die. So as she watched her little girl writhing in pain, all she could do was wring her hands and pray.

"Now, the little girl also had a wicked grandmother, who wished her nothing but harm. The grandmother was jealous of the little girl, who was young and pretty. The grandmother was old and toothless and ugly; she had a long pointy nose, and her hair was pulled back into a tight little bun. On that fateful night, she stood over the little girl's bed saying: 'She's going to die, she's going to die! Mother of God, she's going to die!' The little girl imagined she was smiling as she said it.

"There was only one person who could save the little girl, and that was her father. He picked her up and carried her out of the house to where a taxicab was waiting and took the little girl to the hospital. And all the way in the taxicab, in the dark, he stroked the little girl's hair and told her 'Don't worry, honey. It's going to be all right. The doctors will make you well, and it won't hurt any more.'

"So the doctors took the little girl from her father's arms and brought her into surgery and cast a magic spell on her so she would sleep. And when she awoke and the spell wore off, her head was wrapped in bandages, and she could still feel a terrible pain. And when she finally went home, she could see that some of her hair had been shaved off, and that she had a hollow behind her left ear. And from that day on she knew that all grown-ups lied.

"Because her grandmother had said she would die, and yet she was still alive. And her father had said it wouldn't hurt any more, but it did. So from that day forward, even though the pain eventually went away and she felt much better and her hair grew long enough to hide the hollow behind her ear, the little girl never trusted anyone. And long after, when she was grown to adulthood and had children of her own, she still never believed what anyone told her but always had to sneak around behind people's backs trying to learn what she called 'The Truth.' She spied on her children, accused them of lying to her, drove her relatives and friends away. Soon, only her husband stood by her, because by then he had no friends either, and she was all he had. And deep inside she was still a little girl who knew that all adults lied."

*That's a very sad story,* Fuchsia says after a long silence.

"Yes, it is, isn't it?" Karen says thoughtfully.

*But very well written,* Fuchsia suggests, suddenly a critic. *A good piece of fiction.*

Karen smiles. This was exactly the response she was hoping for. She springs her trap. "Except it's the truth. The little girl is my mother."

Fuchsia is taken aback. It's all in the tilt of hir head.

*But you just made that up!* s/he protests.

"The event itself? No, it actually happened. You can find it in your memory banks." She waits while Fuchsia does so, though there's no acknowledgment that she has. "As for the little girl's emotions and the conclusions she reached, okay, I had to extrapolate those. But if you look at her behaviors seventy years later, she's still that frightened, suspicious little girl."

Fuchsia works on this for what seems a very long time.

*I don't get it.*

"Neither do I," Karen sighs, "and I've been working on it for forty-eight years, but—"

*No, I mean, I don't get it.*

It's very hard for Karen not to hear the refrain ". . . another 'real' book . . . another 'real' book . . ." still, hard not to grab Fuchsia by the throat *in loco parentis*. But if Fuchsia's puzzlement is sincere, she has to respond to it.

"Granted, that may not have been the best example. We'll come back to that story another time. Let me tell you a different story.

"My mother has an imaginary daughter. Her name is Karen, just like mine. She was born at the exact moment I was and looks a lot like me, and the events of the first fourteen years of her life are identical to mine. Where we differ is that this Karen never met Father Russell and never got counseling in high school. Instead, she seems to have had some sort of breakdown right after she graduated, or maybe just before.

"She never went to college because her grades were so poor, and her father said he didn't see the point of sending a girl to college anyway, since girls got married and their husbands could support them. Karen wanted to point out that this contradicted what her mother had always said, which was that no man would ever want her, but she bit her tongue because she knew that if she contradicted either of her parents things would not go well for her.

"So she spent a few years after high school taking low-paying clerical jobs. But her parents told her that she wasn't happy and said that if she wanted to just stay home and keep her mother company, she could stop working, for now. So that's what she did. And whenever she thought about going back, she realized she didn't have the skills or the experience. And whenever she spoke about going back, her mother would suddenly get sick and Karen would have to look after her. So after a while the idea of working seemed frivolous and she abandoned it. . . ."

Karen's fairy-tale voice has gone elegiac. She can almost feel Fuchsia shiver.

"Karen's friends were the daughters of her mother's friends, because she knew her mother had never approved of the friends she chose on her own. And after a while even those friends got married and had babies and lost touch with Karen. It was just too unsettling for them to have this shy, awkward, unattached woman at the dinner table.

"After a while she no longer went out of the house at all except to take her mother to the doctor or the supermarket, so she never met anyone, and after a while the idea of marriage and children seemed unfathomable. After all, her mother had long ago told her these things weren't possible for her. Besides, as her mother pointed out almost every day, what would happen to her parents if Karen didn't take care of them?"

Fuchsia is shrinking away from her, inching off into a corner of the hayloft, hir brightness fading; s/he seems to be hugging hirself.

"Now, maybe Karen began with the same urge to write that I have, but she probably decided a long time ago that whatever she wrote wouldn't be interesting to anyone, so she either kept her writing hidden away where her mother wouldn't find it, or never bothered to begin.

"She's almost fifty years old now. She wears the same kind of clothes her mother wears. Her hair is cropped short because her mother tells her it looks 'most becoming' that way. She still lives with her parents, in the spare room where her mother keeps the sewing machine and the empty aquarium, which is empty because all the fish died. All the houseplants in her mother's house die, too, no matter how often they're watered, and the cat's too frightened to come out from under the bed. Karen looks after both of her parents, who are getting kind of elderly now. She cooks for them and cleans for them and drives them to church and takes her mother shopping, and—"

*Stop!* Fuchsia has clamped two of hir largest tentacles over where hir ears should be. *I can't listen to any more. It's just too awful!*

Karen smiles wryly. "It happens all the time. Among certain ethnic groups it's almost a tradition to choose one girlchild out of the whole flock, usually the plain one or the 'slow' one, and groom her for a life of servitude. In return, the unmarried daughter gets to keep the house after her parents are gone. And in most instances, there is at least a little love."

*There's no love in this story!* Fuchsia announces, an expert on this now, too. *It's horrible. And anyway, you're not in the spare room, you're here. You* definitely *made this one up.*

"No, I didn't, but my mother did. That's the daughter who lives in the soap opera of her mind. *Now* do you see the difference between reality and fiction?"

Karen can see that Fuchsia's trying very hard, but still s/he shakes hir head. *I'm not sure.*

"All right," Karen says with infinite patience. They were making progress. And whatever else might be said for spending the rest of her life halfway between nonexistence and a hayloft, it was better than working the day job. "Then let me tell you a third story. . . ."

She doesn't get the chance.

# SIXTEEN

As they spin out, Karen swears she hears Fuchsia mutter: *I'm glad I don't have a mother. If I were writing this, I'd write a better one!*

Making Karen wonder: Does s/he get it yet or doesn't s/he?

Well, stop and think about it, she tells herself as she shakes the mud off the hem of her skirt. They have "arrived" in the sow's enclosure behind the house Grethe shares with Kit, and the sow immediately trots over to nuzzle her. Karen scratches the sow behind the ears; the beast leans against her contentedly, nearly knocking her off her feet and rubbing mud from her hairy hide all over Grethe's apron. Karen starts to shove the sow away until she realizes: The sow can see and feel her. She is substantial, wholly here, not stuck between dimensions as she was in the hayloft in Bourges. Okay, part of the problem is solved, then; now to the rest of it. Consider:

Unless we view the Common Mind as the mother of all S.oteri, the concept of progenitors doesn't really register. For an S.oteri, there always has been All There Are, not some who came before and subsequently produced those who came after. And, if you stop to think about it, the whole concept of oogenetic reproduction is pretty damn weird.

The way S.oteri reproduce, if it can be called reproduction, is a kind of parthenogenesis, like amoebas, two splitting into one. No, check that, Karen thinks. It's more like having a big lump of clay or bread dough (is it the smell from Kit's bakery, wafting above even the stink of the sow's enclosure, which suggests the simile?) and breaking off pieces, each of which has the same characteristics as the main lump, only not.

Well, anyway, Karen thinks, as meanwhile she takes stock of the situation (the weather is cool, either early spring or late fall, both of which were places she visited thanks to Fuchsia last time; will she climb to the *solar* to find the queen speaking of figs, or gone?), as if S.oteric reproduction wasn't bizarre enough, consider the human:

Two people participate in an act so furtive their children grow up thinking Nah, they couldn't have!, the outcome of which, at least for postwar Catholics, was so overt that baby showers were thrown and christenings performed, and the next twenty years or so were spent on diapers and school clothes and trips to the dentist until the product of this strange and furtive act was old enough to initiate the process all over again.

Looked at that way, it was enough to make sticking to a wall in a cave and eating fungus look positively glamorous. What boring little novels we humans make, after all. And, therefore, as far as Fuchsia is concerned, mothers are a fictional construct, a device to move the story along. And if s/he were writing this, s/he'd write a better one.

"You and me both, kid," Karen remarks, nudging the sow out of the way at last and letting herself out through the wicket gate. Fuchsia follows. Karen's still wondering about that. "Do you have to follow me, or are you doing it because you want to?"

*Yes.*

"You know, I'm getting *really* tired of that. I thought we'd reached an understanding back in Bourges. If you're only going to give me one-word answers, I may miss something important. And it's my impression TQ expects you to get this straightened out before it will let you go home. It *was* TQ that just yanked us into the proper time line just now, wasn't it?"

*Yes.*

"I thought it had a different feel to it. I don't feel like throwing up this time. Okay, now that we've at least gotten that much straightened out—"

"Talking to y'self, Grethe, or to the sow?"

Kit had come around the side of the house quietly for once, or else Karen was so far into her conversation with her suddenly invisible fishy friend that she hadn't heard her. She starts guiltily. This wasn't the streets of New York, where a person could get away with these things. In these parts, this much woolgathering could get a person accused of madness or witchcraft or both.

" 'Tis—'twas a prayer," she says, thinking quickly. "I was missing my Jacob and thought I'd have a word with him."

"Sounded like you was scolding him," Kit observes. Karen, meanwhile, notes that the girl looks only a little thickened about the waist. Good. TQ has dumped them back where it all began, well ahead of the Third Crusade.

*Good?* You idiot, you're back in the same quandary you were in before! Do you tell Eleanor about Acre this time or don't you?

Mindful of Berlin and saving Anna, Karen realizes the answer is no easier this time than it was the last. What if she tells Eleanor the dream of the fig merely means Richard shouldn't eat strange fruit in an unfamiliar climate unless he wants the runs? Since he's going to get dysentery in Acre no matter what, it will only confirm yon Grethe's reputation as a prophetess. Unless, of course, Eleanor's dissatisfied with the answer, and Grethe suffers for it. Even that could change the time line long after Karen's gone. Why can't temporal anomalies be as simple in real life as they are on TV?

"I've just come from the kitchens," Kit is saying, giving her no time to think. The empty bread basket swings idly in the girl's hand. "Gervase is in a tear again. Says he needs two measures of hippocras for a sauce, and there isn't any more. Says someone's been sneaking it, and he'll have the truth or woe to us all. Three guesses, says I . . . or at least I wanted to. If there's anyone's sipping at the hippocras wine, it'll be your paramour Gilbert, only I can't say that to Gervase, can I? Firstly, I'm not supposed to know the two are pouffin' each other; second, I'm not supposed to accuse his lover of being a drunk. Which he is, but never mind—"

"Kit, God's bones, give it a rest!" Grethe scolds her with Karen's full approval; the girl does go on. "It's none of it a disaster. Gervase knows I've always got more fermenting. All he's got to do is send someone for it. I'll fetch some this instant before he starts throwing things."

A shriek and the sound of smashing crockery tells her she's too late.

"Well, at least mayhap we'll get a new chamberpot out of it!" she calls over her shoulder to set Kit giggling as she gathers up her skirts and hurries to the brewery.

Hippocras was wine mulled with sweet herbs and honey, often used in sauces, but also potable on its own. A little cloying for most tastes, but then it was said that Gilbert would put anything in his mouth.

Suppressing a laugh, Grethe changes her apron and fetches a heavy copper-alloy jug decorated with vines and standing on three animal feet, draws some off, and wrapping her apron around it for purchase, lugs it toward the castle kitchens thinking: Last time it was the new beer; this time it's a jug of hippocras. Is Fuchsia writing this script or is TQ? Does it matter? What in God's name am I going to tell the queen? And meanwhile, where is Fuchsia?

Karen swears s/he was just behind her when she arrived in the kitchens—a feeling like goosebumps more than a visual, since s/he went invisible as soon as Kit came round the corner. Karen's getting to the point where she can sense whether an S.oteri is in the vicinity or not.

She whiles away her time pretending to admire the custard three of Gervase's apprentices are constructing in spite of the mayhem; Gervase is in the back by the ovens hurling pots now, and no one wants to get close enough to tell him Grethe's here with the hippocras. Well, actually she *is* admiring it; how could she not? The work is labor-intensive and rather creative. One boy chops dates while another whips eggs while a third presses out the pastry "coffin" to contain the entire mixture of ground meat, herbs, dates, ginger, vinegar; the whole thing held together with the eggs before it was enclosed in a crisscrossed overcrust and baked in a slow oven. Karen's tastebuds remember Grethe's memories even as she scans the corners and in under things for the telltale purplish twinkle and not seeing it. Damn!

"Thank God!" Gervase announces, sailing in and relieving her of the jug. He pointedly avoids touching her, unlike Gilbert who apparently needs to touch everyone. At least she's spared that part of it this time around. "No one else seems to appreciate that when we run out of things, it's *my* head on the block and no one else's. The Countess Marie was looking for you."

"I'm not surprised—" Karen starts to say, affording herself one last peek under a long trestle table where the puddings are left to cool even as the rustle of brocade and the dropping of curtsies announces the countess's arrival.

"My mother, the queen, wishes to speak with you."

"At once, milady."

*Déjà vu* all over again. Sort of. This part of the scenario runs pretty much to format as Grethe follows the queen's daughter down the corridors as before. Only this time as Grethe walks, Karen is thinking:

Forget about Fuchsia. You can't control hir anyway. Either TQ's keeping hir on a leash, or it isn't.

Last time you fretted yourself into a frenzy wondering if one of your ancestors was a Crusader. You had no reason to connect any of this with Raymond then at all. Well, what if his ancestors were as likely to have been among the Crusaders as your own? The point is, you can't change the big picture, so don't even try. Just go with the flow and hope that TQ's agenda includes sending you back with Fuchsia to leave the major portions of history intact while you search out one loose thread and weave it back into the whole, and while you're doing that, consider this: Maybe you're on trial as much as Fuchsia.

•

*Put me down, put me down!* Fuchsia shrills in a tangle of tendrils. *I didn't* do *anything! Lemme go!*

Gentle Reader, we're going to have to ask you to imagine this part because, as humans, you're not allowed to see. There will be no genuine descriptions of TQ in this narrative, so you can imagine anything you want, and you'll probably be just as right as you are wrong. Imagine, for the sake of argument, something attenuated and cool-colored, with very long arms and an indeterminate number of digits, holding Fuchsia by the scruff of hir neck and shaking hir.

Or just watching hir struggle, knotting and gnarling hir tentacles, creating hir own momentum, spinning round about hir own axis. Whatever. All you need to know is that Fuchsia's in trouble again.

*I said: Lemme go! There's no telling what Karen will do if I'm not there to keep an eye on her. Lemme go!*

{As if!} TQ replies. {You don't have eyes,} it points out. {And just now there's some question as to whether you have a brain.}

Fuchsia finds hirself dropped in a heap on a flat surface. Floor, ground, tabletop? Indoors, outdoors, underground, in a windowless room, a lab, a ship, a kitchen? As s/he refuses to give Karen answers, so s/he gets none now. S/he untangles hir tentacles and tries to look dignified, trips over one unaccounted-for tendril, rolls into a ball like a sow bug, unravels and starts again. TQ is not impressed.

*I didn't* do *anything!*

{Why did you set her down fifty years earlier? Why Bourges?}

*Because Bourges is Avaricum.*

Can TQ look surprised? Remember, we can't answer that; you're not supposed to know. It would bring us into the heavy topics like not only what TQ looks like, if it/they look(s) like (because there's always the possibility of invisibility, ephemerality, interdimensionality, and whether they/it have faces and/or if we'd recognize them as such). And what might look like surprise on a human face could just as easily mean "I want to have your baby" or "Die, fascist pig!" on someone else's.

And that's before we even get into the parameters of whether TQ is omniscient and is just toying with Fuchsia because it already know that the medieval city of Bourges was built on the ruins of Avaricum, or if it really didn't know and had to ask. And it might all just be smoke screen on Fuchsia's part, a lucky guess, or something about the specific gravity of the place.

Yes, we know, Gentle Reader, there was some mention of that in a previous book, specifically regarding Tessa McGill, the Jesus of the Jellyfish, and her belief that certain places on Earth had different gravitational fields. Turns out that, flaky as she was, she was right about that much.

Apparently (and we're reporting this from a secondary source, so it's only as accurate as the original research), not only does the Earth's radius affect the pull of gravity (as, for example, gravity is denser at the poles than it is at the Equator, but you knew that), but mountains are different from valleys (and you thought it was just oxygen depletion that keeps killing those Yuppie fools on Everest), and the density of the rock beneath a site can have an effect as well.

No, we're not making this up. An eighteenth-century French scientist named Pierre Bouguer actually drew up a series of anomaly maps for places in Europe, and his techniques have since been applied to sites in the Americas as well. The gravitational values we're about to give you are measured in milligals (another word to add to your lexicon), meaning one one-thousandth of a gal, which is a unit of acceleration equivalent to one centimeter per second per second. (And you thought a gal was just someone you tried to pick up at a Saturday night line dance.)

Confused? You should be. Suppose we just reduce it to plus and minus numbers and tell you that, say, the city of Boston is a 0 (on the Bouguer map, for God's sake! Damn Red Sox fans, so sensitive about everything), New York is a +30, Washington D.C. a +40, meaning the gravity is pulling that much harder in both places, which may explain why it takes so long to get anything done in either town. Los Angeles, on the other hand, clocks in at −70 (Cool!), although we don't want to even guess what that might mean.

Now, if you want to get into extremes, there's the Mauna Loa volcano in Hawaii at +300 and Breckinridge, Colorado at −300. Since both are high altitudes, we can't presume to speculate about why they're so different. And there are some extremes of density in very localized areas that might be enough to drive some local citizens bonkers.

There is a man in Oregon who considers himself a kind of environmental guerrilla. Not an overt screwball, he's a serious professional man with a good income, a stable marriage, two cars in the garage, and a garbage disposal in the kitchen. He lives in Eugene, a pleasant white-bread college town where local issues are debated at town meetings and genuine poverty is a myth, and rents a vacation house on the coast near a little town called Yachats.

The shortest way to Yachats is to drive straight west from Eugene until you get to Florence on the coast, then hang a right along the coast highway until you get to Yachats. There are any number of state parks along the way where you can stop and enjoy the view. Our professional man does this several times a year. But he doesn't just stop and look at the view. He gets down in the sand and starts pulling up the sea grass.

It is, he will explain to you if you ask, not native to the state of Oregon but was imported from California by the then-governor of Oregon at the turn of the century to stop the erosion of the dunes which threatened to wash away the entire coastline. In the intervening decades, the soft gray-green fronds have proliferated luxuriantly, sending prolific runners out to fix the sand in place, creating tide pools where countless aquatic species flourish, turning barren sand into a sea creatures' playground.

"But it's not *native*!" our friend will shout, all but stamping his feet in his urgency to make us understand. Thus he spends an hour at a time pulling the grass out by the roots until his hands bleed, knowing that at his present rate, assuming the grass did not grow back (it always does), it would take him a millennium to return a single state park to its "native" condition.

A question: Does the sea grass know it is not native to Oregon? Does it stop at the California border and refuse to cross?

A point to ponder: The man himself is not native to Oregon. He comes from one of those cities back East where the gravity is denser than it is in Eugene (which is a −30 on the Bouguer scale). His ancestry lies in several places in Europe. Which tempts us to suggest that *he* should be pulled up by the roots and sent back where he came from, and also brings us back to our theory:

Eugene is a −30. Yachats, where the man and his wife will spend the weekend after he has ripped up sufficient sea grass to soothe his conscience, rates a +50 on the Bouguer scale. Does traveling in and out of the two anomalies have an unforeseen effect on this man's brain which causes him to think that his actions make some sort of environmental sense? Perhaps someone should do a study of other Oregonians who travel the same road with any frequency. Shake a tree anywhere in Oregon and you'll find a sect, be it survivalist or New Age, tumbled out of the branches. Schoolchildren open fire on their peers in lunchrooms. A lot of science-fiction writers live in Oregon. Far be it from us to suggest that any of this is interrelated.

All we're saying is: keep that man away from Mauna Loa and Breckinridge, Colorado.

And beware of jellyfish who cannot tell a lie, but who can obfuscate the hell out of a truth.

•

{You're suggesting that you tossed Karen into both Bourges and Avaricum because they're actually the same place.}

*You could say that,* Fuchsia offers, amazed at what s/he's apparently accomplished quite by accident. Imagine what s/he could do if s/he were really trying?

{Then why Berlin?}

Oops. Caught. Fuchsia shrugs. *It's in Europe.*

Which, considering what the average human knows about geography, is as good an answer as any. What does geography mean to something that lives in a cave?

If TQ could sigh, it would. {The place is not as important as the time. You were trying to keep her away from Eleanor. Why?}

*That's on your say-so. I never said that.*

TQ has unlimited patience. {Why?} it persists.

*Because you're going to take the power away from me anyway, so I wanted to hold onto it as long as I could!* Fuchsia all but shouts.

{Is that what you think?} TQ can play this game, too.

*Well, um, aren't you?*

{When?}

The question throws Fuchsia for a moment.

*Um, well, I just assumed . . . as soon as Karen and I got the time lines straightened out.*

{Then is it possible you're finally beginning to grasp the concept of Time?}

*Heh-heh. Hmm. Well, if you put it* that *way . . .*

•

Queen Eleanor sat before the open Gothic windows of the *solar* contemplating the turmoil in the bailey below over against the serenity of the hills beyond, her hands folded in her lap, her expression far more serene than her thoughts.

"I had a dream last night, Mistress Grethe. Perhaps you can tell me what it means."

"Certes I shall try, Lady."

"I dreamt of Richard."

"Did you, Lady?"

"He was in the Holy Land," Eleanor began. "It could be no other place for, God's breath, I know it well. . . ."

Karen tries to pay attention, but a memory intrudes, just as it had last time. Only this time the memory is more than complete.

•

She knows Jacob entirely, from the twinkle in his October eyes, to the pattern of the freckles on his back, to the slight webbing between his second and third toes, which means he always goes shod in public.

"Witch toes," he told her once. While Elspeth was still alive, or after? "They killed my mother for it. Oh, they said she'd killed a neighbor's swine by evil-looking them, but it was because someone noticed her toes. I was eight when she died. The priest had driven her out of the church: the village shunned her. It broke her heart. She sank into a sleep from which she never woke. Just before she stopped breathing, she stirred, once. I thought I saw her beckoning to me, begging me to join her."

Grethe held him while he wept, half a century later. "I'm ever so glad you didn't, husband mine."

She knew the feel of him, cool in all weathers, the only man she'd ever known who didn't sweat, knew the heat of his kisses and his passions. Knew the curve of his arms as he labored over the vats, the sweet yeasty scent of him, the softness of his hair, the whiteness of his teeth as, smiling up at her, he—

No, that was Govannon.

Yes, but it was Jacob, too. And might have been Johann, if you'd stuck around long enough. Karen shakes her head, trying to clear the cobwebs. Queen Eleanor is still speaking, and she has to pay attention. Fuchsia's done hir job too well this time.

"Stop it! I'm trying to concentrate here!"

The words slip out involuntarily. Eleanor stops abruptly, looks at her oddly.

"Are you ill, Grethe?"

"N-no, Lady. Only . . . beset."

"The spirits, or whatever it is that speaks to you, are troubling sometimes?"

"Y-you could say that, Lady."

"And what do they say about my dream?" Trust a queen to bring the conversation back to what was important.

Karen shakes her head again. Something stands between her and the queen, a pinkish-purple blur that twinkles like a migraine aura. Karen scowls at it ferociously. To Eleanor, it looks as if Grethe is concentrating mightily.

*Not here!* is all Karen hears Fuchsia say. Meanwhile, Grethe, it seems, is speaking.

"It's only an ignorant woman's opinion, Lady, but meseems your dream means nothing more than that you might caution Milord the King not to eat too much fruit in a warm climate, particularly those fruits he's unfamiliar with."

"Oh." Eleanor's disappointment is written on her face.

Karen's is written on her soul. Before she can say another word, she feels herself being pulled out of herself, as if she's about to faint. Not that she's ever fainted, but she's been told what it's like. There is a sense of floating, like those out-of-body experiences people talk about. Below, she can see Grethe still talking to the queen, advising her on the herbs to take for diarrhea, should Richard choose not to heed his mother's advice about figs.

*Not here,* Fuchsia said. Meaning the broken thread of Raymond's existence is not to be found at Chinon? Too late now anyway, because something—Fuchsia, TQ, who can keep track any more?—has yanked her out of the *solar* and is sending her on her way.

Which means, among other things, Karen thinks as the scenery spirals past, that Grethe will have to deliver Kit's baby on her own this time. Will it make a difference? She had this thought the last time, that the whole purpose of her being here was to bring twentieth-century methods to a twelfth-century birth, and now, in light of Raymond, she has the thought again, but with a twist:

What if Kit's baby dies? That won't affect Raymond, who's already missing. But what about Anna? No need to worry about rescuing her in a Berlin cellar, because she is a descendant of Kit's baby and will never be born? It's a reach, and yet, pluck out one thread in this century, and it affects a multiplicity of threads intertangling down the ages. Why not assume the missing thread is as likely to be about Anna as about Raymond?

Or maybe none of the above. Maybe another thread entirely. Or not. Trust Fuchsia, take hir at hir word, or not. Too late, no time.

•

It takes much longer to get where they're going this time. Usually, the change of scene is instantaneous; it's why Karen always feels nauseated, adjusting. This time she finds herself turning and turning, dizzy-making, and she can see as well as feel it. Not quite the cheap f/x of being caught inside the tornado that ends up in Oz, but close.

And—this is different—Fuchsia's along for the ride.

*Help me!* Hir slithery suckery tendrils stream out behind hir like Medusa's hair, all snakey spirally in the widening gyre, except when s/he gets caught in currents, eddies, backwash, and they tumble intertangling all about hir little domed transparent head. Sometimes s/he hirself goes ass over teakettle like a tumbleweed, a kid rolling down a grassy hill again and again until hir knees buckle and hir insides heave, who has insides but no knees to speak of.

*Help!* s/he yelps again, spinning by like strawberries in a blender and Karen, who's not feeling all that well herself, is torn between ignoring hir (as if she could!) and, in the interests of enlightened self-interest, grabbing ahold of the little pest so she at least knows where s/he is.

"Oh, for God's sake, hold still, will you?"

She grabs the closest tentacle, which wraps around her wrist like a vine, and for the briefest moment, they are spinning contralaterally, she and Fuchsia against the momentum of the tornado thingie, spiral, helix, circumbendibus, sinuous tortillary rivulation, tortuous undulatory anfractuosity (suggesting that many such journeys are possible), whatever. (You didn't expect it to rhyme as well, did you?) Like that scene in *The Red Shoes* where the girl dances herself to death. (In fairy tales, unlike real life, nice girls marry the prince, adventurous ones die.)

We're getting very far afield here. Ahem. As we were saying, for a moment there the two of them hold hands and do-si-do, and the next thing they know. . . .

•

The world was made of smoke. Where it wasn't made of mud and horseshit. Karen coughs. It doesn't help. She only inhales more smoke and has to cough again.

"Shit!"

*You can say that again!* Fuchsia grumps, scraping something off a tentacle or two.

They are in a clearing in the wood, and everywhere there is burning. The remains of campfires smoulder, singeing the grass around them. A garbage midden flares fitfully, too full of fresh offal to really burn. From beyond the trees there is a roil of denser, blacker smoke, rank-smelling, scattering a fine dust of ashes intermixed with motes the size of snowflakes down around the two of them whenever the wind shifts in their direction. At least the woods themselves are not on fire. Chalk that up to the torrential rain a day or week ago, the day Govannon died. The trees are still wet. If they were ablaze, there would be no escaping here. Wherever "here" is.

But, the Gentle Reader wants to object: "They're not in any real danger. All TQ has to do is pluck them out of there as handily as it has everywhere else since Bourges. Even Karen's figured out by now that TQ has its hands over Fuchsia's at the controls, to make sure there won't be another of those interdimensional blunders like the hayloft."

But Karen also has the sense of being plunked down firmly in the too real mud, and no rescue until she's done whatever she's been sent here to do. No easy fixes. If anything, the permutations grow more complicated with each trip backward. And, just as before, there is the sense that she could die here.

Wherever "here" is. It doesn't take a rocket scientist to examine the yellowed patches of dead grass where tents were pitched and think: Aha! This must have been the Roman camp! Past tense, because there are no tents here now. No Romans, no horses, just horseshit and human, the occasional bit of broken tack or fluttering rag of tattered garment, fooling the eye with its sudden furtive movement into thinking it's alive, fragments of scrap iron and a rusting breastplate in a heap beside a makeshift forge, rotting food and near-dead cooking fires. Oh, and the rodent brigade, of course. Rats and mice of the field variety rummaging through everything, with the occasional fox lying in wait for them. Karen only sees the rats, but Grainne knows about foxes.

That the campfires haven't been carefully doused is a telling sign. The battle is over, and the Romans have moved on, not caring if the whole province burns to ashes in their wake, perhaps even hoping that it does. Cleaner that way, less likelihood of plague. They can come back next year after the spring rains, plow the ashes under, grow their own crops, and pasture their own herds on the bones of dead Celts. Ground bone yields good lime for sweetening an acid soil.

Karen realizes they're standing, highly visible, in the center of the open campground. What if there are sentries still on the tall wooden palisade enclosing them? Perhaps stragglers, walking wounded taking their sweet time following the main troop, hoping they'll be forgotten so they can stay behind to rape and loot once their wounds heal? But there is a quiet like death hereabouts. As she looks about her, nothing is moving. Even the rats have gone to ground, which is more than strange.

On the far side of the trees, there is a racket of carrion birds. Occasionally, some of them rise above the smoke, circling lazily before plummeting down into the thick of things again. Karen knows where she must go.

# SEVENTEEN

When are we?" Karen asks as they trudge along. Rather, she trudges. Fuchsia, as usual, floats. But s/he did land in the horseshit back in the Roman camp. Karen files that, not yet certain what it means.

It's not quite clear from ground level exactly how the Romans launched their attack. Karen and Fuchsia have left the camp as the Romans did, through the main gate of the palisade, a flimsy affair compared to entrance to the Celtic *oppidum*. For all their attention to detail in building their walls, Karen thinks, the Romans were downright cocksure in just sealing them off with a pair of wooden gates, two meters high and fastened with a simple log-bolt. Then again, they knew the Celts had no siege weapons, no battering rams to make splinters of the gate. Of course. She, and possibly Grainne through her, was learning all the time.

In any event, the deep gouges in the soil churned up by the pounding of a thousand hooves made it easy to see where the cavalry had headed, round about the forest in two divisions. After that, where had they gone? To ring the *oppidum* and wait for the infantry to catch up? More likely, they'd hidden themselves in the trees to wait for the foot soldiers to do the bulk of the fighting before they moved in.

As if anyone could hide a horse, much less several hundred of them, from a Celt. Their own few horses would have gotten the scent of the intruders' horses and called out to them, to be answered in kind. It would have tipped off the Celtic sentries more readily than sending up a flare.

If it was that simple, Karen wonders, knowing Grainne knows more about horses than she ever will, then why did the Romans win?

The infantry had tramped through the woods, then. Maybe they'd gone first, before the cavalry; hard to tell in the aftermath, with bootprints sometimes overlapping hoofprints and sometimes the other way around. If I were running things, Karen thinks, I'd send the foot soldiers in first. Wasn't that the way it was usually done? Wouldn't horses be virtually useless against a barricaded city? Out in the open field, cavalry against cavalry, facing the Celtic chariots, they'd serve their purpose. But ringed about an ancient rubble-filled wall, they'd be like carousel horses, easy pickings. Maybe once the walls were breached they'd come in handy in riding down civilians and sending torchmen through to burn the houses. Maybe that was how they'd done it?

All that mattered was that the Romans won. Let the military historians play with it for the next few thousand years. It wasn't why she was here.

Or was it? Her presence in the aftermath of battle suggests this much: Grainne survived. To do what? To bear witness, obviously, but perhaps to learn and bring her knowledge with her so that the Celts would live to fight, or fight to live, another day. How else, after Caesar alone killed more than a million of them, had they survived to extend themselves from the banks of the Indus to the Pillars of Hercules, from Brittany to Cornwall and Scotland and Ireland, leaving behind their artifacts and place names—Iberia, Bohemia, Hibernia, Galicia—newer variations on Grainne's childhood poem?

In any event, Karen thinks: I can't help it; I'm a writer, I observe. And if Grainne retains my observations after I'm gone, there's nothing I can do about it. Once again I'm stuck with bifurcate perspectives, mine and Grainne's, and I can't always tell which is which, and if I become so overwhelmed with detail that I miss the forest for the trees, so to speak—

She catches her tunic on a bramble and, annoyed, yanks it free, turning her ankle in a chuckhole in the process. Okay, that's enough! Focus and click.

"When are we?" she asks Fuchsia who, though s/he's floating just above ground level as usual, seems to be taking inordinate care not to brush up against anything.

*Don't you mean "where"?*

"No, I mean *when.* In Berlin we returned just hours before the shell struck the cellar where Anna was. In Eleanor's time you screwed up completely, and TQ had to set you straight, and we ended up arriving just in time for Eleanor to summon Grethe about her dream, again. Here we're obviously too late to prevent the battle. It's over. When?"

Fuchsia sighs. S/he seems too tired to even obfuscate. *Two days ago.*

"And what I'm looking for is here, in this time." Karen does not ask so much as state it. "Whatever was changed here made Raymond's time line disappear."

Fuchsia seems to hesitate before s/he answers. *Yes.*

Karen knows she won't get an answer to her next question. It would be too easy. She asks it anyway: "What was it?"

Silence.

So we're back to yes/no answers, Karen thinks. Still, something's different. Fuchsia actually landed in the horseshit, and s/he's acting as if s/he's tired. These are not S.oteric traits as I know them. Something's changed.

Karen's throat hurts. She's desperately thirsty. The smoke is thicker here, wafting through the Mother Trees, clinging to them like cobwebs in places. Karen's always felt claustrophobic in deep woods without ever knowing why. Even Grainne's persona can't protect her. Yet she dreads what she knows she'll find on the far side of the trees.

Grainne seems to have been prepared for fight or flight, she only notices now. Her feet are shod for once, thank God, and she's wearing a sleeveless coarse-wool tunic and loose riding breeches. She wishes she had Grethe's or Margarethe's apron to tie around her face to filter some of the smoke. Still, the writer can't help making note of everything.

Sometimes the breeze lifts the smoke a little, but mostly it seems to be coming right at them, burning her eyes, closing her throat. It has a greasy quality to it that sticks to the skin. She remembers reading about Auschwitz, the smoke of burning flesh, genocide in any century.

"Smell that?" she asks Fuchsia without thinking. She is surprised by what happens next.

A little vestigial nose appears, morphing out of the blank dome of the jellyfishic head, forming the start of a momentary pseudoface. It sniffs. *Smoke?*

"Yes. That's what smoke smells like. What do you think?"

In the time it takes her to ask it, the little nose has disappeared.

*Nasty!* Fuchsia offers.

Karen files it. It might come in handy at some point.

•

"What if you could travel between times? Come to the places where the life you know intersects with other times?"

Had Govannon truly asked her that on the night they spent together, or had she only dreamed it? Dream or reality, it had been Karen who answered it, not Grainne:

"Are there such places? I've never bought the theory of parallel universes."

Then again, maybe Grainne had also been a smart-ass. Growing up with a name like Ugly can do that to a person.

"Can one 'buy' a theory where you come from?" Govannon had asked it with a chuckle, then grown serious: "I can show you."

He'd been tracing circles on her belly, interweaving invisible Celtic knots on her pale flesh, his living pre-Christian precursor to the *Book of Kells*. The effect was mesmerizing. She felt herself fighting the sleepy-wonderful sensation. She slid out from under his gentling fingers, propped herself up on one elbow, scowled at him in the dark.

"Show me? Show yourself! Find a hole in time to slip into and escape your own death."

The whiteness of his hair and beard, a glint of teeth, phosphoresced in the imperfect dark. "Is that what you think I should do?"

"I don't know!" She sat up cross-legged, striving to keep her voice down, took his hands, and kissed his fingertips. "I only know I don't want you to die!"

"Then I will not." With that, he touched a finger to her lips to stop the thousand questions, stretched her out on the borrowed bed, arranged her roanish hair like an aura about her head, and made love to her again.

•

No! Karen thinks with a sidelong look at the blank-domed Fuchsia. The lovemaking, yes, but that particular conversation? No. This is revisionist history, and I'm not playing!

Or was it? She'd accepted the added information about Jacob back in Eleanor's court. Why not this much more about Govannon?

"Because the memory of Jacob was Grethe's, not mine!" she says, making Fuchsia stop when she does. "It was out of Grethe's past."

They stand glaring at each other across a deer path in the woods. Hard to say which one is the more adamant, nor how exactly Karen can tell Fuchsia's glaring. Once s/he speaks, of course, there's no mistaking her snotty tone: *And Govannon's out of yours.*

"Or Grainne's." Karen's having trouble keeping it straight herself.

"But it was recent. I remember everything Govannon and I talked about that night."

*Everything? Could you recite it all from memory?*

"Maybe, given enough time." Where was this conversation leading? "Not that you weren't watching and listening."

Fuchsia wants to deny it; Karen can see it in hir sideways floating, shilly-shallying, looking to change the subject.

*It was very—enlightening,* s/he offers at last, a little shamefaced.

"Too bad there's nothing like it in your experience!" Karen shoots back. This is getting petty. "He never said that to me. About slipping through time."

*Are you sure?*

The answer is, she isn't. Too much has happened in the interim. But she's not about to tell Fuchsia that, not yet.

"We really don't have time for this now!" She strides off toward a clearing in the trees. The smoke is making her squint. Add that to her nearsightedness and—

She steps on something soft and recoils instinctively. She used to have cats and knows what it's like to set her foot down on something that isn't supposed to be there before it shoots out from under you with a squawk of protest.

This thing doesn't move, though the cloud of flies covering it does. She's found the first of the dead. Her skin crawls, her heart flip-flops. "Jesus Christ!"

*Not for half a century yet,* Fuchsia observes.

It's a Roman soldier, Karen notes, with a satisfaction she can't entirely suppress. His head's been hacked nearly off, and his left arm is missing. The flies have done a good job of obliterating his face.

He's got plenty of company. The underbrush is planted with Arverni and Roman dead alike. Their armament lies scattered about them where they fell, short knives and longer swords, some with sword arms still attached, a shield embossed with two boars, another with spirals, a plainer red-hued Roman shield. Here a plumed and earflapped Roman helmet, there some pot-shaped Celtic helms terminating in points or with eagles on them. An overturned chariot with a splintered whiffletree, dead horses. And everywhere corpses, hacked or with their entrails trailing, adding new smells to the stink of smoke.

Karen finds herself scanning the Celtic faces now to see if there's anyone here she recognizes. All male, so far, and all of them unknown to her. Past the clearing, the trees grow close together again. It's darker, but there are also fewer dead, less room to maneuver, more places to hide. Again she wonders about stragglers but makes no move to conceal herself.

Here is the spring where she and Aoife met Govannon. Wistfully she searches the leaf-filtered sunlight for the brightness of him. Let him appear to tell her this is a nightmare that she need not take part in. Of course he is not here. Desperately thirsty, trying not to think that the water might be contaminated by the nearness of so much death, she drinks, washes her face and neck and arms though she knows it's futile; the sifting ash will only add a new layer to her skin to replace what she's washed off.

A terrifying thought strikes her: What will she do if she finds anyone still alive? Did the victors walk the battlefield after, to make sure no wounded survived? She didn't know enough about war in any age to know that. And Grainne's knowledge for once does not seem to be forthcoming.

Which way to go next? Through the underground passage that she and Aoife took once before? Or around the wall and through the main gate, where the fighting was fiercest?

Easier on the soul, much less the stomach, to sneak in under the wall. There will be dead enough inside the city. Does she have to wade through them at the gate? But she doesn't know what she's looking for, or how long it will take her to find it, or if she'll recognize it once she does. Will slogging through the thick of the carnage make that simpler?

Her stomach starts to heave. She hasn't vomited in decades and isn't about to allow herself to now. Breathing through her mouth, one bare tattooed arm shielding her face, she makes sure Fuchsia is still with her and goes the long way around to the front entrance of the *oppidum.*

•

It is impressive even in defeat. Walls three meters high and four meters through, gates four meters wide built into the inturned thickness of the walls so that any enemy has to enter through a kind of man-made valley, with Arverni spears bristling on the palisade above them, raining death. And death is all that remains. The corpses, male and female now, are piled so deep there is no getting through them. Unaware that she is weeping (from the smoke or simple grief?), Karen retreats. Back to the underground passage, in hope it is not also crammed with death.

•

She finds Flidias on the beadmakers' street, her throat slit and her sprawled limbs hacked severally, her staring eyes not yet plucked out by the carrion birds that flap rustily like beady-eyed rags in furtive, hopping clumps, too many and too brazen to number. Does Karen expect to find Ryalbran beside her? For she must find Ryalbran. She has convinced herself that he is the key, his resemblance to Raymond too like to be coincidence. Ancestor, avatar, or time traveler like Govannon, she must find him.

And what of Govannon? she wonders with a shiver. She didn't think she had so many emotions to spare. Is the pit nearby? Does she dare find it?

How much carnage can one human witness and still be human? Karen has done the only thing she can do to survive—distanced herself from everything around her. This is a documentary, she tells herself—remarkably detailed, impressively three-dimensional—but the fact remains that all these people died millennia before she was born, and she cannot invest any feeling in what she sees and hears (how many flies can there be on a single planet? How do they know where to come to feed, and how far does the news travel? What do they feed on, to survive in such numbers, when there are no battle dead?) or she'll go mad.

Say the same about Govannon! she taunts herself. Or Ryalbran, for that matter.

Flies and wild dogs and carrion birds are all that is alive here. Karen swears she recognizes some of the dogs as recent pets. Is it savagery or a kind of practical love that causes them to forage among their former masters for sustenance in this place of death? The dogs, she thinks, probably feel more grief right now than she does.

She wanders aimlessly, stepping over and around scattered casualties like so many broken dolls, some of the bodies charred by the fires the Romans set, some grotesquely swollen in the heat. The wind has shifted, carrying most of the smoke away, though here and there a thatched roof still smolders fitfully.

There is one-eyed Arawn, blindsided forever by a Roman sword, silver-throated Ferchu who will sing no more. In the king's house, the bodies of Glewlwyd and his two wives have been mutilated and their heads taken, probably carried as trophies back to Rome.

Karen forces herself to enter Sequanna's house, finds her huddled protectively over the bodies of two of her grandchildren—dead though, mysteriously, none of the three has a mark on them. She covers her childhood friend and the two children with their winter cloaks, for now. The rest of Sequanna's kin, including pregnant Aoife, are nowhere to be found.

Nor is Ryalbran. Did he and Flidias truly ride off to Vercingetorix for reinforcements, or did Grainne only dream it? Why is Flidias here and Ryalbran not? Has he somehow survived?

Karen alternates between shivering almost uncontrollably and burning with a freakish inner fever; rivulets of sweat streak the ash blanketing her skin. Fuchsia bobs beside her like a half-filled helium balloon. Does Karen only imagine the beginnings of eyes, like the vestigial nose, on the nonexistent face?

*If it hurts so much, why do you keep doing it?*

"What?" Karen croaks, her voice destroyed by smoke and grief. Beyond exhaustion, she keeps moving, afraid to stop, wary of the thoughtful sideways look in the eyes of the carrion birds, some of them the size of turkeys. She is afraid they will mistake her stillness for weakness and close in. She is no longer even looking at her little purple nemesis, doesn't care if s/he hears her or not. "War, you mean? Killing each other? Don't ask me. I've never indulged."

*You've killed characters in your novels.*

"Oh, for God's sake! That's enough! This is a game for you; it doesn't mean anything. If you haven't figured it out by now, you never will." She stops, collapsing none too gracefully on a bench outside an unfamiliar bathhouse. "But you have, haven't you?"

*Have what?* Fuchsia asks warily.

"Back there in the woods, when I stepped on the first body. . . ." Karen tries to say it without thinking about it, but it haunts her. She can feel a kind of pestilence creeping up her leg from the sole of her soft boot where it made contact with the dead man. If she doesn't keep talking, she'll feel that impact again, almost hear the squish of guts. At the time, she couldn't twist out of the way fast enough. "I yelled out 'Jesus Christ,' and you said, 'Not for half a century yet.' You *do* understand the concept of Time."

Fuchsia doesn't answer. S/he doesn't have to. It's written on hir face, along with eyes, nose, mouth. They are still impermanent, morphing in and out, a cartoon face which would be almost amusing under any other circumstances.

"You know what's ironic . . . ?" Karen is so weary she hears her own words through a buzzing in her head, more annoying than the flies which, not content to feast on the dead, light on her continuously no matter how often she brushes them away. Does she only imagine some of them are touching down on Fuchsia, too? "You started all this because you were afraid of my writing. As if my fiction, my mind, could reach across time and space and alter your world. . . ."

She speaks deliberately, marshalling her thoughts, clutching at wisps of sanity in this Boschean aftermath, echoing madness long after the battle is done. "The joke is, you were the one who reached across time and space to interfere with me and all these time lines, and look what's happening to you."

The eyes, at least, stay permanent for a minute. Are there tears in them?

"I hate this!"

There is that little squeaky voice again. Karen reaches out and touches the nearest tentacle, which does not retreat. She takes it between her two hands and strokes it gently. It is solid enough, warm to the touch, almost velvety.

"What exactly is it that you hate?"

The tentacle withdraws then; the eyes disappear.

*You still haven't found the glitch!*

The voice is back in Karen's mind again, taunting. Karen pulls herself to her feet.

"But I will."

•

It was mid-morning when they arrived; it is past noon now. Karen thought this was Grainne's reckoning at work, but she is beginning to realize that Grainne is no longer with her. If she ever was, this time around. As bizarre as it seems, she's actually hungry. She retraces her steps to Sequanna's house, where there is always a pot of oatmeal on the fire.

The fire has burned down; the oatmeal is crusted around the edges of the cauldron, but soft in the center, and too hot for the flies. There is dried salmon hung from the rafters, berries in a covered pot on the herb shelf, and beer, of course. As she eats and drinks, Karen wonders what she should do about Sequanna and the children. Bury them? Impossible. She might be able to dig a shallow hole and carry the children, maybe even drag Sequanna that far, but the labor would take the rest of today and part of tomorrow, and there weren't enough stones about to cover the graves to keep the dogs off.

When, if, she found what it was she was supposed to do, Karen thinks, she would come back afterward and complete the burning the Romans had begun.

She borrows one of Sequanna's tunics and washes again in cold water from the well in the courtyard. The fire in the bathhouse is down to embers, almost out. Karen takes her time. There is no hurry in this city of the dead. She even finds some hazel twigs to clean her teeth. As she unbraids and combs the tangles out of her roanish hair, she hears something.

The wind? An animal? No. She has birthed; she knows that sound. As she makes her way cautiously around the perimeter of the courtyard, listening with her whole being, she almost trips over Fuchsia.

"For God's sake, don't do this now!" she snaps. Ever since they entered the city, she's been treating the S.oteri like a pesky housecat, stepping over and around hir as s/he weaves about underfoot, alternately floating out of reach and all but rubbing against Karen's ankles, needy. It hasn't been amusing for a very long time. Karen has an urge to punt hir across the courtyard, but the sound intervenes. "Be quiet, will you? I've got to find where that's coming from."

She glances down to notice that Fuchsia now has ears.

"Well?"

*That way,* the S.oteri offers sheepishly, one tentacle pointing.

"Thank you!" Karen manages. She hurries.

•

Aoife half-sits, half lies in a corner of the lean-to behind the bathhouse. Here is where the extra kindling and the rare oils and liniments are kept; there is a kind of platform built into one wall, where men and women, especially those who work in the fields and the salt mines, take turns massaging each other after a hard day's labor. Karen seems to remember Grainne meeting a lover or two here. Why do all of her avatars have more interesting sex lives than she does? Well, maybe not all; Margarethe seemed awfully grim, but that might have been only the war.

Stop it. No time to slip into shock and start dreaming now. Focus and click. Only one thing matters: Aoife is alive.

Barely.

There is a great deal of blood, almost more than surrounds some of the dead outside. One possible explanation for it is mewling weakly at his mother's breast. His cries were what drew Karen here.

He lies on Aoife's belly for warmth, small and perfect and unharmed. His robust limbs are unmarked, but he is strangely still for a hungry newborn. The flesh around his eyes seems puckered in a way Karen has seen before, though she can't quite remember where. Lapped in an old shirt, the cord still attached, he has soiled himself and doesn't smell very nice. Nevertheless, he has been bathed since birth; there is none of his mother's blood or amniotic fluid on him. But Aoife's gown is sticky with blood, and the puddle she half sits, half lies in is fairly fresh.

It is not coming from between her legs; she has bound herself up to contain the bleeding following the birth. Nor are there any signs of a placenta, no trail of blood suggesting that one of the dogs has dragged it off. Aoife did not give birth here.

Trying to make sense of what she sees, Karen kneels beside the girl, whose own half-opened eyes are sunken and whose brow is feverish. When the infant stops suckling, there is no expected trickle of milk from his mouth. Something is very wrong.

"Aoife, child of my heart—" Karen can't finish her thought. She eases one arm under the girl's narrow shoulders and strokes her hair. Aoife frowns at the voice, and her eyes seem to search for the source.

The only light is from the open door; it is dim but not that dim. Aoife seems too weak to move. This is about more than childbirth. "Where are you hurt?"

"Grainne?" It is a whisper. "I thought you were dead."

She does not wait for Karen to speak. "Perhaps you are. Are you come to bring me to the other side? I will go with you if I must, but my son—"

"I am alive," Karen assures her. "I am not here to claim anyone, not you or your son. You're going to live," she adds with a confidence she does not feel. Afraid to move her, she asks again. "Where are you hurt?"

"No hurt . . ." The girl falls into a kind of half-doze and, in truth, she does not seem to be in any pain. Then where, how—?

The infant begins to wail, not the lusty cries of a healthy child, but the desperate, hoarse sounds of a starving one. Aoife is dehydrated, if nothing else, and she has no milk.

Moving quickly, Karen takes the baby from Aoife's limp arms and rests him in the crook of her own, slops water out of one of the row of heavy jugs lined up against the wall and washes the shit off him, searching him carefully for wounds and finding none. He continues to wail, flailing arms and legs weakly as his cries grow weaker, too. Karen pours fresh water, dabbles her fingers in it, trickles it drop by drop into the corner of his mouth. He moves his head to suck at it, swallowing avidly, coughing, swallowing more. It fools his stomach temporarily; he shudders into sleep.

A clean shirt from Sequanna's house to swathe him in, a basket where he can sleep for now, and Karen devotes her attention to Aoife, who slips in and out of something that is not sleep.

"Where are you hurt?" Karen asks again, giving Aoife small sips of water, which she knows somehow she shouldn't do if the girl has a gut wound. But she's examined as much of her as she can without moving her, and the blood smearing her belly does not originate there. "Try to tell me what happened."

Perhaps the water revives her. Perhaps the proximity of death makes her feel she must give an accounting of herself. Whatever the cause, Aoife finds strength enough to speak.

"Conchobar—?" she asks first, coming out of her strange half-trance.

*The baby*, Karen realizes. She brings the basket closer so Aoife can see.

"He's fine," she lies. How long can a newborn survive without sustenance? He's too young for cow's milk, assuming a cow could be found alive; it is mother's milk or death in this time and place.

Aoife manages a smile. "I was in the wood near the spring when the labor started. It's why I lived. I thought I would just rest a while, then come back home so Mum could help me, but I heard the thunder. . . ."

She breathes for a few minutes, dreamy. "Not thunder. Hooves. I knew it had begun. I crawled off into the little grotto where the rocks meet like two clasped hands. You know the one. . . ."

Grainne does. Karen nods.

"He was born at moonrise. I never made a sound. Betimes the fighting was so near I could see them running back and forth and wondered why no one from either side saw me. I watched some of them die. . . ."

Karen remembers the bodies strewn about the sacred grove. "I know. We have just come from there."

" 'We'?"

*Stupid!* Karen chides herself. "Another was with me then. Not now."

In truth, Fuchsia has taken refuge beneath the massage table and is watching everything with hir new-morphed eyes, hir little transparent body pulsating softly.

"He was born. I could see him in the moonlight, quite perfect. I suckled him. I had milk then. You can see. . . ."

In fact, the front of her gown is stiff with dried milk stains. It has been more than twenty years since Karen nursed her babies; her own breasts ache, remembering.

"What happened—?" she starts to say, but Aoife does not hear her.

"It was quiet then, except for the cries of the dying. The animals in the wood were very still, waiting, and there were no old spirits about, only the new ones just leaving the bodies of the dead, and I knew they would not harm us. As the moon went down, I heard soldiers coming. Knew them to be Romans by the clanking even before I heard them speak. They had been sent to finish off any who were still alive. I heard screams, prayers. By dawn it was over, except for the burning.

"I put the baby to my breast to keep him silent and, tree by tree, began to make my way back to the city. I knew no matter what else happened, we could not spend a second night in the woods, for then the spirits of the dead would be in earnest. More fool me, thinking I could protect my son from spirits, when it was spirits caused me to stay behind when Cumaill went away with the cows. . . ."

# EIGHTEEN

"Spirits'?" Karen says carefully, aware of Fuchsia in the corner of her eye. "Tell me about the spirits."

But Aoife slips away again, into something between coma and sleep. She has said nothing hurts. Is she so deeply in shock that she cannot feel a wound? She needs to be moved, examined more thoroughly. She is small; Karen is sure she can lift her. As she slides one arm each under shoulders and knees, Fuchsia scrambles out from under the table, pulsing agitatedly. Wrapping as many tentacles as s/he can spare around Karen's right arm, s/he tugs.

*Don't!*

"Butt out!" Karen snaps, blocking the thought: You have to let her die! She is already dead, centuries dead, in the reality you know. Well, that was then, this is now. Twenty thousand children died daily in her century's Third World, and there was nothing she could do about it. But here whole time lines intersect, and she feels responsible. "We'll play mind games later. I've got to—"

*Don't move her!* Fuchsia tightens hir grip, tugs harder. *You'll only make it worse.*

"Make what worse?" Karen has already started to lift the girl, but her left knee, the one that always threatens to give out when she's running for a bus, threatens again. Fuchsia's tugging (remarkably strong for hir size; make note of that, also) doesn't help. Karen stops, repositions herself. Aoife stirs in her arms, opens her eyes. Defeated, Karen sets her down again, offers her water, sits back on her heels, and waits. Something tells her the most important thing she can do right now is listen.

". . . saw the dust on the road which was the last of the Romans, I thought . . . came back and found Mum and Dannan's two in the house. She must have tranced them so they'd die without pain. No need to go far to see that everyone was dead. . . ."

She braces her hands against the floor, her thin shoulders against the wall behind her, trying to sit up. Karen wants to help but stops herself. There is something odd about the way Aoife moves, but what?

"I'll help you move if you . . ." she begins, but Aoife is very far away.

". . . meant to do my grieving after, to take whatever I could carry and bring my son to safety, over the mountains, to find Cumaill and the cows. He'd said that if the siege continued, they would winter at Gergovia. . . ."

Gergovia, where Vercingetorix was. A chorus of voices crowds Karen's head suddenly. She has no time for this.

"And Caesar first took Vellaudonum of the Senones, then Cenabum of the Carnutes, then Noviodunum of the Bituriges. Following a long march, he laid siege to Avaricum, where forty thousand died. The rest, a fragment, fewer than one thousand, journeyed over the mountains to join Vercingetorix in his capital at Gergovia. There many Romans would meet their doom, the rest retreat after the loss of forty-six centurions and a hundred times as many men. . . ."

They are the voices of men and women both, perhaps even the voices of children, reciting an oral history she knows by heart. It makes her wonder if Grainne is her ancestor, and if she carries this race memory somewhere in her DNA. No time, no time. She shakes her head to still the voices, when the only one she wants to hear right now (Not Ryalbran? Not Govannon? Not now; no time) is Aoife's.

"I knew I had to stay as still as I could in case there were soldiers left about. . . . I'd heard that was a trick the Romans had. But I could not stop the tears, and I must have been keening. That was when he found me. . . .

"He was no more than a boy. Younger even, I think, than I. What he wanted was rape, a way to celebrate his first kill before he ran to catch up with his troop. Mayhap he was a deserter, mayhap he was even looking for a bride in the only way he knew. When he saw that I'd just birthed, I could read the disappointment on his beardless face. That was when he drew his sword. . . ."

Karen sees what happened next with a sudden frightening clarity, as if she has become Aoife, reliving it.

"He said something in his mumbling city tongue. I know no Latin, but his intent was clear. It was as if he was saying 'If I can't have you, no man will.' I started to run, but he had me cornered. There was a sudden, sharp pain, and then my legs . . . I was so afraid of dropping Conchobar, I didn't—"

Karen reels and has to catch her breath. She can not only see the boy severing Aoife's spinal cord, she can feel it, as well as the numbness that follows it. She understands now why Aoife does not move her legs, why there is so much blood but no pain.

*I told you!* Fuchsia says impatiently. *If you move her, you'll only hasten her death. She's dying anyway. Soon she'll no longer be able to breathe on her own because of the cord damage, but given how your kind cling to life, I thought—*

"Spirits!" Karen hisses, spitting the word out. "Aoife, child, tell me about the spirits. It's important."

Her ferocity does two things simultaneously. It brings Aoife out of her stupor, and drives Fuchsia back under the table.

Aoife laughs, then coughs. A tiny trickle of blood forms in the corner of her mouth, bubbling a little when she speaks.

"Strange . . . I was just about to tell you, that day beside the spring. But then Govannon was there. Not appeared, so much as simply there. A shape-shifter, thought I, though you would know better than I." Is the child actually giggling? "If there had been time, I might have asked you what shapes he took, that night you spent together. But you were so bedazzled by him that day beside the spring, I never got to finish my tale. . . ."

She pauses, as if breathing has become more difficult. Karen wishes there were something more she could do. But the look on Aoife's face is strangely peaceful.

". . . and now Govannon's gone to the other side, and we've lost the battle anyway, I can at least tell you about the spirit . . ."

She breathes as if she has to think about it.

"Mum was praying, as I said, to learn the sex of my child. She didn't know if Sulis would appear to her, though she had betimes in the past. . . . Mum said something began to shimmer in the corner of her eyes. . . . When she turned to study it front on, it tried to take a human form. But she could see it was a gyre."

•

"A what?" Karen doesn't recognize the word. She wonders if Grainne would. To this point she's been able to understand the language in whatever place she finds herself, as if Fuchsia's game came with a free Universal Translator. This is the first time she's been stuck.

"A gyre," Aoife repeats, the blood bubble bursting and trickling down her chin. There is more where it came from; her voice is thick with it. She frowns, searching her memory for a clearer word. "Mum didn't think an evil one could inhabit a sacred place, but there it was. . . . She spoke to it, but it did not answer. . . . Then she sang an incantation, and it shimmered away, as if she'd freed it. . . . Before it did, it completed a shape, the shape of my namesake, the goddess Aoife."

Where does her strength come from? Karen wonders. She is holding the girl now, regardless of the blood. There is nothing she or anyone can do for such a grievous wound in this time and place.

The baby begins to stir feebly in his basket. Which will die first? Must she bear witness? Is *this* why she was brought here?

". . . don't need to tell you the tale," Aoife is saying, "of how Aoife the Jealous turned her stepchildren into swans for nine hundred years. The other gods punished her. She became a demon, cursed to float on the air until they chose to free her."

"But what has that to do with you, dear heart?" Karen has to ask, though she knows she should remain silent and listen. The girl's flesh, which before had been feverish, is now like ice to her touch.

"Mum wasn't sure." She breathes. "It's why she didn't want me to go when Cumaill chose to leave with the cows. . . . There were sharp words exchanged between her and Cumaill, you remember. . . ."

Grainne might, Karen doesn't, but she whispers "Aye" all the same.

"I'd have gone with Cumaill, if it hadn't been for the gyre. . . ."

•

She has slipped away again, into a realm that is neither life nor death. The baby is stirring in earnest now, his little fingers flexing desperately, his cries a high-pitched keening like a small animal dying. Karen eases her arm out from under the comatose girl and lunges at Fuchsia, grabbing whatever comes to hand, dragging hir out into the light.

"This is it!" she seethes, no doubt in her mind. "You're responsible for this! You and your fucking 'tweaking the reality.' This was not supposed to happen! She was supposed to go with her husband. If her mother hadn't seen you, she'd be safe in Gergovia by now."

*People will die in Gergovia, too!* Fuchsia protests feebly, trying to wriggle free.

"Granted." Karen tightens her grip. "But that's what was supposed to happen, what happened in the first reality, and maybe the baby at least would have survived. You changed that, and you've got to change it back!"

What is the sound of a Third Thing chuckling?

*I . . . I don't know how.*

"Yes, you do."

Karen is thinking of an artist she once knew, back in the twentieth century, a woman whose nervous system was so damaged that an S.oteri was able to join with her and heal her, leaving not a little of its own personality intertwined with the human's. It was the very kind of "contamination" Fuchsia's most afraid of.

S/he can hear what Karen's thinking, and s/he struggles harder. Karen grabs two handfuls of tentacles and holds on.

"No!" the squeaky little voice protests, as Fuchsia digs in hir metaphorical heels. S/he sounds like nothing so much as Conchobar, wailing his protest against a world that would let him go hungry for this long. "I don't want to! I'm afraid!"

"Afraid of what?" Karen demands, not a little cruelly. She does not relent in dragging the squirming S.oteri across the packed-earth floor. "You can't feel pain, and you can't die, unless you stay out in the sun on your own planet. For all I know, you're not even really here. Just some sort of projection. Dammit, quit resisting!"

"Noooo. . . ."

Hir cries blend with the baby's; Karen can't decide which grates more on her nerves. She has never been able to bear the sound of an infant crying, wants to pick them all up and comfort them. Aoife's breathing has gone alarmingly shallow; there is no color in her face at all. Is it too late?

The more Karen pulls, the stronger Fuchsia seems to get. Up to now, Karen has focussed all her energies on saving Aoife. Now she realizes Fuchsia is feeding off her determination. She lets her attention wander, thinks of Govannon's hands on her, his body against hers. A wave of pleasure washes over her; she almost laughs. God, she's exhausted! She hears Fuchsia giggle in her mind. It's all the distraction she needs. She heaves the little monster off the floor and throws hir, jellyfish floppy-squiggly, plop on top of Aoife.

Holding the wriggling mass of Fuchsia as tightly as she can with one hand, Karen gently rolls Aoife onto her side. The wound is small but too deep to contemplate; Karen feels her nerves twang at the sight of it, and it's all she can do to keep from dropping her hands and backing away. The sudden movement has caused fresh blood to well, obscuring the source. Karen focuses herself, grabs the nearest tentacle, and shoves it in.

What is the sound of one jellyfish screaming?

•

An instant, an hour, a day? None of the three would ever know how long it took to work. What happened was this:

Aoife lay very still, insensate, only her shallow breathing indicating that she was still alive. Fuchsia was a different matter. The instant s/he made contact with the wound hir entire body went rigid and began to shake, all hir multiplicity of tendrils and tentacles straightening like those of a cartoon character touching a live wire. All that was missing was the smoke coming out of hir ears. It might have been comical, if there hadn't been so much at stake. There was also the screaming.

Karen had just enough strength left to crawl across the floor and prop herself against the far wall, with nothing left to do but watch. Only then did she notice that she was as covered in blood as Aoife.

"Please . . ." Fuchsia had whimpered at first. Karen had held the tentacle in place, afraid the instant she let go Fuchsia would escape. As the S.oteri's tendrils unfurled and went rigid, Karen realized s/he was all but welded there by whatever process was taking place. Half wondering why it didn't grab hold of her as well (she felt only a mild tingling in her fingertips running up her wrists, no more than what a day of typing medical reports would do), she tentatively let go.

Fuchsia stuck there, unable to pull free although s/he was clearly trying. Strangely indifferent to the struggle, Karen had tucked her knees up under her chin and watched. She wouldn't help no matter how much Fuchsia pleaded.

"Please . . . !" Fuchsia whimpered again, a sound from between clenched teeth. Karen had been known to make such sounds herself in the dentist's chair when the novocaine didn't take. But S.oteri didn't have teeth. Something else must be hurting. At one point, Fuchsia managed to pry a few tendrils and waved them like seaweed in Karen's direction. *Help me! It hurts!*

"I'll bet it does," Karen said grimly, at the same time wondering why. Aoife had felt only an instant's pain as the boy's sword severed her spine. Shouldn't Fuchsia have felt the same? Or was s/he suffering for more than Aoife? How many life threads had s/he pulled out of the weave? How many generations lay between Conchobar and Raymond? And were they the only ones?

Stop extrapolating! Karen warned herself, one eye on the baby, who had come fully awake and seemed to be listening. You don't know for sure that Conchobar's the answer. You may never know.

Fuchsia went rigid again, taken by a new spasm; they seemed to come in waves. The sounds s/he made were sounds no human should have to listen to. Concerned for whatever effect hir agonies might have on a newborn psyche, Karen scooped the baby out of the basket and held him against her one-handed out of long practice, carrying him out into the sunlight. His little mouth went rooting instinctively, his tiny fingers scratching at her neck as he searched for a nipple to latch onto.

"Sorry, little one. Can't help you there. Weaned my last baby a long time ago." Karen tried to soothe him as he rubbed his face against her collarbone, sucking and clutching at the fabric of her tunic, squalling weakly, frustrated by the fates yet again. She stroked his tiny head with its fuzz of soft hair, smelled the wondrous baby smell of him, the same in any era. "Not much longer now, I think."

She stood swaying in the sunlight, singing anything that came to mind to comfort him. The pestilence of flies notwithstanding, at least it was quieter here. But at last the sounds within were subsiding.

"Please . . . !" Fuchsia whimpered once again, reaching out tendrilly.

"You're almost done," Karen assured hir, not knowing how she knew.

Things were falling into place in the RealWorld the way they sometimes did in her writing. She could actually foresee what would happen next. The effect was exhilarating. Would the S.oteri have to die to save the human? Karen didn't think so. They'd all know in a moment.

Aoife opened her eyes.

•

Again, there was no measure to time as the girl sat up as if from a deep sleep, yawned and stretched and reached for her baby, opening her gown with her free hand and putting him to her breast. Cautiously now, as if he expected to be fooled once more, Conchobar rooted around, found what he was searching for, and began to suck. His mother held him close and crooned to him, knowingly pressing her arm against the opposite breast as she'd seen her sisters do to stop her suddenly abundant milk from flowing from both at once.

Exhausted as she was, Karen felt like dancing. Aoife regarded her with bemusement.

"What happened?"

"How much do you remember?" Karen countered.

"A Roman . . . a boy with a sword . . ." Aoife reaches to find the wound, notices the blood as if for the first time. "Arragh!"

"You're all right," Karen supplies, thinking quickly. "It was a small wound, but it bled a lot. It's stopped now. How do you feel?"

"Thirsty!" Aoife announces like the child she is, laughing giddily. Karen cannot fill a cup with water fast enough.

"Slowly!" she cautions futilely as Aoife chokes and sputters, spattering her son, who stops suckling only long enough to give his mother a quizzical look before he returns to the very serious business at hand. He makes little grunting, snorting noises until, finally sated, he indulges in a fit of hiccups interspersed with the occasional burp and fart.

"Piglet!" Karen says fondly. "May I . . . ?"

She holds her arms out, and Aoife surrenders him. Karen sets him against her shoulder and pats him on the back. He spits up all over her tunic. Now it is her turn to laugh. "Oh, Jaysus!" she says without thinking, sounding like her own grandmother.

"Who is Jaysus?" Aoife scrambles to her feet with her old grace, completely healed, slipping out of her blood-fouled gown with the casual nakedness of a Celt.

"A god I believed in in my youth," Karen supplies quickly.

Aoife plunges her arms into an amphora almost as big as she is and tries splashing the water over herself, but it will not do. "I need a proper bath. . . . Was he a worthy god?"

Karen considers her answer carefully. "I think he meant well. But his people expected too much of him."

"Don't we always?" is the wisdom Aoife offers, retrieving her son from his foster mother.

Conchobar drowses against her shoulder, his belly full for the first time in days. They all repair to the bathhouse. Sifting the ashes, they find a few coals still burning. How long will it take to get it built up again and the water hot enough?

•

And what of Fuchsia?

S/he had dragged hirself, limp as an old sock, back into the gloom beneath the shelf against the wall. The humans, taking one of their interminable baths, seem to have forgotten about hir. When at last they return, carrying food they've foraged from a nearby house for an impromptu evening meal amid the carnage, s/he is weeping softly.

Both women are dressed in plaid breeches and sleeveless tunics, riding clothes, if there had been anything in Avaricum to ride. There is nothing but death and the threat of disease in Avaricum. Traveling clothes, then. They have scrounged a pot of curds for Aoife, as well as bread and bacon and dried fruit. Aoife settles her sleeping son in his basket, and they set to. Karen would have preferred a clearing in the wood, away from the stink of death, but Aoife knows the woods are filled with spirits. The very suggestion would frighten her.

"How do you feel?" Karen asks the girl.

"I've never felt stronger," Aoife says. "Isn't it odd? I should be mourning. But my son and I are alive. That's all I can think of for now."

"There will be time enough for mourning later."

The strange light emanating from under the shelf catches Aoife's eye. She crouches to investigate it and, finding the source, announces without fear: " 'Tis the gyre."

Karen isn't at all sure this meeting is supposed to take place. Well, too late now. She also peers at Fuchsia.

"Had enough?"

*Yes.*

"I think you'd better come out now."

Shuffling across the floor like a Horta, s/he does.

"You've been crying," Karen observes, sitting cross-legged on the floor to minimize the size difference. She keeps forgetting how small S.oteri are.

*I . . . I never realized.*

"But you do see now?" Karen finds herself caressing the little domed head. "It was a painful way to learn it, but you do finally understand the difference between what you did and what I do?"

*There are times when fact and fiction overlap,* Fuchsia mutters defensively.

"Well, yes, that's true, but—" Karen begins, then stops herself. The two of them seem to have forgotten they have a witness.

"Is it . . . is it your familiar?" Aoife asks cautiously. She seems more wary of her mother's old friend Grainne than of the gyre. Before Karen can answer, she takes a step forward, putting herself between Fuchsia and her child. "It was you I feared. I thought you would come back to the spring to claim my son. That was why I returned to the city, more afraid of you than of the Romans, and now I find you here. Is that what it's all for, then? Do you mean to take my baby?"

*No.*

Karen watches the exchange. "Can you hear what it's saying?"

Aoife seems surprised by the question. "Yes. It speaks in my mind."

Karen wonders if Fuchsia has left some portion of hirself in Aoife's consciousness, or if it's simply that Aoife is Sequanna's daughter and knows the slipstream between the worlds.

"Maybe you should explain yourself," she says to Fuchsia.

•

Suddenly, they are all sitting cross-legged on the floor, except for Conchobar, who stirs in his basket from time to time, snuffling slightly in his sleep. As she doles out the food, Karen has to stop herself from offering Fuchsia some.

*I never meant to change anything at first. I was only watching. But I found I could change shapes. Sequanna was thinking about Aoife when she came to pray. I merely plucked the image out of her mind and formed it on my own face, like this. . . .*

For a moment she bubbles like a kind of iridescent stew, then hir featurelessness morphs into a human face. It looks like oddness itself hovering above the tangled mass of tentacles, but it is enough like Aoife to impress the girl.

"That's very good!" Aoife giggles past a mouthful of curds, covering her mouth with her hands. "Do I really look like that?"

"You know you do," Karen tells her, tearing a great loaf of oaten bread in half and passing it to her. "Only your head isn't quite as easy to see through."

It is Celtic humor, biting and not a little cruel, but necessary even here. She has to keep the girl's spirits up until this little drama has played itself out.

"Go on," she says to Fuchsia.

*There's really nothing more to say.* The Aoife face disappears back into the blankness. If the S.oteri had shoulders, s/he would shrug them. *Sequanna misunderstood.*

Karen can feel Aoife bursting with questions but, well-schooled in the proper protocol when dealing with spirits, the girl waits. Besides, she knows what Fuchsia is, or thinks she does. It is Karen who has suddenly become a stranger. The girl's eyes fix on her even when Fuchsia is speaking.

"So why didn't you correct the error while it was simple?" Karen asks. "Tell Sequanna you were just passing through, that your mimicking Aoife didn't mean anything?"

*Because I wanted to see what would happen next.*

"A plot twist," Karen suggests. Fuchsia answers with silence. "Then why not just let it play out? Why drag me into it?"

*You're a writer. I thought you could fix it for me.*

Karen doesn't know whether to laugh or scream. Not only is this revisionist history at its worst, it's a song she's heard from every wannabe writer she's ever met, as if these same people would ask a doctor to set a broken arm for free. She sighs.

"Would you do it again?"

*You know I'll never get the chance.*

"That isn't what I'm asking."

*No.*

"No, you wouldn't do it again, or No, you're not going to answer me?"

*Yes.*

Aoife giggles.

•

"We're better off at night, at least until we reach the foothills," Aoife insists as the sun lips below the horizon and the long, late-summer twilight sets in. "After that we'll go by day. But you know I have a cat's eyes for the dark."

Conchobar, fed and changed again, lies snugged under her ribcage in a carry-sling. The rocking motion as Aoife walks will comfort him and keep him from crying, and she can move him around to either breast without breaking her stride. They are going over the mountains to Gergovia, to Vercingetorix.

Those mountains, Karen reminds herself, just happen to be the Alps. She looks at the slight figure of the girl and wonders. But there is at least another month of warm weather, and Aoife knows how to feed off the land. On her other hip, balancing Conchobar in his sling, is a saddlebag crammed with dried fish and jerky and herbs and uncooked oats. When those run out, she can forage for berries and roots and set traps for small game while she sleeps; the short spear she uses as a walking stick and the forged steel knife at her belt will come in handy for fish or anything too large to trap.

Karen keeps waiting for her own part in this to end, for TQ to pull her out of here and send her home. She's taken Fuchsia aside to ask about it and gotten no answer. What now?

"Are you coming with us?"

Not "aren't you," but "are you," Karen notes. She has a choice. It doesn't help her decisionmaking. Fuchsia, who has been following them both like a puppy, is noncommittal. But Karen has some unfinished business here.

"I need to finish what the Romans started. They meant to burn the city so the land would be habitable in the spring. There's nothing we can do to prevent that—"

"We'll see about that, once I tell my tale to Vercingetorix!" Aoife says fiercely.

"Aye, well," Karen says carefully. "But I would start the fires up again, to lay to rest the dead we cannot bury."

Aoife considers this. "The Mother Trees are still damp from the rain. I think they'll be safe if the fire stays within the *oppidum*. Do you want me to remain and help you?"

"If you didn't have the baby with you—"

"Aye." Aoife is relieved. Courageous as she's been these several days, she doesn't know if she could set the fire that consumed her mother's body and the only home she's ever known. "But you'll join us later?"

Dare she speak for Grainne who, for all Karen knows, is lying dead somewhere in this vast city and only awaiting the flames?

"Mayhap. Take the gyre with you," she says on a sudden impulse. If it's wrong, TQ will intervene, won't it? "It will light the way for you, perhaps warn of pitfalls, and if it choose to vanish, you'll know it's gone to its rest."

She gives Fuchsia a warning look. No words are needed. The S.oteri twinkles at her, hir faceless face unreadable.

The two women embrace, cradling the infant between them. Karen kisses his little fuzzy head. Though he is asleep, he frowns, knitting his brows ferociously like someone she once loved, someone who hasn't been born yet.

"If you find him," she hears Aoife say. "Tell him Aoife, Sequanna's daughter, bids him greeting."

" 'Him'?" Karen starts, She'd been thinking of Raymond. Can Aoife read her thoughts as Sequanna used to?

"The Thunderer. Don't tell me you aren't going to seek Govannon?"

*Govannon's dead!* Karen wants to shout: *You and your kind saw him to his execution!* But does she know this for sure?

"I . . . I'll tell him," she says, shaken by the thought.

If she's going to start setting funeral pyres, she ought to do it while there's still some light.

"Go!" she tells Aoife abruptly, knowing she will never see her again. "If I can follow your trail, I'll catch up with you in a few days. If not—"

Aoife nods. "I understand. And if you choose to go with him instead, I'll understand that, too."

# NINETEEN

She dares not watch Aoife go, because if she does she will want to follow her, protect her, as if she could, interloper in this time and place. Instead, she retraces her steps to the borrowed house where she spent the night with Govannon. Wherever the mob brought him later cannot be far.

Inured to the sight and stench of the dead by now, she threads her way among them. Even the carrion birds, eyeing her warily, hop aside to let her pass. A certain wearing of the cobblestones in one street leads her footsteps in the grooves worn by a million others, and she finds the pit.

He is not here. Some trick of the late evening light allows her to see all the way to the bottom, to the sharpened stake strewn about with sacred artifacts and fresh flowers. There is no sign that it has been recently used. It stands naked, obscenely phallic, awaiting a sacrifice not yet offered. Is this the only pit, or are there others? No. The bare, worn earth around it and the remnants of dried flower wreaths indicate recent activity continuing a tradition as old as the city itself. If Govannon had died within the walls of Avaricum, it would have been here.

The sky just above where the sun disappeared is the color of his eyes. Karen can almost hear his laughter, the low generous rumble of it rising from deep within his powerful chest. Govannon is not dead. Lost to her forever, perhaps, but not dead. Unfinished business, like so much of her real life; small wonder she seeks solace in her writing. Will she be able to find that solace again, having witnessed all of this?

She wipes one last tear from her cheek. "I want to go home," she says softly, then louder, in case the Third Thing doesn't get it: "I want to go home!"

Nothing happens, and she begins to doubt. Was there something else she was supposed to do? From the moment she realized the connection between Fuchsia and Aoife, she has known precisely what to do. It had all come to her like a plot outline, the first time real life fell into place as seemingly structured as her writing. Would it work that way from now on?

The fire, that's all. She had promised Aoife she would start the funeral pyre for an entire city of the dead. She looks about her one last time, wondering where on this site the cathedral of Bourges would someday rise. Where was the hayloft where she and Fuchsia waited? Was there a modern French city on the site? Her ignorance of geography amazed her sometimes.

Would Fuchsia behave hirself in Aoife's presence? Karen could only hope. Out of her hands in any event; let TQ worry about it. She fetches a torch and flints from Glewlwyd's house and sets to work.

•

She begins with Sequanna's house (she owes Grainne's friend that much, at least) then tries to remember to stay upwind of anything else she puts to the torch. It isn't easy. The wind is whimsical this time of year, running about itself in alternating gyres; Karen finds herself choking and scurrying out of the way more often than not. She can smell her own hair burning, and she's covered with soot again. The dogs have already fled and the birds, getting the message at last, rise in griping, flapping twos and threes, scary against the night sky. By the time Karen's gotten a half dozen structures burning seriously, she's exhausted and the sky is dark. She supposes she might keep working by the light of the fires she's already started, but—

Not a moment too soon, she feels the familiar tug, the gentler tug that is TQ, now that Fuchsia's otherwise engaged. Can this be the end of it, please?

•

It takes longer than she thought. For some reason she assumed (too much TV, maybe?) that passing forward through time this time would take no time at all. Instead, there's a feeling like gridlock, the inertia of a doctor's waiting room, the eternal moment between when the landing gear comes *Thunk!* out of the wheelwell and the actual squeal of contact with the ground, as you remember reading somewhere that most plane crashes occur during takeoff and landing.

What are we waiting for? Karen wonders.

The in-flight movie, obviously. The trailer, the infomercial on the TV in your doctor's waiting room, radio commercials while you wait for the traffic to crawl. Coming Soon to a Theatre Near you:

An infant bundled in an army blanket lies on a drift of rot-blackened leaves in a clearing in the deep woods. She is cold and wet and hungry, but deeper than all of this, she is alone. A face she knows, the pale face of the child who bore her, drawn with an anxiety which makes her older than her thirteen years, floats between the infant's still focusing vision and the jagged, clawing shapes of November trees.

*Mama!* The small fists flail and the little mind cries out, though the words would not have formed in the questing, toothless mouth for nearly a year. *Mama!*

"I got no choice!" the infant's mother tells the unfeeling trees. "You hear me? I got no choice. It ain't me that's doing this, it's them. I can't help it. They made me. It's not my fault!"

What the infant cannot know is that the trees are in a churchyard, and in less than an hour the church bells will ring, summoning the congregation to Sunday services. The cold iron clanging of the bells will frighten the child, and she'll begin to cry, her cries summoning the curious until someone picks her up and takes her inside where it's warm.

Or so her mother tells herself as she turns away without looking back, trudging through the dead leaves toward the highway taking her—wherever. She was afraid to bring the child too near the church lest someone recognize her. Though she lives in the next county, there is still the fear that someone might connect her with this—this thing that has happened to her. Or so she tells herself.

She blocks the little voice in her head that tells her she may have lost track of the days and today might be Saturday, not Sunday, and by the time anyone happens upon the small body, it will be blue and still. She doesn't want to know these things and so will never know, just as she managed not to know about the child which seemed to grow inside her like some perverted inverse miracle until the day it was born.

She doesn't remember what her uncle did to her, though he'd been doing it since she was six. No one else in the family noticed, why should she? They think she simply ran away, if they think of her at all. She knows they no longer speak her name. She went missing just after school let out in June, so big around the middle that she wondered no one saw. No one did. No one ever noticed anything she did.

She'd hidden in her uncle's hunting cabin all summer and into the fall. It was off-season and no one came, and there were canned goods enough to hold her until she gave birth. No one went looking for her. When her uncle showed up at the start of deer season, he didn't seem at all surprised to see her or the newborn.

"You're gonna to have to get rid of it," he told her, though he made no move to do anything about it, and for the next couple of months they lived like a makeshift sort of backwoods family, with him stopping by once a week to bring cordwood and deer meat and fresh fruit. But as the weather got colder, he did, too.

"You're got to get rid of it. Your brothers are wanting to come up here with me Thanksgiving week. You've got to be gone by then."

She'd waited until he'd gone back into town that time, knowing he'd be away for the next few days. That was when she'd first hit the highway, yesterday afternoon, just as the sun was going down.

A few minutes from now, she would hit the highway again, thumbing a ride to anywhere that wasn't here. She will spend the rest of her foreshortened life convincing herself that her daughter was found in the churchyard and put up for adoption, where she had a chance to grow in one of those families she'd always heard about but never knew, a family where there was love.

Karen looks down at the pale infant against the dead leaves as if from very far away, and recognizes herself.

•

Too depressing. Channel surf. How's about an adventure flick?

South Africa, 1901: A white man's encampment on the edge of the veldt:

There is a war going on. The sound of rifle shot has echoed up and down the kloof all morning, and most of the farmers have sent their womenfolk and the children down to the village to wait out the fighting in the low hills. Andreas's wife, Rachel, had refused to leave.

"We don't know it's any safer from the English down there, husband," she'd announced stubbornly when the first shots, and what sounded like thunder but Andreas knew as cannon, had woken them even earlier than the sunrise that morning. "There's families have been shot in the towns, too. We stay together."

"You'll make me choose between the farm and my family!" Andreas had raged, but Rachel held fast. Cursing under his breath, Andreas had gone to clean the shotgun and hope the fighting passed them by.

Rachel had left the baby sleeping in her cradle and taken the two boys, one by either hand, out with her to feed the chickens. The two-year-old, Micah, clung to her skirts, his other hand jammed in his mouth as he sucked on his three middle fingers. Rhys was nearly five and independent with it.

"Don't go outside the yard!" his mother warned him, but Rhys seldom listened. He wanted to climb the fence and play by the stream the way he usually did, and didn't see what all the fuss was about.

"Those are rifles!" he announced when they heard the distant popping again, and his mother stood still as a gazelle, listening, while Micah whimpered and sucked harder on his fingers. "Papa told me!"

"Did Papa also tell you they can kill you if you don't listen to your mother and stay inside the kraal this day?"

The boy didn't answer, his cinnamon-brown eyes growing darker as he drew his brows down in a scowl. Unusually dark-haired for an Afrikaner, he didn't look like either of his siblings, and there were those in town who whispered that Andreas might not be his father.

Rachel shook the last of the feed out for the hens fluttering around her feet and pried Micah's hand loose from her skirt. "Come inside now!" she said to Rhys, who was still eyeing the fence as if he meant to bolt for it.

He looked as if he were about to protest but gave in and went with her instead.

Nevertheless, he *would* stand in the open doorway on this hot January day. The British sniper never even saw him. His target was a company of Afrikaners pinned down in a clump of rock a full thirty kilometers to the left of the farmhouse, but the bullet ricocheted and caught young Rhys in the throat, felling him without pain or a chance to cry out. He was dead before he hit the doorsill.

•

*Raymond!* Karen thinks, reaching futile fingers out to him as the (vision, memory, might-have-been?) flies past.

And Now for Something Completely Different:

The millennium, or thereabouts. Interior: Hospital. Semi-private room, night. One bed is vacant. A short, fat woman in her seventies sits propped up in the other, a glucose IV resembling nothing so much as a jellyfish tendril attached to the back of one wrist. Her frizzy hair is strictly *Bride of Frankenstein,* crowning the face of a troll. Her complexion is the color and texture of suet; her downturned slit of a mouth has been drawn outside the lines with a matte red lipstick that bleeds over into the cracks around her lips and ends up on her teeth. She is wearing a quilted nylon robe in an improbable shade of turquoise; her short neck disappears into the collar like that of some alien brood hen. There is dandruff on her shoulders.

A pair of half-glasses, the cheap nonprescription kind bought off the rack in a pharmacy, sits crookedly on the tip of her pointy nose. Her gnarled little hands move endlessly on the surface of the blanket, alternately twisting her diamond-solitaire engagement ring around and around and around on her finger and scribbling at a legal pad with a blunt-pointed pencil.

*(I'll get you, my Pretty, and your little dog, too!)*

She scribbles furiously for a moment, her letters overlarge and sprawling and full of exaggerated loops, then stabs the pencil against the bright yellow surface of the pad for emphasis *(So there!),* snapping the point off in her fury. She shoves the pad toward a shadowy figure seated in a plastic bucket chair just beyond the aura of the track lighting above the bed. The figure takes the missive without making contact with the woman and reads in a low voice:

" 'When Am I'm Going Home?' When '*am I'm*'?" Karen repeats, holding the pad out for the old woman to take it back. "Capital letters in the middle of a sentence? Come on, Ma, you can do better than that. Start with a fresh piece of paper and write it correctly: 'When am I going home?' "

Once upon a time, when Karen was in grade school, her mother read all of her English compositions, marking over them in pen. Having already tried and failed to find fault with the spelling, grammar, punctuation—even as a child Karen excelled in these—she made stylistic corrections according to her own lights ("Don't ever end a sentence with a preposition! You know you're not supposed to!") just because she could. The goal was not to instruct but to thwart, to stifle, to humiliate. Too naive to make two copies and submit her original, Karen had meticulously recopied everything. The ideas and the execution, she reasoned, were still hers. When she got straight A's, her mother took the credit. Karen knew a few editors like that. But now it was payback time.

The old woman screws up her mouth, clamping her lips together more tightly than ever, trembling with rage. She opens her mouth to deliver yet another rant out of half a century's practice and—

Nothing. She grunts and pants and gapes like a goldfish, red-faced, the veins ropy and pulsating in her forehead, but there is no sound.

Gloria Rohmer, it seems, has had a stroke. Or, as the medical community prefers to refer to it, "a transient ischemic accident." Part of her brain, assaulted like all the cells in her body by a passion for eclairs and bacon and an inability to let go of the salt shaker, has shut down in protest. According to her doctors, there was no loss of consciousness, memory, or cognitive function, no visual or auditory disturbances, no bowel or bladder dysfunction. The temporary paralysis in her legs has been responding well to physical therapy. There are, in short, no long-term sequelae, except for one little thing. The TIA went directly to the most overused part of her brain, the speech centers, and destroyed them.

Speech therapy has been weighed but, given the patient's age, recalcitrance, and the extent of the damage (dozens of little whiteouts on the CAT scan—My God, it's full of stars! Karen thought when she saw them), ruled out. Gloria Rohmer will never speak again.

At first she refuses to take the legal pad from her daughter, folding her arms tightly across her chest, her entire posture saying: So there! Karen regards her imperviously. Gloria balls her little fists and pounds them on the bedclothes, huffing and snorting and mouthing words in a language only she understands. Karen offers her the writing pad a second time.

"And to answer your question," she continues, as Gloria snatches the pad from her and starts writing again (the broken-pointed pencil thwarts her; she jams it against the page until the paper tears) "the neurologist says you can go home as soon as you stop trying to rip the IV out of your arm and act like a responsible adult."

She braces, able to map the tantrum as it happens. First her mother throws the pencil at her. It misses, landing in a far corner of the room. Karen doesn't even flinch. Next the legal pad comes frisbeeing toward her, its trajectory slowed by the inertial flapping of the pages. Still, it strikes her a glancing blow on the chest before splatting on the floor at her feet.

"Are you finished?"

Karen doesn't expect an answer. She is already planning how she can use this in her novel. (What if Gret's mother had been a Null, jealous of her daughter's Telesper traits, and determined to break her, prevent her from fulfilling her destiny? Interesting potential for flashbacks, though she can hear her editor doing his It-doesn't-advance-the-narrative chant.) Later. She snaps back to the present as a half-filled plastic water glass strikes the foot of the bed, soaking the blanket and the sheets. Gloria is grabbing at everything on the nightstand—a box of tissues, one of her ubiquitous Harold Robbins paperbacks (Interesting, Karen notes that, like L. Ron Hubbard and, more recently Asimov, Robbins has written more after his death than before) that slams spine-first against the wall near Karen's head.

Karen watches as if from a great distance. Déjà vu all over again. When she was a kid, she would duck and cover as her mother threw anything and everything that came to hand, waiting out the firestorm, which would have been comical (her mother's aim was bad even then) except that it invariably preceded the hair pulling and the fists and the little pointy shoes. And the rant, the endless rant.

There would be no more rant, not ever.

Karen watches Gloria go for the water pitcher. It's almost full, and too much for her, even two-handed. The old woman is hyperventilating and tears course down the desert of her cheeks. The pitcher trembles violently in her hands. Karen gets up from the chair at last and relieves her of it, eluding the clutching fingers, setting the pitcher back on the nightstand. She leaves everything else where it's fallen. Gloria continues to clutch at the air as Karen heads toward the door. Her mouth forms two soundless words:

*Help me!*

Karen glances at her watch.

"Oh, I will, Ma, believe me. Your doctors say you're healthy as a horse. You could live to be a hundred. I sincerely hope you do. I'm going to help you in ways you can't possibly imagine. We have *so* much to talk about. . . ."

The room breaks up like glass shards all around her.

•

*Dammit, she wasn't supposed to see that!*

*She wasn't supposed to see any of them—not the baby or the boy or the old woman. So what? Nothing we can do about it now, except maybe be grateful those are the only variations she saw. . . .*

•

It wasn't a matter of waking from a dream this time. Karen was simply *there*. Returned to the moment before she'd gone to her quiet place to speak to the S.oteri and find out what went wrong. This suggested that everything which followed might have been a dream, but she was no longer so easily fooled.

Returned, she is melancholy, almost afraid to move. Everything is just as she left it, because she never left it. The fridge is empty, the laundry hamper full. The little stack of manuscript pages is entirely too thin given how much time she's spent on it. Her deadline ticks softly in the background, ominous. Tomorrow at 8:30 A.M. she will be back in the doctors' office, headset on, eyes fixed on the screen, ears straining to hear the words in and around the head neurologist's smoker's cough. What fun. Better to be Gret the Telesper, whose thoughts can power a spaceship. At least now Gret's pining after Darymon made sense again.

*Raymond . . .*

What she ought to do at least is check her Rolodex to see whose names are there and whose are not. She is afraid to do even that much. Too much knowledge has been given her lately. She's not sure how much more she can take. That last bit in Avaricum has left her with a stink of blood and smoke in the back of her throat that may never go away. Her hands tingle and, like Lady Macbeth, she feels compelled to wash them.

The phone rings. Karen jumps. It's been a few millennia since she's had to deal with such sounds. The number on the caller ID solves one mystery, at least. Virtually paralyzed, Karen waits for the voice on the answering machine.

"Hi, Karen, it's Raymond. I know it's been a small eternity since I called you last—or last called you, I guess I should say—" He's stammering again, she notes automatically. Meaning he's had to rehearse a statement as simple as that. Meaning that even after all this time he's still uncertain of his feelings for her. Or perhaps too certain of them, and at least one of them is guilt. "—but things have just been so busy, I—"

The machine cuts him off. It does that to him and to no one else. Karen waits to see if he'll call back. He doesn't. And if he'd had time to finish his thought? Or if she'd intercepted the call? What would they have talked about?

Oh, doubtless he'd regale her with tales of his wonderful middle-class life, the house, the two cars (no more truck?), the DVD player, the gas grill, the wide-screen TV, the best computer, all the Right Stuff. It wasn't what he'd aspired to when Karen knew him, if she ever truly had. Laments about the job that made all the Stuff possible; so what else was new? Maybe a hint at how empty the house was now that Angelica was away at college. Then the questions would start.

"So what are you up to these days? I see you're still in New York. Didn't you talk about moving on someday? And how's your sex life? Are you at least dating again? You know, you really shouldn't just sit around the house for the rest of your life. You've got to get out more, meet new people. . . ."

. . . so you'll stop thinking about the old ones. Thank you, Mr. Diplomat. They'd had the conversation before; Karen had always dreaded it. Raymond never seemed to grasp that, having walked out of her life, he had no right to ask her any of this. She'd fielded his inquiries and waited for the next call. In between she'd write to him, innocuous chatty letters that he could have easily read aloud to his wife. She wanted her end of this documented as much as he wanted his to vanish on the airwaves without a trace. Would she write to him this time?

*"Sitting around the house," indeed! If he had any idea where I've been and what doing, he'd be livid with envy. He gets off on that kind of thing. . . .*

As the minutes tick by and it becomes clear he's not going to brave the Answering Machine from Hell a second time, Karen finds herself inexplicably giggling. Then she checks her pulse.

Usually, the mere sound of his voice sends her heartrate skyrocketing. This time, for the first time since he stalked out of her life, it doesn't. Is it simply that she has no adrenaline left, or is it something else?

Never mind. He's back. She's done what she set out to do. Why isn't she turning cartwheels? Instead, she reaches for the Rolodex, even as it occurs to her what a strange relationship this is.

*Strange? Don't tell me from "strange," Kemosabe, not after where I've been and what I've done!* Her voice, even in her mind, is shrill. She flips through the Rolodex quickly, before she loses her nerve, avoiding the alternate thought: *Relationship? What "relationship"?*

She goes through the Rolodex twice, then checks the B's a third time. There is no card for Anna Bower.

No! Karen thinks. Don't do this to me now! It isn't fair.

She checks every other possible source—the address file on her computer, e-mail addresses, the stray bits of paper in the drawer of the phone table. Nothing.

"But—" she starts to say, then stops. What is she going to say, and to whom? *Hey, look, I saved Anna's life even before I went back and made Fuchsia change Aoife's fate, which meant Conchobar survived, which meant Raymond's timeline was restored or so I hoped, and that phone call just now proves it, so what's the deal? What happened to Anna, huh?*

Stops herself because the answer is: Any one of an indeterminate number of things. Like Conchobar's having a few million other descendants in addition to Raymond, any one of whom might have crossed the time line of any one of Anna's ancestors and killed someone, let someone live, had a child with someone or not, died in a war, a plague, a fall down the stairs, whatever, and changed all the subsequent time lines. Or hadn't you thought of that when you went barreling back through the ages in search of a local hero named Ryalbran who just happened to resemble someone you knew in your own time? And has it occurred to you how ironic it is that Ryalbran had nothing to do with the outcome after all? And did you think Raymond would come back to you just because you saved his existence, when he never even knew that his existence was in jeopardy?

"I—" Karen starts to say.

*Um, Karen—?*

It's a good thing she's interrupted just then, because there was no way in hell she'd have been able to finish that sentence.

"What?!"

*It's going to have to wait a while. We need you to do something else for us first.*

•

Of course they do. For a species with such a sketchy concept of time, S.oteri are damn insistent when they want something.

Karen, it seems, has been called as a character witness at Fuchsia's, for want of a better term, trial. New York City Housing Court *and* an interspecies breach-of-contract case all in the same year? Talk about unfair . . .

Where is she? The scene is strictly blue screen all the way around, and she's standing out over nothing. Not nothing as in standing in midair looking down into a chasm or like that, but nothing as in *nothing,* okay? Above her (with apologies to John Lennon) not even sky. Just a pretty blue nothing.

"Hey!"

She can hear, at least, though the sound of her own voice is slightly muffled, and there's a hint of bounceback, as there might be on a foggy day. But that's not fog out there. She stretches her arms out and touches nothing, reaches down as if to touch the palms of her hands to the floor (she still can), and though her feet are planted solidly, her hands touch nothing. Even when she reaches under her feet to determine what she's standing on, she finds nothing. It's quite a trick, really.

"Is anybody out there?"

And since apparently no one intends to answer her, she may as well keep exploring. She notes the atmosphere is just a tad chilly for her in her T-shirt and jeans which, for Karen, who rarely feels the cold to notice, it means it would probably be downright uncomfortable for anyone else. There is neither taste nor smell to the air she's breathing, and it isn't damp because she doesn't see her breath on the exhale.

Does that cover the five senses? She walks around a little but can't really tell how far she's gone or in what direction because there are no landmarks to help her get her bearings. She thinks of all those horror stories about people getting lost in blizzards and decides it might be better to stop moving. When she tries to sit, she starts spinning on own her axis as if she'd tried sitting down under water. It's disorienting.

No, come on, admit it: It's downright terrifying. She struggles to rebalance and stand straight again but can't remember where she left that solid surface she was standing on. She flounders, thrashing like a nonswimmer in deep water. This only makes it worse. There isn't even the give of water to hold onto. She lets out a yell, hugs herself, rolls into a little ball, but the ball starts spinning. Maybe if she shuts her eyes she won't panic. She can hear her own breathing, her own heart, the opening and closing of every valve, the rush of blood behind her eyes—

{Karen?} Tertium Quid speaks. She knows it's the Third Thing without knowing how she knows. She rolls up tighter and doesn't answer, afraid her voice will be snatched away in the vortex she's creating. She feels rather than hears the Third Thing inhale and start again. {Karen, what's wrong?}

"I . . . can't . . . see . . . anything!" she manages to gasp. What she hears next is genuine surprise.

{You can't?. . . . We hadn't anticipated—bear with us for one moment longer. . . . }

Well, at least she's finally bumped up against a species with a concept of time, Karen thinks as her world stops spinning and her own internal noises recede. She stretches out her arms and legs and finds herself upright, standing on a beach somewhere. Hasn't she seen this movie already? Any minute now, Jodie Foster will walk out of that clump of palm trees and stand beside her. . . .

{It was the best we could do on such short notice} Tertium Quid explains wryly. {Especially since we know how terrified you are of forests.}

She is. She always has been and never knew why. She thinks of the infant in the churchyard. What does it mean?

{It means Fuchsia lost control. We have decided hir kind isn't ready for what we gave hir.}

"You've already decided? Then what do you need me for?"

She's addressing the strange green-tinged sun that is either rising or setting out over the ocean whose edge she's standing on, shading her eyes against it, noticing how, incongruously, it tinges the too-blue ocean a kind of orangey color. If she were a scientist, or even a good s/f writer, she'd be able to explain what it was that TQ was doing to her optic nerves to get the colors not-quite-right. But she's just Karen. She never saw the need to reinvent the sun just to tell a good story.

All her other senses seem to work. The wet sand is cool between her toes, the sun warm on her face, but winter-warm, not you-didn't-bring-your-sunblock-and-boy-are-*you*-going-to-be-sorry warm. The air tastes of sun and salt; the sough of surf tickles her ears. She's amazed that after all this she feels hungry again. She could use something chocolate, a piece of fruit, some of Kit's bread or Sequanna's oatmeal, anything, but it can wait.

The surface of the ocean, there in the center where the orange hues are deepest, begins to roil and patter, as if simultaneously beset by heavy swells and incongruously gentle rain. A something rises out of it, long and tall and attenuated at its stellate ends, rather ponderous in the center, its color indistinct against the greenish sunlight, but darkish and denser than the gravity of the place might suggest. The Third Thing? One of them, all of them?

{What do we need you for? To do what you have always done. Bear witness.}

Karen thinks about this. "That doesn't seem to be enough somehow. . . . But, all right. You saw everything I saw. Maybe felt everything I felt, too. What more do you want me to say? Fuchsia fucked up. But I don't think s/he meant to. It was a new experience for hir, that's all. It doesn't mean another of the S.oteri might not—"

{We're not asking you to pass judgment.}

"Fine!" Karen is getting tired of staring into that sun. She's convinced TQ has situated itself this way on purpose. "Then let me go home. I've got a book to write."

{Temper? Aren't you afraid of us?}

"You know whether I'm afraid or not. Just once I'd like to meet a species that isn't superior to humans! What are you? What's the fascination with all of this—humans, S.oteri? Explain it to me, and maybe I can understand."

{You too are not ready. . . .}

"If I can ask the question, I'm ready for the answer!" Karen shouts. She earns the expected silence, then considers her next words carefully. "I think there's a strong possibility you're actually just an aspect of the S.oteri. A dimension of them even they're not aware of."

{An interesting supposition.} TQ begins to lower itself into the waves. {Thank you for your time. . . .}

"Yo!" Karen, true New Yorker, yells and waves her arms at it. "That's it? What about the trial?"

{The trial is over. You have acquitted yourself well.}

*Glub.* It slides back into the sea even as Karen the wordsmith considers the several meanings of acquittal. Fuchsia apparently wasn't the only one on trial.

# TWENTY

Okay, the good news is, Fuchsia won't be playing at telekinesis again any time soon. Karen can just hear Gray kvetching at hir as the Mind goes off into the metaphoric sunset:

*TQ was going to give all of us the power, yew Noh. You were the test case. But having watched you run amok, they've called off the deal. Further negotiations could take eons. Here's another fine mess you've gotten us into. . . .*

Over and out and Gee, guise, don't bother saying goodbye. Will Karen ever hear from them again? Does she want to?

Take stock: Raymond is back where he belongs, and Anna is . . . unaccounted for so far, with no answers forthcoming from the S.oteri. What else has changed?

More to the point, what hasn't? Start with the deadline on her manuscript. Back to work, in between fielding phone calls.

"Hi, Ma." Guess the vision of her having had a stroke was just that, huh? As usual, her mother talks and Karen listens. Déjà vu all over again.

". . . and the cat did the funniest thing this morning, but I'll tell you about that in a minute, because first I wanted to tell you I ran into Mary or Maryann Somebody that you went to high school with. You know the one I mean; I can't think of her maiden name. But she told me to ask you when are you going to write another 'real' book. And I also wanted to tell you before I forgot that there's an apartment for sale in our building. It's a one-bedroom on the first floor, and they're only asking fifty thousand for it."

This is followed by a few seconds of palpable silence. For a moment Karen wonders if the phone's gone dead.

"Hello?" she says.

"Did you hear what I just said? I said there's an apartment for sale in the building for only fifty thousand. You're not going to get a bargain like that anywhere else in this neighborhood. . . ."

Karen's parents live in what is considered a luxury co-op, really an old, prewar, multiunit building overlooking a patch of the Narrows (well, at least the units on the upper floors in the front of the building do, if you squint beyond the highway and the sewage treatment plant) gussied up and privatized and filled with elderly people congratulating themselves for having bought into a building with a tenants' committee to keep the undesirables out. Why is her mother telling her this? Gloria Rohmer's factoids always have teeth, hidden snares, and poison pockets. Tread carefully.

"Gee, Ma," Karen says, thinking quickly. "I don't know anyone with that kind of money who's looking for an apartment. I don't know anyone with that kind of money, period, but—"

"I meant you."

Oho! Now we're getting somewhere. "Me? I don't have fifty grand, and even if I did I—"

"You can get a mortgage," her mother says flatly.

"No, I can't. I've only had this job for six months. Before that I was self-employed for twenty years. I can't even cosign a mortgage. I—"

"There's a woman across the hall who's just a secretary like you. She got a mortgage."

Karen waits. The only answer her mother wants is "Yes" and there'll be ski lodges in Hell before she hears it. Until she does, she'll just keep talking.

". . . because you're not going to get a bargain like that again in a hurry, because there was only a widower living alone, and he just passed away. He was in a wheelchair for the past six years, and I don't think the place was cleaned since his wife died. It's in the back of the building on the first floor, which means you get the noise from the park at night, but—"

Wow, great salesmanship, Ma! Karen wants to say, but what's the point? She knows where this is leading, has already made the not-quite-quantum leap. She is supposed to buy the apartment (with what? A halfway intelligent person would have taken the checkbook out by now and offered to at least lend her the money, but Karen's mother has never had a carrot, only the stick), squeeze into it with Matt and all their stuff (she apparently to sleep on the couch while he gets the bedroom, or is it the other way around—an incentive to him to move on that much faster?). Then picture it: There is Karen, rattling around alone in the same building as her parents, when the calls begin:

"What are you doing down there all by yourself? ("You have no friends and you never will and no man will ever want you. . . .") Come upstairs and have supper with us while I tell you about the funny thing the cat did today. . . ."

"Your mother and I were wondering if you'd like to have the car. My knees are so stiff I can't drive any more, and if you just promise to drive us to church and take your mother shopping once or twice or three times a week, we'd be willing to sell it to you for the book value. . . ."

"And it makes no sense for you to be down there by yourself now that Matt's out of the house. You don't need that much space. We've got the spare room; we can move the fish tank and the sewing machine out of there, though your father's going to want to keep the desk. You can sell your place and move in with us and quit your job. As long as you help me with the laundry and the shopping and the cooking and the cleaning and take me to the doctor and to church and give me my medicine and bathe me and—just because we've ignored you for more than thirty years doesn't mean you have to get nasty about it. . . . Hello?"

Imaginary Karen will take her rightful place in the scheme of things, and all will be forgiven. Not in this universe.

•

"How long do you think you can continue to postpone the inevitable?" Govannon asks her.

"What are you talking about? What she wants is never going to happen. All that's inevitable is that I'm going to hold her at arm's length until she dies."

"Really?"

Now there's an interesting phenomenon. When did she start talking with Govannon in her head? Karen considers this.

Once upon a time, actually from adolescence until quite recently, she'd had hypothetical conversations with Benn, a fictional alien from a sixties space opera. Once she'd met the actor who played Benn, it had changed everything. Now Govannon, a real person out of a past she'd recently lived as if it were her own, had begun insinuating himself into her thoughts to the point where she was thinking aloud. Was this an improvement?

No point in asking questions to which there are no answers. Better to take advantage of what is without examining it too closely. Govannon's presence, real or imagined, is comforting.

"Yes, really. She's got nothing to offer me and, more to the point, nothing to threaten me with. Until now, she was a nuisance. After what I've been through lately, the places I've been, and the things I've seen, she's not even on the map."

"If you say so. . . ."

She wants to stop what she's doing and rest her head in the hollow of his shoulder, feel his arms around her, but all she has of him is his voice and the mind behind it. If she tries very hard, Karen thinks she might be able to see the occasional Cheshire-cat flash of his smile. She no longer questions her sanity. What is, is.

"May we talk about this later, please? I have a book to write."

"And when you've finished? What happens then?"

Karen doesn't even have to think about it. "I'll crash. I always do. I'll curl up in a little ball and not talk to anyone for a few days, a week at most. Sleep more than I need to. Then uncurl and start thinking about the next project. If there is a next project. In today's market—"

"And why do you suppose you 'crash'?" Govannon's tone is gentle, genuine inquiry.

"Because I'm never sure if I'll be able to write again. I mean, intellectually I know I can, but emotionally . . . and no matter how often it happens I never seem to learn from it. I have to go through the same crash every time."

"And what else?"

"What do you mean, 'and what else'? Do I have to tell you my writing is usually more interesting, more *real* than my so-called life? At least it was until this current spate of adventures. Between you, me, and the lamppost, as me Irish grandfather used to say, I'm looking forward to a long stretch of uneventfulness from hereon."

"And what else?"

Karen stops pretending that what's on her screen is more interesting than the conversation. Truth to tell, her heart's no longer in the tale of Gret and Darymon, hasn't been for a long time. Now that she no longer feels more than a little wistful might-have-been for Raymond (and when did that happen, exactly?) the story of his alter ego and hers has become a bit of a struggle. Her agent had warned her not to make it autobiographical. Well, it was about a thousand years too late now:

•

". . . can't tell you how unsettling it was to sit in that cave staring at those silent little pulsing blobs while the rest of you were all but coming in your pants with excitement. . . ." Darymon muttered, pouring himself a skotj from a real bottle set into a wall sconce. From the level of it, he'd been savoring it in small sips for the entire voyage. "Unsettling, hell. It was positively creepy. Only the glow on Jeska's face kept me from running out of the cave screaming."

They were back on the ship following their first encounter with the New Species. None of it had gone as smoothly as they'd hoped. First there was the awkward moment when one of the humans mistook a patch of fungus for an S.oteri. There followed an untoward amount of bumping into each other before the team managed to settle themselves comfortably on the cave floor without accidentally sitting on someone. They'd barely gotten past the preliminary exchange of greetings before Petra noticed a funny readout on her oxygen level and had to go back, retracing the footprints in the talcumlike sand until she reached the landing site, only to find the ship wasn't there. An emergency hail told her that Carm, the chief 'kinetic, had moved the ship, he said, because the ion fluctuations had had him worried and he'd tried to find a more sheltered spot, with every intention of leaving a marker to tell the landing party where they were, but there hadn't been time. He said.

All the while they'd been sitting cross-legged on the cave floor communing with the S.oteri, a prickling at the back of Gret's neck told her something was fishy back at the ship. She'd tried to Send as much to Jeska, but the girl was in a kind of rapture with the Gray One, and there was no distracting her. Finally, Gret had had to speak aloud to Darymon.

"Something's wrong with the ship" was how she put it, hoping neither her own kind nor the S.oteri would read between the lines to what she was really saying, which was that a shipful of unsupervised 'kinetics, who'd already threatened mutiny on the way here, was a formula for disaster. Darymon, with the one-track mind of a Null, was able to read her loud and clear.

"Gotcha. People, we have to go back now. We can continue this tomorrow."

They'd made their apologies to the S.oteri and shuffled back the way they came.

Once everyone was back on board, the landing party's paranoia about being marooned by the 'kinetics for whatever reasons seemed just that—paranoia. Still, there were too many half-finished conversations left dangling in the corridors; to Gret it seemed like walking through an abandoned house, brushing the cobwebs aside. She'd gone behind the Door to request a private conversation with Darymon and share her concerns.

"Me, too," he admitted, dropping his guard and letting her see just how uncertain he was for the first time since he'd told her he loved her five years before. "I . . . I don't know how long I can hold them together, Gret. They've got nothing but contempt for a Null like me. And there aren't enough of you—" (he meant the 'espers who, ever since the threat of a strike, he'd assumed were all on his side) "—to balance them if they decide to treat with the S.oteri on their own."

"They won't," she tried to assure him. "They can't. 'Kinetics have no diplomatic skills. They move things, not minds."

It was an old prejudice between the two schools, though clearly Darymon had never heard it put quite that way before. He laughed.

"Besides," Gret reminded him, "the S.oteri themselves have said they'll treat with all of us or none of us. That includes you."

"What if they change their Mind?"

"They won't."

"You're so sure of that."

"Yes. Because Jeska's the key, and I'm sure of Jeska. Aren't you?"

"I . . ." He faltered, studying the play of light in the skotj glass to keep his voice steady. "I'm sure of her inasmuch as she's my daughter, and I know she's gifted. But it's a gift I can't begin to understand."

This was the moment, Gret thought, to suggest it to him.

"You could, if you wanted to."

He put the glass down with a too-emphatic thump. "Not that again!"

"Yes." She waited.

"I don't *want* to be an 'esper, Gret! Even if I thought it was possible for you or anyone to Open me, which I don't, I don't want it. I'm afraid."

"Are you?" Her tone said *You protest too much.* He almost seemed to hear it.

He hesitated. "It's been a long time since I was a virgin. All right. Tell me—start with today, in the cave. Meeting them for the first time, talking to them. What was it like?"

She started to think it to him, stopped herself, started to speak but found no words. "It was . . . *like* nothing else. It was what it was. I can't—"

"Don't do this to me!"

"Darymon—" His name was the hardest word she knew. "I'd have to show you. . . ."

•

The novel wrote itself whenever she wasn't at the keyboard which, with the day job, was most of the time. Having so much of her time and energy sucked up by other things took away a great deal of the joy of process. Analogies about fast food versus gourmet meals bounced around in her head. As if that weren't bad enough, whatever free time she had was spent in an almost fanatical search for information that had nothing to do with her novel.

"Your friend Jacob could be a former monk," Karen Jenner told her when she asked. "It wasn't uncommon for monks and nuns and even priests to simply walk away from their vows, especially those who'd been promised to the church in infancy by overzealous families. If you gave him that as backstory, it would explain how he knew the brewer's skills as well as herb lore. Beyond that, it would be unusual for a layman to be a brewer."

"I see," Karen said thoughtfully. She'd given Jenner what she knew about Jacob as if he were a potential character for a novel. No point in telling the truth.

"You might want to watch out, though, that he and Elspeth aren't burned as witches for their combined knowledge," Jenner went on. "As for pre-Christian Celts, they're really not my area, but there are several good research texts I can recommend. Just off the cuff, though, it seems to me that to kill forty thousand with the weapons of the time you'd need several days, not one. And there should have been more hardship evident from the siege—trade brought to a standstill, real food shortages, with children and old people dying, that kind of thing. Then again, I could be wrong. The only chroniclers of Avaricum were Suetonius, who wasn't there but heard about it later, and Caesar himself. You can believe his version as readily as you'd believe Nixon on Cambodia. . . ."

•

Wasn't it interesting, Karen thought, how often the experts disagreed on what might have happened, back when no one with a stylus or a quill pen, much less a camcorder, had the presence of mind to record things as they were happening? She wants so much to tell Jenner what she knows—that in fact the Battle of Avaricum took only a day and a night into the next day, that it was possible for a layman and two of his wives to be both brewers and herbalists without being killed for it. Then again, how does she know Jacob *hadn't* been a monk? There'd been no time to ask. Yet, why doesn't she say something? It's not as if her telling someone now is going to change the past.

Is it? She's getting as confused as Fuchsia.

Enough. Real life is messy. Fiction conforms to the outline. Sometimes.

•

"I want you to know I'm only doing this for Jeska," Darymon pointed out as Gret prepared herself.

*Shut up!* she thought, her concentration broken. Did she only imagine she saw him flinch as if she'd said it aloud?

•

". . . In other news, the Smithsonian Institute announced today that a heretofore relatively unknown art historian named Anna Bower has been instrumental in recovering several paintings stolen by the Nazis in World War II and presumed lost forever. . . ."

Matt has left the TV on in his room and disappeared on some errand or other. Ordinarily, Karen can't hear it at her end of the house. She is on her way to the kitchen when the name catches her ear, and she finds herself drawn toward the screen. It's a common enough sounding name, she tells herself as the CNN announcer continues his spiel and the camera cuts away to a kind of hurriedly organized press conference in one of those anonymous windowless rooms every institution seems to have set aside for such matters, where cameras whir and buzz and click, their focus a tiny dark-haired woman with deep, dark eyes, wearing an expression of vague bewilderment, standing beside what, to Karen's minimally schooled eye, could be a Raphael or a Giotto or a John Doe—well, something Renaissance-ish, anyway—that looks as if it's spent the past five decades in someone's root cellar.

Which, from the little she knows about World War II and stolen art (bad movies starring Paul Scofield as a Nazi general notwithstanding), it probably was. But it's not the painting Karen's interested in, it's Anna.

Because it *is* Anna, no question about it, the Anna Bower she knew in an alternate universe, and suddenly it explains everything, sort of. It at least explains why she and Anna wouldn't know each other in this universe. Art historians who work for the Smithsonian don't exactly run with the same crowd as midlist s/f writers.

The news coverage is over before Karen can do more than get a glimpse of her once-upon-a-time friend. She decides to wait for the story to come around again on the half-hour. She will watch it five times altogether over the next three hours (during one segment it's deleted for a report on a riot during a performance-art performance in Manhattan amid the usual controversy over NEA funding). Each time she learns a little bit more.

Take a, perhaps, hour-long press conference held most likely sometime around noon today, and edit the Q&A down to a one-minute news story which is the same, only different, each time it's aired—or not aired—several hours later. The reporter's voiceover interprets Anna's answers for the audience at home:

". . . said that the paintings were found in the subbasement of a middle school in the small German town of Salzheim, where they had apparently remained undisturbed, hidden behind a pile of old lumber in a boiler room, since before the war. . . .

"When asked how she and her team knew where the paintings might be found, Ms. Bower was understandably evasive. 'This is serious business,' she told us. 'Some of these works are priceless. People have died. My sources help me only because they know I will never reveal them. . . .' "

It's quite a different Anna after all, Karen thinks as she watches, mesmerized. Instead of a desk jockey, a Federal flunkey, here was a confident, skilled professional, one of the top ten percent in her field, a woman who knew who she was and what she was about. It was enough to make one wonder what Raymond might become if he ever gained similar insight.

Karen has had some interesting thoughts about Raymond lately. Raymond had loomed on her event horizon at a time when she'd been surprisingly vulnerable. One would think that someone with a *New York Times*-reviewed novel on the stands and a guest appearance at an s/f con would be anything but vulnerable, but she had been. And the first thing she'd noticed about Raymond (well, the second thing she'd noticed, after his voice and his face and his body and his—) was the glimmer-glint of S.oteri in his eyes.

Now, having just spent several months working with three actors who were also visited by S.oteri—one of whom "got it," one of whom who never would, and a third who, depending on where in her post-menopausal mood swings she was on a given day, wavered somewhere in between—you'd think she'd have known better, wouldn't you? Would have known that sometimes having the S.oteri in your eyes was simply not enough. You had to *do* something about it.

Anna Bower had no S.oteri in her deep, dark eyes, at least none that Karen had seen on that life-altering evening which—here, now—had apparently never taken place. There had been instead a terrible sadness, which might only be watching her mother die in a bomb shelter when she was four years old, or—

As the *CNN Sports Report* rattled through the day's football scores, Karen considered this. Would this universe's version of Anna's life contain any mention of the special little factoid about her origins? Since they didn't know each other, there was only one way to find out. . . .

•

Karen became obsessed with the story over the next several days, coming home with bundles of newspapers, scanning the newly downloaded Internet access at the office, reading the same predigested wire service report again and again, varied with the occasional attempt to tie the Stolen Art story in with Nazis and the Swiss Bank Accounts. Gradually, though, the column inches shrank, the TV news moved on to something else; within forty-eight hours the story was no longer news. It wasn't until *Newsweek* and *Time* carried it a week later that two interesting details came to light. One was that Anna's husband, a D.C.-based psychotherapist, was a Holocaust survivor. The other was that Anna herself was a German orphan adopted by an American family just after the war.

There was, however, no mention of her being rescued from the bombing by a nameless stranger. Karen was strangely relieved.

Then, there was *Nightline*.

"Tonight's story: Stolen art and some of the people who recover it after decades of oblivion. Between 1933 and 1945, the Nazis looted the museums and private collections of Europe, taking anything that was not nailed down. Before the war had officially ended, Soviets and Americans alike made off with the very same paintings and sculptures, unearthing them from salt mines and hidden bunkers, shipping them back to their own countries and, more often than not, into their own private collections."

It has been a long time since Karen's watched *Nightline*. Ted Koppel's voice and delivery are as Just Right as ever. She listens, rapt.

"Over the intervening decades, only a fraction of those paintings and sculptures has been recovered and restored to the original owners or their heirs, by those like our guest tonight who, with an almost Simon Wiesenthal-like obsessiveness, have turned their very considerable skills toward tracking down the missing. We'll have that story next, when we return. . . ."

Karen finds herself gripping the arms of the chair as the car commercials zoom by, her thoughts awhirl with possibility. She can just see herself calling the Smithsonian and asking to be put through to Anna Bower. "Hi, you don't know me, but I'm actually the woman who rescued you when the ceiling of the bakery collapsed in '45. You were with your mother, and when the bomb hit, you—yes, I know I don't sound old enough to have—in fact, I'm actually a few years younger than you, but I can explain—Hello?"

The car commercials are over. Ted Koppel has returned.

"Our first guest tonight began her career as an apprentice art restorer in a Georgetown antique shop when her children were small, doing graduate work in art history at night. In the past twenty years she has built herself a reputation as a maverick researcher, an expert at spotting fakes, someone who, apparently, has never heard the words 'It can't be done.' Anna Bower, welcome."

"Thank you, Ted."

The voice is the same; the face in the studio close-up is the same;

the centered sense of self is the same, only everything else is different. Karen wonders why she didn't have the presence of mind to tape this. For what? she wonders in the next thought. This is going to be more about the recovered paintings and not about Anna at all.

The camera is on Koppel again. "With Anna is her husband of thirty years, Dr. Jacob Bower, a noted Washington area psychotherapist and, until recently, an invisible force behind the search. I'm almost wondering, Dr. Bower, if we're doing you a disservice by putting you on camera. Your days of going undercover, at least in this country, are now over."

"Not necessarily, Ted." The voice catches Karen's attention even as the camera highlights the too-familiar face. Dr. Bower is now putting on a phony German accent. "Ve haf many possible disguises, you know!"

Dr. Jacob Bower is a distinguished-looking white-haired man of about seventy. He sits beside but slightly behind his wife in the Washington studio, as if to let her have the greater part of the glory. His very blue eyes look confidently into the camera, into Karen's heart.

Well, she thinks, strangely numb to it all, at least now she knows what has become of Govannon in her time.

Wait a minute. No, impossible!

How can he be two people in the same era? He'd have been born while Timothy's friend Johann was in his prime. Karen is barely listening as the three people on her screen play Talking Heads. She is thinking in several realities at once.

". . . and I believe the windows of your hotel room in Prague were shot out at one point," Koppel is saying.

"Yes." Jacob Bower nods, the ghost of a smile playing beneath his mustache.

". . . You were detained for several days at the Yugoslav border after your passports were confiscated—"

Anna says, almost brightly: "That's right."

". . . I could go on, but the question is: Why? Why not stay home and clean the cobwebs off the Whistlers in the National Gallery? Why put yourselves at risk this way?"

They look at each other with undisguised fondness, and Karen imagines him squeezing her hand just below camera level.

"I think, Ted, that each of us feels as if we've been given our lives to live not once, but twice," Anna says. "Jake's family's story is very similar to your own, getting out of Europe one step ahead of the Nazis." Koppel is nodding now. "As for me, I was born in Germany in either '40 or '41 and adopted by an American family after the war. . . ."

This is the part Karen tuned in to hear. Why isn't she listening? She is visited with a sudden anomie—as nothing she does from hereon matters, as if the events of the past few millennia have finally caught up with her, and all she wants to do is melt into a little puddle and cry.

Or maybe she's just jealous because Anna has Govannon? Nah!

". . . at least as my late father told it to me, I was rescued by someone he referred to all his life as the Mystery Woman, a stranger who threw herself over me just as the roof collapsed, killing my mother and all but two other people who had taken refuge in the basement. . . ."

Well, Karen thinks bitterly. Nice to know *something* I've done matters. She thinks of spending the rest of her life doing what she's doing—holding down marginal jobs while she writes s/f novels for marginal advances, listening to editors lament over her refusal to write Just Like Everyone Else. She can hear the current one carping already:

"It's too soft. All that stuff about telepathy, which is not legitimate s/f as far as I'm concerned. *And* your protagonist's infatuation with a younger man. Nobody's interested in a love affair between people that age. They want young. Youth sells. Make him fifty and her twenty-something and write it from his POV and you might have a mainstream novel. Except you can't, because I'm not paying you to write a mainstream novel. No one will. And while it's perfectly all right for male writers to write female protagonists (and a lot of s/f writers are using that as their hook these days), it doesn't work the other way around. At least not for you.

"I mean, jeez, I asked you for something big, apocalyptic. Instead you've got all these characters sitting around getting in touch with their feelings. It's a Girl Story; I hate girl stories. I want jeopardy, tension, something blowing up occasionally. Explosions. Yeah, what your manuscript really needs is more explosions. . . ."

•

Maybe Jacob isn't really Govannon? Or maybe Johann wasn't? Maybe only Govannon is Govannon, and she's missed him by more than two thousand years? Then why is she still having conversations with him in her head?

"Does it occur to you that something's wrong with this reality, too?"

"Of course it has. You're living two overlapping lives. I doubt even you're that talented."

"Don't you want to know why?"

"Not now, please!" She wants to snap at him but finds herself whining instead. "Something's wrong with most of life, or haven't you noticed that in all the lives you've lived? Excuse me, but that's why I right . . . er, write. To write the wrongs. I mean—"

"Is it hard for you to write about characters you no longer care for?"

"It's not that I don't care for them, it's just that—"

"You're not sure how you feel about the real people they're based on," he finishes for her, and she does not contradict him. "How do you feel about Raymond?"

Since I've met you? she wants to ask. Instead she says: "I . . . I don't know."

That answer seems to satisfy him. "If you could do anything at all right now, what would it be?"

She knows that lofty answers like "end poverty and disease and war" are not going to cut it here. Her own needs are so much simpler; they only seem as unlikely to be met.

"Quit my job and earn a solid living as a writer?" She tries it out, as if it's bound to be hypothetical, even in the universe Govannon inhabits. "Write an erotic novel under an assumed name. Write mainstream novels again, under my own name. Be taken seriously. Be with you."

How's that for a Girl Story? she wants to ask her editor in absentia. Fifty-something midlist writer runs off into an alternate universe with the Two-Thousand-Year-Old Man. Will she Live Happily Ever After?

The statement seems to take Govannon by surprise. "Do you? Really? An old man like me?"

"It's a good guise, but it doesn't fool me. You're not old. You're immortal."

" 'Good guise'?" His voice is Bogart. "Are you saying I'm one of the Good Guys?"

Karen giggles. What is it about him that makes it feel as if she's about twelve years old and the world brand-new?

"You're the Third Thing, aren't you?"

"That's TQ to you, sweetheart! Do you mean it? You want to come with me, really?"

Her voice is that of a little girl: "Yes!"

"You're so cute! Are you frightened? No, don't answer that. We're all frightened, aren't we, most of the time?" He seems to be weighing something. "Why?"

"Because I want to see the worlds you see. I want to know the things you know. I want your wisdom. I want you."

He accepts, extending one big strange hand to her. Their fingertips touch, and she holds on.

"Come on, then," he says. "This is going to be fun!"

# EPILOGUE

The phone rings. The answering machine takes messages. The little red light blinks frantically all night long. In the downstairs hall, catalogs and MasterCard bills shoot through the mail slot and plop on the floor, accumulating. In some cybernetic limbo, e-mail messages accrue unsummoned. Clocks tick or blink, analog, chronolog. Dust settles, houseplants grow, window blinds creak. Karen is not there.

Rather, Karen is not *here*. She *is* . . . there. Somewhere elsewhere. Disappeared into her own narrative, transformed into a fiction of her own creation? She always was a character. Where has she gone? Or is it when? And more importantly than either of those: how and why?

In a cardboard box beside a secondhand computer on a generic particle-board desk, a manuscript lies. The header dubs it *Preternatural Too*. Within, a group of space-suited humans sits cross-legged on the floor of a cave, interspersed among S.oteri. It has been determined that the air is safe for the humans to breathe, and that human viruses don't affect S.oteri. In short, helmets have been removed; faces are visible.

One of the humans, Gret, watches as Darymon, the only Null in the group, finds himself surrounded, tendrilled about, and his mind awakened. Let's listen. . . .

"Gret could barely credit what she saw, but it was happening.

The look on Darymon's face—transfixed, childlike with awe—said it all. His mind had been touched and found receptive, and at last he was able to See."

•

{Tee-hee . . . }